ZODAK - THE LAST SHIELDER

TEMPEST RISING SERIES
BOOK 1

MAX MOYER

FOXHALL
press

Copyright © 2024 by Max Moyer; Foxhall Press

All rights reserved.

No part of this book may be reproduced in any form or by any electronic or mechanical means, including information storage and retrieval systems, without written permission from the author, except for the use of brief quotations in a book review.

❦ Created with Vellum

For my family, and the heroes that they all are.

JOIN MY MAILING LIST

Sign up for my mailing list for news, exclusive content and special releases and access. Also, for now, new subscribers receive a free copy of *Throne Born*, a novella that predates the events in *Zodak - The Last Shielder* by 200 years.

Go to: MaxMoyerWrites.com to sign up and get your free book!

MAP FROM THE TUKS

YIDUIIJN (yid-wee-YIN)

Directions, Weights & Measures

Directions

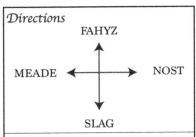

FAHYZ / MEADE ← → NOST / SLAG

Measurements

jot - 1/12 an inch
inch - 1/12 a measure
measure - 1/6 a marq
marq - length of an average man
lynk - 9 marqs
cliq - 888 marqs: measured as the width of the mouth of the Swath (~ 1 mile or 1.6km).
span - 41 cliqs Standard; a day's journey on a galloping horse.

Currencies

Zo'ol   = 49 Dunt
Dunt   = 49 krown
du-krown = 2 krown
krown = 9 corq
corq   = 1 bite std silver
dither   = ½ corq
shim   = ¼ dither
spat   = 1/8 shim

Weights

crimp = 1/7th chip
chip   = 1/13 dok
dok   = 1 wellish shell (1 lb)
chub = 1 1/5 dok
dokkert = 7 dok
slab = 77 dok
wagon = 11 slabs

Cut out and use as bookmark:

PROLOGUE

Hallah's eyes flashed at her husband. "Leave it on a doorstep. Drop it in the river. I don't care! I want that thing out of this house!"

"This is madness!" said Ardon, shaking his head. "That *thing* is a child. My only nephew."

"A nephew you didn't know you had, from a brother you never knew. He may as well be a kin cousin!"

"He's an innocent child! My flesh and blood!" Anger smoldered in Ardon's eyes.

"A mouth we can't feed. That's what he is!" A sip of bandi sloshed from her wooden mug, and she tottered, adjusting her stance.

"Bandi," Ardon growled. "How many cups have you drunk tonight?"

"It doesn't matter," she snapped, regaining her footing. "What matters is the dirt! The ground's been stone hard for seasons; ever since that boy was forced on us. He brought the drought."

"The drought's got nothing to do with him. For Color's sake, his parents are dead! Taking him in was the only honorable option."

"So you've said. But we both remember that night," replied Hallah. "The way the ground trembled the night he arrived. Rumors of a giant, of all things! And the rain stopped the very next day."

Ardon just shook his head.

"What happens to us without crops?" she pressed. "Barst isn't a patient man."

Ardon dropped his face to his hands and rubbed his forehead. "Barst has more money than he could spend," he replied. "I've got but two quarter-seasons to pay. I'm sure I can reason with him. He knows I've been nothing if not dutiful."

"Ha! If you knew anything of duty, your children—your true flesh and blood—wouldn't be asking for food from bare cupboards. Instead, we're running an orphanage."

Ardon flinched at the jab. "Where is the Hallah I married? The girl who used to lie beside me in the leopard grass?"

"She's gone. She and her dreams died long ago."

"Please, Hallah," he persisted, his wedding vow of ample provision echoing in his head. "You know I've been in those fields from dawn until last light tending the silka seeds. And each morning on my knees pleading with the Figure in the Clouds for rain—"

"Silka seeds, the Figure in the Clouds, the Color!" She spat the words with a fine mist of bandi. "Foolish mind rot, all of it! I told you not to buy those cursed seeds. That's two seasons of our wages locked in the barren ground. If that Figure you pray to cares a dither for us, then where is the rain? Can you eat a silkeen scarf?" she slurred.

"Of course not, but prices for threshed silka in Pol Dak are as high as—"

"It doesn't matter!" she shouted. "We have no threshed silka! No food! We have no money!"

"Please," urged Ardon, holding up his palms. "The children," he added, glancing up to the darkened loft.

She scoffed, waving him off as she crossed the small room to the shelves. "They've been asleep for hours." She uncorked the bottle of homemade bandiroot broth and poured another foaming cupful.

∼

"We gonna starve?" whispered Ergis to his sister, eyes brimming with tears.

"If we do, it's 'cause a Zodak," Alana whispered back to her younger brother. The two huddled close in the dark on the shared straw mat where they had been listening to their parents argue. At seven seasons, two older than Ergis, Alana was the authority on all things. "He cursed us," she added. "He's why the plants is all dead. If we die, it's a-cause of him." She stabbed a finger in the darkness. A few measures away, in a large drawer repurposed as a bed, lay young Zodak, his soft chest rising and falling rhythmically, the only one oblivious to the firestorm.

1

"Argh. Empty," Zodak scoffed, restringing the orko snare even as his stomach groaned.

Collecting dried zheibak dung patties for the fire, checking the snares for any hapless orko trapped during the night, and collecting armloads of kindling were but a part of his daily chores and duties. When the darkness came and he felt like punishing himself, he'd imagine himself a young rising lord to a royal family, dining at the table of one of the Pol Dak nobles. He could picture biting into a thick steak like those he'd seen wrapped in paper at the butcher's stand in the market or opening a box of pepperfruit carted in from far away. But a young lord of Pol Dak he was not. Instead, he'd have to settle for the stringy orko meat from the oversized haunches of the squawking rodents cooked with earthy potatoes or misshapen carrots.

Zodak leaned his weight into the sapling, clipping it to the tiny snare. A darting movement caught his eye. A shadow the size of a dog slipped behind a thicket and froze. Zodak carefully released the sapling and, drawing himself up, slowly pulled the knife from his belt. He crept a step forward, then another, his eyes ever fixed on the thicket. His foot cracked a twig and three zheibak shot from the thicket. They bounded on springy legs, launching higher than his head with each jump as they glided through the forest like whispers of light, their painted stripes making them all but invisible in the brush. Zodak released his tensed muscles and his shoulders sagged.

The delicate creatures had once captivated him. Five seasons past, he had freed one whose ornate latticed antlers had gotten tangled in the underbrush, he recalled marveling at the beast's bounding retreat, only to meet his uncle Ardon's disappointed longing gaze as the week of meals sped away. That day killed his pity and wonder for the splendid little animals. He soon learned to pin the spindly legs of a trapped zheibak to keep its sharp hooves from thrashing, and swiftly slice the throat to bleed it. Ardon often reminded him to be grateful for the forest's bounty, truly a gift when the poor in the cities didn't have a roof overhead or a warm meal for days.

With nothing to show for his efforts, Zodak turned back to the house. The forest was silent and inviting. *Try it*, a tiny voice urged. After a step, he sank to his knees. He stilled his body and breathed deeply of the morning forest, digging his fingers into the rich soil. *"The trees around us, the earth beneath us, the creatures of the wood, they were all created by the Figure in the Clouds and so they are touched by the Color,"* Ardon had told him a season ago. *"Silence your mind. Let the Color cover you. You'll see the Figure."* So here he sat, extending his hope again, ignoring past disappointment. He tried to clear his mind, tried to empty it of the unceasing cacophonous swirl of thoughts and memories and fears.

"Hurry with the spate wafers, boy!" came Aunt Hallah's shout from inside, cutting his meditation short.

His head twitched involuntarily, a regular movement of his that now came unbidden. *"Another of Zodak's broken parts,"* his cousin Alana had jabbed recently. She wasn't wrong. He couldn't control the twitching or the subtle shaking in his hands. They had been there for as long as he could remember, only getting worse.

A hundred measures from the house, circled by trees, his eyes closed again against the weak morning light. Even as he tried to clear his mind, the same question pecked at him: *Why not leave? Why not run from this pack of jackals without a glance back?* Every day he felt like a prisoner under his aunt Hallah's cruel watch, tormented by his cousins Ergis and Alana. But was he a prisoner, really? There were no guards watching him, no chains keeping him here. He could easily slip out and never return.

Even as he asked the question, he knew the answer. At sixteen seasons old, Zodak was no child—though undersized for his age, he *had* grown a half measure in the last season—yet he was far from a man. Without family or guardian, he would be vulnerable. This village was too small for him to get away from his problems, and while the city of Pol Dak was plenty large, stories of the child stealers made his blood run cold. Tales told of bands of grizzled hunchbacks, armed with nets and sacks, hired by the Governor to clear the city of urchins and child beggars. It was said they delivered captured children to group homes for education, but fragmented stories of these homes brought nightmares to even the bravest boy. And for older ones, it could be far worse.

The other reason Zodak knew he'd stay was his uncle Ardon. The worst day with Ergis, Alana, and Hallah was tolerable knowing Ardon would come back at the end of it. Zodak deeply longed to call him "Father," but this word was wrong. Too sacred for a nephew, for a bastard. If that word were ever to leave Zodak's lips, Ergis and Alana would make him suffer. *The Wickeds*, as Zodak called them, put on a pathetic façade of kindness in front of Ardon, but when he was gone, their potent venom came out.

Zodak shook his head, again seeking silence, digging fingers deeper into the earth the way Ardon had taught him, feeling for the Color. *This is foolish.* He brushed the thought away, listened to the breeze dancing through the trees, and quieted his mind.

A bird's cry carried from far off. Silence.

There! Had he heard something? Sensed it? A scrap of feeling, a faint thrumming from beneath his fingers, through the soil. Or was it imagined? He quieted himself, receding deep inside, listening for the quiet voice.

"The wood, boy! Now!" Hallah's cry came again from the house, shattering the moment.

With a deep breath, he abandoned the failed ritual and rose, wiping dirty hands on his pants. *Stupid! It never works,* he scolded himself. *There's nothing out there.*

Zodak heaved the long pole to his shoulder, finding the midpoint that would balance the bundle of sticks in front and the basket of spate behind. The stiff spate wafers carried only a hint of manure odor and the impressive pile of sticks stood as evidence of his morning efforts. Walking back to the house, he chased visions of the city of Pol Dak: the lords, street rats, and the child stealers.

He was so lost in thought that he didn't notice the unusual log standing upright on its end in the middle of the path near the edge of the woods, or the curious flecks of blue that speckled the bark. He absently raised a boot to the top edge of the log and pushed hard. Instead of giving way and rolling into the underbrush, the log stood fast. A burst of energy shot back against Zodak's kick, knocking him backwards. He fell to the path, his basket and kindling crashing to the ground.

What? Zodak crept forward cautiously on hands and knees, inspecting the odd-looking log in the middle of the path, the blue bark glittering. As he stared at the log, water began to seep up out of the end grain onto its surface.

Strangely, it neither ran off the sides nor soaked into the wood. It pooled into a shallow dome before his very eyes. Then the water began to vibrate. He drew back, startled as tiny peaks appeared on the surface, like a round of dough pinched by an invisible hand. Zodak stared, transfixed, as a small pyramid of water arose from the center of the pool and transformed into a small figure. Before him stood the form of a person made entirely of water, no taller than the head of an axe. The form shimmered translucent blue in the morning light.

Zodak blinked rapidly and smeared an eye with the back of his hand, trying to return to reality. *Am I dreaming?* He shook his head, trying to clear the vision. Yet there the watery form stood, defying all his senses, a tiny figure with smooth, delicate features. Then it spoke.

"Zodak."

He leapt backward and looked around wildly to see if anyone else had witnessed this vision. An electric tingling flashed through him. *It knows my name!*

The figure raised a diminutive arm towards the boy. "Your call has come," said an ethereal little voice that cooed like a dove, hollow like wind sweeping over a bed of reeds. "You are needed."

"How... what *is* this?" he stammered.

"You have questions, young one. But know this: you are not alone. You never have been. And you shall have company every step, whether you perceive it or not."

"Every step where? What *are* you?"

"Your journey will not be an easy one. Much will be asked. Much will be taken. But in you, there is courage and strength."

"What? What journey?"

"Patience, young one. Patience," replied the creature. "Your call has come."

"Zodak, how's the gathering coming?" Ardon's familiar

voice came from the house. The liquid figure collapsed into a pool of water, then ran off the edge of the stump.

"Wait! Come back," Zodak called after the puddle that even now soaked into the earth surrounding the log.

Ardon strode from the house, his tall, strong frame moving to the boy in an effortless glide.

He laid a hand on Zodak's shoulder when he reached him. "Everything okay— Oh, looks like you had a stumble?" He surveyed the path. "Goodness, you've collected a lot this morning. Let's get it inside." He stooped to gather the kindling, but Zodak didn't move. Ardon noticed Zodak's face for the first time. "Are you all right, son? You look like you've seen a ghost." He smiled, but Zodak's expression didn't lighten. Ardon's smile faded. "What happened, Zodak? Was it Ergis again?" A flash of anger danced over his face.

Zodak looked up into Ardon's inquisitive eyes. "No, not Ergis. I... it's nothing," he muttered, and began gathering wood, shaking the vision from his mind. He knew how ridiculous his story would sound.

Ardon put down his stack of wood and gripped Zodak's shoulder. "I don't think nothing happened," he said. "What is it?"

"You wouldn't believe me. I'm not even sure if I do..." Again, he trailed off, staring at the log.

"Try me," said Ardon.

With a resigned sigh, Zodak quickly recounted the fall and the words of the sprite. Even as he spoke, he saw his folly. He asked too much of a grownup, or anyone, to entertain such a fanciful tale. "I probably imagined the whole thing," Zodak added quickly as he hurriedly returned to gathering the wood.

Ardon didn't move. "I'm not so sure," he said, shaking his head.

"You're not?" Zodak slowed his gathering. He had already convinced himself the whole thing had never happened.

"This world is filled with mystery, both visible and hidden." Ardon put a hand on Zodak's shoulder. "Many people don't believe anything beyond what their own eyes see. They're small-minded, afraid of the unknown. But the Figure in the Clouds made our eyes and hearts to see so much more. Maybe He sent a messenger." He stood up and walked over to the log.

"I've never seen blue bark like this," said Ardon, rolling the log over.

The bark sparkled with sapphire flecks. Under their gaze, the blue faded and disappeared, returning the log to an unremarkable brown.

"You see?" said Ardon with a knowing smile. "Mystery."

"The spate for the fire, boy!" came Hallah's angry cry. "You'll feel my belt if I find that you—" Hallah had marched out the kitchen door into the dewy grass to the edge of the forest. "Oh, Ardon... I didn't know you were out here." She offered a shallow smile and nervously flattened the front of her skirt. "We've been waiting on the fire all morning. Would you please have him bring the wood?" his aunt asked in a tight voice. She avoided speaking directly to Zodak whenever possible.

"It's my fault, Hallah. I've kept him. We'll bring it in now." Ardon winked at Zodak. "Come on. Load me up," he said, ruffling Zodak's hair. Ardon shouldered the pole while Zodak secured the kindling bundle, and the two walked back to the house.

Aside from their occasional snickering, Ergis and Alana were uncharacteristically quiet during breakfast. Whatever hidden joke they shared, it would certainly come at Zodak's expense. They knew he had spent time with Ardon this morning, and they'd almost certainly punish him for it on the walk to school. After breakfast, the children fastened their boots, and Zodak heaved the leather bag full of school supplies over his shoulder.

"Let me look," insisted Hallah, inspecting Alana as if she

was a prized auction bull. At almost eighteen seasons, Alana should have aged out of the school experiment already, but so far, Hallah's desperate search for a suitor for the sour girl had been fruitless. "This is a mess." She tugged at Alana's thick dark hair.

"It's fine, Mother."

"Hardly," Hallah scoffed. She herself went to great lengths to ensure her carefully manicured appearance. "Now remember, chin up to avoid those terrible neck rolls."

"I'll make sure not to look downward today," Alana quipped. The girl shared a few of her mother's attractive features but was not as fair. She also possessed some of the hard angles of Ardon's face and an "offensive beak of a nose," Hallah often reminded her.

"I doubt you do much of that anyway," Hallah said, spinning the girl to inspect the back of her drab dress. "If you did, you might accidentally find yourself reading your school materials." Hallah gave a pressed smile as Alana rolled her eyes and stormed off. Ergis, a head taller than Zodak and dozens of doka heavier, shouldered past him on his way out.

Zodak took a breath and then he stepped through the door, out of the safety of the house. Out from under Ardon's shield of protection.

2

Zodak accompanied Ergis and Alana to school every day, but not to learn. Like the others in Laan, the family was allotted just two students in the experimental school established by Barst the overlord to bring Pol Dak culture to the agrarian village. Though Ardon had promised each season to find a way to enroll Zodak, the spaces were few. At his age, Zodak was already growing out of the program. He knew the mines were more likely his fate. For now, though, Zodak went to serve his cousins. They certainly couldn't afford one of the massive golyath snails and cart—only one family in town could—so he carried their tablets and bags, brought them lunch, and walked them to class.

Ergis and Alana walked ahead of Zodak, without so much as a glance back. *This isn't good,* he thought. The straight driveway to the main street, still in view of the house, served as neutral ground, but once out of sight, Zodak was on his own.

Alana whispered and giggled to her brother, but Ergis remained dangerously silent. Ergis, whose name meant "valiant knight," fell woefully short of his title. Bossy and tubby, at almost seventeen seasons, he stood taller than most men, with an unkempt shock of black hair always hanging over his brooding eyes. When they were younger, Zodak could recall a handful of happy moments when he and Ergis had laughed or played together. But even those sunny memories often ended in anger or pain, and the seasons had washed away any remnant of friendship. Zodak had outdone Ergis too many times, beat him at some little game or contest. As the joyful moments grew fewer, the hatred festered, until every interaction became a strategic assault in Ergis's war of aggression.

"Look!" Alana stopped, pointing at the spider weed beside the path.

"Hmm?" grunted Ergis, his cold anger stifling his full participation in her charade.

"It's a little goblin made of water, and he's talking to me! He's telling me secrets!" Alana put her palms to her cheeks in mock surprise. Embarrassment and then anger stabbed through Zodak. "He said I'm not alone. Oh, you don't believe me, do you?" She pouted.

His pulse quickened and his hands trembled with fury. *You fool!* he scolded himself. The Wickeds had overheard the morning's events.

Ergis puffed his chest and screwed up his face into a scowl. "Why, of course I do, my half-breed, cursed *son*." Ergis spoke in a deep voice mimicking Ardon. Even in charade, Zodak knew the last word tasted bitter on Ergis's tongue.

"The water goblin said I am to be king of the Midlands," sang Alana in falsetto, clearly relishing Zodak's torment. "He said I will be a hero."

"Now that's going a bit far, my little bram dropping." Ergis furrowed his brow and stuck out his lips in ridiculous exaggeration. Thespians these two were not. "I can bear your lies only for so long, you little bastard. No matter how many water goblins are in your head, you'll never be a king. Just a cursed bastard!" Ergis wrapped a meaty arm around Zodak's shoulders and clamped down on Zodak's neck, pulling him into a headlock. Zodak lurched forward, yanked into a bowing position as Ergis squeezed hard, cutting off his air and pinching Zodak's folded ear painfully. Zodak dropped his bag and thrust Ergis's arm over his head, pulling free from the hold. Ergis and Alana exploded in shrieks of laughter.

Seasons of rage bottled inside Zodak bubbled over. He screamed as he snatched up the heavy leather bag with the slate tablets and hurled it straight into Ergis's face with a satisfying crunch, knocking the larger boy to the ground, blood showering from his nose.

Then Zodak turned to face Alana. "You're a selfish poison dart worm!" he snapped. "You know our father loves me, and he can't stand you! Who could? You're the most pathetic, horrible person I've ever met!"

Alana burst into tears and collapsed in a heap on the ground.

So went the fantasy in Zodak's head. He had played dozens of scenarios like this over in his mind, but as always, he remained silent under their jabs. Instead, he stood panting, his ear throbbing as he stared into the eyes of the Wickeds, fighting off the rage that welled within.

"Come on, hero! What's wrong?" taunted Ergis. "You gonna cry?" He swung to cuff Zodak on the back. Zodak dodged to the side, avoiding the blow. Ergis had earned the satisfaction of Zodak's tears in seasons past, but those days were long gone. Instead, Zodak lifted the school bag, his eyes still fixed on Ergis as his body fought to keep the shaking at bay. *Throw it! Hurt him,* the voice inside goaded him.

"Is carrying our slates to school your big journey?" taunted Alana.

"Careful," warned Ergis, looking around. "He's not alone!" Now Ergis joined Alana in laughter. Zodak knew the worst danger had passed. After a long minute, the cackling finally subsided.

"Don't you dare tell lies to our father, boy!" hissed Alana. "Play with your slagging wood fairies in your mind, but don't you bring your cursed pathetic little world into our home!" Zodak dropped his eyes under her barrage of words, hurled like darts. "Even a little sich moth like you can see your extra mouth to feed is killing our father."

The shame and embarrassment welled in Zodak. Alana wielded her biting words with precision compared to Ergis's blunt abuse. Her rants only encouraged Ergis.

"That's right," he added, moving close to Zodak. "If I ever hear you talk that foolish mind rot again…" He grabbed Zodak's shirt front and raised a meaty fist. "Even a stupid sich like you knows these woods got nothing but trees, orko, and skupp. No slagging goblins, no water creatures, no magic gnomes. Keep that scat in your pathetic empty head." He cuffed Zodak hard on the back of the head and let him go. The surge filled him again. Zodak clenched his teeth and ripped away from Ergis's grip.

"And Father doesn't need to carry your lies with him down into those horrid mines," added Alana, fixing Zodak with her challenging stare. "Don't worry, you'll be marching with him soon enough."

Still, Zodak said nothing. Trying to explain himself would be a fool's errand, and any retort would only make the situation worse.

"The goblin-loving moth can't even speak for himself," Alana taunted. "Lots to say when you're whispering your filth to Father, though."

Zodak tightened his grip on the heavy school bag, staring Ergis down. *Do it!* the voice shouted. It had been seasons since Zodak had fought back, and a part of him relished the opportunity. Zodak knew Ergis was afraid, afraid of one day unleashing the darkness deep in Zodak, fed by seasons of insult and abuse. Hallah had once promised him that the day he laid a hand on her children was the day he found himself in the woods. Whether just another of her manipulative childhood stories or a true promise, Zodak didn't know.

"That pill isn't worth the scratch on your knuckles," Alana said to Ergis. *She knows it too,* Zodak realized. Ergis hesitated long enough to show he had made up his own mind and then spat at Zodak and turned to go. Zodak sighed with relief, smearing off the spittle with his cuff. The teasing and jabs would no doubt continue. The intimate moment with their father was too rich and painful a prize to squander. But for now, Zodak had succeeded. He had survived another walk to school.

The dirty mustard-colored schoolhouse hadn't had a fresh coat of paint in all the seasons since the experiment had begun. *A building just for learning, like in the big cities.* "A waste of time for growing children who should be learning a craft or helping in the fields," many complained. The first season only three students attended, but the trickle had grown to a steady flock of children who congregated there each day.

Viera Folba, one of Laan's only inhabitants with two names, was brought in by Barst himself from Pol Dak for the schooling experiment. Some villagers said his vision for an "oasis of culture" was a thinly veiled scheme to recruit for his growing krius mining empire. Ms. Folba had very much been an outsider when she arrived, but most in Laan had come to appreciate her teaching and the school itself as a luxury for such a small, sleepy farming village.

Zodak situated Alana and Ergis in the classroom with their slate tablets and chalk sticks. Then he was excused to the stable until classes ended when he would return for their things. Most days, only a few children gathered in the stable with Jup the grounds hand to shoe horses, stitch saddles, or learn simple carpentry and farm work. Most were either too young for school, third children, or children of families indebted to Barst, and therefore declared ineligible for school. Hallah, it seemed, didn't care much what Zodak did as long as he was out of the house.

Zodak had only been to the stable a few times when he discovered the hallway storage closet behind the classroom. Exhausted, he had slipped in to catch a nap, but once inside, he found the wall planks had flexed and bowed over time, making a slit between the closet and the classroom. From his secret spot, he could watch the entire class.

That first day Ms. Folba taught on the enthronement of Kaen the Great, urchin turned king, and Zodak was hooked. He never returned to the stable. From his cramped haven he absorbed Ms. Folba's every word, even without being able to see the leather books passed around in the class. The other children casually glanced at the sketched charcoal pictures on those pages before passing the book, but Zodak closed his eyes and imagined every detail of the scene. The smoke from the villages razed in the Great Seaborne Battle burned his nostrils. He could hear the trumpet blasts announcing the arrival of the Seven Judges. The wind atop Atlas Peak in the Direth Range blew and tussled his hair and he tasted the cool mountain spring water where the spade fish spawned. He longed for the next season when he could walk in as a real student as Ardon promised.

Today, though, his mind was not on the lesson. His thoughts flitted back to the water sprite. *Was it even real? What is my call? Or am I truly crazy?* He had heard about the tailor's apprentice, who swore he was seeing his dead ancestors walking about in the dye shop. The boy was sent off to Pol Dak and two seasons later had still not returned.

"And in what season was the Octarch Queendom established?" Zodak heard Ms. Folba ask. Silence. *Seventy-nine seasons into the Second Span,* he thought. She had taught this only last week. Ms. Folba was thirty-five seasons, although, with her hair pulled back into a tight ponytail and the hints of urban flair in her dress, she was sometimes taken for younger. She had a soft, kind face with warm eyes when she smiled, but she had never married. In response to the students who regularly asked, she would say she had married the love of learning.

"All right then, in what Span was it established?" she asked patiently. *Second...* thought Zodak. Still uncomfortable silence.

"Third," blurted a child near the back.

"Not quite," replied Ms. Folba. "The Queendom became disrupted and fell during the Third Span, just before the Goblin Swarm. But actually, it was established a good bit earlier."

"There's no such thing as goblins!" cried a child.

"Well, history is actually full of accounts that they do exist," replied Ms. Folba levelly.

"H'ol Chazkar controls them's minds," chirped a mousy girl from the back.

"Jelda!" gasped Folba, her face suddenly drained of color. "That name is never to be spoken." She gripped the desk to steady herself.

"Why?" replied Jelda. "'Cause yer afraid the Ice King is gonna come back?"

"Those are just dumb stories made up to keep us from traveling!" declared Alana. "The wicked Judges invented the Ice King to keep control over all the people."

"Where did you hear that, Alana?" asked Ms. Folba, her voice brimming with alarm. "The seven noble Judges forged the peace in the Midlands that has endured for hundreds of seasons."

"My mother has a cousin in the Venerable Council in Pol Dak," said Alana, lifting her chin. The class murmured admiration. Actually, Morzi, the daughter of Hallah's aunt, had been a servant in the washroom of one of the Council members until she was caught stealing silver spoons and thrown out of the Sisters' Keep. "She told my mother about this conspirity," Alana proudly declared. Zodak rolled his eyes. Ergis and Alana were among a handful of students who challenged all accounts outside of their reality. History class was largely a wasted hour because it invariably broke down into arguments among children infused with their parents' uneducated politicized views of the past. From the way her mouth tightened into a thin line, it was clear that Ms. Folba, who had studied royal lineage and history herself at the Institute of Forgotten Learning in Pol Dak, fought to keep from joining the obtuse debates.

As the class drew to a close, Ms. Folba announced, "I have a special project for you all." A few groans. She paused patiently. "You will each have a writing assignment." Now muffled whispers rippled through the class. "To complete the assignment, I will be giving you each a black coal marker...and paper." The questioning murmur turned to excitement. *Paper?* Zodak perked up, and then just as quickly sank back into disappointment. Paper was a treat. The students did all of their writing on slate tablets. Nobody in the village other than the money counters wrote on paper. Writing paper belonged to the elite city folks and in old leather books, not in the hands of country children. But sure enough, Ms. Folba, ever a devotee to knowledge and learning, produced a short stack of writing paper.

"You must each write about an experience you have had. You can describe something that made you feel happy or something sad. Choose whatever you like. Have fun with your writing. It should be just like writing on your tablets, but you'll use both sides of the paper like this." She demonstrated how to keep the letters in line. The large room was full of whispers and squeals as the twenty-two children lined up to get their coal markers and two sheets of paper each. "I will collect your papers in three days," concluded Ms. Folba.

Zodak burned with envy. He had practiced his writing

along with the other children during class on a broken piece of slate he had found in the closet, but he could only imagine writing on real paper.

"This is stupid," complained Ergis, returning to his desk with the supplies.

"I don't know. I think it could be fun," said Alana. There was a gleam in here eye, replacing the typical scowl.

As the classroom cleared out, the stable children shuffled in, collecting the tablets, chalks, and supplies. Zodak moved especially slowly. He desperately wanted to try writing on paper. Asking Ms. Folba for the supplies was out of the question. He wasn't even a student. His eyes roved from desk to desk, but none had been left behind. His mind raced. Ms. Folba collected her things up front, and without knowing what he would say, Zodak found himself walking towards the front of the room. As he approached Ms. Folba, he froze.

She glanced up. "Ahoi. May I help you?"

His throat was suddenly dry. She smiled patiently. After what seemed like an eternity, he croaked, "Pa—per."

"Oh? For Ergis. I see," she said, shaking her head, handing him the supplies.

Zodak didn't speak. He clutched his prize and slowly backed away. Glancing over his shoulder, he carefully slipped the paper between the two tablets in the bag and pocketed the coal marker before nearly skipping out of the room.

"What's taking so long, skupp?" Ergis's bulky figure blocked the doorway.

Zodak's breath caught. "Uh, n-nothing." He felt the weight of the marker in his pocket. Ergis looked him up and down, his accusing gaze finally settling on Zodak's face. Zodak averted his eyes, praying for the silent inquisition to pass. Ergis peered over Zodak's shoulder into the classroom.

"Psheesh," he finally grunted, shaking his head as he walked away. Zodak breathed again.

3

For the next two days, Zodak slipped away every chance he could to work on his story. Writing on the fragile paper was like handling a dried snakeskin. Marking the paper while holding it on his lap like a tablet was very difficult. He finally found that laying it down flat on the worktable in the shed worked much better. He knew exactly what he would write about: the water creature from the woods. He would pour every detail he could remember about it, and then he would burn the paper so Ergis could never find it.

Ergis, it appeared, had completely ignored the project until Ms. Folba announced that any student who failed to turn in their story would be required to read aloud to the group. That night Ergis hurriedly wrote a sarcastic and sloppy story about when he had won a first-place ribbon for growing the largest fire squash for the Harvest Festival. Conveniently excluded were the details that he had actually won third place, had stolen the squash a day earlier, and consequently had his victory denounced and his ribbon reclaimed.

To Zodak's surprise, Alana seemed genuinely excited every time she discussed the project, though he hadn't actually seen her start writing. Despite Hallah's dismissive comments, Alana continued to share the details of the story she planned to write.

The classroom hummed with excitement on the second day. The students chirped and chattered about their stories and their adventures writing on paper. A few had ripped their paper and needed a new sheet. Bluef, a stocky boy with a slow drawl, had somehow burned both sheets and the marker and he had the charred paper to prove it. Most, though, eagerly shared the snippets of writing they had completed. As he sat in his closet, Zodak cursed himself for leaving his story back in the shed. How he longed to pore over every word.

On the way back from school, Alana hurried ahead of Ergis and Zodak.

"Why do you even care so much about this stupid project?" he overheard Ergis call after her.

"I don't know," she admitted, slowing. "It just somehow makes me feel...alive or something."

"Boring as pith if you ask me," huffed Ergis.

"Maybe," she replied airily. Once at home, she skipped off and went straight to her room. That night she missed dinner, claiming a stomachache.

"Wouldn't hurt her to miss a meal now and then anyway," Hallah had said. From the candlelight dancing on the ceiling over the curtained-off section of the house that was Alana's room, Zodak guessed she was working on her story late into the night.

On the morning the assignments were due, Alana was dressed and finished with breakfast, reading her story when Zodak went out to get the morning wood and spate. He couldn't remember the last time that had happened. She usually stumbled into the kitchen irritable and half-asleep, hurling sharpened insults, shoveled food into her mouth, and tromped off to school.

"Good morning," he said, immediately regretting opening his mouth at all and bracing for the barbed retort.

"Good?" she replied. "It's a trimidious morning!" Again, he waited for the attack. She must have sensed his hesitation. "It's the day we turn in our stories in class," she explained. "Ms. Folba gave us real paper. It's…it's amazing." She spoke fast as if trying to catch the thoughts. "Before I knew it, I was at the bottom of the page. And then the second." She was nearly breathless. Their eyes met and Zodak quickly looked away. An awkward silence landed as they both sat in the foreign, intimate shared moment.

"Are you going to Far Market tomorrow?" she blurted suddenly, changing the topic.

Zodak had no idea what to make of Alana. She had never spoken to him like this. "Yes," he answered carefully. In all the excitement, Zodak had completely forgotten about his upcoming trip to the town of Komo. He felt proud of his responsibility to buy provisions for the family and usually counted down the days to the trip, though he never understood why Hallah granted him this gift. But whatever the reason, she entrusted him with the family's money, their horse, and the cart across the rocky vale to the river town of Komo.

"Lose a dither of this money and you'll never set foot outside the house until you're old enough to be shipped off to the mines!" she warned on his last visit. But Zodak considered her routine threats a small price to pay. He made the trip only every mooncycle. Most of what the family needed came from the local market. Yet Hallah demanded fine herbs, oils, and the occasional fabric whenever she had stashed enough of Ardon's money to afford it. Laan produced no such finery.

"Oh, good." She clapped her hands together. "Mr. Kanes gave me a corq for helping him pickle his pig turnips last week, and I was wondering if, well, I was hoping you could buy me a blue scarf when you go. Dyna at school got one and said they only cost a corq."

Zodak turned the question over in his mind, searching for the trick or insult. *Will she claim she gave you two? Or that you stole her corq?* That seemed unlikely, even for her.

"Okay..." he answered guardedly.

"Really?" she chirped.

"Mm-hmm," he answered, now looking around for Ergis. But they were alone.

"Great!" Alana beamed.

"What's all this?" Hallah's voice cut in. "Where's the wood?" She shot a glance at Zodak. "And what's gotten into you?" She turned to Alana.

"It's this writing assignment, Mother. It... it feels like drawing back a heavy curtain letting light and color rush in."

Hallah snorted. "Foolish indulgence if you ask me. You have better things to do than playing make-believe on expensive paper."

Zodak grimaced, backing through the open door.

"I don't know," said Alana, finishing off a bite of cold cheese and rusk bread. She dashed out to finish getting ready for school. *What's happened to her?*

Before collecting the wood, Zodak slipped off to the shed to get his treasured story. He wouldn't turn his paper in, but he hadn't brought himself to burn it yet. The words from the encounter with that strange water creature came alive again on the pages and now haunted him anew. Today he would read and re-read his story again and again, relishing every word. Zodak swept aside a dusty canvas sack and lifted a wide floorboard out of place. Ever since discovering this secret spot a few seasons earlier while patching a skupp hole, he had used it to hide his most precious items. Most were boyhood treasures only to him. Among them, three colorful glittering stones from the stream, a very old glass lens, and a smooth silver ball just larger than an almond. Zodak carefully removed his paper from the hiding spot and replaced the board. He unrolled the story on the worktable just to look at it once more.

"What are you doing, half-wit?" Ergis darkened the only doorway to the shed. Zodak's stomach twisted.

"Just... putting the axe away," replied Zodak, not turning.

"I heard no chopping," accused Ergis, stepping into the shed. "Why are you at the worktable? You came in here yesterday, too."

His back to Ergis, Zodak slowly rolled his papers, his heart galloping.

"I asked you what you're doing!" Ergis's hot breath was on Zodak's neck.

As subtly as he could, Zodak slipped the roll under the front of his heavy linen shirt. "Nothing. I told you." Zodak turned around to face Ergis, trying to look calm. Ergis pushed him aside, searching the table. Zodak moved to step around Ergis, but Ergis blocked his path.

"Why are you rustling about in here before school?" His dark eyes searched Zodak.

"I'm not," replied Zodak, again trying to step around Ergis, only to be cut off again.

"Then what are you doing here, worm?" Ergis pushed Zodak, causing him to stumble backward.

"It's nothing," insisted Zodak. He lowered his head and again tried to shuffle past.

"What are you hiding there?" Ergis asked, reaching for the slight bulge in Zodak's shirt.

"Nothing!" Zodak lunged forward and shoved Ergis with all his might. Unlike Ergis, who rarely exerted himself, Zodak had grown strong from his many daily chores. The push launched Ergis backward. He tripped and fell to the ground against the shed wall, a shock of his messy black hair flopping over his eyes. For a moment he just sat, stunned. Zodak hadn't raised a finger against Ergis in many seasons. *What have I done?* The look of fear flitted from Ergis's face, and his cheeks turned from white to bright red.

He jumped to his feet, rage in his eyes. "You," panted Ergis.

"I... I'm sorry... I—" Zodak stammered, holding out a hand.

"You will be sorry. Just wait!" he seethed and turned and ran out of the shed.

Zodak shook uncontrollably. He had dreamed of and dreaded the day he would stand up to Ergis, but it felt nothing like he'd imagined. He hadn't thought or planned. It happened too fast. He simply reacted. Ergis couldn't know about his story. Zodak carefully removed the roll of paper, put it in his coat pocket, and walked back to the house.

Ergis didn't say a word on the walk to school. A thick icy wall separated the two boys. Ergis hid his shame and anger expertly, yet Zodak knew how he loathed being humiliated. Once, a small village boy named Simpeon landed a lucky blow as he flailed about in a pathetic attempt to shield himself from Ergis's merciless bullying. The punch bloodied Ergis's nose and drew laughs and jeers from the knot of onlookers. Ergis didn't retaliate in the moment but fell into a dark brooding silence until a few days later when Simpeon's beloved pet ram died mysteriously. Ergis never claimed responsibility or gloated, but Zodak found the empty bag of weed poison and feed in the shed. The very day Simpeon shared the tragic news, Ergis snapped back to his boisterous, impetuous self.

Alana, meanwhile, appeared a different person, changed somehow. She didn't offer to carry the slates or compliment Zodak on his outfit, but a new, unfamiliar glow covered her. Even her face seemed free of the morning shadows and persistent scowl that normally clung to her like bogmoss. She spoke excitedly, talking to no one and waiting for no answer, then whistled a melody of some sort. Her high spirits couldn't lift the cloud over Zodak, though. He feared his inevitable punishment for the clash with Ergis. The attack could come anytime, maybe today, maybe in a month, but he would hold nothing back. It would be terrible. Zodak was in danger.

As soon as they arrived at school, Alana hurried inside to show Ms. Folba her written pages before the other students arrived.

"I'm afraid I didn't finish my story," Zodak heard Alana say as he entered the classroom. "Actually, it felt like I had only just begun when I ran out of room..." Zodak caught Ms. Folba's surprise, but her eyes twinkled.

"Oh, I know that feeling," she said, reaching into her desk and removing at least five more pieces of paper. Zodak pretended to straighten the desk as Ms. Folba drew close to Alana. "I don't have enough for the entire class, so you mustn't tell the others." Alana nodded, wide-eyed. "Though I think it important that you finish your story," Ms. Folba added. Alana gleefully snatched the paper and slid it under her tablet, just as two other children arrived.

After setting up, Zodak hurried out the door towards the stables under Ergis's searing glare. As was his routine, once outside, he turned back to the road and circled around the schoolhouse. He slipped through the building's side door and glancing around furtively, cracked the closet door, and stepped inside. Blades of light from the classroom cut in through the cracks in the wall. Zodak had turned a crate upside-down as a makeshift table, and carefully unrolled his story. When most of the children had arrived, Ms. Folba began collecting the stories. The students shuffled to the front of the class, chatting and giggling, sharing in the grandness of the accomplishment.

"Anyone who likes may read their story to the class tomorrow," Ms. Folba announced.

Zodak could have finished reading his story in a few minutes, but he wanted to savor the experience, to re-live the encounter with the water creature. Reading and re-reading every sentence, he returned to the woods, to the magical encounter, whether real or imagined. He was picking through the second page when his thoughts were interrupted.

"... we'll finish talking about the Tszoi people and the Nomadic Nost Clans after lunch," said Ms. Folba. *Lunch?! Could it be lunchtime already?* It was just as Alana described it. His story had sucked him in, and he had completely lost track of time. He would have to leave the rest for after lunch. Snatching up the wax cloth bundle with the children's lunch, he crept from his room. Today they would have biscuits and salted orko jerky with a chunk of cheese and a misshapen apple each. Zodak had the same, but saw there was no orko for him, and only the most meager slice of cheese. But today nothing could topple him from his joyful perch. He peered out of his hideaway, slipped out, and pulled the door closed behind him.

He hurried into the multipurpose room where the children settled into lunch. He handed Alana her meal and nearly fell over when she said, "Thank you." In all the seasons living under Ardon's roof, Zodak couldn't recall anyone other than Ardon thanking him for anything. His service was almost always met with a snide remark or complaint.

"You're... welcome," faltered Zodak. Ergis still fixed Zodak with the cold stare, yet he said nothing as he collected his food. He took Zodak's apple as well in a subtle, but clear declaration: the war had begun.

Zodak didn't need the apple today, though. His story would be his food. After delivering the waterskin, he hurried out, skipping ahead of the other stable children. He checked over his shoulder and scurried down the slender hallway. But as he rounded the corner, he stopped short. From a few paces away, he could see the door to the closet, his closet, was wide open. He always closed it. And it looked like someone, or something, was moving inside. Zodak's stomach twisted. *I'm found out. No... No!* Fear welled up and burning tears flooded his eyes.

He had been so careful to conceal his hideout, the only escape he had from his grueling days. *What if I'm caught?* he had wondered many times. They would throw him out of class, that was a given. But the thought of being relegated to the stable every day felt like a prison sentence. Hallah would positively erupt. But much worse than all of that was the shame it would cause Ardon. The entire town would hear of it: Ardon's stableboy breaking into school. He took an unsteady deep breath and crept a step closer. As he approached the opening, a figure stepped out, nearly colliding with him. It was Ms. Folba.

Zodak's breath caught, and his mind spun. *Should I turn and run or start talking? Spouting excuses? Or I could just break down and tell the truth.* As he opened his mouth, fumbling silently for words, Ms. Folba walked right by him, not even glancing up. Zodak released the breath he had been holding. But then he noticed what had her so transfixed. She stared intently at something she held in her hands. *No,* said Zodak silently, gripped by a new terror. Ms. Folba glided down the hall as if in a trance, a perplexed expression on her face. She was reading his story.

4

Zodak cautiously trailed Ms. Folba, chewing his nails so low they bled. His mind spun. *What does this mean? What's going to happen to me?* Ms. Folba walked ahead, flipping a page over as she continued reading his story. As she turned into the empty classroom, Zodak reluctantly abandoned the pursuit. He stalled for a minute and then scampered back to his closet. Once safely inside, he peered through the crack into the classroom. Alone at her desk, Ms. Folba pored over his paper. *What's she looking for?* he wondered. *Is she trying to recognize the handwriting? Could she know? No.* She had never seen him write anything before, and with twenty children in the class, it would be all but impossible to identify him. Zodak whispered a pleading prayer to the Color. Ms. Folba suddenly gasped, covering her mouth with her hand as she read. When she finished the story, she dropped the paper on her desk. Her gaze drifted toward the window. Her face looked pale, and though it was hard to tell from his closet, Zodak thought she was trembling.

"Hi, Ms. Folba!" Both Ms. Folba and Zodak jumped at the

voice of the returning student. The rest of the class began streaming in from lunch.

When everyone was settled, Ms. Folba strode to the front of the class and rapped for attention. "Has everyone turned in their stories?" The general murmuring seemed to imply that they had. "Did every student walk right up here"—she signaled to the floor—"and put their paper on my desk?" she asked again. The students replied again with a muffled affirmative.

She doesn't know. Zodak's shoulders relaxed a bit.

"We'll try another way. Please raise your hand if your paper is not in this stack," she said, holding up the papers from her desk. She peered into the sea of children, looking for the missing student. No one raised a hand. She stood in silence, waiting. *No, no, no!* Zodak scolded himself. *Why didn't you burn it? The sprite, its warnings. You wrote too much!* At least he had left names out. Surely Ms. Folba couldn't track it back to him.

Finally, a young boy named Cilac shyly raised a trembling hand, glancing around self-consciously.

"Oh. Interesting," said Ms. Folba softly, wearing a quizzical expression. "Please come to the front and put your name on your paper. I have it here," she said, holding up Zodak's story. Cilac looked flustered. "It's all right, Cilac, come up front."

Obediently, he rose on unsteady feet. After two steps, Cilac faltered. "B-but I didn't have a chance to...to write mine," he whined. "My pa took my paper and marker from me." Whispers shot across the classroom floor. Cilac's father Circes was a local farmer and an exceedingly private man whose family had been on the same land for generations. In town meetings, Circes often warned of travelers and city folk passing through Laan—"thieving outsiders" he called them. His was one of the families that swore off all the old legends as fable.

"You didn't hide your paper somewhere?" Ms. Folba asked encouragingly.

"No," answered Cilac almost inaudibly, his face bright red. He smeared his tearing eye with the back of his sleeve.

"Okay. You may sit down, Cilac. Thank you."

Cilac raced back to the safety of his chair.

"Please work on your addition tables," said Ms. Folba, shaking her head. She counted each of the papers again, and marked a list. When she had finished the entire stack, she wore a confused look.

"Alana," she called, gesturing for Alana to come up front. Zodak couldn't hear what Ms. Folba said, but Alana's face lit up and she hurried back to her desk, returning with her story. Ms. Folba smiled politely, but her shoulders sagged.

Zodak found himself sweating in the closet. He desperately wanted his story back. *I can try to steal it after class,* he thought. But Ergis and Alana would be waiting for him, and Ms. Folba might take it with her. *I could tell her the truth.* Ardon had often reminded him that however hard, telling the truth was always best. But that might get him thrown out of the schoolhouse. *And what would it do to Ardon?* He had been dishonest, stealing the paper and hiding in the closet. They would discover that he had been skipping the stable work. *But maybe Ms. Folba would give me the story back. Isn't it mine?* Hallah wouldn't be happy with him if she found out, but when was she?

The questions gnawed at him on the walk home from school. He was distracted at dinner and while doing his evening chores, earning a switching on the legs from Hallah that he all but ignored.

"Everything okay?" asked Ardon while cleaning the cramped kitchen beside Zodak. "NO!" Zodak wanted to shout.

"Yes," he finally answered. "I was ... thinking about a lame foal we birthed today." He rarely lied to Ardon, and a cold, dark feeling crept over him.

"Hard to see new life suffer," answered Ardon with a nod. Zodak fought to keep from saying more.

That night, alone in the dark in bed, Zodak's lie echoed through his mind. The only other time he recalled lying to Ardon was about losing his pocketknife. "You must always take responsibility for your mistakes," Ardon had said when he discovered the truth, "no matter how hard it is, or how bad the mistake. This will make others trust you more, not less." Zodak made up his mind: he would tell Ms. Folba the next day.

He tossed and turned that night and found himself lying awake well before dawn had cracked the corner of the night sky. Today he would measure every word and watch each step. He couldn't afford a tangle with Ergis. To his relief, the cold stare was Ergis's only reprisal, and Alana was in the clouds again. Were it not for the pit in his stomach, Zodak would have relished the almost pleasant walk to the schoolhouse.

All day he anguished in the closet, waiting for the right time to fulfill his pledge. But none came. Morning recess came and went, and Ms. Folba spent lunch in the classroom with Djinda, who needed help on her addition grid. Zodak didn't touch his lunch. When the day was over, after the students had cleared out of the classroom and the stable children were packing bags, Zodak approached Ms. Folba on unsteady legs. He had never spoken a word to the teacher in three seasons, yet now, in a few days, he would have come to her twice. As he approached, she stood to leave. The words caught in his throat as she walked past him.

"Did you have a question for me?" she asked, catching his pleading glance.

"I... uh, yes," stammered Zodak. She nodded impatiently. On nice days, she always sipped tea after school under the huge copner tree as the children dispersed, waving goodbye.

"What is it?" She glanced up at the door. *This could wait until tomorrow,* thought Zodak.

"Uh... never mind. Sorry," he said.

"Okay." Ms. Folba smiled. "Have a nice evening," she added,

turning to go. Zodak's stomach was in his throat. She reached the doorway, pausing to let the last stable child shuffle out.

"I wrote it!" blurted Zodak.

Ms. Folba stopped short and cocked her head. "What?" she asked, turning and stepping slowly back into the room.

"I am the one who wrote that story."

"What story?" she asked with carefully measured words, her brow furrowed.

"The one you found in the closet," he replied, resigned to his fate. The blood pounded in his ears and his breathing was fast and shallow.

She pursed her lips. "I see." Her eyes darted back and forth. She was quiet. "I think... I think we'd better talk," she finally said. Ms. Folba directed him to her desk, pulling up a student chair. "Okay. Now, first tell me what—"

"Been waiting, scupp!" Ergis charged through the door into the now empty classroom. He froze when he saw Ms. Folba. "Oh, Ms. Folba. I... uh...sorry. I was looking for Zodak."

Zodak glanced helplessly up at Ms. Folba. His stomach twisted.

"Oh, yes, of course," she replied, turning back to Zodak. "Actually..." She hesitated. "Why don't you go ahead, Ergis? I need to talk to Zodak. I will walk him home when we're through."

Ergis opened and closed his mouth like a frog, but no sound came out. Finally, he murmured, "Yes, Ms. Folba," and backed out of the room.

"All right. Well, we got your name out of the way, Zodak. I am Ms. Folba. So please, tell me about this paper."

Zodak took a deep breath and blurted his confession. "I took the extra paper you gave me."

"I see," she replied, nodding thoughtfully. "But Zodak, tell me about this story. Did you write it?"

"Yes, ma'am," replied Zodak, now uneasy again.

She was quiet for a moment, searching his face. "I am impressed. This writing is quite good." Zodak blushed, blindsided by the compliment. "But I am more interested in the subject of your story," continued Ms. Folba. "The tiny water figure. Where did that idea come from? Did you hear it somewhere?"

Zodak's brow furrowed. "No, Ms. Folba. It happened to me just three days ago."

"Are you sure, Zodak?" she pressed, her face intent.

His heart sank. Now he understood. *You're here because of your fanciful story and overactive imagination. No, it's worse. She thinks you're crazy. Maybe dangerous!*

"Yes," he answered in defeat. "It was out on the path behind our well..." He stopped short. *What's the point?* "You think I'm making it all up," he said, exasperated.

Ms. Folba looked solemn and held his gaze. "Zodak, come with me, please," she instructed.

He followed obediently with heavy steps. She led him out of the classroom and down the hallway. This wouldn't go well. All the excitement he had from opening this door and letting Ms. Folba in now melted into dread. *You've made a huge mistake.* Even if Ms. Folba didn't think him crazy, he couldn't prove his claim. *You should have kept this secret locked in your mind where it would be safe!* the voice inside accused. *At least you could have told her you invented it. Fool!* he scolded himself. *What will this do to Ardon?*

She continued past his closet, walking to the end of the hallway. He glanced longingly at the safety of his dark little refuge. Maybe Ardon would attest to the blue sparkling bark that changed color... *No, even that sounds crazy.*

"Bring that lantern," said Ms. Folba, pointing to the lamp hanging in the hall. At the dead end of the hallway, Ms. Folba reached up and pulled a lever. With a creaking squeal, a panel in the ceiling lowered, revealing attic stairs. Zodak hadn't even known these stairs existed. The flickering lamp stretched its dancing fingers across a dusty storage space that spanned the length of the school building.

Ms. Folba led him through a maze of boxes and papers, a few dusty books, and more towers of boxes. Tucked back behind a small mountain of old school chairs and desks stood a short, sturdy wooden cabinet. Ms. Folba pulled an iron key from a fold in her dress. It fit snugly into the weathered lock. *Click.* The doors groaned open.

"Could you bring that lamp close?" she asked. Zodak complied, craning his neck to see what she was doing. "Ah," said Ms. Folba, pulling a cloth bundle from the cabinet. She heaved it up on a nearby crate and slowly unwrapped the oiled canvas to reveal a thick leather-bound book. She pulled the lamp nearer and ever so carefully lifted open the cover and began gently turning the pages as if they were butterfly wings. A puff of dust escaped the old book. Her searching stopped. She turned another page. After a moment, she asked, "Is this what you saw?" Zodak searched her face but found no hint of irony or a joke in her voice. He drew near to the book.

Filling most of the yellowed page was a painting, cracked and faded by time. To Zodak's shock, he immediately recognized the image of the little water creature that had spoken to him just days before. "So I didn't imagine it!" he said with triumph. His heart raced and his palms were clammy.

"No, you did not," replied Ms. Folba. "Listen." She read from the dusty book, "*The elusive water sprite is rarely viewed, and never by chance. They have been reported to speak in riddles and deliver their message at seemingly random times over the span of hours, days, or even seasons. (Footnote: see e.g., visitation of De'Olandria, during the First Span at the Bond of Elven Ŕih't*— Yes, yes, yes..." She skipped ahead.

"*The more urgent the message, the more clearly it is delivered. The Memoirs of a Fallen Sisterhood claim that King Keanor's nursemaid saved him as a baby from Mokala, the Sea Wolf Captain, after a warning from a water sprite. Again, in the first wave of Judges, Judge Oleon is said to have communicated with the Gray Ambassador through water sprites*—Okay, okay, here it is," she continued.

"*The words of a water sprite are to be heeded. The recipient of such a sacred message carried by the Color receives on his or her shoulders the burden of destiny. By heeding or ignoring the prompting of water sprites, great nations have been established and destroyed, races have been devastated and redeemed, and the schemes of the Ice King have been vanquished or empowered.*"

"The Ice King?!" The name sent a chill down his spine.

"Well, yes, but we won't speak of that here," she replied quickly.

"So, what does this mean?" asked Zodak.

"I had read of sprites in my studies in Pol Dak," replied Ms. Folba. "Your story described them exactly like the ancient texts, which confirmed to me that they still exist!" She looked at him with wide, hopeful eyes. "What this means, Zodak, is that something important is happening, and I believe you may be involved somehow."

He looked down self-consciously. *That can't be true.*

"You have a role to play, one that may affect not just Laan, but this entire region of Rislaan, or even Yiduiijn." She laid a hand on his shoulder.

Ha! Impossible! Zodak liked Ms. Folba, he really did, but this was too much. He slept in a glorified closet. He collected dung patties. He was hit and insulted daily, relegated to a barn every day to learn to shoe and clean horses—clean horses! He wasn't wise or brave or handsome or valiant. He couldn't shoot a pike melon from a galloping horse at a hundred mounts. That was what heroes could do. *"It's thick-headed fools who believe fanciful tales and mystical creatures."* Hallah's voice rang loudly in his ears. Maybe she was right. He knew one thing: he wasn't what this kind, misled schoolteacher thought he was. Anger and confusion flooded his thoughts.

"I know this might seem overwhelming," reassured Ms. Folba. "It must feel like the world is turned upside down. You may not even know if you believe it or not. But this book isn't just some collection of fairy tales. This is *The Greater Collection of Knowledge*, compiled by the Buruth Scholars at Hoonk Point hundreds of seasons ago, with works of Zebubo the Chronicler himself," said Ms. Folba, carefully closing the heavy book and dusting off the front so Zodak could read the gold words etched in the book's leather cover. "It may be the only one in Rislaan other than in the Elder's Keep. My grandfather, a great inventor and amateur historian, was gifted this copy for warning the scholars of the coming thunder tide that would have destroyed the ancient library. Zodak, I assure you, this is no joke."

"Okay," said Zodak blankly, his thoughts jumbled like tangled fence wire. *What is she saying? Can any of this be possible?* He tried to shut the voice down, but the spark of exhilarating possibility remained. The two sat in silence.

"I need to speak with your parents—your guardians," she said.

"You can't. Uh, Ardon doesn't get home until one or two past," said Zodak.

"I will speak to Hallah, then," offered Ms. Folba.

"No!" he blurted. "I mean, she isn't going to like what you have to say."

She looked at him questioningly.

"We must wait and tell Ardon," Zodak pleaded more than demanded. He wasn't sure how Hallah might respond, but he didn't want to find out.

"Zodak, you can't know how important this is. Maybe Ardon will be home early today."

Ms. Folba wrapped the book up and locked it in the cabinet. The two climbed down from the attic. Zodak had been at school long after the last class. Pink hues stained the golden light. *How will I answer Ergis's questions?* Zodak noticed he had already begun to worry less about Alana, though her fragile transformation could crack at any moment. Ergis wouldn't sleep tonight until he knew why Zodak was kept so late. Zodak was a stable child. He had no business even being in the classroom, much less staying late in secret conversation with Ms. Folba. *And what about Hallah? She'd never understand this, would she?* He could feel it: a storm was gathering, and he was heading straight into it.

5

Zodak trailed Ms. Folba out of the schoolhouse as the pair started down the dirt road towards the small cluster of houses just outside of town. The ruby sun cast long shadows that stretched across the road and melted into the dark grain fields. Zodak tried to put words to the dread that welled in him. Ms. Folba had agreed to his begging to withhold the details about his hiding in the closet and writing the story and to speak with Hallah and Ardon privately, away from his cousins. *"I'm well aware of the cruelty that can infect children,"* she had said knowingly.

Ms. Folba and Zodak arrived at the house just as the sun dipped below the horizon. Zodak looked anxiously for signs of Ardon, but the horse and wagon were still gone. Before they had even reached the overgrown stone path leading to the front door, Ergis appeared.

"What did Zodak do?" asked Ergis as innocently as he could, but Zodak could see the eagerness in his eyes. Hungry for news of Zodak's transgression and punishment, no doubt.

"Ahoi, Ergis," said Ms. Folba with a smile. Zodak cringed,

bracing for her reply. "Zodak's going to help me organize some of the supplies at school," she replied.

Ergis's face dropped as his anticipation evaporated.

"He'll be arranging stacks of books and papers in the attic. Would you like to help?"

"No! Uh, thanks," replied Ergis, slinking behind the house.

Ms. Folba winked at Zodak, and he released the breath he had been holding. The two approached the front door, stepping around a pile of wood shavings and Ergis's pocketknife, carelessly discarded once he had lost interest in his whittling project. She knocked.

Hallah opened the door a bit too quickly. "Oh, Ms. Foley," she said with an artificial smile, then shot a glare at Zodak. "What has the boy done now?"

"It's actually Ms. Folba, but please just call me Folba." She smiled warmly. "And Zodak hasn't done anything wrong, but I would like to talk to you in private if I could."

"I... I don't understand," said Hallah curtly. "If he's not in trouble, why did you keep him? Why must we talk?"

"May I?" asked Ms. Folba, gesturing inside. Hallah hesitated for an instant too long.

"Of course." She wore her long silkeen house robe, now showing its age, and toted her tall cup of bitter bandi. They walked to a small alcove in the back of the snug house.

"Hi, Ms. Folba!" Alana waved, excited to have this celebrity in her home.

"Ahoi, Alana."

"I'm on page six of my story!" Alana exclaimed.

"That's trimidious! I can't wait to read it."

"I think you'll like it," Alana called. Ms. Folba smiled.

"We'll just be a minute, dear," interrupted Hallah, glaring up at Alana as she ushered Ms. Folba into the study.

"Please excuse us, Zodak," said Ms. Folba. Zodak longed to listen in, but Hallah pulled the heavy curtains across the entrance to corner of the house referred to as the den. At least behind the wall of wool that greedily swallowed sound, the Wickeds couldn't hear either. Zodak slipped outside and crouched at the corner of the house, where a wooden patch covered the rotten siding. Sounds from the den could be heard clearly here, as he had learned one summer evening when fleeing the tumultuous house.

"Now, what is it?" he could hear Hallah asking. He pictured her settling into her favorite chair.

Ms. Folba began cautiously, "This may be hard to believe, but I believe Zodak may be... special. He may have an...important role to play. I think you should take him to see the High Elder of the Venerable Council."

Hallah burst out laughing.

"I know how this sounds, but Hallah, I assure you, it's no joke. Zodak was visited by a water sprite that—"

"Yes, Alana told me about this imaginary chipmunk made of water, speaking fate to the boy. Ms. Folby, if you've come to encourage these delusions, I'm afraid you're wasting your time."

"Actually, what Zodak saw was no illusion. I spent several seasons studying ancient texts at the Institute of Forgotten Learning, and the type of water sprite described by Zodak has been documented throughout history. Its appearance signifies something of great importance." Ms. Folba launched into a detailed narrative of the sprites, and the history surrounding their appearances.

Hallah was uncharacteristically quiet as Ms. Folba spoke. Then, her tone changed abruptly. "And you're sure you have the right boy?"

"Absolutely," replied Ms. Folba.

"What would the High Elder tell us?" asked Hallah, her voice now sounding almost earnest. *What's she doing?* thought Zodak.

"Well, she may be able to help interpret the message Zodak

received. There could be much hanging in the balance here. We simply must understand the visit with as much clarity as possible. It's quite exciting!"

Hallah was quiet again for a moment. "I suppose it would be helpful to have the Elder hear of the incident," replied Hallah finally. Zodak almost fell over. "I will discuss it with my husband and we will send the boy before the week is out."

"Oh, thank you! I think you're making the right choice. And I'm sure your sister can help you gain an audience before the Elder."

"My sister?" asked Hallah.

"Yes. Alana told the class about her position on the Council."

"Oh," Hallah replied. "Yes, I'm sure she can." *Something's wrong.* "Well, thank you very much for coming by. I am sorry to have reacted strongly to your suggestion at first. You must understand, it was quite a lot to take in."

"I understand. Shall we tell Zodak?"

"Yes. I think that would be good." Hallah called for Zodak. He tore himself away from the woodpile and hurried to the front of the house. There was still no sign of Ardon, and it was one past already. Ms. Folba told Zodak about the plan while Hallah looked on. He couldn't believe what he was hearing. *Hallah agreed to this?* It sounded amazing. *There must be a catch.*

"Well, thank you again for coming," said Hallah the moment Ms. Folba finished, now moving to the door.

"Oh. Yes, it was my pleasure," responded Ms. Folba. "Zodak, you're welcome to join our class any time."

"But we don't have an allocation for him!" Hallah cut in.

"I'll speak to the administrator. For Zodak, I'm sure we can make an exception this season," she said, smiling at him. "Will you be there tomorrow?"

"Yes!" he replied, feeling like he was floating.

"No," cut in Hallah. "Have you forgotten your trip to the

Komo market tomorrow?" she asked with thinly feigned sincerity.

"Oh, yes." Zodak suddenly remembered, sorry to miss his very first day as a real student in class. "I suppose not."

"Well, I must get dinner on the table," Hallah said curtly. "Goodnight, Ms. Fobley."

"Goodnight," replied Ms. Folba, even as the door swung closed.

No sooner had the door shut than Hallah spun to face Zodak. "Come with me!" she hissed. She marched him back to the study and drew the curtain. "Listen and listen well, boy. I am willing to play along with this nonsense. I will even arrange to have you brought to Pol Dak. But when they tell you that you're a slagging fool given to childhood fancy—that you're nothing but a cursed stableboy with too much imagination—I don't want to hear another word about this ever again. Do you understand me?" *There it was. Now it made sense.* Hallah would quietly play along and protect her reputation. Any objection risked escalation.

"Yes," replied Zodak soberly. In truth, he had expected much, much worse. *I'm going to Pol Dak!* The thought shot a jolt of excitement as it flitted through his mind.

"And another thing," snapped Hallah. "I don't want you to speak a word of this to Ardon until you return from Pol Dak. There's no need to fill his mind with this filth. Besides, we both know he'd insist on going with you, and we'll not forego two days' wages so he can babysit you on this fool's errand. You leave for Komo in the morning. I will make plans to have you brought to the city after you return from market, but speak one word of this to Ardon, and I promise you I will make sure you never set foot in Pol Dak until you're a grown man. Do you understand me?"

Zodak hesitated. He burned to tell Ardon every detail from the day. Keeping this news to himself for even two or three days would be excruciating. But Hallah would make good on her threat. She was as vindictive as Ergis. *Besides, what if what Ms. Folba told me could be true? What if the High Elder confirms what Folba read? That would change everything!* Zodak could march triumphantly back into town and tell Ardon the whole, beautiful truth. It was worth the wait. Zodak nodded his understanding to Hallah.

"Good. Now start the fire and prepare for your trip to Komo tomorrow."

Zodak obeyed, his spirits soaring. As he packed his bag, he considered telling Ardon about his paper, and how Ms. Folba had complimented him on his writing and had invited him to join the class; after all, Hallah had said nothing about mentioning that. *But how could I explain the way it came about?* He couldn't bring himself to lie to Ardon again. No, it would have to wait until he returned from Pol Dak. *What will Ardon say when he learns I'm gone? That Hallah kept this from him?* He pushed these worries from his mind. No matter what the Elder said, Zodak would return a real student. Maybe much more.

"Hello, my family!" called Ardon, walking in through the side door. He said the same thing every day. Hallah hastily finished scribbling a message in grease stick on a square patch of smoothed leather. She rolled it and slid it into her robe just as Ardon walked in.

Zodak struggled to hold his tongue during dinner. Staying quiet was his best tactic. Later, lying awake in bed, he replayed everything that had happened that day. After hours of staring into the dark, his mind spinning, he finally dozed off.

6

The charred husk of dawn enveloped Zodak as he stepped from the small house. The smell of morning fire hung in the air. Ardon was already awake, fitting the horse and wagon.

"Good morning, son." He smiled. "Ready for your trip? You were awfully quiet last night."

"Yes. I am ready." Zodak tried to sound casual, as if he weren't holding back the most important news of his life.

"It's a long ride. I could come with you." Ardon always offered, and Zodak always declined. He could think of nothing better than a full, glorious day with Ardon, but he dared not be the cause of lost wages.

"I'll be okay, but thank you." Zodak climbed up into the wagon.

"Be safe. I will see you tonight, son."

Zodak clapped the reins against the tired silver mare, Sal, and she jerked her head up. Without Sal, Ardon would have to walk the cliq and a half to the mines today. Ardon never complained, but Zodak had heard stories of how grueling the work in the mines could be, and he hated to think of Ardon walking all the way home at the end of the day.

"Ardon—" The call came unbidden.

Ardon stopped. "Son?"

"I... I..." *I am going to see the Elder! I might be marked by the Color! I read legends of the sprites with the Kings!* His head spun.

"What is it?"

Hallah's warning flashed through Zodak's mind. "Thank you for waking with me," he finally said blankly.

"It is my joy, son. May the Color light your path today."

"Thank you." His whole inside shouted. The cart creaked and shuddered, crawling away from the house. As Sal picked up her gait, Zodak turned and waved. Ardon returned the wave and watched the boy until he was out of sight.

Once on the road, Zodak's whirling thoughts returned. *What did the sprite mean? What adventures call me? What great purpose?* He strained to imagine such a purpose in Laan. But Folba had also promised school. Zodak imagined himself entering the classroom, not as a stableboy but as a student. *Ergis will be that much more jealous and bothersome, but he can't match me in the classroom.* Zodak knew and remembered dates, facts, and stories from history. He could already add, subtract, multiply, and divide. This new competition at school would fuel Ergis's jealousy, but that battle had rules, and playing by the rules, Zodak could crush Ergis. Outside the classroom, though, outside of the rules, Ergis would be ruthless.

He shook the thought from his head, and his mind skipped to Alana. *What happened to her?* Zodak could feel the weight of her corq bouncing in his shirt pocket. He had long since abandoned any hope for friendship that had flickered in her rare acts of kindness when Ergis wasn't around. But he could feel hope rising again. He found he actually looked forward to doing this simple favor for her. Ever since the writing assignment, she was a new person. What had she written about? If he hadn't seen it with his own eyes, he would never have believed it possible.

Finally, he let his thoughts drift to Pol Dak and the Venerable Council. The idea, the hope. They were almost too big to hold. He had never been to Pol Dak. Most villagers in Laan hadn't. Though back when the farm was prospering, before Zodak could remember, Ardon had traveled to Pol Dak to buy silka seeds for planting. Trading in the impossibly soft silka pods, later spun into silkeen, could be a lucrative business. That's what Ardon had dreamed of. He struggled to imagine Hallah in her prime, without the biting bitterness, but he recalled hearing Ardon speak wistfully of memories of the two, working side by side after sunset planting rows upon rows of seed as the babies played in the dirt. Hope. That's what they shared. Before the drought. Before Zodak.

Ardon had described Pol Dak to the children many times – not one of Yiduiijn's great cities, like Epis Kopol or City K'andoria, but a true city nonetheless. Zodak couldn't quite picture the long streets with houses stacked atop one another, or the constant humming noise of people in those streets. They would be teeming with golyath snails and teams of stallions, drawing huge wagons of goods and passengers. He had studied the map and the stately governor's mansion and sprawling courtyard, that stood at the dead center of the city, flanked by the hearing hall, commerce center, and city guard stronghold and barracks. The cluster of official buildings all stood elevated above the shoulders of row houses, inns, and shops, and were encircled by a high block wall. The rest of the city fanned out in all directions, eventually relaxing into a skirt of farms and fields, interrupted only at the edge of the patchwork where, high on a bluff overlooking Pol Dak—looking down on it, some said—perched the imposing Venerable Council Keep and pristine grounds of the Revered Sisters.

A gust of wind blew past him, shooing away the lofty thoughts of the grand city. As the swirl of dust in the road dissipated, it revealed the hunched profile of Komo's lone lookout tower on the horizon. The trip had passed quickly. Zodak had barely scratched the surface of his thoughts. How could he grasp or understand the possibilities that lay in Pol Dak?

He pulled up to Komo just before midday. The village was larger and wealthier than Laan, but, excluding traders and travelers, not much more populous. Aside from the market, there was no town center to speak of, just a sprinkling of modest homes and a handful of farms, arranged in a circle around the marketplace and the cluster of inns and eateries, the heartbeat of the village. A teetering weathered wooden wall surrounded the market square and nearby houses, but free passage in and out of Komo had long been prized over its security. The wide gates were perpetually flung open and now sagged. Long grass and vines grew up, around, and over the slats and cross braces. Zodak doubted they could close anymore, even if they had to.

"Come for trade today?" Zodak nearly lost his seat in the wagon as he lurched in surprise at the scratchy whine of a voice from below. "A freshness of face in there, boy." Zodak had first taken the old woman for a heap of rags and even now, the shriveled and creased face seemed suspended in a lumpy pile of discarded shreds of cloth.

"Um. Yes. I've come for market." He tried to smile politely and push ahead through the gates.

"May the Elder keep us."

Zodak slowed, seeing a woman behind the face now for the first time. Pale blue, washed-out eyes stared vacantly from hollowed eye sockets in the leathered face, speckled with a faded ink pattern from many seasons past. Piles of tattered fabric covered her like the feathers of a decrepit old bird. One gnarled hand grasped a wooden bowl, and with the other she ground some sort of blue chalk fragments into powder.

"Keep us she does." He recited the reply that remained locked away somewhere in the recesses of memory.

"And for that we should be daily thankful." So the adage

went. He nodded. "Much she protects us from," added the woman. *That wasn't part of the recitation.*

"Goblins, you mean?" he asked, intrigued. The village children regularly told stories of these malevolent imps roving distant forests. A nuisance, but only truly dangerous in numbers. The woman gave him an inscrutable stare. "The Elder protects us from all margoul and keeps them at bay," he added quickly, pride swelling as he parroted back what Folba had said a few days before in the classroom.

"Boy, it's not the silly beasts in the woods she shields us from. Were these villagers able to grasp even a hint of the true evil she defends us against, terror would paralyze them. Horror would own them."

Zodak swallowed hard.

"H'ol Chazkar," she cooed. Something stabbed through him like a freezing pinprick.

"The Ice King? What do you know about him? Is he real?" asked Zodak.

"Is he real?" The old woman echoed the question, as if weighing it on her tongue. "The very ground rumbles with his waking. May I not live to see that day." A shiver ran through Zodak's body.

"Hiyah!" Zodak started as a horse and wagon rumbled past, the driver muttering loudly.

"What does it mean he's waking—" Zodak turned back, but the woman was gone. Or at least her hands and face were gone. The heap of cloth remained, still and silent. "Hello?" Zodak called. He considered poking the mound but thought better of it. With a reluctant snap of the reins, he urged Sal ahead into Komo, trying to shake off the chill of the woman's words.

Traders and visitors from several nearby towns and villages frequented Komo, but the crowd was far from exotic. Most of the goods were second-rate, even if unavailable in Laan. Still, Zodak enjoyed the market's buzz. He visited the vendors, methodically working through the list, collecting exactly what Hallah had requested. After a couple of hours, he had found everything with one minor substitution. As he made a final pass, he spied scarves of all colors dancing in the breeze under a sturdy white tent. Zodak pointed to a rich blue scarf nestled between the deep emerald and blazing orange ones. The tall, wiry vendor wearing a faded multicolored patchwork coat unclasped it and handed it to Zodak with a watchful eye. The material felt amazing, like fine oil running through his fingers. He could just imagine the look on Alana's face.

"Five corqs," grunted the man behind the table.

"Five?" said Zodak, looking up, surprised. "I thought these were one corq each."

"Hrrmph," snorted the man. "Nie. They're five."

"But a friend bought one just last week for a corq," persisted Zodak.

"Week past, an old fellow from the Slag had some small, cotton ones for a corq, but he'sa packed up and moved on. This is silkeen, boy."

"All I've got is one corq," replied Zodak, his shoulders dropping.

"Well then, all I've got is a handshake and a 'thanks for stopping by,'" retorted the vendor, snatching the scarf back.

Zodak counted his money again. Hallah always gave him just enough to buy what she needed and expected exact change. He had one corq and a couple of dithers change for Hallah, not enough for the scarf. Besides, he dared not spend Hallah's money. Only minutes before he had imagined returning with the beautiful scarf and the new bond forged with Alana, but there he stood, empty-handed. Crushed by the defeat, Zodak slowly turned back to the wagon when a call from a nearby booth caught his attention: "Pay a corq, win a krown! Pay a corq, win a krown!" He slowed his gait. Earlier in the day, the gamer's tent was buzzing with people, yet it seemed rather empty now.

"Ya look like you have some luck about you!" shouted the gamesman, who stood stacking coins. "Why don't you come on down and try Roll of Fate!" The game was simple enough, the man explained. The player pays a corq and rolls a giant multi-faceted wooden die. The number that ends facing up is the pay. The die was the size of a hog's head. It must have had over a hundred faces, most of which would probably take the corq. How would he ever explain to Alana if he lost her money? *No, I can't.* He glanced longingly back at the silkeen scarves fluttering like rainbow feathers in the wind.

"Worried about losing a corq?" The gamesman had perfected his pitch and could read most every face. "Watch me." He gave the die a roll. When it settled, it showed a "1c." "A corq! See, I lost nothing!" Zodak took a deep breath and stepped up to the table. "That's a boy!" encouraged the gamesman.

Zodak slowly unbuttoned his shirt pocket and handed over Alana's corq. He lifted the carved wood block with both hands and inspected it. There were more than a hundred faces. Many showed a zero.

"Go on, youngster!"

With a deep breath, Zodak tossed the die across the table. It tumbled and bumped, then slowed and stopped.

"Let's take a look!" said the gamesman. He and Zodak walked to the other side of the table. The polished triangular wooden face pointing up showed a zero.

"Oh, I'm sorry!" said the gamesman, quickly pocketing the corq. "Would you like to try again?"

Zodak fumed. *How could you have been so stupid?* He had lost his only corq, Alana's corq. Whatever fragile bridge had been growing between them would certainly shatter.

Wait, he thought. *I do have one other corq.* Zodak took

Hallah's small leather purse from his pocket. As he was deliberating, a tall woman with broad shoulders and deep red hair strode up to the table. She seemed to tower over the pudgy gamesman.

"You keeping things honest, Pritch?" she asked.

"Well, yes, ma'am, I am. Just like always."

Zodak could tell from her tall shiny boots and the sword she brandished that she carried some sort of authority. "You sure you want to do that?" she asked Zodak, who stood dumbly with the corq in his hand. He wasn't at all sure.

"I... I think I have to..." he finally said.

"There you have it!" boomed the gamesman's voice, as he snatched the corq from Zodak's hand. "Give her a whirl, young fella."

Zodak picked up the die. He thought long and hard. He pictured the *K* mark facing up, showing he had won a krown, nine corqs, and collecting his money. Opening his eyes, he realized he had been holding his breath. He let it out slowly and released the die. It tumbled out of his hand, bouncing across the table. Time stopped. The die crashed against the far wall, teetered, and came to a stop.

"Let's take a look, shall we?" The gamesman's musical voice broke his trance. Zodak, the gamesman, and the woman, now curious about the outcome, walked to the other side. As he neared the other end of the table, Zodak's heart plummeted. He could see the zero as he approached. He was lost. Alana would hate him, and Hallah would be apoplectic. *What have you done?* He started to panic. *Will Hallah rescind her offer to help me get to Pol Dak?*

The gamesman's sputtering and choking interrupted Zodak's frantic thoughts. The pudgy man was white and looked like he couldn't breathe. His eyes bulged, and he gripped his chest. He stared at the die. Zodak glanced down. He saw now that what he had taken to be a *o* was actually the top half of a *Q*, which was followed by a lowercase *w*.

"My Color!" exclaimed the woman, staring in wonder at the die.

"What does 'Qw' mean?" asked Zodak, glancing around, surprised by the reaction.

"It means Queen's-weight. You've just won a queen's-weight gold piece, boy!" exclaimed the woman, her eyes still fixated on the die.

Zodak's heart skipped a beat. *Gold?* The word was too high for him to reach. Gold was kings. Gold was power. Gold was fairy tale. From the look of the gamesman, though, this was no fantasy. Zodak couldn't speak.

"Queen's-weight equals half a Zo'ol. That's more than ten thousand corqs! You could buy a manor with that!" exclaimed the woman. She grabbed the babbling gamesman by the lapel and ordered him to pay, looming over him as he counted to be sure. Zodak's brain felt empty and his lips numb and tingling. He gaped in wonderment, unable to understand what was happening. The gamesman, of course, had no queen's-weight gold piece, so he counted the amount from what he had. Dejectedly, he swept piles and piles of coins into a leather sack. When the shelves were empty, the count was still 910 corqs short. The leather bag bulged, its rippling walls stretched tight. While only the size of a pumpkin, the gamesman groaned as he lifted the sack off the floor. Zodak still couldn't speak.

The woman heaved the bag over into Zodak's arms. He stumbled under its weight and cradled it with both hands, straining.

"Boy." She bent low. "Take that and leave right now!" She spoke urgently, glancing around. "A fortune like this doesn't stay hidden long; you should be far from here when the word spreads." She reached into the gamesman's pocket and pulled out Zodak's first two corqs, flipping them to Zodak. "Now go!"

Zodak lumbered across the road to the scarf tent. He set the bag down at his feet, checking over each shoulder, and slapped down a krown and a corq. "The blue scarf, please," he said in the most respectful tone he could summon. The rude vendor wore a confused look. "And the orange one," Zodak added. When the vendor returned, Zodak grabbed the scarves and hurried to his wagon. He could feel the searing stares on his back as he waddled across the road. He thudded the coins in the wagon and jumped to the seat. A small knot of people had begun to form at the game hut. Someone pointed in his direction, and his stomach twisted. He whipped the reins again and again. Sal lazily plodded ahead. Zodak kept snapping the reins and yelled at the horse, not daring to look back. After an eternity, Sal's trot finally built to a canter, and Zodak fled from Komo, smiling from ear to ear.

7

As he bumped along the road home, Zodak constantly looked over his shoulder, certain he was being followed. He was soaring. Still in disbelief, he reached back to feel the firm bulge of the bag under an oiled canvas cover. He knew exactly what he wanted to do with the money: he would give it to Ardon. It would pay all of Ardon's debts and free him from the krius mines.

Zodak imagined it: *Riding triumphantly to Barst's manor, beaming with pride as Ardon dropped the coins on the desk and purchased back every cliq of his family's farmland, and then some. There would still be plenty of money to build a new barn, to stock the storehouse, and more. He'd work the farm beside Ardon the rest of the season. The entire glorious future played out in Zodak's head. Might the rest of the family accept him? Alana would adore the scarves, that he knew. Hallah couldn't help but be pleased with the riches, could she? Maybe, just maybe even Ergis would forgive Zodak... No. Likely not; but with the rest of the family on his side, Zodak would be free.*

He was so lost in thought that Zodak failed to hear the horse's hooves behind him until they were close. He jolted out of his daydream. Two men approached fast from the rear. The cart continued at a trot, but the riders were galloping, headed straight for him.

Zodak looked around frantically for something to defend himself with. He reached back into the wagon, his fingers groping for a weapon. They closed around a weathered axe handle missing a head. He pulled it to the seat next to him, his knuckles white and every muscle in his body tensed. The riders slowed as they approached. The dirty tub of a man riding behind eyed the cart. But the man in the front froze Zodak's blood with his black searching stare. Dark brown hair framed the man's hard features. His large, dark eyes gleamed, whether with friendliness or fierceness, Zodak couldn't tell. A long thin scar trickled from his left eye to his chin. He wore a stiff emerald riding coat, fastened with brass buttons. At his side hung a short sword, its black wood handle studded with silver, and dark brown leather pants hung over black boots spattered with mud. He rode a chestnut horse—a fine animal—tall, sleek, and powerful. It bore a small circular brand on its flank that Zodak couldn't quite make out. Zodak met the man's stare, his stomach in knots, hand clenching the axe handle. Time stopped.

"*Hiyah!*" the man shouted. Zodak started, nearly falling from the seat, and the two tore off down the road. Zodak exhaled, his heart still pounding. *They weren't after the coin. They weren't after the coin!* He threw his head back against the afternoon light and breathed deeply, letting out a loud sigh, then a deep laugh.

The sky was stained pink with blooms of red as Zodak approached Laan, but his joy hadn't dimmed. He was dying to see Ardon. *Won't the fortune change Hallah's mind about the missed wages? Maybe I can tell Ardon everything now! Should I just march into the house holding the fortune in my arms, or should I bring the family out to the cart? No. I must act as if nothing has happened until Ardon returns, then I will tell the full, glorious tale. It* was safer that way. He slowed the horse and pulled quietly up to the shed. After coming to a stop, he waited. Hearing nothing, he leapt from the wagon to retrieve the coin. Zodak looked around cautiously before peeling back the canvas. The bag full of promises lay just where he had left it. He heaved it out of the cart and waddled into the shed. He hurried to the corner, dropped the bag on the floor with a thud, and hurriedly removed the loose plank. For once, there was real treasure in his secret spot. He replaced the board and returned to the cart.

As Zodak unpacked the goods from the market, Alana emerged from the house. He smiled to himself as his fingers flitted over to the box where he had carefully stowed the two scarves.

"Hi, Zodak. How was your trip?" she asked.

"It didn't exactly...go as expected," he replied, enjoying the unusually cordial conversation.

"Well... did you find any scarves?" she asked hopefully.

"I'm sorry. I didn't see the scarves for a corq. The man selling them had left just this week." He cast his eyes downward in feigned disappointment. *Is this act a mistake? Could this break the spell?*

"Oh, burn!" She looked down. "I was so hoping you'd find one."

"Here's your corq," said Zodak, handing her the compact wooden box.

"Thanks," she said, taking the box. "*Ooh,*" she gasped as she opened it and the scarf billowed out. "You *did* find it... *Amazing!*" she squealed as she pulled out the length of the blue silky azure fabric. "What?! *Two?* Zodak, thank you!" she said, her eyes sparkling at him. "How? They are absolutely beautiful." She squealed and skipped away, flying the scarves overhead.

Who was that girl? Zodak shook his head and unloaded the rest of the cart.

After he had fed and watered Sal and hung up the tack, the

sun dipped just below the hills. That meant Ardon would be home in an hour or two. Zodak could barely contain himself. He tried again to imagine Ardon's reaction. This would mean a new life for them both. *"Ardon, we can get your farm back."* Or, better, *"Father, our troubles are over!"* Ardon looks at him questioningly. *"What are you saying, son?"* Zodak tells him everything: *the greedy little gamesman, the woman*—no, better yet, *he takes Ardon to the shed and dramatically peels back the floorboard to reveal the fortune! Yes! That's it.* He could see the look on Ardon's face.

Zodak paced anxiously in the front yard, letting his thoughts run free as the time stubbornly crept by. The sun was gone. *Another hour at least.* He decided to bring in Hallah's things from Komo to pass the time. He had hoped to avoid her altogether until Ardon returned, but it would give him something to do. Zodak returned to the side of the shed. Something had changed. *Where are the boxes from the market?* He had unloaded everything and stacked all of it neatly beside the shed. That was only minutes ago. Hallah couldn't have brought it in so soon. Zodak heard a shuffle in the shed. *No!* his mind screamed. *The money!* He ran for the shed and burst into the room.

Bam! The door slammed behind him. Zodak whirled around. There stood Ergis, blocking the door.

"What is all this, Zodak?" asked Ergis in a singsong mocking tone, his hands on his cheeks in feigned surprise. Zodak spun back, surveying the room. To his relief, the secret corner appeared untouched. But there in the middle of the shed lay the crates from Komo, smashed and broken. Pillot oil seeped into the cracks on the floor. A piglet sniffed and chewed at the herbs. "It looks like you had an accident!" mocked Ergis, a sick smile on his face. "Mother has told you not to balance the boxes on top of each other. They can easily tip."

Zodak breathed a sigh of relief. *The money is safe.* "I'll just tell her what happened," said Zodak unconvincingly.

"No, you won't," replied Ergis. It was true, of course. Hallah would never believe Zodak over Ergis. Besides, if Zodak *could* somehow convince her that Ergis had engineered all of this and managed to escape blame, Ergis wouldn't have his revenge, and another, worse attack would follow shortly. Any other day, Zodak would be desperate, frantic. But today it didn't matter. When Ardon returned, broken oil bottles and fouled herbs would seem like such small and petty problems.

"You're right," said Zodak. He walked to the pile of crates, carefully removing an unbroken bottle of oil.

"Zodak!" It was Hallah's voice from outside. Ergis's face lit up with an evil grin, watching Zodak expectantly, waiting to savor the fear and horror.

"But you know what?" Zodak's eyes stayed fixed on Ergis's. "I don't care," he said, calmly letting go of the bottle. It shattered on the floor. The piglet scampered away.

"Huh?" Ergis frowned in confusion and his untethered gaze darted around the room. Footsteps sounded outside the shed. Zodak turned calmly to greet Hallah. With a crash, the shed door flew open, slamming against the wall. Instead of Hallah, there in the door stood the scarred man in the emerald riding coat who had passed Zodak earlier that day. Hallah edged in beside him.

"There he is," she said, pointing to Zodak. The man and his stout companion pushed into the shed. Zodak's stomach lurched. *Are they here for the treasure?* In the seconds before, he had decided that, when Hallah entered in her tornado of curses and screams over the broken crates, Zodak would reveal the bounty, turning her rage to joy. But everything had changed. *What is this?*

"Mother, look what—" Ergis began.

"Quiet!" snapped Hallah, her eyes never leaving Zodak. "Zodak, you'll be going tonight. Now." *Going?* In the excitement of the day, he had nearly forgotten about the trip to Pol Dak.

"I thought I was leaving tomorrow." He couldn't go before Ardon returned.

"Leaving where?" asked Ergis.

"Things have changed," replied Hallah, ignoring Ergis. "The meeting is set for... uh, noon tomorrow. You must leave."

"Wha... Who are these men?" demanded Ergis. "What meeting?" Hallah scarcely glanced at the mess in the middle of the shed. The scarred stranger's squat companion lurched ahead, roughly sweeping Ergis aside with a thick arm. Ergis stumbled on a broken crate and fell backward, landing hard on his backside. Hallah said nothing.

"Come," growled the stocky man, reaching for Zodak's arm.

"Can't we leave at dawn?"

"No. Now!" Hallah hissed. "You must make haste," she added more gently. Zodak felt like he was being torn in two. He desperately longed to see Ardon before he left, but Hallah had actually kept her promise. Pol Dak and the High Elder and the Keep would all be amazing. *The money will be safe here,* he reasoned. *You can always tell Ardon about the treasure the moment you're back.* Still, two days seemed an eternity.

"We haven't time, child!" barked Hallah.

"Yes," said Zodak finally with a sigh. "I'll get my things." He tried to pull away from the dirty man beside him, who smelled faintly of sweat and fish.

The man's grip tightened on Zodak's arm. "We go now," his voice rasped in a strange accent.

Zodak reluctantly complied. He had asked for this trip, after all.

Ergis still sat awkwardly among the shattered crates on the floor as they led Zodak away. He found himself suddenly alone in the silent and dark shed.

Hallah's face reappeared in the doorway. "Not a word of this! Not a word... dear." Her glare turned to a poisonous smile, and she was gone.

Hallah spoke in hushed tones with the scarred man while the short companion seemed almost to guard Zodak, as if he might try to run. Zodak turned his gaze to the horses. Beautiful animals, both. These beasts were huge, at least four measures higher than his mare Sal. Zodak patted the nearest horse's flank. Firm muscles rippled beneath the skin, a strong animal. He wondered what noble deeds it had done in the past. His hand passed over the brand, which he inspected. A circle with a profile of a head inside. The features of the face were small and soft, the circle perfectly round. The image tickled his mind with familiarity, but he couldn't think why.

"Get up," barked a thick voice from behind him. The scarred man leapt into his saddle. "Up ye go." Zodak was suddenly whisked off his feet and deposited behind the scarred man. With a kick, the horse sprang away from the house. Zodak nearly fell off the back, but he caught the rider's jacket just in time. He looked back once more, searching for any sign of Ardon. Nothing. His eyes landed on Hallah, who wore a strange, inscrutable expression. They galloped off, engulfed by the deepening dusk.

The scarred man smelled musty, yet Zodak had to hold close to keep from being thrown. At the edge of the town, the riders slowed their gait. *Who are these men?* wondered Zodak. The dirty companion certainly wasn't distinguished enough to serve the Venerable Council Keep, but this man, with his fine emerald riding jacket and tall boots, seemed important. Zodak wondered how much the men knew about him. *Hallah wouldn't have told them the story of the water sprite, would she? No, she would have invented some cover story to get me to Pol Dak as quietly as possible.*

The sound of approaching hooves echoed in the dark. A shape emerged from a wooded patch on the left and the scarred man grunted, "Ho!" This new dark rider nodded silently and fell in beside the other two, slowing to a trot.

This caravan was better planned than Zodak had first thought.

The new rider glanced at Zodak and nodded. "A bit old for the pit, this one," he croaked, earning a hard glare from the scarred man. His dark oily hair twisted in locks that hung over his long, gaunt face. He was clad in brown and black from head to toe. His rough face bore pock marks, and around his head he wore a dark green band. Zodak couldn't picture this man serving in the Keep either. *Ah, he and the short man are bodyguards to the leader,* he thought.

The odd procession pushed into the darkening night, moving at a healthy clip through the forest. The men continued in silence until the dark, oily man broke the quiet, speaking in a rasping voice. He spoke a strange language that sounded like hissing. The scarred man answered in the same tongue. The speech sent chills down Zodak's spine. A dark feeling crept over him like a heavy tarp. He clung closely to the scarred man. The dirty companions felt dangerous. Pol Dak could not come soon enough.

8

As Ardon walked to the mines that morning, something troubled him, gnawed at him. Farmers on either side of the road scurried like roaches in the thinning darkness, readying their fields for the day. When Laan awoke, they would be well into their routine, a routine he longed for, craved. The deep satisfaction of dropping to his knees in the cool of the morning and digging his hands into rich, damp soil of his very own to plant, to grow, to cultivate.

He had frozen the moment, framed it, and tacked it to the wall of his mind: a decade and a half earlier, standing up after patting dirt over the last silka seed. Groaning slightly from the stiffness in his legs and back, but then feeling the rush of deep satisfaction and contentment as he surveyed the field. Rows upon perfect rows of freshly planted silka seeds, the dark soil damp from the sprinkling rain the night before. The hope, the promise. That was the moment he clung to.

Why that one, he wasn't sure. There had been so many moments since. Days upon beautiful days of sunshine. Too much sun. In fact, that last day of planting marked the end of the rain. The silka seeds had sprouted, but the delicate shoots quickly stiffened and then shriveled, the glowing green streams of life turning brown and then black as the wind carried them off. The blackness of his own failure. His farm, the farm of his father, had been sustaining. *Why then borrow the money from Barst for silka?* He didn't need to ask himself the question, yet he constantly did. *But for the drought, it would have been a shrewd business decision, wouldn't it?*

That very same night, just hours after his frozen picture, he had been awoken by shouting and a rumbling noise. He ran outside to find the odd trio of villagers holding a bundle. A baby. His own nephew. Yes, that was the heaviness that perched on him like a great black bird this morning. The children. Hallah. Zodak.

Ardon never once doubted bringing Zodak into the family. It was the right thing to do. Hallah objected at first, of course, but he had trusted that would pass. He believed motherly instincts would prevail. How could he have foreseen the mutiny? First from Hallah and later his own children. The curse-speak was nonsense, of course. The timing of the drought was just an unfortunate coincidence. *But how did it get so bad?*

Ardon lived a simple life, yet he wasn't the simpleton Hallah accused him of being. He saw it all: Alana's brokenness, Ergis's fear and hardening. The cruelty toward Zodak. *Under my own roof!* It wasn't the life he had pictured. It wasn't the family he had imagined. He had sworn to be the kind of father he hadn't had: a man who loved and understood his children. Not like his own father, whose trade pulled him away for weeks every moon cycle. He had vowed to be the light that filled his house and all in it. *Wasn't that the man I was when the children were young? When I came in from the fields, tired but filled? There was laughter then.* It was different now. By the end of the long dayshifts in the mines, his head ached, and his lungs burned. When he got home, every fiber in his being wanted to dissolve into sleep, only to awake hours later to return to the mines.

"Hie!" The voice shook Ardon from his thoughts. He leapt aside just as Obe, the massive golyath snail, glided past in surging jerks, leaving a glittering slick smear in the road behind. Ardon's lunch basket unclasped and tumbled to the ground as Barst's houseman sneered down at him and spurred the snail ahead, the sleek wagon bouncing behind. *He's at it early.* Ardon shook his head, turning to gather his things. He glanced down to find the clay pot of orko stew overturned and its contents seeping into the dirt.

"No, no..." Ardon scrambled to catch the pot and save some of the precious orko meat snared the day before, tossing it from hand to hand as he fumbled with the waterskin to rinse off the layer of dust. "Burn me!" Another day of the aching pain in his stomach and parsing out the crust of bread through the afternoon.

When Barst had first returned from Pol Dak with Obe, the creature was a true fascination. Children and adults alike streamed out of their houses to see the exotic beast, said to descend from enormous ancestors that could shift continents from within the fissures deep underground. The little children rapped on its massive, striated shell, bands of brown, emerald, and pearl with the occasional silver flecks that twirled into a tight spiral at the shell's center. The brave ones dared to touch the creature's gelatinous neck and skirt, the pebbled surface slightly damp to the touch, but not slimy. What most delighted the children was how the snail's massive stalk of a head swung toward anyone who touched exposed skin, long fleshy horns waving wildly in the air, to a shower of cheers and giggles.

The Pol Dak streets were filled with them, Barst had reported. Pulling carts twice the size of what any horse could draw. Obe still drew the occasional squeal or wave from the children it passed, but for the adults, the novelty had long since worn off. A season later, months after the snail had accomplished its task, sniffing out the vein of krius that ran underground through Houndstooth Cave by the old mill, Obe was just another reminder of Barst's outsized wealth and influence that he lorded over the villagers.

Like the snail, the krius mine began as a symbol of hope and promise of a better life for the villagers of Laan. The freshly minted town council, of which Barst named himself Steward, quickly and enthusiastically approved the proposed project. If they found krius, it would buoy the village's wealth and serve as a safety net for those without work. But while prosperity came, it was Barst and his inner circle who fed like gluttonous gumrats on the village's bloated carcass.

The dawn was lifting when Ardon arrived at the mine.

"Our days go from dark to dark," Sigree, a fellow miner, had complained just the day before. Ardon fought against the bitterness that spread like a virus among the miners.

"Yuh late," barked Amos, the dumpy assistant foreman with the pointed nose and webbed neckline running from chin to chest that gave him the appearance of a turtle straining from its shell.

Ardon glanced at the sunrise. "It couldn't be more than a quarter hand past," he objected.

"And what wouldja call that?" sneered Amos. "Late. That's a quarter sum docked from pay."

"Please, Amos. I'm without my horse today and was nearly trampled on my way—"

"Don't want to hear it. You know the rules."

"Amos, I'm here. Ready to work. Just let it go this time, eh?" Ardon tried a smile.

"Keep at it and it'll be a half sum!" A bloom of angry red appeared on Amos's pasty cheeks.

"It's a handful of minutes. I'll add back twice the time at midway break, Amos. Please." Ardon put a hand on the man's shoulder. "The family needs every corq we can get."

Amos glanced down at Ardon's hand as if it were a fresh

swill dropping on his shoulder. "Well, isn't that a generous offer, Number 072?" Now Amos trembled. Ardon withdrew his hand. "And we'll take it. No midway break *and* docked a *half* sum." He was nearly yelling, glowering up at Ardon in challenge. And there it was: the cobweb-thin line between employment and servitude. Barst knew well that the miners weren't here by choice. It was all they had, and he extracted every last shhf of work he could from the miners. Ardon clenched his teeth, the anger rising like a tide as his hands balled into fists at his sides. He wanted to tear this self-righteous gowk in two. *Wasn't it Amos's wife who had borrowed an upsully of threshed wheat when the drought first set in? That grain had literally kept that family alive.*

"Looking ta get feisty? Go on, big fella," challenged Amos, even as he edged backwards, chalk marker poised to register a full demerit. Ardon swallowed hard, and with one more piercing glare at Amos, spun and marched away. He snatched up the last lamp and toolbelt from the line of pegs on the wall. The hammer, pickaxe, and assorted chisels clinked as he marched down the dusty path into the mine's yawning mouth.

"Anus at it again?" chirped Geras, without looking up from his kit laid on the ground.

"How'd you know?" asked Ardon.

"He's had the look all morn," rumbled Ridge from across the tunnel. "Snubbed by his lady, I'd wager."

"I barely slipped in," added Geras, "and Anus was already spoiling for a fight. Seemed almost hoping for a straggler this morn."

"That sherking moth deserves a hammering," added Ridge, spitting on the ground. And at over a marq tall with bulging forearms, Ridge (short for Reginor) could surely have delivered.

"They all do," added Geras, strapping the assembled toolbelt to his thin waist. "What I wouldn't give to grab that piece of scat Barst by the neck and—"

"Ger!" cut in Ardon sharply. "Careful. The walls have ears."

Geras shook his head and batted a hand in the air, his mop of unkempt hair flopping over his eyes. "'Course they do. Cause *the Baker* owns 'em." He drew out Barst's nickname with emphasized disgust. "Just like he owns Laan. Like he owns us all." Geras started tapping his blunt chisel on a section of wall.

"He doesn't own me," answered Ardon flatly, cupping the lantern wick as he lit it.

"Come off it, Ard," chided Ridge. "You're no better'n us. Jus' a sherking slave like we all are down here."

"Burn me if I am," Ardon said, strapping the belt to his waist and drawing himself up to his full height. "These hands may belong to the Baker, but he'll never have me."

"He may take ya yet," Geras growled, pounding the blunt chisel angrily with his heavy two-dok hammer.

"Go easy, Ger," Ardon cautioned. Ridge wedged a long pry bar in behind a rock formation jutting from the wall and, with a grunt, jammed it forward with a powerful thrust, dislodging a chunk of rock that thudded to the ground. He examined the freshly exposed crater in the wall for the shimmering veins of precious green krius crystal.

"Hrrmph," he exclaimed.

"Even if the Baker don't get you direct," said Ridge over his shoulder, "these tunnels will. This dust is like poison."

"You saw what happened to Silt," Geras growled. "Had to be carried out last week. Blood all over his kerchief. His boy said he might not even make it to harvest. Think a' that!" He slammed the wall with the hammer. "Here one day and gone the next. All while the Baker dines on suckling zheibak and angel mussels!"

"Easy with the chisel, Ger," said Ardon over his shoulder. "Word is the Baker sucks on handfuls of this stuff every day." Ardon pried a small green glowing nugget of krius out of the wall and inspected it a moment before flipping it into a metal pail on the ground. "He must be high as a kite most days."

"The Pol Dak high towers have all taken to the habit," added Ridge. "Least that's what that toad Florian tole me. Says he's kept a stash himself for those tough days if you know what I mean."

"Not me," Geras was nearly shouting as he pounded the wall. "I ain't gettin' trapped in that hole." More pounding. "Just another way for the sherking Baker to clamp down on ya. To own you." *Slam.* Geras swung furiously now. "Last thing I need is to pour my scat wages into the Baker's greedy pockets for the bram I'm pulling out of the earth all day!"

"Ger, slow it—" The words had barely escaped Ardon's mouth when Geras's chisel broke through the rock crust of the wall with a crunch and then a *pop*. It happened all at once. A blinding green-white flash filled the tunnel and Geras shot backward as if punched in the chest by a giant invisible hand, crashing to the sandy ground. Ardon instinctively threw an arm over his eyes but was knocked backward to the ground as well.

For a moment, all was still and dark, a persistent whine ringing in the passage. Ardon opened his eyes to the dim tunnel awash in the crimson ghost of the brilliant green flash moments before. The crisp odor of charred krius tinged with the earthy, organic reek of singed hair and skin filled his nose and throat.

"Ger! Ridge!" Ardon called out, coughing on all fours, his back hunched and arms sweeping the space before him searchingly.

"Unnngh," came a nearby moan. Ardon shuffled that way, the world still veiled in monotone green.

"Ard?" It was Ridge. He grunted as he raised his massive frame from the ground. "Can barely see nuthin'. 'Bout you?"

"I... I think it's coming back," answered Ardon, who could

now just make out indistinct forms around him and the yellow halo of a lantern. And there at his feet lay a body.

"Ger!" Ardon rushed to the crumpled figure, blinking rapidly to clear his vision. "Can you hear me!" The man lay on his back, eyes closed, and leg twisted at an odd angle. Ardon put a hand to Geras's chest. "He's breathing!" he barked up to Ridge, who rifled through a large pack.

"I got salts," he declared, removing the top from a wooden tube and waving it under Geras's nose.

"Enngh," Geras moaned and then sputtered and coughed, his eyes flitting open. He looked up searchingly through the haze to Ardon and then to Ridge. "Well, sherk me. Guess I found a streak." He smiled weakly.

"That you did, Ger," Ardon answered, searching for words of comfort. "A char downy of a streak!"

"What in the downs happened in there?" Stren, the mine lead, snaked into the tight passage from the tunnel beyond. "Everyone okay?"

"We've got a man down," called Ardon. The declaration stabbed at him. Geras had two little ones at home.

"Ger's been blown!" cried Ridge.

"Scat! We got a sparker!" Stren's voice echoed up into the body of the mine. "One fallen!"

"Everything work?" asked Ardon, turning back to Ger. The left side of Geras's face was raw and blistered circles of flaky black carbonized flesh, flecked with green krius powder, ran from chin to eye. Ardon had seen a burn scar before; the massive heat from a krius spark burned hotter than fire. If he made it, Geras would never look the same.

"Not sure about these," answered Geras weakly as he lifted his shaking arms closer to his face. His left pinky and ring finger were gone and his tattered gloves and the mauled flesh beneath looked as if he'd thrust his hands into the den of a ravenous razormouth. Ardon tried not to show his revulsion, but his heart sank. Barst would toss the man aside like a used pot rag. The sound of running boots grew as a handful of miners rushed into the corridor with the all-too-familiar stretcher.

Ardon tore open his shirt and pulled off the kerchief around his neck. He gently wrapped the charred and mangled flesh that used to be Geras's fingers.

A quiet, wiry miner named Krell shuffled in, carrying the front of the stretcher. Krell suddenly froze and dropped the stretcher, its wooden handles clanging loudly on the rock.

"Scat, Krell! What the downs!" came Stichel's voice, the other miner carrying the stretcher. Krell stood frozen, staring at Ardon's chest. Ardon glanced down at his torn shirt and saw what held Krell's stare: the family medallion around his neck, the diameter of a fist, its golden face glittering in the dim light. He quickly pulled his shirt closed and turned back to Geras. As if breaking from a trance, Krell looked up and around at the men in the corridor with budding recognition. Then he slipped quickly through the crowd out into the main passage, trailed by an annoyed "Where you goin'?" from Stren.

"You'll heal up," Ardon said, turning back to Geras. "Lucky to be alive. That's what you are." He tried to sound upbeat. Ridge shot a knowing glance at Ardon. Ardon only nodded slightly.

"Could'a been worse," Ridge added. Geras closed his eyes and gritted his teeth as the first wave of pain rolled in. Stichel gently lifted Geras's head and gave him a long draught of distilled glugg for the pain.

"I'll come by the house to check on you in two dawns, Ger," said Ardon as the miners lifted the stretcher.

"Thank you," he replied weakly, his eyes tightly shut. "I'ma sorry," he added.

"My tin you are," said Ardon with a forced chuckle. "Got

yourself a paid-up ride outta here, is what you got," he called after Geras as they whisked him away.

"Back to it," called Stren as the last of the stragglers dispersed. "And char! Be careful with the hammers on those veins."

Ardon fought against the burning in his eyes and turned back to collect his tools scattered on the ground.

ARDON HUNG his toolbelt and left the krius mine staging area. The weight of the day hung like a coil of anchor chain around him. He wearily began his trudging walk home. Not one hundred mounts from the mouth of the mine, he spotted a figure standing beside the road, waiting. When he was within a few measures, the woman approached him.

"Excuse me, sir," she said.

He instinctively glanced over his shoulder, though she couldn't have been speaking to anyone else. "Yes?"

"Are you Ardon of Nost Laan?" she asked.

"I am."

"My name is Ms. Folba. I teach your children at the schoolhouse." The woman sounded earnest.

"Yes, yes, Ms. Folba. I have heard your name around the house," said Ardon.

"Please, call me Folba. I have something I would like to discuss with you. May I walk with you a bit?" she asked.

"Me? Alone?" He eyed the sky, hours past sunset. It was no small risk she took being seen alone past last light with a married man.

"I know what you may be thinking, but I simply must speak with you. It's urgent."

"Oh?" Ardon cocked his head, appraising the woman again.

"It's about Zodak."

His eyes widened. The tension between the children had been rising. An incident at school was inevitable.

"Very well. What's happened?" He braced himself for the worst and began walking.

"Please stop me if your wife has told you this," said Ms. Folba. With hardly a breath, she launched into a rapid recounting of the last two days. She explained her encounter with Zodak, and how she discovered his secret spot in the closet and his paper, and even shared what she had read Zodak in the attic regarding the water sprites' significance. He listened intently to every word. "Have you heard any of this?" she asked.

"Zodak told me about meeting this... water sprite, but Hallah has mentioned nothing."

"When I visited last night—"

"You came to my house?" asked Ardon, stopping in the road and straightening. "Hallah told me nothing of this."

"Yes." Folba took a deep breath. "I am loath to bring news against your wife, but it's what I feared and why I wanted to speak with you directly. Zodak cautioned me that Hallah wouldn't like what I had to say, yet she *did* agree to send Zodak to Pol Dak. She even said her sister would help get an audience before the High Elder."

"Her sister?" Ardon's head snapped up.

"Yes, I understand Zodak leaves soon," answered Ms. Folba.

"Thank you very much, Folba," said Ardon. "But something is wrong. I must go now."

"Of course."

With a hasty half wave, Ardon dashed off towards his home.

ERGIS HAD STORMED off to his room in the loft after Zodak was taken, wiping angry tears from his stained face. He had poured himself into his plan to sabotage Zodak and then, in the moment of his triumph, those strange men had stormed in and ruined everything. *They swept you to the floor like a ragdoll and no one even cared.* He rubbed a swollen elbow and felt the lingering throbbing in his head. *Mother didn't even notice. She barely noticed the terrible mess on the floor either. Zodak must pay! And where did those men take him?* He shivered, recalling the face of that fat man. *What did Mother mean "the meeting is set"? And what was all the talk of secrecy?* There was something in his mother's countenance though that stirred a dark hunger deep within him. *Her urgency in sending Zodak off with those brutes; what did she plan? Where did she send him?* The questions blossomed, tinged with excitement. *Zodak. Gone. Does it matter where?*

A commotion from the main room broke his thoughts. He could make out Hallah's voice, sharp, but unsteady. A deep voice roared at her. A man's voice. Cold pricked Ergis's scalp and his heart pounded in his chest. He grabbed the heavy wood stick he kept behind his bed and crept to the edge of the loft, hands shaking like a shriveled leaf in the wind. Peering cautiously down into the dimly lit study, he spied the owner of that terrifying, booming voice: Ardon.

Ergis had never heard his father raise his voice beyond a stern rebuke, even when Ardon punished him. But now, the house seemed to shake with his yells.

"STOP WITH THE LIES! WHERE WAS HE TAKEN?" demanded Ardon, his powerful hands gripping Hallah's arms. Ergis had never seen such wild terror in his mother's eyes either. True fear plastered her face, but still she said nothing. Ardon's chest heaved, and his voice grew soft and grave. "If you do not tell me where he is, you will not spend another night under my roof. Ever. And I don't think you'd fare well in the streets."

Ergis gasped. Ardon spoke of Zodak. The sickly-sweet seed of dark hope inside him shriveled. A new shadow passed over him. *Such anger! Such threats. Would Father pursue me so?* The forbidden question loomed, unspoken but ever present. *Does he love me like that?*

"Okay..." Hallah finally stammered. "All right. They... left... out the Mead Road." She pointed feebly.

Ardon released her with disgust and raced to the door. Hallah slumped to the floor, visibly shaking. Before leaving, Ardon stopped and turned back. "You had better pray nothing happens to that boy!" He stormed out.

Ergis raced to the window. Ardon quickly saddled old Sal. He leapt onto the mount and tore out of the yard off into the pitch-black night. Hoofbeats faded and suddenly all was quiet except the pounding of Ergis's heart and the trembling of his hands against the glass from the fear, anger, and confusion that swirled like a cyclone within him.

9

For over two hours, Zodak clung to the man in the dusty green riding jacket, begging the Color that he wouldn't fall off. Finally, the group slowed to a stop at an opening at a fork in the road, lit by a dim moon. *At last!*

The men dismounted, the oily dark rider and scarred man speaking in a raspy tongue. Zodak knew Pol Dak was a large city, but this strange language sounded like nothing he had ever heard. He strained to decipher even a word but got nothing.

"Speak the common tongue!" the short companion barked. "We be makin' camp, then? Figured we'd a push through the night to Pol Dak." The thought of clinging to the scarred man all night made Zodak groan.

"New plans," replied the scarred man, staring down his companion as he slowly coiled a whip. "We wait here for the meeting." The words slithered out in his scaly foreign accent.

"What meeting?" asked Zodak. "Is the Elder sending an escort?" *Maybe she's coming herself!*

"Hrrhmp," the scarred man half laughed, half grunted. "Yes, worm, your escort is coming." The reply carried an edge.

"Sa long as I gets paid," huffed the short companion. Quick

as a snake, the scarred man unfurled the whip and cracked it at the short man just inches from his face. The short man reeled. His hand slipped into his coat, but he didn't draw his weapon.

"You want off this crew?" demanded the scarred man. The short man's eyes darted between the two, and he shook his head. "Cross me again and I'll open ya," hissed the scarred man. Zodak shrank back from him. *Pol Dak has harsh customs,* he thought with a shiver. *Best to keep a distance from this one.*

The horses drank from a nearby stream that glittered like a liquid silver ribbon against the ink-black canopy, and the men passed around a fistful of foul-smelling gray jerky from the short man's pack that Zodak politely declined. The scarred man suddenly jerked his head up and hissed an order.

The dark man shuffled to the edge of the camp. "They approach," he called, staring into the blackness and edging back beside the group. The squat companion scurried back behind the duo. Zodak peered down the paths, one curving right and one curving left, into the night, but saw nothing. The scarred man straightened, and Zodak noticed how his hand flitted nervously to his sword hilt, then to his belt, and then fell to his side. *Finally, some respect for the Elder,* Zodak thought self-righteously. He too straightened, readying himself to meet the convoy.

A branch cracked from the path that wound slightly downward and to the left. The rhythmic thud of footfalls slowly grew, and a sliver of torchlight flickered between the dark tangle of branches. A horse whinnied. Straining to see, Zodak finally spotted a figure, then a second and a third. As the group approached, Zodak could make out a cloaked rider, sitting astride a stately black horse with a coat that shimmered in the moonlight. Affixed to the horse's head was a black iron headpiece shaped like a skull. Two—no, three—men trudged beside the rider, brandishing weapons and carrying torches. Zodak's heart stopped. Behind the four men, ghosted at the edge of the torchlight, loomed two hulking shapes. They stood as tall as two soldiers and moved like men underwater, their huge frames towering over the others.

"Boss..." The short man let out a gasp.

Zodak had heard ancient stories of giants, sixty, seventy, eighty measures tall, tossing horse carts as a child might toss blocks. These grotesque beasts were something different altogether. They were wrapped in tattered black and gray from neck to toe, with full sized swords dangling like whittling knives from thick belts that crossed their massive chests and waists. Knotted hair hung like swamp vines.

Behind the giants came two more men. As they approached, Zodak beheld the full group for the first time. He had thought the scarred man and his companions grimy, yet these men were twice as filthy and wretched. The men on foot wore tattered black jackets, each more ragged than the next. Their faces were tattooed with strange markings, and rings and chains hung from noses and ears. A sour odor seeped into the glen ahead of the procession. *Something is terribly wrong.*

"We brought the child," said the scarred man as the convoy came to a stop and squared off with the trio.

A hand clamped on Zodak's arm. *This can't be the Elder's convoy, can it? No. This is all wrong. What has Hallah done?* The voice inside rose to a panicked shout. The dark man yanked Zodak forward. He tried to pull back, but the scarred man grabbed his other arm and they dragged him before the group. Zodak shriveled under the gaze of this horrible company. The man on the horse wore a sleek black robe, its hood shadowing his face. Moonlight glinted from the shards of gems and jewels embedded in the back of his hands. He drew back his hood and Zodak gasped. His captors drew back a half step as well.

The rider's weathered bald head shimmered dully, and his gaunt face was decorated with more rings and chains and gems than all the others. Sunken black eyes roved over the group.

Beneath his heavy, arched nose, his slit of a mouth ran across his face and opened into gaping blackness as he spoke. "Is this the one?"

"Yes, we brought him as agreed," said the scarred man. "Son of the Shielder."

"Are you sure this is him?" croaked the rider again.

"We took the one you asked," replied the scarred man. "Where's the gold?"

Zodak's stomach knotted. He had been tricked. Deceived. *Hallah!* It was too much. His vision danced and his legs threatened to collapse. The bald rider threw a pouch at the scarred man.

"It feels light," said the scarred man, testing the satchel's weight in his hand.

"There's the half. The other half when we have the Shielder."

"What in the downs is 'e talkin' about?" snapped the short man to the scarred man.

"The deal was for the boy," said the scarred man, his voice rising. The grip on Zodak tightened. *What's happening? What deal?* Zodak's heart thundered in his chest.

"The boy's just bait," the rider hissed.

"Dis sherking moth," grumbled the short man under his breath.

"We can't know if the Shielder will come," the scarred man protested.

"Not to worry, Eirik," snorted the bald man. "He'll come. We're told he's departed already."

"The deal was for the boy, Griss," repeated Eirik. "Pay us our due now or—"

"Or what?" challenged Griss, moving his horse a step closer and letting a spiked ball and chain fall to his side. The men behind Griss drew weapons, and in a flash Eirik and his two companions had blades drawn as well. Zodak felt a sharp point under his chin.

"Or you don't get what you came for..." threatened Eirik. One of the giants moved forward, lugging a huge black angular blade over his shoulder. Griss held up a hand, and the giant froze.

"You'd be digging your grave. Or maybe Droggth would save *you* for the plunge. Might still have use for the dead boy, too." The dark man hissed something urgent to Eirik.

"This ain't what I signed on for, boss." The short man's voice quaked.

Eirik spun on the short man, hate wild in his eyes. "What did I say—" He groped roughly for the short man's collar and lifted a clenched fist high overhead.

"I am here for the boy!" A strong voice shattered the night. Eirik froze, his head cocked as the short man wriggled from his grasp. There stood Ardon, alone in the road beside Sal. The Pol Dak riders hissed to each other.

"Right on cue," croaked Griss.

"Stop! It's a trap!" Zodak yelled. "We're not going to Pol Dak. They're not from the Elder—"

"Quiet, boy!" Eirik struck Zodak on the head, sending searing pain over his scalp.

"Zodak." Ardon's voice was pained. "These men are child stealers."

For a moment, Zodak couldn't make sense of the words, his brain struggling for their meaning. Eirik hissed a command to the dark man. Zodak's legs became wobbly, and his mouth filled with a metallic taste, nausea hitting him like a punch to the gut. Eirik held him tight as he swayed, gasping for breath. Suddenly it all came into perfect focus: the grimy men, the slippery hissing tongue, the horse brand. He *had* seen that symbol before: that was no man in a circle. It was a child, in a net.

Zodak struggled to twist out of the hold, but Eirik's grip was like iron.

"You're far from home, old man!" The dark man spoke, and his companion shuffled beside him. "Crossed into the wrong clearing, ya did. And now ye gonna—"

"YOU LET MY BOY GO!" roared Ardon. For a split second, no one moved. The mercenary beside Griss glanced up at his leader's ghoulish face, but Griss held up a hand and shook his head slightly.

"I'm gittin' my money," declared the short man, drawing a long dagger from his coat, the black blade reflecting no moonlight. Another wave of nausea hit Zodak. He tried to shout again, but he had no voice.

Ardon stood planted like a tree, his chest heaving and eyes burning. His right arm rested on Sal, who still panted from the long run.

The short man closed in with the menacing blade. His voice rasped. "Ye should'a gone home when ye could. Now ya gonna—"

Crack. Ardon whipped the axe handle from Sal's saddlebag, smashing the small man on the side of the head. The man crumpled, his legs folding awkwardly under him. Ardon's savage eyes locked onto the dark man.

"Let my boy go," he snarled, stepping forward. The dark man unfurled a chain with three walnut-sized metal balls hanging from it and began swinging it over his head. Ardon never slowed his advance.

"Old fool!" cursed the dark man as he lunged forward, whipping the chain down on Ardon. With hardly a break in stride, Ardon darted forward and dodged to the left, ducking the arc of the chain. He swung the axe handle at the nape of the dark man's neck, and with a crack the man's body crumpled. Ardon glanced up at Griss's amused face, but neither the rider nor his company moved. If the sight of the giants startled him, Ardon showed nothing.

Eirik threw Zodak to the ground and snatched the long whip from his waist. Zodak rolled aside and watched, dumbstruck. *Ardon?* He didn't know the man before him. That morning, Zodak would have sworn that Ardon had never been in so much as a scuffle. Eirik whirled the whip high above his head and then snapped it at Ardon. The whip caught Ardon on the cheek, painting a thin red line that trickled blood. Ardon didn't flinch.

"You'll have to do better than that," Ardon growled.

Eirik's eyes flashed. Drawing back, he snapped it again, wrapping the serpentine whip around the axe handle. The two stood frozen, tethered together by the leather strand. Ardon grabbed the whip with his free hand and yanked with terrific force. Eirik flew through the air, crashing at Ardon's feet. Without a pause, Ardon slammed Eirik in the head with the butt of the axe handle. Eirik collapsed and was still. Zodak gasped. Ardon stood, chest heaving.

"Better them than us," came Griss's voice, hollow and gravelly. "Thank you for joining us. Droggth will be pleased we have both father and...son."

"Turn and crawl back into the filthy hole you came from, and you'll be spared this night," Ardon bellowed.

The dark clearing fell silent. Zodak felt the cool, damp soil beneath him and the thick smell of moss and forest around him. Framed before him, bathed in blues and reds of moon and torchlight, the scene looked like a painting from the halls of the ancient kingdom K'andoria: The man Zodak once knew stood alone, face hard as an anvil, axe handle in hand. Across the clearing crouched that hideous horde with its two colossal monsters. *Let me wake from this nightmare,* pled Zodak to the sky. Thunder rumbled in a distant reply.

A grating sound like flint scraping steel broke the silence.

Griss was laughing. The sound grew until the man shook in his saddle with bellows. And then, as quickly as it rose, the laughing stopped.

"Spare us?" Griss hissed with rage. "How dare you even speak to me, you pill! Droggth will have what he seeks. He'll have your blood tonight!" With that, the giant wielding the shard of sharpened steel as long as Zodak himself sprang at Ardon, knocking the closest man to the ground. The forest floor rippled with each thunderous footfall.

"*No!*" Zodak screamed as the monster lunged forward, bringing the blade down on Ardon.

The axe handle splintered with a mighty *crack* as it met the giant's hungry blade. But Ardon managed to deflect the swing, sending the blade thudding into the earth. In a flash, Ardon sprang forward and buried the splintered axe handle into the beast's neck. The giant reared back, screaming as it clawed at the butt of the handle. Ardon snatched up the massive, angular blade, and with one swipe, severed the giant's head from its body. The group stood in stunned silence as their champion's headless corpse teetered on stiffened muscles before toppling like a felled copner tree. Zodak had frozen, planted to the earth where he sat.

The mercenaries exploded into attack. Weapons out, they swarmed Ardon in a thick knot. Dread stole Zodak's breath. He couldn't follow the battle in the low light, yet no man could stand against a half dozen and a giant. Suddenly frantic, Zodak jumped to his feet, searching for a weapon, anything to help Ardon. He spun and found himself staring at dirty black boots. He looked up just in time to see Griss's jewel-knuckled fist slam him in the face. The night exploded in searing white and gold, and he crashed backward to the ground. A rough hand grabbed him by the hair and yanked him back to his feet, cold steel pressed against his neck. The stench of rot choked him, and the horizon rocked precariously back and forth.

"Stop now!" shouted Griss. "*Stop!*" he screamed again. The world slowly faded back to a sickly red as Zodak's vision returned. The scrum before them halted. A man lay dead, his own blade buried in his chest. Another staggered from the group in a daze, pawing at his shoulder where his arm once was. Ardon had a third in a choke hold, a dagger raised for a deadly strike. Zodak's mind went blank, and he felt ice running through his veins. *Who* are *you?* he asked silently of the stranger before him.

"One more blow and I will bleed this boy!" Griss sounded wild, unhinged, and spittle showered Zodak. The blade stung as it bit into Zodak's neck. A quick slicing motion and it would be over.

"Wait!" said Ardon. He threw the man to the ground as a cold, wet wind whipped through the glade.

"It's not the boy we came for," said Griss. The forest flashed white, and thunder boomed. The tapping of the approaching rain dancing on leaves grew as the storm pushed closer.

"I know what you want," seethed Ardon.

"A simple trade," said Griss. "The relic for the boy's life." Zodak's heart pounded like a herd of zheibak and his face throbbed. Nothing felt real, yet it was all so horribly real.

"Again, I say it: let him go or you will not live through the night," Ardon growled.

This time Griss didn't laugh. "A slice and he's done. You want to carry his body home, Shielder? Put him in the ground? That what you want?"

Why won't Ardon just give them what they want? Ardon said nothing. His eyes met Zodak's, fixing him with a knowing stare brimming with sorrow.

"Very well, we shall see," said Griss and he cocked his arm to ready a slice with the knife.

"STOP!" boomed Ardon. "Let him go. You can have the medallion. Just let the boy go."

Griss snorted a chuckle and spoke a slithery command to the others. *The medallion?* Zodak had, of course, seen the medallion Ardon wore around his neck. He recalled asking about it as a child. *"It was passed down through my family,"* Ardon had said. *"It's a bond and a promise, and besides my family, the only precious thing to my name."* Ardon never removed it. *How can these wicked thugs know about that?* Zodak swallowed. *Please just hand over the thing so we can leave!* he silently urged.

"Give yourself up," said Griss. Slowly, Ardon raised his hands, dropping the long black knife to the ground. The pressure of the blade on Zodak's neck withdrew.

"Now release him!" demanded Ardon.

"I'm no fool," retorted Griss. "Bind him!" he hissed to the giant.

The beast grabbed Ardon's arms and yanked them behind his back. Ardon looked like a child beside the musclebound giant. The creature wrapped a heavy rope around Ardon's arms and torso. Once Ardon was tied, the thug he had been choking approached him, still rubbing his neck, and kicked Ardon hard in the back of the leg, sending him to his knees, and spat on him. Another man backhanded Ardon across the face.

"Stop!" yelled Zodak. Rain began falling.

"You have what you want. Let him go!" said Ardon. Griss threw Zodak to the side like a mutton bone chewed clean of meat. Zodak stumbled but caught himself. He wiped rain and tears from his eyes as he backed away from this throng of evil men.

"Let me see it," Griss said greedily, rushing to Ardon. The giant pulled Ardon up by his hair until he sat on his heels. In one swipe, Griss ripped Ardon's shirt from neck to hem. A man with a torch leaned close. Griss staggered backwards.

"We've found it," blurted the grizzled henchman with the torch.

"Zodak, go!" yelled Ardon, shaking Zodak from his trance.

"Go? But you're coming with me." The quiet statement was a question, a plea. Their eyes met. Behind Ardon's urgent stare Zodak saw love, sorrow, and regret. Zodak knew, as if he always had, Ardon wasn't coming home. *The trade was never just for the medallion. You knew it!* His mind raced. Then the beating began. Fists, kicks, spit, and sticks rained down on Ardon. *No!*

Zodak had continued to inch backwards and now bumped into the belly of something large. He spun frantically only to find Sal chewing lazily, hair wet with rain. He turned back to the scene. He couldn't watch but couldn't tear his eyes away either.

Then he spotted it: the sword handle glistened from beneath a dripping fern ten measures away. A vision flashed through his mind: Zodak taking the enemy by surprise from the dark, cutting and hacking. Saving Ardon. He turned back to Sal. Then back to the sword. *I'm just a boy.* His hands shook and his mind felt empty. He sprang up to the saddle. He suddenly felt sick and leaned over the side of the horse and vomited. *But Ardon. I have to do something.* Every fiber in him wanted to be cliqs away from this horrific scene and these dirty men. *You're nothing. What can you do?* accused a voice inside. His stomach felt like a rag being wrung of rainwater.

"Hold him!" Griss bellowed. With the giant and three of the men holding Ardon's beaten body up, Griss ripped the medallion from his chest. A brilliant flash pierced the dark glen. Griss screamed and dropped the medal. At the sight of the flash, Sal whinnied and sprang off down the path.

Zodak's eyes burned green from the bright light, and he fumbled for the reins. His foot lost the stirrup and as Sal swerved, Zodak launched from the saddle and crashed to the damp earth. He scrambled on hands and knees through the dripping thicket, back to the clearing. Thorns tore at him, but he hardly noticed. Elbow over elbow, he dragged himself, blinking away rain, his eyes fixed on the flickering torches. Two dark shapes rushed from the group towards him. He dropped his face to the dirt and froze. The henchmen raced past, nearly stepping on him as they ran down the path. When they passed, he breathlessly clawed himself forward to the edge of the clearing. He could just make out Griss, holding out a stick with a hastily bandaged hand, fishing the medallion off the forest floor.

"Don't know what Droggth wants with this trinket," Griss said, "but the Magistrate parted with a bag of gold the size of a hog's head for it. What power does it carry, farmer?" he asked, holding up the stick with the medal dangling from its chain. Ardon moaned hoarsely.

"Such a pity," Griss added, bending low to Ardon. "Trading your life for nothing." He gave a nod at one of the men holding Ardon. The man whipped a knife from his belt and thrust it into Ardon's stomach. He doubled forward and moaned. The man stabbed a second time. Zodak stifled a cry. Griss pulled Ardon's head up by his hair to meet his taunting gaze. "Fought like a lion you did. But guess what? We're gonna kill the boy anyway," he jeered. "Sent a pair after him already." Even through the darkness, Zodak saw Ardon's eyes flash. His moaning grew from anguish to primal rage.

It happened fast. Ardon whipped his head backwards, slamming his captor under the chin, and sprang forward like a frog towards the dangling chain, his arms still bound. Another flash blinded Zodak. He heard screams and the sounds of battle. When his vision returned, he caught sight of Ardon, unbound and atop the giant, the medallion glimmering around his neck. His body reared back, pulling hard against the rope that now encircled the giant's neck. The man who had stabbed Ardon lay in a heap. Griss scrambled to his feet a few measures off, his left arm hanging awkwardly, and unfurled his ball and chain. Footsteps pounded from behind Zodak as the two henchmen returned, running up the path.

"He weren't on the horse—" The men stopped short as they beheld the scene. They both drew weapons, one an axe and the other two long knives.

"Well? Kill him!" shouted Griss. One of the men flipped his knife, snatching it by the blade, and hurled it. Even as he did, Ardon heaved the giant's massive torso up in front of him as a shield. The blade buried itself in the giant's chest and Ardon dropped the monster to the ground. Ardon staggered backwards, wincing and gripping his stomach. His tattered shirt was stained dark red. Screaming, both henchmen charged. Ardon dodged an attacker's slashing knife, turning the man's wrist with a snap, burying the blade in its owner. As the second man brought the axe down on Ardon, he caught the man's hand overhead, arresting the blow. The man lashed out with his other hand, jabbing Ardon in the shoulder with a small blade. Ardon smashed his forehead into the man's face, sending him staggering backwards.

Movement caught Zodak's eye. Griss had slipped away from the battle and was struggling up onto his horse.

"Ardon!" Zodak stood from his hiding spot. "He's getting away!"

The axe whined as it sailed through the air in front of Zodak and caught Griss between the shoulder blades. He tumbled from the saddle as his horse galloped off into the night.

"Ardon!" Zodak ran to his side, burying his face in Ardon. Sobs came unbidden.

"It's all right." Ardon put an arm around the boy. "It's all right now."

"I should have told you. Told you everything!"

"You didn't know. You couldn't. You were deceived."

Zodak suddenly pulled his face back from Ardon's chest, his eyes red and burning.

"You are a warrior!" he blurted. "I've never seen anything like it! You beat a whole army!"

Ardon only offered a pained smile.

"We must ride back to town. You can ride Sal. I'll walk. We'll mend your wounds. The guard's watch will surely find who sent these men and—"

Ardon suddenly staggered, falling to a knee. Zodak tried to pull him to his feet. Ardon struggled to rise but faltered again. Zodak put his arms around Ardon's waist to pull him up again. When he pulled his hand back, it was covered in blood. Ardon collapsed. Zodak stared at his glistening hand and suddenly couldn't breathe. Tears ran uncontrollably down his face.

"No. You're okay! Get up!" Zodak struggled again in vain to pull Ardon to his feet. "Please. Get up!" he sobbed, throwing himself on Ardon.

"Son." Ardon's voice seemed as calm as if he was sitting by the fire at home. "I can't... get up." He reached for Zodak. "You can't stay here. More of them... two are not dead... more will come. You must go."

"No! We're both going," insisted Zodak, hugging Ardon tightly. "I won money. We're going to buy a farm. Folba said I'm special... that I might change things. It will be better. No more krius mines. Please." Zodak's tears flowed, falling on Ardon's chest. "Don't leave me... Father."

"Zodak... I love you," said Ardon, struggling to push himself up on an elbow. "You *are* special. You will be great, son. I know it... You must listen." He lifted a shaky arm to his collar and removed the cord from around his neck.

Zodak covered his eyes against the bright flash as the medallion left Ardon's chest. Zodak felt the smooth, heavy relic pressed into his hands. He expected it to burn him as it had Griss, but the surface was cool. He lifted it by the cord, the gold medallion dangling between his face and Ardon's.

"Hear me, son." Urgency rose in Ardon's voice. "You must do whatever you can to keep this safe. At all costs. It is..." He winced. "It is a key to... to hold... the darkness." Ardon winced and squeezed his eyes closed. "Find the... Order. In Uth Becca...."

"Go to Uth Becca? The city? What's the Order?" Zodak protested. "How can I find it?" His voice trailed off.

"Go!" Ardon demanded, falling to his back again. His labored breathing rattled now with the sound of a twig stuck in a wagon wheel.

"I can help you onto Sal." Zodak lay on Ardon's chest, his own body shaking and convulsing with the waves of sobs. "We'll be free..." He lifted his head. Ardon's eyes were closed. Suddenly, a cough and hiss came from the dark a few measures off. Zodak gripped Ardon tightly. "No," he cried softly. Now another voice hissed at the first.

"The medallion!" Ardon's eyes flitted open once more in an urgent flash. "Go!" A tremor rippled through his body and he was still. The medallion throbbed with a purple glow and then returned to its dull gold sheen. The sound of shuffling came from the clearing. Zodak took his father's large hand between his own one last time and squeezed. Finally, he tore himself away and stood, placing the medallion cord over his neck. As soon as he did, the medal sucked to his chest as if by some unearthly magnet and flashed brilliantly again. He felt like someone kicked the air from his lungs. He struggled for a breath beneath the medallion.

"Who's there?" hissed a raspy voice from the dark.

Zodak turned to the blackness and ran.

10

Tears stung Zodak's eyes, and cold raindrops whipped his face as he ran. He gulped the thin air in struggling gasps. His body was a living contradiction: he had burst from the clearing with a sudden surge of newfound energy, bounding like a deer, hungry to run with new power he didn't know he possessed, and yet his chest felt heavy, a gaping pit sucking his energy. Beneath the medallion, his skin seared, emanating fire through his torso and limbs. The medallion itself clung to his skin, neither swinging nor bouncing, even as he thrashed through underbrush. A constant pounding noise filled his mind, draining his head of thoughts, and an electric tingling hummed through his very veins.

He tripped, banging his knees as he fell. On all fours, he paused, fighting the fire that raged in his chest. Nausea rocked him and he heaved and retched. *What is this? Am I dying?* He dropped his head to the dirt, wishing the very ground would swallow him. A twig snapped and his head shot up. *Are they coming?*

Zodak stumbled to his feet and lunged ahead, again touching some untapped power. His head pounded, but he pushed on, without thought for what direction he aimed. One singular thought cut through the empty thoughts: Escape. Ardon's dried blood stiffened his right hand, jerking his mind back to that cursed clearing in the woods. His father dying in his arms. Zodak felt no stab of sorrow, just the overwhelming rushing numbness that swallowed him like an oily black bog.

Zodak ignored the sharp pain of a cramp that shot through his side. He had never run like this, yet he refused to stop. His body pulled him on and his mind burned against those wicked men, deceivers and murderers. Thieves. Child stealers. Hallah's face flickered in his mind. He ran faster, his legs flying beneath him. *Hallah sent me away with the scarred man. She planned it all. Hallah finally won.* Zodak crashed through thickets, his feet almost unable to keep up as he tried to fend off the branches that whipped at his face and arms. Tears of rage blurred his vision. Shrubs and brambles tore. He roared at the top of his lungs, ignoring the billowing inferno within, pushing as fast as his body would let him.

A gnarled root caught his foot and with a gasping cry, he let himself fall to the forest floor, feeling a thousand needles rising like a swarm of hornets within. He coughed and struggled for breath. After what felt like an eternity, Zodak slowly lifted himself to his knees, and then raised up on shaky legs. He stood in a thinning forest bordered by an open meadow or field. Far ahead through the trees, Zodak spotted a flickering light. *A farm!* He couldn't see a farm building or cottage, but he staggered ahead towards the glow.

Out in the field he could make out a small house in the distance. Painful blisters covered his feet, making each step burn like walking on coals. The claws of the dense wood had left Zodak scraped and bleeding from head to toe. Around him, tall shaggy piles of zip grass crouched like sleeping monsters. *A farmer's field!* He longed to knock on the door, to ask for a bed, but each step felt like dragging a millstone through a thicket of stinging nettles. *No, that house is still half a cliq away. I have to stop.* Zodak approached the closest pile of freshly threshed grass, about twice his height. He cleared a small hole just large enough for his torso and squirmed inside, curling up into a tight ball and pulling loose grass over the entrance. The fire in his chest had calmed, but a dull heat still radiated beneath the medallion and Zodak's head pounded as he shivered uncontrollably in damp clothes. Everything burned, and even as he hugged himself against the frigid night air, he started to sweat. He closed his eyes, trying to leave the horrible night behind him.

Darkness collapsed around him, and he dozed. After what seemed like only seconds, he jolted awake. Without opening his eyes, he tested his surroundings. The itching zip grass and bite of the air snuffed the flicker of hope that he had dreamed it all. Suddenly, not more than ten measures away, a horse whinnied. Zodak froze. All was quiet. A hissing voice broke the silence. That rasping sound sent chills down his spine. Another voice answered in the same tongue. The hisses were now sickeningly familiar. He had run like a deer. How had they found him?

Then a new voice answered, gravelly but strong. "Could he have gotten this far?"

"We found torn cloth in those trees that matched the boy's tunic," answered the first voice. "You two, go, check the house." Horse hooves pounded off. "If he's not there, we'll bring the bonehounds and continue the search at first light. Droggth said this boy must be found. The relic must be found."

"Griss didn't tell us. How could we know?" the first man snapped. An argument erupted, but Zodak couldn't understand the strange tongue. After what felt like an eternity, the horses returned from the farmhouse, and the foreign voices exchanged hissing words. Finally, the group thundered off into the night.

Zodak guessed he had only slept an hour at most, but he knew he couldn't stay. His body shivered and ached from hunger and fatigue. He had not eaten since Komo, and his very bones ached as if he had been poisoned, yet the burning in his chest had turned to a dull ache. The cuts on his face and hands and legs had stopped bleeding, but with each slight movement brought burning as the rough zip grass raked across his superficial wounds.

Those evil men will be back with others and bonehounds. No. Get up! You can't stay, he scolded himself. After lying still and listening for a few more minutes, he poked his head out of the zipstack. The night was quiet and still and the rain had stopped. The smell of a cooking fire made his stomach rumble. He slithered out into the night air and rolled painfully to the ground. It was cold. He lifted himself to his feet and took a step, then two, noticing the bright glow in the distance. *No,* he mouthed. There was no cooking fire. Hungry flames enveloped the farmhouse. *That's because of me.* He forced the thought from his mind, and slowly, with stiff, aching strides, he began to jog. With each step, pain shot up his leg. It felt like hot wax running through his veins, but once again, his strides were fast and somehow powerful.

He tried to ignore the blisters and clear his mind to think. He rewound the night's events, trying to retrace his steps to the fight. *I crossed back over the road to Laan as I fled; that means I'm pointed nost. What if I double back slag towards Laan?* he wondered, but then stopped.

Why go to Laan? Nothing awaits you there, the voice said. *What about the fortune?* he objected. The treasure awaited him, but the thought of it only turned his stomach like sour milk. The money wasn't wealth, not really. It was a promise, a promise of a better life with Ardon. It now seemed so empty. *Even if I could get it back, what would I do with the money? Where would I go?* Those men and the bonehounds would cover the road to Laan. *No, I can't return to Laan now. Maybe never.*

Zodak had wasted enough time. He turned back to what he thought to be nost, towards the famed city of Uth Becca. That's where Ardon told him to go, wasn't it? With painful steps, he jogged and then ran, drawing on the deep well of sorrow or fear or whatever power fed his steps. The night deepened, yet on he ran. He came to the yawning edge of a dark forest with twisted, towering trees and ran in without pause. He tried to leave no trail, but above all, he had to keep moving. The pain throughout his body didn't abate. The burning turned to ice, and he fought bouts of dizziness. His throat dried up, and his tongue felt fat and sticky in his mouth. But still he ran. When his legs became unstable, he didn't stop. When it felt like a thunderstorm inside the walls of his head, and his fevered body cried out for rest, he didn't stop.

After hours, when he finally came to a clearing in the woods, he could go no farther. His steps were unsteady, and his body screamed for a rest. Zodak leaned heavily on a fallen bough as though it alone kept him from being sucked to the ground. He vaguely noticed the deep plum color of the sky. Night was lifting. He must have been a dozen cliqs from where he began, but it still wasn't far enough. His body begged him to stop. He wanted to sleep. Every fiber in him burned, and the heat had returned to his chest. He was unwell and his body cried for rest and water but stopping meant giving the bonehounds time to catch up. It felt like the time he had eaten bad river oysters and shivered in bed for two days. It took all the strength he had to rip himself free from the log. He staggered forward into the trees.

As he entered the grove, his vision spun, and the ground suddenly heaved violently to the side. Zodak threw himself at a nearby log to keep from falling. When the ground stopped moving, he took a measured step, releasing the log. The ground suddenly lurched, and he fell hard. Lying with his cheek against the forest floor, panting like a dog, Zodak couldn't move. He felt like he was sinking into the dirt, and his body no longer responded to his will. Even the fear of being caught, which had carried him this far, didn't help. In that moment, no feather bed could have offered a softer spot. *This may be your last night alive.* The detached thought floated by without emotion. If he didn't freeze to death, he would die without water. He knew a little about forest berries and nuts, but even if he somehow found food, his fever would overcome him. And if he survived all of those, the bonehounds with their long spindly legs, swift, deer-like grace, and two rows of yellowed teeth would tear him to pieces.

"*Go! Find the Order.*" Ardon's voice pierced the mental fog.

With strength he didn't know he had, he pushed himself back up to hands and knees. On all fours, panting and spitting, he heard it: a muffled tinkling sound. *Water!* He forced one leg up and, summoning all his might, he pushed against screaming muscles until he was standing. The forest thinned off to his left and gently sloped downward. Gripping saplings and boughs, he pulled himself forward on unsteady feet like a bannuk swinging through the trees. The air smelled crisp and fresh. He felt a cool breeze. A hundred measures ahead, the forest gave way to a grassy hill cut by a pair of well-worn wagon tracks before it fell away to the most beautiful sight he could imagine: a stream. He propelled himself forward with reckless abandon.

Even as Zodak careened down the bank towards the stream, arms whirling like pinwheels, the world tilted, and colored streaks passed before his eyes. He fell too fast, his weak and wobbly legs no match for gravity's unrelenting thrust, and he crashed down onto the packed mud road, his head thudding hard. Darkness choked the light, and lying in the road, just a few measures from that beautiful, lifegiving water, Zodak's world went dark.

11

Black boots clapped against smooth polished marble floors as the slender figure with the dark face and long black coat approached the vaulted throne room doors of Uth Becca's Magistrate, each an ornately carved towering slab of wood telling ancient stories of conquest and travail.

"Halt!" boomed a mountain of a man with slate-gray eyes standing as straight as a banner pole before the entrance. "Nobody sees the Magistrate without an appointment." Two dangerous-looking sentries flanked the man on either side. The guard who spoke wore a fitted and pressed ash-gray uniform that plunged like a rock face beneath his polished black belt. He gripped a spear at least eight measures tall. For a moment, the man in black stood, silent, considering the soldiers before him.

"No, I'm sure you see to that," the black-clad figure replied in a high, singsong voice. "And believe me, that wretched shell of a man you hail as Magistrate will soon wish it were so."

The guard's sneer slowly hardened as he understood the threat. "Suggest you leave now, moth," growled the guard. "Unless you wish to be snapped in two like kindling and thrown from these steps." He took a menacing step toward the smaller man and grasped a fistful of collar. "How did you get into the keep anyway—" The guard suddenly spasmed and went stiff, the spear falling from his hand and clattering to the ground. His eyes flashed with panick yet his face was rigid as his body quivered, foam gathering at the corners of his mouth. There came a soft pattering sound and acidic odor as the guard soiled himself.

The slender man calmly removed the guard's paw and straightened his wool lapel. The torches affixed to the wall flickered with a gentle gust of wind. A muffled scream from outside the castle drew the two other guards' gazes down the long corridor behind the visitor. The bright archway at the end of the hallway suddenly darkened as a massive figure ducked slightly through the entrance.

"Droggth—" moaned one of the guards in horror.

"Well, you know him at least," chirped the slender man. "I trust you'll have those doors open before he asks. He's far less... understanding than I." The two ambulatory guards scrambled to open the giant doors as the hulking figure approached. The first remained paralyzed.

Droggth was a dreadful sight. According to rumor, he was a foul crossbreed between man and half-giant with a portion of gorgol blood. Whatever his origin, he had the appearance of neither man nor pure monster. His block head was sunken in the twisted mass of rippling muscles comprising his neck and sloping shoulders, twice or three times the width of any man's, and his massive body tapered down to a distinctly human waist and legs, not the stumpy legs of a gorgol. Dead yellow eyes glowered, and pronounced lower fangs jutted up through cracked plum-blue lips of his wide mouth, even when closed, betraying the gorgol blood in his veins. Spikes of various sizes and dimensions covered Droggth's body, some adorning his armor, and others, like the black diamond clusters on his shoulders, sprouting straight from his mahogany skin by some tainted art. A strip of wild, matted black hair ran from his forehead to the nape of his neck, flanked on either side by some sort of hard carapace, like black tortoise shells fused to either side of his skull.

The marble floor trembled slightly under the heavy footfalls of his massive black boots, once tan leather, but stained over the seasons by blood and dung and filth. Over his shoulder, Droggth toted his infamous war hammer, with its crushing iron head as big as a molasses barrel, the jagged diamond face permanently stained a dark, sticky red. By the time Droggth arrived beside his slender companion, who looked like a child by comparison, the guards had indeed flung wide open the doors to the Magistrate's inner quarters. Each decorated soldier now cowered out of the path of the monster.

"You're late! You were to have followed me in," snapped the slender man.

"Yes, Lord." Droggth grumbled a reply, his voice like a rockslide in a deep canyon. "One of 'em looked in my eye."

"I see. And I suppose the poor cutter won't do that anymore."

"Won't do much of nothing no more," Droggth blurted with a sneer that approached a smile.

"Such a brute," answered the slender man, shaking his head. "Very well. Let us tarry no longer. We have an appointment with the Magistrate." The pair crossed through the doorway into a low-lit antechamber that smelled faintly of lilac and cedar chips. A heavy blue curtain separated the space from the Magistrate's inner quarters. The slender man pushed through the curtains with Droggth close behind.

Two rows of alternating statues and olive oil urns tipped with yellow flame lined the Magistrate's receiving hall. Some thirty measures from the curtain stood a heavy man in blue robes, hunched over a table beside a raised platform that held an ornate golden seat. The heavy man reviewed drawings of some sort surrounded by a cluster of colorful figures, festooned with feathers, tassels, and reams of velvet and silk.

"Alarm!" came the guard's cry from a fold of tapestry behind one of the grand doors.

The startled company at the table looked up. One of the fancy men covered his mouth and shrieked at the sight of Droggth. Another grabbed an armful of fabric from the table and ran. Guards materialized from the dim recesses of the room like dung wasps and swarmed to the pair. With incredible speed, Droggth lunged in front of the slender man and with an arc of his mighty hammer swatted the first guard like a skupp, sending him soaring through the air and crashing into the closest statue, which toppled to the ground. Another guard jabbed with a spear. With a backhanded swipe, Droggth snatched the spear from the air and snapped the tip off like a toothpick. The slender man just stood, without moving or flinching as Droggth decimated the hapless guards one after another.

"Stop!" cried the portly man in the dark blue robe, who had scrambled up the three steps to his royal seat. The ring of guards quickly retreated from Droggth's terrible reach. When the slender man walked past Droggth, the guards parted like damp spring earth before the plow.

"Müziel," said the portly man, "I didn't know you were coming, or of course... none of this." He waved a trembling hand to the guards and wreckage.

"Your guards need better training," replied the slender man. "I would have expected a more... hospitable welcome."

"Yes, my apologies, my lord. I... I... I haven't had the opportunity to... prepare them properly," sputtered the Magistrate, shooing the guards from the throne room. Droggth watched them with hungry eyes as they scampered out.

"But I see you've had ample opportunity to expand your

wardrobe." Müziel approached the table, examining the swatches of fabric and jewelry. He raised his head at the two clothiers still lingering at the table and hissed, baring two rows of sharpened teeth. Squealing, the two fled from the room like startled hens, shedding swatches of fine fabric like plumage as they ran. "And your waistline besides, Magistrate Kuquo," Müziel added, looking back to the Magistrate.

"Well... I, uh, we have had a bountiful season."

"Have you? That's strange, your gates have no fewer beggars than last I visited."

Kuquo fumbled for a response but finally just offered a mirthless chuckle.

"You have the relic for me?"

"My lord?" Kuquo answered, the half-smile still plastered on his face. "Oh! Yes, we received your runner at half-moon. And we acted with all haste, my lord," he quickly added. "I conscripted Griss, the infamous bounty hunter, and four of his most... notorious companions. And paid him handsomely at that. No small sum." Kuquo sank into his royal seat and absently fished a flake of emerald krius the size of a fingernail from the goblet affixed to the arm of the throne and deposited it on his tongue. "You'll be glad to hear I even paid extra for two of those skuller mountain beasts—" Kuquo's eyes shot up to Droggth and he grunted a pathetic chuckle. "No offense intended of course." He dipped his head slightly in Droggth's direction. "I even gave that foul Griss and his lot open access to the armory, you see."

"And? The relic?"

"Yes... uh, well, you must understand—"

"The command was simple, Kuquo," sang Müziel softly.

"Well, yes. I mean, I thought so too," sputtered Kuquo, his smile now pained and sour. "A single man and a boy. A necklace—"

"A medallion," corrected Müziel.

"Right, yes, of course."

"I gave you the hour and the place," snapped Müziel. "I delivered them on a platter for you," he added, never raising his voice, only increasing its pitch.

"And what of Governor Palius from Pol Dak?" whined Kuquo. "Your runner said his soldiers would meet us. They were nowhere to be found!"

"Is that accusation in your voice, Magistrate?" Müziel's words dribbled like oil.

"No! No, no, sire," Kuquo answered hurriedly as he smoothed down his blue robes. "It's just that I thought Palius would have his Pol Dak thugs there as well. But he must have been too busy counting his money or lost in his krius fog. I hear he has a pouch of krius in his cheek from morning until—"

"I will deal with Palius!" snapped Müziel. "Where is the medallion, Kuquo? Where is the boy?"

"Well..." Kuquo took a breath. "My men slew the one who wore the relic."

Müziel's head cocked to the side. "The Shielder is dead?" Müziel asked, his eyes brightening. Kuquo's face wore a blank stare. "The man?" Müziel continued. "The farmer with the relic is dead?"

"Yes!" said Kuquo triumphantly. "I cut him down where he stood—well, my men did."

"I want to see his body."

"His body, my lord?" Kuquo's face screwed up as he fidgeted with the arm of his chair. "You didn't ask for his body. The relic and the boy. That's what your runner said."

"Very well, Magistrate. And where are they?"

"Well, you said bring the boy *if* we could."

"Kuquo." Müziel closed his eyes and spoke slowly. "I will not ask again. Where is the relic?"

"I do not have it, my lord," Kuquo finally blurted. "Griss... he failed me." Silence settled on the room, heavy and thick.

"Bring Griss here," said Müziel finally.

"Well..." Kuquo kneaded his hands. "I can't do that."

Müziel's jaw clenched.

"You see, Griss is dead. As are the skullers."

"He killed the giants?"

Kuquo nodded.

Müziel just shook his head. "Very well. Bring me his companions."

"Companion, sire," corrected Kuquo.

"What?" snapped Müziel.

"Of the mercenaries, only two men returned, my lord. One had lost an arm and succumbed to his wounds the night of his return. The other..." He swallowed.

"The other?"

"My guards may have been a bit... heavy handed in his punishment, my lord."

Müziel pinched the bridge of his beaklike nose and closed his eyes.

"The wretched lot cost me a hogshead of gold!" complained Kuquo.

"Fine. Where is the medallion now?" asked Müziel, not looking up. "Where is the boy?"

"Griss's man said when he awoke, he searched the man's body, but the medallion was gone. So was the boy."

At these words, Müziel flinched as if struck.

"You didn't tell me this man was some sort of warrior! I thought we pursued a farmer!" Kuquo squealed, his beady eyes wide. "How can one farmer kill a troop of famed bounty hunters, and a pair of half-giant thugs?" He fished a silkeen kerchief from his sleeve and dabbed his forehead. "And where were you? Where was he?" Kuquo flung his arm in Droggth's direction, terror rising in his eyes at his own accusation.

Müziel slowly ascended the stairs to the throne. "Kuquo, you are no king," he said quietly. "Yet you have built a throne room for yourself. Statues in your likeness line this hall. You sit here sucking krius and getting fat and rich on the blood and spoils I have given you. Recall that I was the one who gave your name to the High One. He has asked little of you. I have asked little of you. But this we asked, and you have failed."

Kuquo pressed himself back against his chair, his eyes wide, pupils ringed in the thinnest line of green from the krius.

"Not that a sore like you deserves an answer, but Droggth and I were called away on important business. To recover something of great value." Müziel slowly began unbuttoning his cloak. Kuquo watched, transfixed. So captivated was he that he failed to notice Droggth climbing the steps and circling behind him. Droggth's huge arm suddenly encircled Kuquo in an iron grip.

"What's this!" shouted Kuquo.

Müziel pulled apart his collar to reveal a jagged shard of cold midnight-blue stone affixed to a chain around his neck. He spoke quietly in a foreign tongue and the stone glowed. Droggth turned his head to look away. Kuquo's frantic eyes flitted over Müziel until they glimpsed the glowing blue pendant and there they stuck, like a fly on scat. Try as he might, he couldn't rip his gaze away. The shard, nearly black, was infinite in its depth. Light glinted off tiny flecks in the deep navy. Staring at it was like searching the depths of the night sky. A sudden sense of endless wonder and a thrill washed over Kuquo. Joy and delight and pure, dark ecstasy raced through him. As he stared, the exultation receded, and the darkness grew and grew. A muffled and distant voice deep inside shrieked. Kuquo groaned, but the blue fragment now owned him.

"We've found another shard of the Narsk Blade," cooed Müziel. "H'ol Chazkar's power grows. With the medallion in hand, I could be clearing the way for his arrival even now. Crushing his adversaries. But you have failed us."

The wave grew to a torrent thrashing Kuquo's mind, spinning him off into a horrifying reality. The longer he stared at the shard, the deeper it sucked him in. He whimpered as it came on. The corners of his vision darkened and down he went, into the shard, into the blue blackness where his body and soul were ravaged. Fear, like a black bird of death, carried him into the darkest corners of his soul. Into the very Wyther Downs. Ice shot through his veins and a torment he never could have imagined enveloped him. It devoured him. Kuquo's screams and shrieks filled the room as nightmarish terrors swirled around him, pecked at him like a million undead ravens in a persistent prison of fear and death and ice while he thrashed in his throne. What lasted no more than two minutes for Müziel and Droggth seemingly stretched into seasons of torment for Kuquo until Müziel finally spoke again to the stone, causing it to cease its glow. He buttoned his shirt and closed his coat.

Kuquo's heaving frame crumpled to the slate floor and lay in a heap on the ground, drenched in sweat and tears. Müziel examined his fingernails and Droggth picked at something in his lower teeth as Kuquo lay, slowly returning to reality.

"Now, Kuquo," sang Müziel finally. "I think we've made it quite clear what is expected. When His Might requests something, failure is not an... appropriate outcome. Is that clear?" Kuquo groaned a smear of vowels. "I will accept that as your agreement." Kuquo rolled over and vomited.

"Quite a mess you've made here. But mind me, pill, this is but a taste, a shadow. It's nothing compared to the mess you'll be if I have to come back here. I doubt you want a longer look into the shard—"

"Nooooo, noooo!" howled Kuquo, terror filling his eyes, as he scrabbled backwards a marq.

"That's right. So, listen and listen well, you despicable pile of filth. Never forget you're in this paper castle for one reason:

because I want you here. Because He wants you here. A snap of my fingers and everything vanishes, and the little trip you just returned from will feel like a holiday."

"Wha... What do you want?" Kuquo blurted, wincing from the foul taste in his mouth.

"The same thing I wanted before, Kuquo." Müziel looked to Droggth and nodded at the throne. Droggth lifted Kuquo like an obstinate child and dropped him on his chair. "I want the medallion. Somehow, your flock of moths managed the much harder task of killing the Shielder yet failed to simply pluck the medallion from his neck." Müziel leaned close and rested his palm affectionately on the side of Kuquo's sweaty head. "However, if that sore you call a mercenary speaks truth, somewhere in your province is a boy carrying the relic I seek. A relic that could turn the tide. I don't care if you have to conscript a hundred skullers down from the mountains. Find it. Bring it to me."

"And what of the boy?"

"I am less concerned with him. If he's alive, send him with the other children to be delivered next moonphase. Perhaps offering the son of a Shielder could speed the Coming of His Might."

"Yesh, my lord." Kuquo slurred the thick words. "It will be done." The Magistrate had regained a bit of his shattered composure and spotted daylight at the end of this nightmarish tunnel.

Müziel nodded to Droggth. A massive fist wrenched open Kuquo's mouth as his muffled cry filled the throne room. Müziel snatched a handful of krius, enough for a week of revelry, and stuffed it in Kuquo's mouth. Droggth slammed Kuquo's jaw closed, crunching the flakes and causing Kuquo to bite down hard on his tongue. Blood, spit, and green krius juice dripped from the corner of Kuquo's mouth. His eyes opened wide, and he shook his head violently.

"Yes. I expect it will be done," answered Müziel. "But to ensure your krius-soaked mind doesn't lose the message, I will leave you a reminder." Müziel slid a fine dagger from the folds of his coat as Droggth pinned Kuquo to his chair. "Find. The. Medallion," said Müziel, as he sliced the front of Kuquo's shirt, sending buttons flying to the floor. Kuquo's horrified screams filled the chamber as Müziel quickly carved a neat circle onto Kuquo's corpulent chest.

Whimpering cries trailed Müziel and Droggth as they departed the castle and left its broken Magistrate in a blood-stained pile on the polished marble throne room floor.

12

In a hazy blur, Zodak ran through blackness so thick it felt wet. Truly, he floated more than ran, suspended in space. His foot caught, and down he fell, end over end, hundreds of measures. He woke with a start. A figure hovered over him. As his eyes focused, he recognized the face: Hallah. Something pricked the back of his mind, a muffled warning cry, but he couldn't place the danger. She had an insipid smile plastered to her face. She slowly and deliberately lifted a pillow, then brought it down over his face, smothering him. He couldn't breathe. Zodak raked and clawed at the pillow. His fingers found a hole, and he pulled, ripping the fabric apart. As he pulled and the tear widened, he found he was pulling open the slats in the closet at school. He stepped out of the closet through the hole into the classroom. He was surprised to find Ergis teaching a class of pear-shaped birds. The birds all stopped, turned, and stared at Zodak. He introduced himself to the nearest one who wore his classmate Cilac's face.

When he looked up, Ergis had become a long snake, and had snapped up one of the birds in his jaws.

"*Stop!*" yelled Zodak. "They're friendly!" Ergis's eyes burned with contempt as he swallowed the bird and snapped up another. The giant snake slithered forward, losing Ergis's face. They were now outside, and the snake towered above him, death in its eyes. Zodak crouched and helplessly covered his head. Just as the monster drew back to strike, a black shape rushed by Zodak and pounced on the snake. The water sprite sat astride a magnificent black panther that ripped and clawed at the snake. One swipe of the cat's claws split the belly of the serpent. The scarred man's body rolled out of the snake, followed by the dark child stealer. The panther bounded away and was gone. Before his eyes, the snake and child stealers dissolved into the dirt.

A dull, rhythmic sound grew louder. A cold wind whipped around Zodak. He crossed his arms, trying to stay warm. The pounding grew louder. Hoofbeats. He shivered uncontrollably. Against a wall of black, Zodak could make out a huge horse and rider galloping towards him. The moon hanging in the darkness began to fall from the sky behind the rider. As it hit the ground, it exploded into a blazing light silhouetting the rider and blinding Zodak. The rider, an armored knight, stopped just in front of him and dismounted. The horse began galloping around the two. The knight knelt down, his metal armor creaking, leaned forward, and pulled off his helmet. Long hair fell down over his face. He looked up, brushing his hair aside, and stared straight at Zodak with eyes that flashed like Ardon's. This face looked familiar, but Zodak couldn't quite place him. The steed continued to gallop in a tight circle around the two, its hoofbeats deafening, as dust rose like a dense fog. The knight put a hand on Zodak's shoulder and spoke, his rich voice undiminished by the sound of the horse. "Zodak, wake up."

Zodak pried his eyes open. The drumming sound from his

dream grew louder, and a cloud of hooves and dust and steaming nostrils thundered towards him. Zodak instinctively curled into a tight ball.

"Whoa!" came a voice. The horse whinnied to a stop as Zodak's eyes struggled to focus. A short, stout rider leapt down from the covered wagon that towered over him. "What do we have here!"

"Be careful!" came a shout from the wagon.

"This one's not dangerous, Mum," the short man replied. "Not even sure if he's alive." The man poked Zodak with his staff. "Anyone there?" Zodak slowly uncurled and tried to sit up. "He's alive all right! Mum, get some water!" Through blurred vision, Zodak could only make out the short man's outline as he bent down. "What'd you get into? Looks like you're in rough shape."

Two smaller shapes tumbled out of the wagon, trailed by scolding shouts. "You two come back here..."

"It's all right, Mum," the little man answered over his shoulder. The two children crept up timidly behind their father and peeked at Zodak. As they came into focus, Zodak started. All three of them were much shorter and stockier than any people Zodak had seen. Their heads were round and wide like pike melons turned on their side, and the man looked nearly a head shorter than Zodak himself. The boys—as far as he could tell, they were boys—were even shorter still, but were almost twice as wide as Zodak; not fat, but thick, as if flattened. One of the boys poked Zodak with a stick.

"Rusty! Stop that!" scolded the father. The boy dropped the stick to the ground and sheepishly retreated. "This boy's not well."

"Is he a... a human?" came the other boy's voice. Even in his delirium the question struck Zodak as ridiculous.

"That he is, Quaram," replied the father.

Another, more melodic voice joined the group. "Tell me you're not bringing another stray along with us, Lumpy... *Oh!*" she gasped when she saw Zodak. "What *is* he?"

"He's a human," replied Quaram proudly.

"Is he, Lumps?" She looked to the father. "He's so small."

"He's a human all right. A young one. And he's in bad shape. Now let's give the poor boy some water"—he paused—"and get him up to the wagon."

"Lumps!" gasped the mother.

"He's coming with us, Fah?" squealed Rusty.

"Look at him," the father answered under a glare from his wife. "If we leave him here, he'll certainly die." The two boys danced over this news.

"But Lumps, where's his home? What if he lives nearby? Or what if he's dangerous? You've heard Jaspar's stories!" objected the mother.

"Bah! Have you ever heard Jaspar say anything reasonable about anyone from the Open? That fool wouldn't know a human if he shared a huffinpuff sack with one!" The boys snickered. "Look around. Only one road through here. There's nothing for cliqs." They stood in silence.

"Can't we just leave him some food?" the mother offered weakly.

"How we've been smiled on," said the father, embracing her. "What if this were one of our rascals?"

Her eyes swept over to the boys, and she shook her head weakly.

"Come, boys," the father finally barked.

Zodak felt his body being lifted from the ground. The tiny hands that carried him to the wagon felt surprisingly strong. The mother cleared a space long enough for Zodak in the back, where they laid him on an impossibly soft blanket and covered him with another.

"Boys, up to the front," the mother ordered.

"But can't we..."

She gave a hard stare, and the two scurried out of the wagon. With a slap, the horse began its plod forward. The mother sat in the back with Zodak, administering more water and trying to make him comfortable. In the dim, warm wagon, sleep already clawed at him. As she inspected him, the mother suddenly cocked her head. She pulled back a flap on the wagon and sunlight splashed the inside of the dim caravan. She tugged back the collar of his shirt and gasped. The medallion stuck to Zodak's chest like a fixture, a red halo of rash encircling it. Tendrils of deep blue ran from the medal in all directions like serpentine rays of a blue sun, climbing his neck and winding over his shoulders. She gently touched his skin, shaking her head, and began to remove the cord.

Zodak's eyes flashed open. "No! Please," he added weakly.

She frowned down at him but replaced the cord. Working quickly, she ground a foul-smelling powder and stirred it into a lumpy black liquid. He choked it down at her urging, and soon he was fast asleep.

ZODAK AWOKE to a crisp square of blue morning sky framed by the wagon opening. He was starving, and for the first time in a long time, he wasn't shivering. The wagon creaked to a stop.

"Everybody out," came the father's voice.

Zodak still felt weak and gingerly climbed from the wagon, testing a few shaky steps.

"Well, look who's up!" said the mother.

"Join us for some breakfast," said the father.

The little family laid out a spread of strange looking food, but Zodak devoured it all hungrily.

"You look to be feeling better?" said the father.

"Much better," replied Zodak, breaking apart an orange, melon-sized pod and hungrily eating the fluffy white insides, as he had seen the father do. It tasted like fresh bread.

"Now that you're awake, perhaps we should start again," said the father. "My name is Quar."

"I call him Lumpy," whispered the mother with a smile.

He gave her a playful glare. "And this beauty here is Sella," said Quar, putting his arm around the mother. She smiled at Zodak with a slight nod, her cheeks turning a soft shade of pink. "And the other two, I'm sure, haven't gone unnoticed. Boys!" The two came running. One gasped. "Don't be rude, boys. This one here is Quaram, and this is Rusty—well, Quarus, actually, but we call him Rusty to help tell 'em apart." One gave an exaggerated regal bow immediately imitated by the other, their heads almost touching the ground.

"Clowns, the both of them," chuckled Sella.

"We are tuks, from Dunshar just Mead of the Myriss Slope," said Quar.

"Oh, he knows what we are," said Sella. "You have heard of tuks before, haven't you?" she asked.

"Well... no, I don't think I have," replied Zodak, ashamed of his ignorance. "But I'm pleased to meet you," he quickly added. "My name is Zodak. I am... just a boy. I am from Laan." The blank stares told him they had never heard of his town. "Must only be a few cliqs off," he said. "Near Pol Dak," he added quickly. Sella and Quar exchanged glances.

"Is your family in this Laan?" asked Sella. "Do they know where you are? Are they looking for you?"

"Yes. Well, no." Zodak fumbled over the words. "It's complicated. But no, I'm afraid nobody is looking for me." Another glance between the parents. "I'm an orphan now," he added quickly. "What are tuks?" he asked, changing the topic.

"Tuks?" said Quar. "Why, we're friendly folk. We hail from the Dell, a cozy spot a couple hundred cliqs to the Mead of Pol Dak, tucked away and circled by the great trees. Most tuks hate to leave the Dell, you know. Any outsider is an enemy, and anything beyond the Dell limits, they call the 'Open.' To be out in the Open for long is the stuff of tuk nightmares."

"But not us!" chirped Rusty.

"Indeed. Well, we should get back on the road. I am sure you have quite a story to tell, and—"

"The open road loves a story," chanted the boys and Sella in monotone unison.

"Heard that one, eh?" said Quar. "Well, go on, gather up the things." Like a practiced circus crew, the tuks packed up the elaborate lunch with amazing speed and in no time had the wagon ready to go. Zodak climbed stiffly in the back with the last bundle of food, handing it to Sella as the wagon began rolling.

Not long after they set off, Quar gave a sharp whistle. Zodak cocked his head and listened. He heard a soft but steady rumble of horse hooves, growing louder.

"Strange," said Sella, shooting a furtive glance to Quar. "Not usually travelers along this road." She quickly pulled the corner of the wagon cover back and peeked out. Two figures approached, riding tall steeds. Zodak leaned to look through the opening but couldn't make out the riders clearly.

"I'll be!" exclaimed Sella. "More humans. This is strange."

Zodak's curiosity suddenly vanished, replaced by dread. As the riders approached, he could see their familiar stately brown horses. One rider wore an emerald riding coat. "No," Zodak groaned, lurching backward into the cover of the wagon. "No! Please. Please hide me!" he begged.

Sella looked at Zodak for a moment, then quickly closed the wagon cover. "Lumps, the boy's got unwanted company!"

Zodak felt the wagon speed up slightly, but the horses

continued to approach. Before long, they had overtaken the wagon.

"Hello there!" came a man's smooth voice, with just the hint of a rasp. Zodak's stomach dropped. The wagon slowed to a stop.

"Ho," replied Quar. Zodak froze.

"I'm sorry to bother you, friend," the man said in an oily voice, "but we're in need of a bit of assistance. I'm looking for an...outlaw we've been tracking for a few days."

"Oh?" Over the din of his galloping heart, Zodak could hear the jangle of the other rider slowly circling the wagon.

"Yes, well, he's just a boy, but without going too far into the business of the Venerable Council, he has blood on his hands, and we need him returned to the city."

"The Venerable Council!" exclaimed Quar. "We must be a hundred cliqs from Pol Dak. Is the boy traveling by foot?" An awkward pause followed.

"Well, he may have had help," replied the voice hurriedly. "Have you seen him?" His voice now carried an edge. There was a pause.

"You're the first human we've seen in Rislaan for days. Not often do we run across a human in these parts."

"Mind if we take a look in the back?" asked the voice.

"There's no need—" But before Quar could object, the other rider flung the back of the wagon open.

Inside sat Sella mending a torn feed bag amidst a jumble of packages and boxes for the journey.

"You wouldn't happen to have any golden marsh wheat from Pol Dak, would you, dear?" asked Sella, holding out a feed bag to the intruder.

The man sneered and recoiled.

"Not this one!" he hissed to the other, letting the flap fall closed.

"If you do see him, he is dangerous," warned the first man.

"Dangerous how?" asked Quar.

The man only sneered, and the horses galloped off.

Sella lifted the grain bags, and Zodak pulled the huffinpuff sack off his head, gasping for fresh air. Immediately, the boys started chattering and squealing frantically to each other.

"Zodak, we need to talk." Quar's voice was stern.

13

Sella ushered the children to the back of the wagon as Quar summoned Zodak to the driver's bench. A wave of anxiousness swept over Zodak. He knew he owed the family an explanation, but what if they didn't believe him? He had finally felt safe for the moment. *Do they think I'm dangerous? I have to tell the truth.* He remembered Ardon's words.

As the wagon bumped along, Zodak told Quar what had happened to him since Komo, leaving out the encounter with the sprite. Quar peppered him with questions as Rusty and Quaram strained as far forward as they could, devouring the tale. Sella moved up beside Quar and listened attentively. When he reached the fight in the clearing, he braced himself for a rush of sorrow, but to his relief, he didn't fumble or shed a single tear. He felt curiously numb. When he finished speaking, the sun hung low in the sky, and for the next quarter hour, no one spoke.

"Them were the men who tried to steal you?" blurted Rusty, earning a thump from Quaram and a glare from Sella. The blunt question sent chills through Zodak. He nodded.

"Amazing," Quar said finally. "You have walked through fire no boy should have to face."

"You were very sick," Sella said. "That medallion of yours looked to be burning a hole in your chest when we found you." She motioned to his torso. Zodak drew back the corner of his shirt. The red around the circumference was gone and the blue lines were so faint they looked like nothing more than pronounced veins. "But you're safe now," she added, with a pat on his back. "We won't let them near you." She stole a glance at Quar.

"Yet it doesn't all fit," added Quar. Zodak looked up searchingly. "I'd need to consult a map to be exact, but the spot we found you must be over twenty cliqs from where you said you escaped those men. That's a couple of days' walking for a seasoned traveler, and twice that, I'd wager, for a fevered boy scrambling through thickets..." His voice trailed off.

Again, dread crept over Zodak and his breath quickened. *They don't believe me.* Had he counted the days wrong? No, the escape had only lasted the night. Possibly another blurred day at most. His mind scrambled for an explanation. *If they think I'm lying, will they leave me here?* His eyes darted anxiously around as he examined the thick wooded surroundings. *What lives out here?* His hands twitched nervously, and he shook his head involuntarily. His fingernail clawed a cuticle.

"How'd he come to be here, Lumps?" asked Sella.

"Says he ran," said Quar absently.

"I did. I promise!" exclaimed Zodak.

"Well, if your story is true—"

"It's true," Sella interrupted Quar, staring into Zodak's eyes with startling intensity, as if trying to discern a shape at the bottom of a streambed. "Or at least he believes it is," she added, nodding.

"Strange," Quar muttered to himself. His attention snapped back, and the hard expression softened. "There is much we don't know about you," he said, "but I know two things: finding you isn't an accident, and you, Zodak," declared Quar, "are no ordinary farm boy." Rusty and Quaram retreated to the back of the wagon in a cloud of conspiratorial whispers.

"I don't know what to say," Zodak finally replied. "This feels like a dream. Or a nightmare."

"Well, like Sella said, you're safe with us now," said Quar. "We'll make sense of what we can, but no reason to toss you into the woods alone… just yet anyway," he added with a wink.

Zodak's knotted shoulders relaxed. "Thank you." His head bowed slightly. After a moment, he asked, "Where are you all going now?"

"We are on an adventure," said Quar.

"A last adventure," Sella cut in, "before we settle down."

"For a bit," Quar added with a mischievous glance at Sella. She shook her head. "She's got the tuk blood in her, you know." He smiled at Zodak. "Like I said, tuks need nothing more than the quiet and slow life of the Dell. Don't want news from afar, and they don't need to go a step beyond their whipple fields. Their lives are family, the harvest, and neighbors."

"That sounds like Laan," said Zodak. "Without the whiffle fields, I mean."

"Whipple," said Sella.

"For most tuks, Dell contests and storytelling are adventure enough," continued Quar. "A favorite hobby is settling—sitting on their padswillow toadstool, or pads, sipping the tuberfruit nectar straight from the stem. Take great pride in our pads, we do. Always pruned and tidy so as to grow the tuberfruit. Ah, the lovely tuberfruit." Quar closed his eyes. "That is one thing I miss." Sella seemed to drift off back to the Dell as well.

"So, why are you out here if tuks hate to leave the Dell?" asked Zodak.

"Well now, that's a story too long to tell before nightfall.

Maybe tomorrow on the road I can swap some tales of my travels."

"What will you do, Zodak?" asked Sella. "Are you certain you won't return to Laan?"

Zodak gazed towards the darkening horizon. "No... no, I don't think so," he said quietly. "There is nothing for me there."

"What about your money?" asked Quaram eagerly. "You're rich!"

Zodak snorted a mirthless laugh. "I guess I am." It felt strange to say that aloud. "But the money will have to stay hidden. Those men might be waiting for me in Laan. No, there's nothing for me there." Again, the group grew quiet.

"I think you're right about those men looking for you," said Quar. "I fear they mean you harm. A couple of goblin friends if I've ever seen one. Wore it all over their faces, they did. I've no idea how they followed you all the way here, but if they find you..." He trailed off.

"Goblin friends?" Zodak asked. Quar exchanged glances with Sella, her face stern.

"There are some who walk Yiduiijn whose minds have been tainted by the Darkness." He hesitated, then leaned closer and whispered, "They keep counsel with margoul." Zodak's eyes grew wide.

"Fah's killed halfies!" shouted Rusty.

"No goblin talk! Not so close to nightfall..." Sella scolded, rolling her eyes and throwing up her hands.

Quar glanced her way with a mischievous twinkle. "Oh, they're nasty creatures, too. Always looking to steal or harm. No bigger than this one here," said Quar, patting Quaram on the back. "But they make up for size with hate. There's no good bone in any goblin body. Not a one. It's why there's nothing but dust when they die."

"No blood," chirped Quaram. Sella glared at Quar.

"You could come with us," Quar finally said.

"And where is it exactly you would say we're going?" Sella shot him a guarded look.

"We'll head up Fahyzward to the Rhunx River," he answered casually. "You know, I've always wanted to see the Grasslands—"

"The Grasslands! That's another two hundred cliqs! We'll not go that far!" interjected Sella. Quar chuckled. This negotiation was a daily affair. "I say we turn back at Uth Becca."

"Wait!" Zodak blurted. "Uth Becca?" The name crackled in his mind like lightning. Sella and Quar looked up. "That's what Ardon said. I remember now. 'Go to Uth Becca. Find the Order.'"

Quar cocked his head. "Yes, well, I don't know anything called the Order," said Quar, "But we're headed to Uth Becca. Want the boys to see the famed White City."

"There's so much I need to understand," said Zodak. "I'm sure I can find answers in Uth Becca."

"Like why them giants tried to capture you?" Quaram asked.

"Ardon died for me," Zodak answered flatly. "He told me to protect this." He tapped his chest. "To find the Order."

"And once you're in Uth Becca, what then?" asked Sella. "It's a big city. Where would you start?"

"I... I..." Zodak's chest tightened. He had no idea. He hadn't thought that far.

"Well, no need to make any decisions this moment." Quar patted Zodak on the leg. "We have a few days yet to sort out such things."

"You won't stay with us?" asked Rusty, big eyes pleading.

"I would love to. I truly would." Zodak rested a hand on the little tuk's shoulder. "But I can't. It feels like stepping into darkness, but I'm somehow pulled. I need to know what it all means, why I'm here. If I don't start looking for answers, I'll never find any."

"You're wise for your young age, Zodak," said Sella.

"I wish I could never leave." Zodak smiled sadly at Rusty and then Quaram.

Just after sundown as the moon took flight in the darkening sky, Quar pulled the wagon off the road into a grassy patch. As always, the tuks made camp in a whirlwind, and in no time, Sella had a fire going with steaming soup for dinner. Rusty dragged Zodak's two huffinpuff sacks from the wagon and handed them over. The stitched leather sacks were filled with fluffy, downy seedlings from huffinpuff pod, an icon of the tuks' Dell, that made for an impossibly soft and warm, if not a bit short, sleeping sack.

The family settled in around the fire, tucked into their huffinpuff sacks. Quar sang a sad ballad from his days on the road, and the boys snickered at jokes until gently scolded by Sella. Zodak stared wearily into the embers, basking in the glow of this little family. In his joy, he felt the pang of sorrow. *Have I been foolish? Should I stay with the tuks?* He felt Uth Becca pulling him, yet there was such richness right here. He put the question away and sighed deeply. For the first time in a long time, he felt he had recovered a piece of himself.

14

Picking his way carefully around the still, shapeless forms scattered in the smoke-black morning, Quar reached out and gently jostled Zodak. Zodak snapped awake in a flash. In one fluid motion, he flipped up off the ground to his feet, landing in a crouched combat position. As the world came into focus, he saw Quar take a step back, a wide-eyed expression on his face and one hand on the handle of his long knife. Zodak's heart pounded, and every sense was alert, but he had no idea why or how. Energy surged through his chest.

"Are you all right, son?" asked Quar cautiously, the concerned look still etched on his face, and his taut muscles betraying his readiness.

"I'm sorry. I... I'm not sure what happened." Zodak relaxed his stance and looked down at his body. *I've never moved like that,* he thought.

"Let's get you some food," said Quar, patting Zodak on the side. The familiar smell of campfire smoke heralded another delicious breakfast of the bready hoopa pod, sweet ruby jelly, and fried cheese, with piping hot pink tea and candy melon.

Zodak wandered into the nearby brush to relieve himself, his mind still spinning from what had just happened.

After stuffing himself, he clumsily rolled his sleeping sack and gathered his water pouch, moving like a blind bushcow compared to the speed of the family as they packed up, cleaned the site, doused the fire, and loaded the wagon with automated ease. In no time, the group was off. Bumping along in the wagon, Zodak's thoughts drifted back to the night before and how Quar's stories of goblins and fantastic creatures and faraway places had cracked open his imagination. He reminded himself that artful exaggeration and embellishment were tools of any good storyteller, yet he couldn't wait to hear more.

Quar had promised what he called "a full and proper storytelling" when they were back on the road.

"You said I should wait until today to ask about your travels?" Zodak finally blurted when he could stand it no longer. He tried to look casual, like he was just making conversation rather than ready to explode from anticipation.

"Here we go..." groaned Sella, climbing to the back of the wagon. The boys squealed excitedly and even Quar's eyes twinkled, betraying how he relished the telling.

"Well," began Quar dramatically, "no tuk had ever ventured out of the Dell in a hundred seasons. Until, that is, my father, Quo."

"Grandpa Quo was the first!" squeaked Quaram.

"Desperation drove him," continued Quar. "When I was a small boy, you see, my mother fell very ill. She was pregnant with my baby sister—"

"Aunt Millie," whispered Rusty loudly.

"Yes. She was pregnant and on death's door," Quar persisted. "But as Color would have it, that very night, a traveler came through the village and shared the secret of the midnight lily."

Like a master silka spinner, Quar wove the fantastic story of his epic journey with his father over the Skulla Range and into the land of giants to seek the midnight lily. Zodak hung on every word, eyes wide with wonder. Quar told how he and his father had scurried like skupp through a land of towering creatures, taller than trees, how they escaped the den of giant horned wasps and lashed together huge, curled leaves into a raft that carried them down a raging river, flashing with great silver, tusked fish. With his audience enraptured, Quar told of their narrow escape from the river gorgol that lurked in the shallows, their bald heads poking above the surface of the water like river rocks until yellow eyes snapped open and the massive gorgol bodies grew out of the muck and started hurling clods of mud the size of barrels through the air.

Zodak breathed quickly and his hands were balled as the master storyteller recounted the desperate rescue by the strange pale-skinned cave-dwellers called the tula people. It was the tula, Quar explained, who grew and harvested fields of the midnight lily deep underground. After weeks of perilous travel, Quar and his father found themselves stumbling back into the Dell on weary legs with the prized midnight lily.

"I sat beside my dying mother, her hand in my two wee ones," told Quar. "Every muscle in my body ached from the journey, but I didn't care. I remember studying her pained face for some sign that the magical lily had worked, that our trip hadn't been in vain." Quar's voice had grown soft. The three boys leaned in close and even Sella had emerged and stopped pretending not to listen.

"'Hurrah!'"—everyone jumped—"shouted my fah when my mum's green eyes flashed open, and she gasped in a sweet breath of life." Sella swatted at Quar. "The midnight lily had saved my mum and baby Millie as well!" Quar beamed. Zodak's heart pounded.

"Every single tuk in the village, without exception, refused to hear our stories. The elders forbade Father from telling any of his tales of the Open, but he couldn't help himself, and no one could really stop him." Quar chuckled and shook his head.

"We were all overjoyed at my mum's return to health and with the birth of my sister. Fah kept a small crop of midnight lilies in a dark box beneath his pad, and lived out his days as the Dell's healer, curing sickness and injuries of all kinds with the plants until the season of the thunder snow wiped out the last of them. It's a good thing for you we have some dried petal powder still on hand," said Quar, winking at Zodak.

"The black stuff?" Zodak's face screwed up as he recalled choking down the liquid Sella fed him that first day.

"I, on the other hand, had been bitten by the adventure bug and was captivated by the Open. As soon as the commotion died down, the Dell started to feel crowded, like it was closing in about me. So as soon as I was of age, I left to travel. I returned to the village every few seasons with new, scandalous tales from the Open which no one wanted to hear—well, nobody but my fah. We'd sip tuberfruit on his pad after dinner, and I would share all of my adventures. But one of those nights, an intruder was prowling around our pad—"

"I was not prowling!" exclaimed Sella indignantly, poking her head out of the back of the wagon. "I was simply out for a moonstroll when the sound of raucous laughter and tall tales caught my ear, so I stopped to listen. After a bit, I simply *had* to see who was spouting these fables. I crept a bit closer and discovered a quite handsome young tuk and his father. This, I knew, must be the traveling tuk my parents so loudly disapproved of. But I suppose I *was* hooked..."

"Mother was hooked, Mother was hooked!" sang Rusty and Quaram in duet.

"The next day in the silver chute field she tried to casually ask about my adventures," Quar said. "I was thrilled to finally find a tuk who wanted to hear the tales, but I had *the hardest* time convincing her they were all true."

"We spent weeks together," said Sella. "It was the longest Quar had spent in the Dell since he had begun to travel many seasons before. After about a season, we pledged togetherness." She took his hand.

"Yes. But only after she agreed to make a go of it on the road with me," said Quar with a wink.

"Reluctantly," added Sella. "I am a tuk after all. But the stories were captivating, and I was young and in love."

"Dwarf's dither! Her parents were *not* happy about that. I might as well have been planning a honeymoon to the Wyther Downs."

"Don't talk like that, Lumpy!" snapped Sella, her face suddenly grave. "No need to mention that place. Not here or ever!"

"Sorry, Mum. You're right. Anyway, I showed her some of my favorite spots as we traveled Yiduiijn. I introduced her to friends I had made across the Midlands. The gnolls, the elves, the foothill elementals—"

"Elves?" interrupted Zodak. "Wait. Elves are real?"

"Of course!" snorted Quar, amused at the question. "Haven't gotten too far out of your village, have you?"

"No." Zodak looked down at his feet sheepishly. "Hombord the traveling bard comes to Laan from Pol Dak with stories of fanciful creatures, but I never knew there was any truth to it. All we have in Laan are farm animals, well, that and skupp and orko and zheibak in the forest, and the occasional marauding bushcow. But no goblins or elves."

"Well, your eyes will be open out here," said Quar. He leaned back toward Sella. "We had great times though, didn't we?"

"Yes, we did," she agreed, if somewhat less enthusiastically. "It has been quite a journey. But a pad and a little house and garden…" Her voice drifted off.

"Soon enough, Mum," answered Quar.

"We want to go on adventures!" blurted Quaram.

"Yeah, like Fah," added Rusty.

"Look! Look how you fill their heads!" said Sella, poking Quar with a stubby finger. "What happened to the quiet life?" Their eyes met and then broke off. The stiff question hung icy in the air between them.

"The pull of the Dell is strong in every tuk," said Quar. "Even an adventurer like this one." He leaned back and kissed Sella on the cheek.

15

The days rolled along with the wheels of the little wagon —much too quickly for Zodak. He rode beside Quar, listening to stories, or played with the boys in the back. When Quar took his daily naps (tuks, Zodak learned, take no fewer than three a day), Zodak drove the wagon, speaking with Sella or trading jokes and stories with the boys. He especially reveled in those two. They were silly and free. They were unguarded, without calculating manipulation or spite, and they had grafted Zodak into their tribe. They became what he only imagined loving brothers to be. For their part, Rusty and Quaram adored Zodak. In him, they found a playmate and a co-adventurer, but also an admired elder. Soon they had begun to adopt his mannerisms.

Even in this season of rest with the tuk family, Zodak occasionally felt death's lingering sting. All it took was a sound or comment to trigger the nightmarish darkness. One day, in the golden wash of a late afternoon as Quar and Sella made camp, Zodak occupied himself in a game of swat the skupp with the boys. Rusty and Quar laughed and hollered at Zodak's wild eyes and grotesque face, chasing him from tree to tree with sapling swords.

Forced back against a hedge of tangleberry bushes, Zodak hunched and covered himself with his arms in mock defeat, bracing for the playful shower of attacks. Whipped into a frenzy pursuing their imagined foe, the boys' swatted Zodak with excited blows.

"Ow! Too hard—" he protested, opening his eyes. There stood the scarred man, bloodied dagger raised to strike. Zodak screamed as play turned to panic, and flung himself backwards into the tangleberry's wall of gnarled claws. He frantically tore at the dense weave of brittle branches, seeking an escape. The limbs and sharp thorns bit back, marking his arms and face with scratches and cuts. He couldn't breathe. Rushing footsteps approached, and terror flooded his body. He sank helplessly to the ground, tucking himself into a ball, and braced for rough gloved hands to rip him from the brambles.

"Zodak," came Quar's voice from far away.

"It's all right, son." Sella spoke softly.

With eyes clamped shut, he felt a small hand gently rest on his back. "You're safe, Zodak."

His heart raced, and he trembled, but his quick shallow breathing gradually slowed. He opened his eyes and let his rigid muscles slowly unwind. The vision was gone. Rusty and Quaram stood back behind their parents, each wearing ashen masks of fear. Quaram had fresh tear streaks on his cheeks.

"You're hurt?" Sella asked, tracing one of the crimson stripes on his forehead.

"I... I'm okay." He looked again at the boys, shame filling him. "I'm sorry. I don't... I don't know what happened."

"No, no. Shh, shh," soothed Sella.

"Let's get you up." Quar offered a hand and pulled Zodak to his feet.

"And *cleaned* up," added Sella, dabbing his cheek with a kerchief. It came away stained with red.

"I... I'm sorry!" blurted Quaram, dropping the switch and burying his face in Quar's side and sobbing.

"No, no," said Zodak quickly. "It's not your fault."

At the wagon, Sella set to work, smearing the laceration on his left hand with balm and wrapping it in a strip of fabric. The boys watched intently from a safe distance.

"It was the man with the scar," said Zodak softly. "The child stealer."

"You've had a scare," said Quar. "Try to relax."

"I'm afraid it won't be the last time those visions haunt you," said Sella, uncorking a dark bottle of pungent liquid.

"But I frightened the boys," said Zodak sadly, looking over at them.

"Quar will talk to them," said Sella. "They don't understand what you've been through." She poured a few drops of a dark yellow sludge onto a wooden spoon. "Take a bit of this." She held the spoon to his lips. "It'll bring calm." The pungent odor overwhelmed him, and the syrup burned his throat, but within moments Zodak felt the tension seep from his body. Sella cleared a space for him in the back of the wagon, and as soon as he lay back, his body surrendered to sleep.

He slept through dinner until just before dawn. When he awoke, every muscle in his body ached. Lying alone in the quiet, he replayed the episode in his mind. It had felt so real, the face of the scarred man, the knife, the look of death in his eyes. Shame rushed in, so he pushed the scene from his mind. As the days stretched on with the tuk family, Zodak slowly released the constant haunting memory of the tangleberry bushes and returned to playful camaraderie with the boys.

Zodak wasn't safe in dreams, though. Sometimes it was the scarred man and sometimes the half-giants or Griss chasing him. Many nights, he awoke to Sella's comforting voice and gentle shaking. "Just a dream." It always felt like more than just a dream. He longed to meet Ardon in those dreams, but somehow, he was always absent as the child stealers closed in.

Zodak drank deeply of this little tuk family. Without so much as a spat to his name, he felt rich. It was a richness he had never known; a richness the coins buried in the barn could never buy. Nothing about his family in Laan had been simple. Navigating the sharp edges required politics and precision. Few and fleeting were the moments with Ardon, like the morning on the forest path, when Zodak could relish the prize of a father's love without fear of reprisal or attack.

But the tuks were different. The boys squabbled and Sella and Quar had their moments, yet Zodak felt spoiled by the loving family. There were no games, no hate to navigate. He could have spent seasons with the tuks, as if they were days. Yet days were all he had, and even as he cherished them, they were shaved away like chips of wood from a whittling stick.

He let himself dream of staying with the family, joining them for good. If he asked, he thought they would probably say yes and make it work somehow. But it never could. The Dell was their home, and while Zodak wished his time with them would never end, he still felt the pull. The words of the water sprite tugged at something deep inside, and the weight of the medallion around his neck served as a constant reminder of Ardon's final words. No, as safe and happy and loved as he felt, this was not his place.

On one of the last nights with the tuks, as the wagon bumped along, Zodak suddenly found himself in complete darkness, sitting across from the water sprite on impossibly tall stone columns, rising hundreds of measures above the amorphous landscape. The sprite sat at Zodak's eye level, locked in his gaze. Zodak blurted the stream of consciousness that gnawed at him daily: how he'd come to love the tuk family; how he couldn't leave them. He recalled speaking no words aloud yet somehow shared volumes. He had known love, real love. A tender mother and siblings he adored and cherished. He looked up to the sprite, who sat motionless with eyes closed. Zodak felt a pang of desperation—*was it even listening? Had it heard anything?*

Then the sprite's eyes flashed open. "Zodak." The voice now rumbled with authority and power that penetrated his chest. "Your purpose pulls you. You have felt it. A gift you've been given. For a time. And that time is ending. Quiet the noise and listen to your call." The sprite paused. "The time has come for you to go."

"Go where?" asked Zodak. The pillar holding the sprite began growing taller and taller. "Where must I go?" Zodak called up again at the figure, fifty measures above him and rising fast.

"To the city, you must go!" called the speck of a figure now a hundred measures away.

"What city? Uth Becca? To find the Order?" Zodak called after the sprite. "Why?!"

"Zodak, it's all right," came the blurry sound of Sella's soothing voice. "You were dreaming." Zodak heaved himself up until he sat heavily against a wooden rib of the wagon. The boys dozed in a tangled clump beside him.

"Quar's been driving all night?" Zodak asked.

"He won't stop here mead of the city. Says he doesn't trust the 'malice of the forest,'" Sella replied.

Zodak dragged himself up to the driver's seat beside Quar. Dawn's dull gray coat blanketed the land. The crackle of hollow swampgrass stems being crushed into the mud beneath the wagon's wheels was the only sound as they cut through a small opening in the dark woods. The wagon plunged back into the dark forest, where the air smelled stale and damp. A thick mist clung to the road. The horse stirred it up and sent it spinning into eddies and swirls behind the wagon. Zodak broke the silence.

"I... I had a dream." He immediately felt silly. Hallah had often scolded him for how foolish it was to discuss such imaginings.

"Oh?" answered Quar. "Can you remember it well?"

Zodak thought for a moment. "Yes. Every detail."

"Oorlo, an elder in the Tuuma tribe of Moon People, once said that the Figure in the Clouds never speaks through our foggy and jerky nonsense dreams, but if you wake remembering every facet of the dream, you would do well to pay attention."

Zodak told Quar about the water sprite and its parting message.

Quar nodded, but for a long moment said nothing. "A water sprite, you say?" He nodded again. "Deep as a well you are, my boy. I'd say we have our answer to the question of you staying on with us. You have places to go."

"Maybe it was just a dream," replied Zodak, fighting back the urge to beg Quar to let him stay.

"Perhaps... yet since the day we found you, I have sensed something about you. Something that churns beneath your surface. You know we would take you with us in a wink, yet..." He softly shook his head. "If the pull comes from the Color, as mightily as I might want to, how can I stand in the way? If you have been called, a tuk family caravan is likely not that purpose."

The wagon burrowed deeper into the dark woods, following the slithering road downwards into its depths. The fog that now enveloped the wagon was so thick that Zodak could see only a ghost of the horse's head. His own head shook unconsciously, as if clearing hair from his eyes. Quar slowed, to keep from running off the road.

"This is dangerous weather," said Quar, glancing about.

"These woods are no friends to travelers, and a cover of fog like this hides wicked secrets." Quar reached into the back of the wagon and pulled out a grain sickle. "Take this, son, and pray you won't need it." Quar put a hand on the hilt of his long knife. Zodak kept a keen watch as they descended into the depths of the swamp. The fog settled here, as thick as foam. Even as he strained to peer into the darkness, the rhythmic thud of wagon wheels on earth and gentle rocking called his thoughts away to his unknown future.

A shriek suddenly pierced the night. Zodak snapped back from his mental wanderings with a start. The hair stood on his neck.

"Steady yourself, boy!" Quar's voice was urgent and sharp.

"There it is again." Sella's worried voice from the wagon made Zodak jump. Something clattered loudly off to the right side of the wagon. Then again on the left.

"Rocks," said Quar. "They're throwing rocks." He increased the speed of the wagon.

"Who is?" Zodak's heart raced as he searched the dark trees for an assailant.

"Goblins," said Quar flatly.

"Here?" blurted Zodak. He had heard the stories. As a child, he had debated their existence with Alana and Ergis, and a few of the villagers had claimed to have a friend or distant relative who had seen one, but never in Laan. Folba had said something about the Elder and Pol Dak keeping them at bay. The horse whinnied and skidded to a stop.

"Burn me!" Quar exclaimed. A freshly felled tree blocked the path. Even as he looked, a darting, black shape caught Zodak's eye just off to the right of the path. Then another.

"With the boys, Mum!" Quar ordered, clicking his tongue and backing the wagon up. A flurry of rocks pelted the caravan.

"Ah!" A jolt of pain shot through Zodak's arm as one caught him on the shoulder.

"Hold on!" called Quar, turning the horse towards the woods and slapping the reins. The reluctant animal pushed into the underbrush, skirting the blockage in the path. Another shriek from the right, answered by one to the left. The cacophony grew, and then came the charge. A half dozen black hooded shapes, each no larger than a child, rushed from the woods. Zodak snapped his head back just as a rusty blade lashed hastily to a long staff whirred by his face and thudded into the top of the side rail.

A goblin ran along the fallen log on the right and leapt through the air, landing on the front right corner of the wagon. The horse whinnied a panicked cry as the goblins fell upon it from either side. The animal abandoned its careful navigation for frenzied flight. It surged ahead into the thicket, its frantic hooves trampling a hapless attacker, while the wagon wheels crushed another. The goblin screams of fury and agony merged with pounding hoofbeats, clattering rocks, and incessant scraping and clawing of limbs and bushes against the wagon in a deafening storm of sound.

The nearest goblin had pulled himself up to the carriage and set to work sawing the leather straps of the harness between the wagon and horse. Zodak gaped at the little monster. Like the others, it wore a tattered black hooded robe. In the dull light, he could make out nothing of a face, just the black void set back in the hood.

"Zodak!" cried Quar, signaling at the attacker.

Zodak suddenly snapped back to the moment, remembering the sickle in his hand. With a lunge and a slash, as fluid as if he had trained for seasons with the curved blade, he cut the goblin down in a single stroke. A screech came from above as a shape leapt from a branch and thudded onto the canvas top of the wagon. The goblin stabbed a black blade into the canvas and began tearing. Without thinking, Zodak turned and sprang up to the roof of the wagon after the attacker. The foul smell of unwashed rags enveloped him as soon as he crashed into the goblin's small, dense body. A chipped knife flashed as the goblin brought the blade down on Zodak. But Zodak was too fast. In one swift swipe, he lopped the goblin's arm clean off with the sickle, and in a sudden surge of strength, flung the goblin off into the night.

"Okay up there?" came Quar's voice.

"Yes!" Zodak tried to sound confident over the pounding of his heart.

Even as he spoke, the wagon swerved back from underbrush to path and surged ahead as the frantic horse found the path again. Zodak slid across the canvas roof and over the edge. As he fell, his left hand grasped the back frame of the covered wagon and he managed to land on the small step at the back of the wagon. With a sigh he relaxed for a moment.

"Zodak?" Quar called again.

"I'm here—" A pole jabbed out from the wagon and struck him hard in the stomach, sending pain shooting through his gut and stealing his breath. Losing his grip, Zodak fell from his perch, landing hard on the ground.

"I got one!" came Rusty's familiar cry from within the wagon as it rumbled away.

"Lump! Stop!" yelled Sella.

Zodak heard a horrible screech from behind and scrambled to his feet, snatching up the fallen sickle. Ahead, the wagon had slowed to a stop, and three sets of tuk eyes were fixed on him. Zodak glanced back down the path at the three charging goblins, twenty measures away and closing. His grip tightened on the sickle. Two more black shapes burst from the woods.

"Come on, boy!" yelled Quar, slapping the reins.

Zodak turned and sprinted, leaping at the back of the wagon as it gained speed. Sella and the boys quickly hauled him in. For a moment he just lay panting as they sped down the path, disappointed shrieks fading into the distance. Sella's face was white, and no one spoke. Quaram and Rusty looked at one another and burst into spontaneous laughter.

"Did ya see me?" Rusty burst out. "I got one!"

"You got Zodak!" laughed Quaram.

"Got me pretty good, though," Zodak added, rubbing his stomach.

"Too close, that," said Sella, shaking off dark thoughts.

"Fah, did ya see Zodak?" called Rusty, pulling open the flap to the driver's seat.

"What an adventure!" called Quar over his shoulder with a broad smile. Sella grunted her disapproval. "The Color has covered us," Quar added. Zodak slithered back up to the driver's seat beside Quar. "That was a nasty troop," Quar said, the smile fading into a grave expression. "Woulda cut us up and left us to die if they could have." Quar sucked in a deep breath as the flap closed. "But I must say," he plucked up, "Rusty's right. You were great! How did you learn to move like that?"

"I... I don't really know," Zodak confessed. "I wasn't thinking, just reacting. But I did feel... strong. Fast."

"Well, you looked it," added Quar. "And a good thing for all of us that you did." They rode in silence for most of an hour. Finally, the fog began to thin as the road climbed steadily from the murky forest. Slivers of dawn lanced through the forest canopy ahead.

"In a couple of minutes, you'll see Uth Becca sparkling in the morning light."

"Is it a big city?" asked Zodak.

Quar chuckled. "Not the biggest in Yiduiijn, but she's a beauty all right, and a good deal larger than you're used to. Have you visited Pol Dak?"

"No," answered Zodak. "I've only heard stories about it."

"Well, it's a sleepy village compared to Uth Becca. She's absolutely marvelous, a true wonder all right." The pungent smell of swamp began to thin and now carried hints of fresh morning and grass and breeze. Ahead, the fog glowed yellow.

"Hold on, here we go," said Quar and he slapped the reins. The wagon lurched forward as the eager horse scrambled out of the throat of the swamp toward an amber wall of mist. Zodak instinctively braced for the moment of impact, but the wagon burst through the fog bank, crashing into a wave of sunlight.

"There she is," said Quar, pulling on the reins. Zodak opened his eyes and gasped.

16

Zodak couldn't speak. The beauty and grandeur of the sparkling white city towering ahead overpowered him. Uth Becca. Before this marvelous sight, Zodak quickly forgot the gloom of the dark forest swallowed by the swirling fog behind. He had never imagined even the legendary City K'andoria from the tales of the kingdom to be so stunning.

"What do you think?" asked Quar, gazing upon the city with a twinkle of pride.

Even from a distance, the sheer size was magnificent. As if shaped by the hand of a master potter from pure pearl clay, the city walls soared upward from the landscape. The spire of the shimmering castle atop a hill in the center of the city nearly pierced the clouds. The endless towering white wall dwarfed the encircling farms, scattered about the city's apron. Zodak could see patches of green, even within the city walls. The wall to the left of the city stood haughtily against a sparkling river, and towering white arches carved into the wall marked the port. Tiny silver sails flared in the morning light. Ahead, the dusty cart path snaked through fields for about half a cliq where it met a road running to the city.

"It's magnificent," stammered Zodak. "I had no idea..."

"She sparkles like a diamond all right," mused Quar.

"Even a diamond has sharp edges," came Sella's voice as she emerged from the wagon. She beheld the sight, and added more softly, "Though I'll never grow tired of that sight. Boys! Shake off the sand and come take a look." Rusty and Quaram dragged themselves sleepily from their nest.

"By Color!" said Quaram, earning a disapproving scowl from Sella. "I told you it was big." He beamed at Rusty.

"You've never seen it!" Rusty replied.

"But I *did* say it was big, didn't I?" Quaram replied as the boys trailed off into bickering about who had thought the city would be grander. After a moment of collective gawking, Quar clicked his tongue, and the wagon creaked forward. Even at this early hour, several wagons and horses plodded toward the massive gates in the pearl wall.

"Uth Becca's majesty is no accident," said Quar. "She once held the castle of a distinguished line of governors during the Age of Establishment."

Zodak sat back in his seat, staring at the glimmering city on the horizon. He recalled Ms. Folba's lessons and tried to imagine the rich history the city had held: the traitorous Governor Flailgore who murdered his mentor for the title and then challenged the king himself to a duel; the disdained Governess who wooed and won the hearts of an entire kingdom; the war of the great lords who almost brought the city to destruction. The family rode in silence, each lost in the city's splendor that echoed with tales from the past.

"Have you decided what you will do, Zodak?" asked Sella, finally breaking the spell. Zodak glanced to Quar in hopes of some escape. Quar gave a slight nod in reply, urging him on.

"I wish I could stay." A pang of doubt stabbed at him. The boys grunted to one another questioningly. "I have had—my time with you all has been like a dream," he said. "You saved my life, and I could never ask for a more wonderful family."

Sella drew her lips back in a half smile and nodded almost imperceptibly as her eyes misted.

"I only wish I could stay forever. I can't explain it, but I just feel I must go." He hesitated and glanced at Quar. Quar's eyes remained locked on the road ahead, but he nodded slowly.

"Wherever that takes me, I will always carry you with me. I will always cherish our time. Always." Even as he spoke, Zodak wanted to snatch his words back from the air and stay. They suddenly felt too permanent, too extreme. He had spoken with conviction, yet he felt none of it. Fear and dread crested inside him. *Would you leave the one truly good thing you've ever known?* the voice challenged. *Strike out into a strange land on your own? All because of a dream?*

As the silence settled on the family, Zodak's inner battle raged. He felt the boys' heavy disappointment. They hung their heads glumly, their sapling hearts sagging with the loss of a playmate. But with some distance, this day would mark the loss of a brother.

Quar's hand rested on his shoulder. "What we've done here is nothing you wouldn't have done yourself," he finally said. The boys moved in close to Zodak, as if coaxing the last heat from a smoldering fire. Before long, the growing buzz of activity around them drew their attention as their wagon merged with the larger road flowing toward the gates of the city. Entirely new sights and sounds—and not a few smells—assailed Zodak's senses. All three boys momentarily forgot their grief and scrambled into the back to peek out from under the wagon flap, occasionally whispering or marveling to one another. Some of the travelers lifted their eyes to inspect the tuk family, but most seemed not to notice.

Creatures and people of all sorts joined the morning flow to the city. Massive golyath snails hauled great loads for trade within the city. Donkeys and mules pulled carts—a familiar sight. But Zodak's mouth dropped open when he spotted a great massive lizard pulling an oversized wagon that looked like it could carry a village. A thick black tongue slithered out to taste the air and wriggled back into the creature's broad scaly head. One hunched figure with no apparent head drove a house-sized beast that bulged at its leathery sides as if it had swallowed a valley cow. A thumping, scratching row erupted behind them as two goggled boys, each saddled atop a giant flightless bird with long, springy legs, whipped past in a blast of dust. Horse hooves clopped, donkeys brayed and veered off the path, and travelers shouted at the commotion. There was too much for Zodak to take in.

As they drew closer to the city, hawkers lined the road, selling to those coming to sell. "Look!" exclaimed Zodak, pointing to a ragged shape of a woman who balanced on a single wheel, doling out some steaming beverage with a long, slender ladle from a pair of cauldrons hanging from either side of a wooden beam, expertly balanced on her shoulders.

Quar chuckled. "Well, mark my line! Hie! Tea ma'am!" he called sharply.

The hunch-backed woman's head snapped up and, catching his gaze, she spun with amazing agility and wheeled over to the wagon. "Tea's up, tea's up, me lovely! How many'll it be?" She balanced on the metal wheel, rocking back and forth next to the wagon and keeping perfect pace, yet her chest and shoulders were so still, the surface of the tea barely rippled in the pots. Her purple-red skin was leathery and deeply creased and her fingers knobby. A fabric wrap covered one eye, but the other shone gladly. Jagged and uneven teeth sporadically interrupted a wide, stretched grin that creased the width of her squat face. And though Zodak recoiled involuntarily at her strangeness, he felt something else. There was a feeling of truth crisp and clear in her, like a faint but distinct bell intoning clearly in his mind amid the cacophony around him. The feeling felt familiar, like he may have felt it before, but this was different. More defined. It brought to mind the inviting and gentle nature of the old man from Laan who swept the same patch of dirt outside the grain house every day. He had never said a word to the man, but on occasion when he met the man's gaze, Zodak had always sensed something. Ms. Folba made him feel the same way, he realized. But those had been just a passing feeling, muffled and vague. This was different—sharper and bright. Indeed, if he had been attuned enough to notice, there prevailed about her almost a luminescence—purple and gray, and lovely. The flicker of feeling faded as soon as it had come.

"Three!" sang Quar, and the woman twirled the ladle, clamping it under her arm as she reached behind her head and produced three waxed paper cones from a satchel strapped to her back. With her other hand, she pulled a pair of strings at her chest, and with a *plop, plop* the lines dropped a metal funnel into each of the two cauldrons. She flipped the cups into the crook of her elbow, lifting her arm to release the ladle, which she snatched up in her free hand and thrust under the end of the metal funnel, dripping wet and steaming. Prattling on incoherently in a cheerful creaky voice as she went, she deftly filled the first of the cups, plunking in a black pellet, before handing it to Quar. Still chirping away, she filled the second and handed it up to Quar, but as she filled the third, she stopped short as she caught sight of Zodak. Her one eye glittered with recognition as she stared deeply.

Then she said softly with a smile, "An' a lump a sugar for this one. Sugar for the newcomuh!" A white cube plopped into Zodak's cup. Quar dropped coins into her hand, and she wheeled away, calling out "Teaaa's up!" in a joyful squawk. Zodak stared bewildered at Quar.

He only answered, "Tea's up! Not gonna stay hot for long.

Drink up, *newcomuh!*" The wagon lurched ahead toward the pearl ramparts with edges that glowed gold in the rising sunlight. Zodak gingerly sipped the sweet aromatic floral tea. It tasted like diving into a brilliant sea of wildflowers. The boys each dramatically gagged and spat after trying a sip of Sella's.

A stone's throw from the Slag Gate, a rank of knights, clad in indigo leather with jangling copper armor, overtook them. Peasants on foot with bands around their heads, and piercings, jabbered in bizarre tongues full of odd-shaped sounds he had never heard. Long-necked gorlans rode toads of burden. Gaunt and spindly Slaggish scavengers sold trinkets. Zodak noticed his tongue was dry from the prolonged staring, mouth agape.

"Are them crickets?" Rusty suddenly squealed, smacking Quaram on the shoulder. Quar jerked his head around, a hand dropping to his knife handle. Zodak followed Rusty's pointing finger through the throng, searching for insects. Instead, his gaze fell on a jailer's wagon, carting three figures in chains, each staring defiantly out into the crowd, daring anyone to meet their gaze.

"Crickets?" Zodak asked.

"Krikkis," responded Quar, releasing his knife. His voice dripped with disdain. "That's the proper name. Call 'em crickets on account of their head spines."

Zodak nodded, recalling the name from somewhere. Sure enough, protruding out to the side from the bony forehead of each stocky figure, sprouted what looked like a half dozen thick whiskers. From the crown of their bald heads encircled by long shaggy hair, like that of an unkempt friar, rose a longer spine, like a thin asparagus spear trailed by three or four more running in a line from the top of the skull down to the back of the neck. The krikkis stood two hands shorter than a man, their heads hung a bit as if permanently hunched. They hissed and spat at any passersby within range.

"They're every bit as nasty as the halfies—goblins—but far more dangerous. They're margoul warriors."

"Ruthless marauders," said Sella. "Kill without thought."

"Right, Mum," he agreed. "Had we run into a band of crickets back in the wood, I'm not sure we'd be here now." Quar glanced back at the boys' wide eyes and gaping mouths. "But they don't frequent Rislaan often," he added quickly. "Not sure where they caught these vagrants."

If the road held so many marvels, what will I find in the city itself? wondered Zodak. But beneath his excitement bloomed his anxiety. The vastness of the city that had captivated him moments before now only intimidated him. When he had decided to leave the tuks, he had pictured himself entering a lively little town, like Komo. But this was another world. He had no idea where to begin or even what beginning meant. Where would he sleep tonight? Where would he wake up tomorrow? The simple decision to leave now felt clumsy and hasty, made without a shred of a thoughtful plan. Deeper than that, though, beneath all the fear, lay the quiet certainty that he couldn't explain: he belonged in the unknown ahead.

To Zodak's relief, as they approached a thickening crowd at the Slag Gate, Quar steered the little wagon off the main road, bumping down a dirt embankment to a dusty road to the left. This path skirted the looming wall, circling the massive flank of the city before merging with other capillaries at the Mead Gate, a detour that took three quarters of an hour. Riding just a few lynks from the city wall made Zodak feel like an insect at the foot of a barn. He squinted up at the rim of the wall, where he could just make out a tiny bobbing head of a sentry of some sort.

Presently, the endless curving wall gave way to a glimpse of the harbor, a cluster of ships moored at the mouth of the Mead Gate. Zodak marveled at the boats, if he could even call them that, for he had certainly seen no watercraft that compared.

Some were sleek vessels that stood tall and proud, with sails that pierced the sky, and others were low and flat, riding just above the waterline, stacked high with boxes and barrels enough to fill two storebarns. Figures scurried like ants on the decks, climbing up and down a web of ropes and lines.

"What brings them?" asked Zodak, waving towards the fleet.

"Trade, my boy," said Quar. "Uth Becca is the center for commerce in Rislaan. Hundreds of ships and wagons come in daily all the way from Thrüt Sound and the Sea of Aras with goods from across Rislaan, the Midlands, and beyond. I've even heard claims about traders navigating through the ancient canals from the Gulf of Dwahini, though I find that hard to believe." The confluence of roads approaching the Mead Gate brought wagons and travelers, though not nearly as many as flowed to the Slag Gate.

Quar called this entrance the gentler introduction to the city. It was certainly less chaotic than the Slag Gate. The volume of travelers and merchants funneled into a congested throng at the Slag Gate, slowing visitors to a halting walk, but here, travelers flowed in and out freely, like a tidal pool. Zodak could remember only a few occasions when the streets of Laan were crowded with villagers: during harvest festival in the season of the cane flies, he recalled gathering sweets tossed in the square with the town children, and when the Pol Dak messenger with the tall shiny boots came to announce heightened land use levies on Laan farmers. The erratic power of a mass of people had always made him uneasy.

"Will you not stay in the city?" Zodak asked.

"Oh, no," replied Quar with a snort. "We're adventuresome tuks, no doubt, but tuks nonetheless. We don't belong in a big city like this. Most of these folks have never seen our kind on account of the Tuk Credo—"

"Never wander, never roam, keep Open out, and mind our home," chimed Rusty and Quaram.

Quar chuckled. "In any case, there's an old elemental named Rumil who lives on a bluff not too far mead in the countryside. It's a bit quieter there, with a wonderful view of the city. That's how I prefer to enjoy Uth Becca."

"An elemental?" Zodak probed. *Had he heard the name from one of Quar's many stories on the road during the week?*

"Ah... an *elemental human*. They look just like you or any other human, they do, but they have some limited control over an element. Earth, wind, fire, water—you know."

"Oh! Hombord used to tell of magicians in Pol Dak who could tame water or fire. Hallah said those people were crazy from the cradle, and anyone who believed in them was a fool."

"Yes. I've heard that before," Quar said with a sigh. "Doubt spreads like a plague in Yiduiijn. We hear the same and more in our Dell. It's one of the reasons I want my boys to travel. Experience is the best remedy for disbelief. Once you've stared down the beady eyes of an angry river gorgol, you tell me they're just fairy tales," he chortled. "Anyway, old Rumil, a fire elemental, lights his stove with a flick of his fingers. Your Hallah may call me a fool, but Rumil's house would still be warm and his food, perfectly cooked."

As the wagon approached the Mead Gate, Quar steered the horse off the path, bringing them to a stop in a patch of scruffy grass beneath the shade of the soaring white wall. Quar jumped down and motioned for Zodak to follow. Sella, who had been in the back of the wagon for most of the preceding hour, pulled back the wagon cover as the boys tumbled out. Quar offered her his hand, and she stepped out gracefully.

"We don't have too much to give, but here are a few things that might serve you," said Sella, reaching into the wagon and pulling out the leather grain sack they used to store camping pots. "There's enough food for a few days, an oiled skin in case it rains, and a huffinpuff pillow I stitched together for you and added a strap so you can throw it over your shoulder." She smiled, but her eyes glistened, and she rubbed his arm the way Zodak imagined a mother might.

"Thank you, Sella." Zodak put his hand on hers. He wished he knew another language. He needed a deeper word for the thankfulness that overwhelmed him, a word reserved for someone brought back from the brink of death itself.

She gave him a long hug. "Please be careful out there, my dear Zodak." She finally released him from the embrace. He only nodded. Rusty and Quaram lumbered forward together, each looking as sheepish and glum as a young tuk can.

"I wish you didn't have to go," said Rusty.

"I know. Me too," replied Zodak.

"Me and Quaram's got something for you," he said, holding out a wrapped leather roll. "We made it..." He trailed off.

"Thank you, Rusty, Quaram," said Zodak, unwrapping the package.

"I hope you have an exciting adventure," Quaram said. "Like Fah."

"Oh, I think I will," said Zodak, forcing a smile and a wink. "I'll tell you both all about it when it's over." They smiled at each other, but Sella only looked away. Zodak unfurled the scroll.

"It's a map of the country," said Rusty. "Fah helped us make it. Fah said that it will help you find us after your adventure." The ink marks from an unsteady hand ensured that the little map wouldn't be confused for a scholar's work, but Zodak suspected it was deceptively accurate. "After you go on your adventures and become a knight or a magistrate, you can come visit us in your royal caravan," said Quaram excitedly.

"Knights don't have royal caravans," said Rusty with an elbow jab. "They ride alone. On horned thunderstags!"

"Well, Zodak will have a caravan," retorted Quaram.

"We marked the Dell," added Rusty, pointing it out on the crude map.

"Well then, the Dell will be the first stop for my royal caravan... of thunderstags," Zodak answered, bowing low. The boys did the same in response. They giggled and Zodak smiled.

"Zodak," Quar called and gestured for him. Zodak drew near and Quar put a hand on his shoulder. "You have your life ahead of you, my boy. It lies unrolled, running far beyond what you can see. There is much to see, much to do. But keep in mind the stories I have told you over the past few days. Each one of them carries a lesson, as does every day. There is purpose behind action whether you know it or not. Chance has not brought you to the steps of Uth Becca. You have felt the current of fate and you have chosen to follow. Don't let anyone tell you that it's just your imagination." He winked and then turned to gaze upon the immense arches leading from the docks into the city.

"Uth Becca is a wonder," he said over his shoulder, "but treat her hungry walls and all that lies within like a glimmering sheet of lake ice, because one wrong step and she'll suck you under. This is a city of strangers. Don't give your trust freely. It must be honestly earned." Quar reached into his pocket and removed a small leather coin pouch.

"Here's one hundred and fifty corqs," he said, handing the pouch to Zodak. Before Zodak could argue, Quar cut him off. "Save your breath, my boy. You'll need food and shelter in the city. Everything costs money. It's not like the farm. We have plenty for where we're going." Zodak opened and closed his mouth, wanting to refuse the gift, but knowing he would not. He realized with a flash of hot embarrassment that he hadn't even thought about money.

"Come here, son." Quar spread his thick fingers and placed his palm on Zodak's chest. "This is something I learned from the elves." Sella and the boys put their hands on Quar. With his palm on Zodak's chest, Quar spoke in a low chant:

Travel swiftly, stumble not on the stone.
At each day's end, as shadows grow long,
May your head find rest when you're worn.
Be kept sound in the dark of deep, deep night,
Shoot straight and resist with all great might.
May the Keepers firm the rock 'neath your staff
And may your eyes never lose your path.
Go on, my Zodak, go on.

Quar removed his hand. The family hugged him one last time.

"We'll miss you," said Quaram. The others nodded their agreement.

"Thank you. Thank you for everything," said Zodak, desperately wanting to stay. He looked at them all one more time. "Thank you." Fighting off tears, he tore himself away. He turned to the Mead Gate and, battling every muscle in his body that longed to dash back to the family, he walked ahead, toward the towering white arches. Within minutes, he was swept into the steady stream of travelers and merchants flowing towards the gaping mouth of the city.

17

Zodak marched ahead resolutely, jaw clenched and eyes glistening. Leaving the tuk family had taken all his resolve, and he feared that if he stopped or looked back, he might lose the will to continue. After climbing the gentle dirt slope from the wagon road, he reached the larger road to the Mead Gate and docks and craned his neck to take in the enormous Mead Gate again. The air was thick with the smell of fish and boats from the dock and wafts of pack animals and fire-roasted meat. When he reached the huge archway, he could stand it no longer. He turned around to see the tuks for one last time, but swarms of people had closed in between them. There were carts in all directions and Zodak couldn't see the tiny wagon anywhere. The pit in his stomach returned with a swell of rising panic.

A loud *crack* startled Zodak. He jumped aside as a team of six stocky blue-gray oxen barreled past into the mouth of the city. The crouched bear of a man in the driver's seat with a long black mustache snapped his short whip with another loud *crack*. Zodak stumbled backwards until his back pressed against the base of the Mead Gate arch where he stood transfixed by the flow of people. The Komo market had felt large and busy, but it was a sleepy flea market compared to this. The stream of merchants and travelers here reminded Zodak of clusters of summer water skippers at the creek, each turning and jostling for position as the current carried them along. Many travelers wore simple gray, olive, or drab white tunics and pants like Zodak, but others were dressed in amazing clothes. Some wore long stately coats or capes, and a few of the outfits even seemed silly: a man, whose green shoes with long pointed toes shone like the back of a beetle, gingerly picked his way along the dirt road as if it were a bed of coals, each leap fluttering a colorful bouquet of feathers jutting from his long, pointed hat.

Zodak considered his own appearance now for the first time in days. He had washed his shirt and pants in the stream two days before at breakfast, but they were worn badly. Sella's graceful needlework mended the rips and tears, but looking around, he felt ragged and out of place in a way he never had in Laan. Though Hallah cared nothing for Zodak himself, she refused to have any member of her household in rags, lest it reveal the family's financial fragility.

Zodak cautiously crossed beneath the Mead Gate into the city, still transfixed by the scene around him. As he ventured deeper into Uth Becca, the streets became busier and more crowded. He stared at the shopkeepers and patrons, at statuesque city guards and scurrying paupers. A few met his gaze, but most did not. *What is the Order?* he wondered. *Where can I find it?* He looked for a friendly face among the throng.

"Pardon me," he finally hailed a young woman with a round face and dark hair wearing a cranberry-colored cape. "Do you know the Order? Or where I can find it?" She snapped her gaze down at him and immediately covered her basket with her free hand, her eyes darkening.

"I have nothing for you!" she said curtly and quickly pushed ahead into the sea of people.

After what felt like hours of wandering, the road opened into what appeared to be a central marketplace, or "da markey" as he heard one man call it as he shuffled by. This sea of people appeared to be a result of the collision of the rush of travelers and merchants from the central road meeting the tide of peddlers and patrons from the Mead Gate Road. Throngs of people crowded the marketplace. Vendors shouted, hawking their goods. Mesmerized by the chaos, Zodak accidentally wandered into the current of bodies that swept him up, bumping and jostling him. Hard faces jeered at him, and strangers shook him off as he bounced and rebounded through the crowd.

Zodak's breath quickened. Everywhere he looked, the landscape of people pulsed and rolled. He stumbled, nearly losing his footing as the mass ferried him past more carts, more vendors. He felt like one of the tiny seed husks he used to launch into the muddy current beside the main road in Laan during spring thundershowers, only to watch the unrelenting water snatch it away, spinning and twirling the craft. He lunged for a pocket of space behind a hulking fishmonger draped in an apron smeared with fish guts who smelled like the inside of a moloth's stomach. Fighting to keep from losing his lunch, Zodak forced himself ahead through the fish stench and fought his way to the edge of the marketplace and around a corner into a side road, out of the chaos. He stooped, hands on his knees, and took a deep breath to steady himself.

Here, the afternoon sun slanted over the rooftops and sliced the street in half, one side bright and warm, the other already painted in shadow. Zodak stared in wonder at the buildings that lined the street. Like farmhouses stacked two or three tall, all standing shoulder to shoulder, these towering rows of buildings made him feel small and confined. He eyed them nervously, quietly hoping that they wouldn't topple over and crush him.

His darting gaze landed on a weathered wooden sign that hung over a nearby door. Carved on the sign was a gnarled old tree, its leaves accented with faded gold. The gold lettering beneath the tree read, "The Golden Oak." The image stirred distant memories of the stately old oak atop a grassy knoll on the farm. This was one of his few fond memories, memories of the way things were before Barst threw the family off the farm and sucked Ardon down into the mines. For the first time in Uth Becca, he felt a comforting hint of familiarity. Zodak adjusted his pouch over his shoulder and tentatively crossed the street to the inn.

The dark wooden door burst open and a round bald man with a very long mustache and wearing an apron emerged, hauling a bucket. He dumped food scraps into a large bin beside the building, reminding Zodak that he hadn't eaten for hours. As the man turned to go back through the door, he spotted Zodak.

"Well, hello there, young fellow," the man called. Zodak didn't answer. "Like the looks of the old Oak, do you?" he asked with a smile, looking up at the sign. "Every time I lay eyes on it, makes me wish I woke up to the rolling hills off to the Mead instead of these cold city streets, it does."

"Yes. It's nice," Zodak replied timidly, remembering Quar's warning not to trust anyone.

"Appears you've been traveling—and a long journey too from the looks of it. I bet you'd like a warm meal and a wash tub. Do you have a place to stay?" he asked. "Have you any coin?"

Zodak's hand instinctively rested on the small coin pouch at his waist. "Well, I... I was going to..." He trailed off, realizing he had no idea what he planned to do with nightfall but a few hours off. *Do you know the Order? Do you know where I can find the Elder?* He tried the questions on in his mind but then thought better of asking.

"I see," said the man, tugging on the thick mustache with a knowing nod. "Well, the Golden Oak is as cozy as they come. Not as fancy as 'The Silver Lining' up the road, but for ten corqs a night, with three hot meals, you'll find nowhere better." He hastily set the bucket aside and wiped his hands on his apron. "Olafsun Matterbrog at your service. Owner of the Oak. Most just call me Olaf." He dipped his head and extended a beefy hand to Zodak. Reluctantly, Zodak took it and shook.

"Ahoi." Zodak didn't give his name. Olaf's fist was solid muscle, but the grip didn't crush Zodak's hand the way the smithy's from Laan used to.

"You have the glazed look of a newcomer," said Olaf, gathering his bucket back up. "I know the city can be a bit much, especially at mooncrossing. If you're not sure about the old Oak here, there's another inn three—no, four streets down called 'The Looking Glass.' But it can be a bit rough around the edges. Also, about a half a cliq to the slag, there's a big inn and game room called 'The Flipside.' The rooms aren't bad, but most of their crowd comes to play flipibip for money. Sure can be a zoo in the evenings."

"Okay, well, thank you," said Zodak hesitantly.

"Well, I've got a stew on the fire and the hot bread in the oven, but best of luck to you, young traveler." Olaf dipped his head, turned, and walked back inside.

Zodak stood alone in the alley, another measure of it covered in shadow now. He shook his head automatically as if to move hair from his face and he picked at the cuticle on his thumb. He wanted to be smart and wary and suspicious like Quar had warned, but his feet ached, and the thought of hot stew and warm bread made his stomach rumble. Besides, it was long past time for his afternoon nap, a tuk habit he'd picked up on the road. Olaf appeared kind, and the Golden Oak looked inviting. *You'll need somewhere to stay as you search for the Order,* he told himself. Zodak gazed down the darkening side street that wound out of sight a hundred mounts ahead, dotted with scurrying figures, and a swirl of breeze sent a chill through him. In the other direction, the marketplace, awash in afternoon sun, still hummed and bustled with no sign of letting up. Just the thought of venturing back into the din made him tired. With a deep breath, Zodak leaned a shoulder into the hefty wooden door and pushed it open, entering the Golden Oak.

The inside of the Oak was cozy—dim, but not dark or dreary. A cooking fire roared in an oversized stone hearth against the left wall and a smaller one to the right, behind the tables. Straight ahead, past the fireplace, was the kitchen, where Zodak assumed Olaf had gone. The walls and ceilings were painted a faint golden yellow and all the wood was a deep brown. A few patrons sat at tables in the main room. Two bearded men smoked pipes off to the right at a long wooden table and played some type of game with smooth stones, and a couple sat off to the side. A wooden staircase in the back right climbed upwards.

Zodak hovered for a moment in the doorway, but the smell of stew from the iron pot drew him in. He dropped his leather sack in a seat at an empty table and sat beside it. Instantly, a wave of relief and weariness washed over him, reminding him of the many hours on his feet. Zodak looked around the room. His eyes met those of a well-dressed older man with a thin mustache sipping a steaming drink at the next table. The man only pursed his lips and, with a raise of his eyebrows, returned his attention to the woman across the table who wore a hat that resembled an exploded pigeon. Zodak jolted as the kitchen door flew open and Olaf barged out backwards, wiping his hands on his apron. He spun with surprising grace to face the room.

"Ah! Hello there." His eyes alighted on Zodak. "I'd hoped you'd come in, young friend. Can I bring you some stew? Bread?"

"Yes, please," said Zodak.

Olaf snatched a towel from his waist and swiped the table in front of Zodak. After a word to the stately couple, Olaf disappeared back into the kitchen. Zodak's gaze drifted to the antler candle holders lining the staircase, taking him back to the quiet edge of the forest in Laan, pausing in the early morning after collecting scat just to take in the still beauty of the wood. Olaf returned with a steaming hunk of bread on a plate and an empty bowl. He served Zodak some of the piping hot stew from the cauldron along with a goblet of water.

"There you go. Enjoy it, sir..." Olaf fished for a name.

"Zodak. I'm Zodak."

"Enjoy your meal, sir Zodak."

And he did. He ate two bowls of stew and three pieces of bread, a small hunk of salami, and Olaf even brought a wedge of milk cake as a treat. Zodak announced he would stay the night and asked to be shown a room. He removed his coin purse and counted out ten corqs.

"Certainly, Master Zodak," replied Olaf. He reached for a key hanging on the wall, then hesitated and took another. He caught Zodak's eye and then flashed his smile. "You have the look of one who could use a deep rest. I'll send you up to the tower instead of in the hall with the others. A bit of a treat for you, young fella. Usually reserved for special guests, you know, but just got word that Thillfurl the feather dealer will miss his reservation and it doesn't look to be too busy in the old Oak tonight." Olaf smiled and turned to the staircase.

A skinny hallway lined with doors ran the length of the second floor. Olaf walked to the end of the hallway and turned up a winding staircase. The stairs ended at an oversized door that Olaf unlocked with the tower key. Zodak followed the innkeeper into a magical little room with windows on three walls that looked over the city rooftops. A plain bed stood against one wall and a small fireplace against the other. The wood floor groaned as they entered. Olaf lit a candle on the wall, though the late afternoon sun still filled the room.

"Will this do?" he asked with a smile.

"It's amazing," Zodak answered with wonder.

"Good. Like I said, it's only for my special guests. The kitchen opens at six and closes at eight. Here's your key. Let me know if you need anything at all. Including directions to the clothier," said Olaf, eyeing Zodak's outfit.

"Thank you, Olaf," said Zodak, looking down, abashed. "Outside. I didn't mean to be rude. It's just... I've never been in a city like this and—"

"No need to explain. You've got good sense to keep to yourself. The city can be dangerous. But if you hang around the Oak long enough, you'll see you can trust old Olaf. How long do you plan to stay, Zodak?"

"I don't know. I am not even exactly sure why I am here..." He trailed off, sensing he had overshared. Still he burned to ask about the Order.

"Very well, very well. No need to go into it just now," Olaf cut him off. "It's been a long day. Anyway, I must get downstairs. Let me know if you need anything. We're glad to have you." Olaf clasped his meaty hands together and gave a slight bow. He turned and grunted his way down the spiral staircase.

"Thank you," called Zodak after him. Zodak walked to the closest window and stared out at the city. He'd never seen anything like it. A world of choppy red rooftops met his gaze, and beyond them, the city wall, then farms, and finally foothills on the horizon.

Somewhere out there, the tuks are bouncing down the road in their little wagon. Together, he thought, trying to ignore the sinking feeling that crept over him. He unconsciously reached for his chest, cupping the comforting shape of the medallion beneath his shirt, a new habit he'd developed. A few people walked along the cobblestone street below, but between the buildings Zodak could see the market, still buzzing with people even as evening shadows crept closer. He moved to the next window to get a better view. This was how he preferred to watch the frenzy. The sea of roofs stretched out in every direction. *How can so many people live in one place?* He moved to the next window and pulled aside a gauze curtain. His mouth dropped open.

A cliq away stood the proud edge of the castle wall. The three layers of the grounds were arrayed in concentric circles around the castle. The first ring, the band between the outer perimeter and the first inner wall, was at least one hundred lynks deep and looked to make a full circle around the inner keep. Zodak guessed three of his villages could fit comfortably in just that space. The wall of the second tier stood almost twenty mounts above the top of the first ring, and closest to the castle towered a third, thick seamless wall like a wedding band, encircling the castle itself.

Sella had told Zodak about the legendary gardens inside that inner wall—thick flowers and groves of fruit trees, ponds, and grassy hills. She never mentioned how she knew that. At the center of the walls, soaring far above Zodak's room, sat the base of the castle. It was immense. Looking up at it, Zodak felt like it was just across the lane instead of a cliq away. Moments ago, he had thought this room was high, but with his neck craned and his face pressed against the glass, he could barely see the top spire of the castle. Its polished white stone shimmered like milky sea glass in the evening light. He wondered if he would be able to see his reflection in the castle wall if he stood beside it. *That's where the Order must be,* Zodak thought. *I must ask Olaf about it in the morning,* he decided. He gaped a while longer, letting his mind wander with thoughts of the royalty within until fatigue fell on him. Weakly, he pulled the curtains, fished the huffinpuff pillow from his sack, and collapsed onto the comforter. It felt like months since he'd slept in a bed.

18

Alana woke with a start. It was the same dream: falling into that black, bottomless pit. The house was dark and quiet. For the hundredth time, she let herself hope that it had all been a dream, that when she arose everything would be as it should. But truth was not so pliable. In just a few hours, dawn would crack open another monotonous day to follow the rotting string of the dozens of vile days that had become her life. She had grown to mistrust the very ground beneath her feet. Rolling over, she forced herself back into a fitful sleep, hoping this time to elude that gaping pit of death.

"OPEN THAT DOOR!" snapped Hallah. The house was full of smoke again as Ergis struggled to keep the morning fire lit with the damp branches he had hastily collected. "Put down that nonsense and fetch some water!" Hallah barked at Alana. Alana knew her morning escape had come to an end, but she had just one more page in the chapter. She sighed and dropped the book, *Pugnulia Nuxious: An Understudy's Exploration of the*

Pudge and Eight Other Yiduiijn Wonders, on the small side table along with the generous pile of other titles on loan from Ms. Folba's personal collection. She rose mechanically, lifted the bucket from its hook, and wandered out to the well.

It had been weeks since Hallah notified Ms. Folba that the children would be withdrawing from school. Folba knew why, of course. Word had spread through Laan like a krius powder flare. Alana ignored the whispers, but it was the pitying looks from other villagers she detested. *What could they know? How could they begin to understand?* Even she struggled to describe it. Wasn't it just days before the incident that she had felt like a Luna moth shedding its cramped and brittle cocoon? A taste of new life birthed by Ms. Folba's writing project at school. Somehow that week made her feel as if she had spent her whole life squinting through a dirty wine bottle and suddenly her eyes were opened to a startling new perspective. She found herself alarmed to see Zodak, not as the villain her mother relentlessly portrayed—as she had treated him—but as the hapless victim of seasons of undeserved hate, her hate. And then there was Ardon. For the first time she could remember, instead of the perpetrator of her discontent, she saw her father for the good, but pitiable man he had become. A man crushed by the world, by his wife, who doggedly pursued the scraps of the elusive life he had envisioned for his family. A fresh wind of new life had begun to fill Alana's sails.

And just like that, they were gone. Both of them. Like all children in Laan, she had heard whispered warnings of bandits and thieves in the woods from as early as she could remember. Few villagers ever left the sleepy town, however, and she couldn't recall a single report of an actual bandit attack—other than one ill-conceived heist involving a krius delivery wagon on the road to Pol Dak a few seasons back, but the addition of a few more thugs in Barst's entourage had put a swift end to that. No, a random bandit attack felt too simple of an explanation.

She couldn't shake the feeling that some inescapably dark and ominous shroud draped the whole affair. One afternoon, Zodak had come home smiling with the prized scarves from Komo, beautiful scarves that put her classmate Dyna's scarf to shame, and the next day he was gone. Ardon was gone.

The feeling returned. It surged up in her like a black geyser. Regret, remorse, shame. *You were nasty. You were pitiless, you were ruthless to that boy for seasons. You were shamefully wicked to the only man who ever loved you.* The accusations fell constantly like a ceaseless drizzle of tiny poison darts. In the days following the incident, she was physically sick. Bedridden. Crushed by her self-hate. She had hoped that drinking Hallah's entire bottle of bandi would end her woes forever. Instead, the miscalculation resulted in a six-hour bout of vomiting until her stomach muscles ached and her throat felt like it had been scraped raw with a scouring pad, all followed by a hammering in her head that lasted two days.

Alana released the well bucket down into the dark void, and she suddenly recalled a shred of the nightmare, of the pit that her wakeful mind had dutifully cataloged and discarded. *It's just a dream,* she reminded herself when it tugged at her mind, but somewhere deep inside she couldn't escape the feeling that her life was sliding inevitably towards that very same dark pit.

She shook the idea away and tried to focus on the ascending bucket. As she watched it rise, she noted the water level slowly but steadily dropping. *Burn me!* The well bucket was leaking again and would need repair soon. *It would have been a quick after-school chore for Zodak. But who will carry out this simple task now? Ergis?* "Ha!" Alana snorted disdainfully, remembering Ergis's feeble attempt to mend the chicken fence last week that ended in cursing, a smashed thumbnail, and not a few scratches on his arms and face. *Another problem for another day,* she thought, splashing the water into the kitchen bucket and tying off the well rope.

"Finally," said Ergis when she returned. He had managed to get a fire burning, though a low ceiling of smoke still hung in the large room. The three ate in silence until Ergis, with much groaning and fanfare, dressed for the fields. Hallah had somehow found a spot for him at the Crilldory farm up the road, at least for the rest of planting season. The meager wages afforded them the essentials, but the family was also permitted to glean the fields and the abundant Crilldory garden for whatever had been left behind. Hallah's disdain for the assortment of oddly shaped vegetables and fruit that decorated the kitchen table outweighed her gratefulness.

"Until this evening," said Ergis with an air of self-importance and dutiful burden. Hallah gave him a hug before he dramatically marched out of the house. He would be the last laborer to arrive by nearly three hours, but Hallah had made special arrangements with Mr. Crilldory, noting that Ergis was the only man of the house. This shrewd maneuver preserved Ergis's fragile employment and saved him from the unspeakable: arising two hours before dawn, a feat he had never successfully performed. Alana worked through mid-morning, preparing a stew and darning the holes chewed in the bedsheets by an elusive family of skupp.

"Good afternoon." Ms. Folba's voice carried through the drafty house from outside the gate, which was as close as she dared approach Hallah's home. Alana's heart skipped at the welcome deliverance from the monotonous needlework. When the weather permitted, Ms. Folba had come to visit Alana nearly every day since she withdrew from class, despite the icy reception she always received from Hallah. Alana and Ms. Folba always left the house, usually to walk by the stream or in the bulbgourd orchard. Ms. Folba had taken to Alana, hoping her attention could offer the girl a rejuvenating mix of teaching, therapy, and friendship. Hallah had initially put a stop to the outings, but Alana quickly regressed to a languid shell of herself, so her mother begrudgingly agreed to reinstate the meetings. The listless ragdoll version of Alana would never do for courting—Hallah's singular focus for the girl.

"Be back no later than two past midrise!" came Hallah's scolding bark from the study behind the heavy curtains. "Burlton will be by for a visit..." But Alana had already dropped her half-finished patching and fled the house, tearing away from Hallah's invisible tendrils that sought to drag her back into that dim and oppressive hovel.

"Eager to be out today?" asked Folba.

Alana just squeezed her eyes shut against the sun, clutching the book to her chest, and breathed deeply. "It's a gift, this sun after three days of solid rain."

"Indeed, it is. I'm sorry I haven't been by for a few days," answered Folba, opening the gate.

"Well, I'm glad you're here now." Alana smiled. "But the Tally Gats?" she exclaimed, flipping open the book as the two turned down the path.

"The Vociferous Tally Gats, to be precise," added Ms. Folba.

"They hold echoes for hours?"

"And amplify one another," added Folba.

"And the Pudge! I can just imagine it! Hanging like a colossal egg sac from a million cobweb roots in the Midli... the Midli..."

"Midlisch Rift ravine," offered Folba.

"Yes! Singing its enchanting song and driving travelers to insanity with its overpowering bellowing!" Alana was beaming. "Though I'm not even sure if it's a plant or animal or even alive at all."

"No, it's certainly alive. Cataloged among the most majestic flora of Yiduiijn."

"Wonderful," mused Alana. "Do you have other volumes like it?" Alana asked. She had been so eager to escape the house and walk with Ms. Folba that she had scarcely even greeted her teacher. She now looked up and took in Folba's face for the first time.

"What?" Alana stopped walking. "What is it? What's happened?" Folba's smile was tight, but her eyes spoke something else entirely. Alana suddenly realized that for their entire conversation, Folba's responses had been soft and reserved, lacking her usual enthusiasm.

Folba put a hand on Alana's arm, pulling her gently back in step with her own gait as they continued down the spongy path. "Nothing has happened, Alana," answered Folba carefully, now looking down at the path beneath their feet. "I am so encouraged to see how you've... grown. Even in the last few weeks. Even with all that has... everything that's happened. It's a beam of light hearing you bring those dusty pages to life. It truly is."

"But there's more," said Alana, ignoring the compliment. "Something else."

Folba sighed. "Yes, I'm afraid there is," she said. "There's no use dragging it along. Alana, I will be leaving in three dawns."

"Leaving?" Again Alana stopped. "Leaving for where? For how long?"

"I'm returning to Pol Dak," answered Folba, spoken almost as a guilty admission. "For good."

"What?" stammered Alana. "No! It cannot be."

"I'm afraid so." The sad smile returned to Folba's eyes. "I've been... asked to leave the school." Another painful admission.

"Asked? By who?"

"By whom," Folba corrected reflexively. "Apparently, the town council voted on it."

"That's impossible! Preposterous!" Alana nearly shouted. "From the moment you set foot here four seasons ago, you've done nothing but good! This town hasn't had a teacher worthy of carrying your slate since they built that rickety schoolhouse!"

Folba looked away.

"You must demand to know why. You must have the decision reversed!"

Folba snorted mirthlessly. "They gave little in the way of explanation, but the declaration carried the stamp of Barst, the Steward himself. You know how Laan works..." Her voice trailed off.

"You're... leaving me?" Tears sprang to Alana's eyes. Folba immediately wrapped the girl in an embrace as her shoulders shook.

"You're a strong and smart young woman," said Folba. "I know your world has been turned upside down, but there is a path for you yet. You will see."

"No, there isn't." Alana now sobbed and buried her head in Folba's shoulder. "There's nothing for me here. They all want me to burn my books and shut my mouth and serve at the feet of some pig until I'm hunched and blind."

Folba searched for comforting words—something, anything—but the truth hammered each of her objections flat. For the thousandth time in the last fortnight, she felt it: the hollowness. She had arrived four seasons ago, the cart loaded with books and maps and drawings, with a beautiful vision of a guide bearing the brilliant candle of knowledge that she hoped would illuminate the hearts and minds of this sleepy town, but day after long day she felt more like a fishnet vendor in the great gum flats. It was the very same futility that made the joy of unlocking an eager mind in Alana such a prize. Folba had only dreamed of witnessing a transformation like Alana's, much less sparking one. So striking, so complete. *And Zodak. What of that boy? An eager student, yes, but wasn't he marked with purpose?* Another thought she quickly pushed from her mind.

"I will be back to visit," said Folba hopefully.

Alana nodded silently, forcing a smile as she wiped away brimming tears.

"And I have dozens of books set aside for you," she added. "There's *Scandals of the Octarch*, *The Crumpled Map: Military Might and Missteps*, and one of my favorites, *Fables from the Fire: A Collection*," Folba offered, hoping to draw Alana into a story other than her own. Alana's shoulders fell and she closed her eyes, her head tilting back and hands covering her face.

FOLBA HAD ARRIVED at school that fateful morning with fresh expectancy. Alana was to read to the class, and with his return from Komo, they would have a promising new student in Zodak. Ms. Folba was almost giddy arranging the desks to make room for him. She had spent most of the night planning for the introduction. She would avoid the mistake her teacher had once made, singling out and elevating a new, star student in front of classmates. Two dozen seasons later, she could still taste remnants of that rotten fruit. But as she greeted the children filing in, the trio was not among them. She assured herself that Ergis, Alana, and Zodak were just running behind, but as the morning dragged on, the absence of the three couldn't be ignored. When they failed to arrive without explanation the next day, she began to worry. Buying bread and cheese from the baker the following morning, she noted not one but two whispered conversations buzzing with scandalous energy. The town gossip usually only betrayed how provincial the place was, but Folba wandered closer anyway, pretending to inspect a loaf.

"You think? Bandits? Got the both of them?" Leselja, the voluble wife of the tailor, eyed her companion with poorly masked delight. Ms. Folba recognized the second woman, whose quiet whispers she couldn't hear, as Persa, a miner's wife and mother of three.

"Dead?" gasped Leselja. "Well, the little stray had it coming, but such a shame about that Ardon. Quite a handsome one."

She leaned in close to Persa. "A chest and back shaped by the Figure himself!" she whispered loudly, earning a playful hit on the shoulder.

"You're terrible!" squealed Persa as they meandered out of earshot, engrossed in their blathering.

The news stabbed Folba like a knife to the gut. She shot an arm out to steady herself on the fruit cart. The two days of absence suddenly made sense. *The stray? Zodak!* The news trickled out in the following days, confirming her worst fears. She had done what she could to comfort the family, but in speaking to Hallah, she might as well have been addressing a rock. And there was something else. Something in the way Hallah regarded Folba. Was it suspicion? Anger? Grief, Folba knew, was a harrowing bedfellow.

Attacked on the way to Pol Dak. That's all Hallah would say. Ergis was no better off, catatonic much of the time. The tragedy had broken the boy. How could a teenage boy's loss of a father do otherwise? Yet it was in Alana's eyes; that's where Folba found the flicker of hope and need. Coaxing the girl out of the dark den of grief and silence hadn't been easy, but in the weeks that followed, the two had grown surprisingly close on the daily walks. From time to time, Folba skirted around the incident, hungry to unpack the mystery that gnawed at her. Yet she probed with the care of an archaeologist. Among the girl's grief, shock, and what appeared to be a genuine lack of information, Alana had little to offer. Folba finally abandoned the fruitless fact-finding and rested uncomfortably with the bandit explanation.

"HELLO, MY FLOWER!" Burlton's pinched, nasal voice sliced through Folba and Alana's conversation. Fingers laced over his substantial paunch, he stood like a stem of cotton, the brown stalk of his riding boots cupping a fully opened cotton boll. A billowy white tunic masked his hefty girth, and how he had squeezed into the short camel-brown riding pants was a mystery. Beside him rested a stately black wagon and an equally stately mare, tethered to the fencepost in front of Alana's home. Hallah stood beside him, an impatient smile plastered on her face.

"Here she is," said Hallah in a singsong voice, glaring at Folba.

"We're back already?" Alana said aloud, her disappointment evident.

"Indeed you are, my button," said Burlton, presenting a bouquet of wilting wildflowers to Alana. "I was beginning to worry you might not come at all!" He chuckled and snorted loudly, triggering a choking cough. He sputtered and spat a wad of phlegm and returned to a smile, his beady eyes roving over Alana. Hallah had known Burlton as a chubby classmate before he left for the fields, like so many others. Were it not for his boyhood companionship with Barst, Burlton would likely be in those fields still. But as it happened, Burlton's standing and wealth rose along with that of his friend, if not as quickly or to such heights. Burlton oversaw much of the krius harvesting, delivery, and accounting. He was one of Barst's most loyal men and constantly strained to stay close to the powerful baron. Yet, even at his age, Burlton had never taken a wife. In some whispered circles, it was said none would have him. Others insisted that the sizable pile of corqs in his bed left no room for a woman.

"Shall we?" Burlton offered his arm. Alana hesitated, glancing at Folba. Hallah cleared her throat loudly, and Alana reluctantly draped a limp arm over Burlton's. When Burlton arrived at their doorstep just three days after the incident to pay his condolences, Hallah was effusive, but when he went on to ask for permission to court Alana, Hallah nearly leapt for joy.

With the offcasting ceremony for Ardon and Zodak just a day away, Hallah prattled on excitedly to Burlton about what a wonderful match they would make. Alana just sat, stupefied at the proclamation, feeling like she was being sucked toward that dark pit from her nightmares. A week later, when Burlton declared his intent to take Alana for a wife, Hallah was overjoyed. She made much of consulting Ergis and requesting his consent as the freshly minted man of the house, consent Burlton never could have dreamed to earn while Ardon lived. Hallah may as well have been asking Ergis to peel another turnip.

A dribbled "I guess," marked Ergis's execution of his paternal duties.

"We will speak again soon," said Folba to Alana as Burlton pulled the girl off to begin their courting stroll. They walked silently for a few dozen paces.

"Just eleven more strolls to go, until our courtship concludes." Burlton beamed.

"Oh. You've been counting…"

"Dreaming," corrected Burlton with a toothy smile and kiss in the air. Alana's stomach turned at the thought of this man's hands on her, his sour breath in her face. She looked straight ahead, forcing her mind to return to the ominous Pudge hanging aloft in the Midlisch Rift ravine, dreaming of what a welcome mercy it would be for that monstrous, sonorous legume to melt her mind into slush.

"I WILL MISS YOU TERRIBLY." Alana heaved a box into the wagon.

"You are not alone in that," answered Folba, hugging the girl for the dozenth time that evening. "I will miss you equally, perhaps more. You are an amazing young woman, Alana. Don't forget that."

"It's not what you told me in class so many times," said Alana with a wry smile.

"That's because it wasn't true in class so many times," Folba teased back. Then she fixed Alana with an intent stare. "You have truly grown to a beautiful woman before my eyes, from the inside out. I could not be prouder." Folba's eyes misted over. "You must promise me you will never cease your pursuit of learning and life." Alana nodded. "Your library is growing!" Folba offered with another sad smile, pointing to a crate overflowing with books.

"It is. Quite." Alana wiped a tear. "Mr. Pig—"

"You mustn't," scolded Folba.

Alana rolled her eyes. "Sorry. Burlton said he would come by for the box tomorrow. Oh! And there is one good thing," Alana exclaimed. "Burlton said he accompanies the krius shipments to Pol Dak once a mooncycle. I asked if I could come, and he said he would see to it!"

"That's trimidious news!" said Folba, stuffing down that tiny inner voice warning of the fragility of courtship promises. "Then I will see you regularly!" she added. They embraced again. "And I will find a way to send letters with merchants or travelers."

"I will count on it." Alana lifted a final box into the wagon. "I suppose it *was* kind of Burlton to lend such a sturdy krius wagon and driver for the trip," said Alana.

"Very much so," said Folba. *The sooner to be rid of me, the better,* she thought. "Well, you must be getting back home, and I have a bit more cleaning up to do here," said Folba. "But before you go, I have something for you." She crossed the empty room and retrieved a small box from atop one of the barren shelves. "This belonged to a world traveler my father knew," she said, unlatching a delicate clasp, lifting the lid, and removing a cloth bundle from within. She pressed it into Alana's hands. "I want you to have it. It will help you find your way." Alana carefully unwrapped the fabric to reveal a small copper disk with a round glass center and a spindly needle that danced in a circle when her hand moved. "It's called a compass," said Folba. "Travelers use them to follow a map. See how this points to the north?" Folba showed Alana how the compass stayed true to its bearings even as she turned.

"North? What's that? It points fahyz," said Alana.

"Yes, it's marked with the ancient cardinal directions," replied Folba, ever the teacher. "But my plea to the Keepers is that truth will remain your compass, no matter what turns your life takes."

"It's amazing," was all Alana could croak through her tears.

"Pol Dak is northeast—fahyz-nost. Here," said Folba, orienting the compass.

"Then I can always find you," said Alana. Folba wiped a tear and the two embraced, said another goodbye, and after one final hug, Alana forced herself to walk out through the door.

Before the sun had risen, the sleepy wagon driver with the lantern rapped on Folba's door. She was ready and waiting. She slipped quietly from the house, turning to give it one last glance.

"Anything else for the back?" asked the driver, looking past her into the house.

"No, it's all packed already. Thank you," she replied and noted his relieved nod. Off through the darkened village, the horse marched, towing the creaking wagon. Folba gazed longingly as they glided past the landmarks that had marked her life here: the bakery, the smithy, the school. The dark silent buildings loomed like squatting figures leering down at her in the dark, silently chasing her out. They continued to the edge of town and passed the long drive leading to Alana's house.

What will become of you? The question hurt to even ask because she felt she knew the answer. *How could this dusty hole of a town provide the fertile soil you need to grow and thrive?* Folba's greatest fear was not harm to the girl, but the prospect of returning in a dozen seasons to find a jaded housewife, listlessly serving that swine and chasing his offspring as daily chores and resignation ground her to mirthless powder.

How could Folba know how the seed she had planted in Alana had sprouted? That the knowledge she had sown had already grown furiously and would shatter the cage that tried to hold the girl. No, Folba couldn't know the wreckage that would be left behind in Hallah's house. She couldn't know that down that lonely driveway, through the gate, beside the quiet kitchen, in her room, Alana's blankets were folded and tucked into her sleeping pad, her pillow propped up, and her bed empty save for a handwritten note. Folba couldn't know that, tucked in among the boxes in the wagon, they carried a stowaway.

19

No sooner had the overstuffed down comforter swallowed Zodak than the sound of chirping birds beckoned him back from the depths of slumber. After a dreamless night, sleep, heavy and sweet, slowly lifted as he bobbed back to the surface of consciousness. The aroma of fresh milk cake snaked in under the door. He cracked his eyelids and reacquainted himself with his new surroundings. Fogged windows glowed like coals with dawn's first rays. After a good scrub, Zodak went downstairs, grabbed a chunk of crusty bread, and slipped out of the sleepy inn to explore the city.

He stepped into the crisp morning, his breath gathering in a cloud before him. His first trip was little more than a stroll around the block of row houses and storefronts. From the safety of the tower room, he'd studied the city's intimidating maze of streets. But if he was going to reach the castle and find the Order, he would need to learn to navigate them.

After striking out and making a series of left turns that successfully led him back to the Golden Oak, Zodak's confidence rose, and he set out again immediately. This time, he wandered a bit farther. He skipped over wagon ruts stiffened into frozen waves of mud during the night. The thick odor of people and animals and trade from the day before had mellowed into a softer smell of dew, morning fires, and baking bread, interrupted by the occasional emptied chamber pot. The handful of city folk that scurried by avoided Zodak. He passed an open stable where a boy his age was brushing a magnificent six-legged bronze ox with a long coffee-black mane. The boy looked up at Zodak as he passed and gave the slightest nod and went back to brushing. Zodak returned the nod, noting it was the first such greeting from anyone in the streets. He made a wide arc out toward the direction of the wall and then methodically worked back towards the inn. His anxiety rose in the face of street after indistinguishable street of the endless jeering rows of unfamiliar buildings until he spotted the market square and, with thrilled relief, the intersection of the side street of the Golden Oak. He quickly learned that when he was unsure about direction, he just needed to reorient himself to the castle to guide himself back to the inn.

Zodak's second outing had worked up his appetite. He heaved open the door of the Oak, and stepped into the warm wave of breakfast aromas and cozy firelight that washed over him and spilled into the street. Four other patrons had made their way to the dining room for breakfast.

"Well, hello, young Zodak!" boomed Olaf as he shuffled past. "Out early, I see. I had taken you to still be snoring." His face suddenly changed. "I hope the room and bed were comfortable enough..."

"Oh yes," Zodak assured the innkeeper with a smile. "It was the most amazing sleep. And the view of the city and the castle! I just closed my eyes and the next thing—"

"You must be famished," cut in Olaf on his way to the kitchen. Moments later, the kitchen door flew open, and Olaf leapt out, glided across the floor, and deposited a piping plate of sausage and fresh milk cake smothered in a sweet cream sauce.

"Olaf," called Zodak between mouthfuls of sweet cake.

"What can I do for you, young master?" Olaf's friendly eyes glittered beneath woolly brows.

"Do you know of the Order or the Elder?" Zodak asked. Olaf's countenance stiffened ever so slightly. "The High Elder of the Venerable Council," added Zodak quickly, thinking he may have been too vague.

"Why do you ask that?" Olaf replied guardedly, his face suddenly hard.

"It's just that..." Zodak scrambled for an excuse. "I've heard that the Elder comes to the city." He hoped his banal answer would quell the innkeeper's suspicion. *Interesting response,* thought Zodak. *Is the Elder disliked in the city? Revered?* The townsfolk in Laan had plenty of grumblings about Governor Palius and the Pol Dak taxes, but the Elder was only ever spoken of with reverence. "I was just hoping I might glimpse her," he added. Olaf's face relaxed a bit. "She's like an original Keeper in my village, you see." Zodak had guessed right.

"Ah, yes. She does cast a long shadow," Olaf said, the sparkle back in his eyes. "Well, I can tell you this." He looked around and leaned in. "She comes to the city once or twice a mooncycle. If you're here for a few days, you just might get your chance." Olaf winked.

"Do you know the Order?" asked Zodak. "Are they in the castle?"

"No," Olaf cut in quickly. "I mean... I've not heard of them." His countenance was stiff again. "Sorry." He tapped his forehead in salute and sauntered off. *That was strange,* thought Zodak.

After devouring the breakfast, Zodak ambled over to the large fireplace and sank into a recliner. From here he watched the two bearded men who had returned to the boardgame again. He had overheard Olaf saying, "Those two play that flipibip every day. Best customers I have too…" Zodak had never heard of flipibip, but it looked a bit like a game they played back in Laan. He stared into the fire, daydreaming of the Elder with memories of his hometown flickering through his head.

Zodak awoke with a start. The hypnotic crackle of the fire and lapping conversation from the sparse crowd had lulled him to sleep. *Too much to do to sleep the day away,* he thought. *I must find the Order.* He rubbed an eye with his palm as he stood. He bade Olaf farewell and headed out to the streets again. Knowing he could find his way back to the inn ignited his excitement. Zodak took off to the north. He still received the typical cold stares from passersby, but otherwise, he felt like he was settling into the city. He expanded the arc of his exploration, and past the stables he came to a store with wooden statues draped in fine, shimmering cloth. The fluid garments dancing in the breeze reminded him of the scarf he had bought Alana in Komo. *What is Alana doing right now?* he wondered. *Is she wearing the scarf? What has Hallah told her? Does she wonder what happened to me? Or Ardon…* Zodak immediately shook the thought from his head. Hallah had no doubt fabricated some twisted explanation.

Zodak suddenly realized his wandering had taken him into the store with the fine fabric. He spun to leave. The streets were beginning to feel a bit more comfortable, but this fancy store stuffed with finery was bigger than his home back in Laan. He felt like an intruder. As he skittered to the door, he passed a tall, polished brass likeness reflector. The metal shone like the surface of a lake. And there in the reflection stood a shabby, homely beggar child. He was struck speechless. While Zodak had never worn fine garments in Laan, he had always looked presentable. The past weeks had been hard on him. His shirt was stretched and ripped and hung limply off his shoulders like a gimble root sack. His hair was tangled and rumpled, and his pants worn and stained. *This would not do for a meeting with the Order.*

"May I help you?" came an inviting voice behind him. The finely dressed shopkeeper wore dozens of rings on her fingers and had yellow-painted eyes and crimson lips against her mahogany skin, with wisps of fire-orange hair slicing through stark black locks. When he turned to face her, she drew back a bit and eyed him up and down. Zodak recognized that stare. It was the same one he got in the streets. Suddenly, her face hardened.

"I am going to have to ask you to leave. I can't give you anything," she stated firmly. "I'm sorry," she added. The woman began shooing Zodak out the door. She smelled like a vine of over-ripened fruit. Zodak didn't budge against her feeble pushing. "Boy, I will call a guard..." she warned.

"It is true, I am new to the city," said Zodak, meeting her gaze. "But is this the way all travelers are treated when they wish to buy new clothes?" He fished his coin pouch from his pocket and mindlessly tossed it from one hand to the other. She jumped back as if stung by a wasp. Even under her heavy makeup, Zodak could see radish red on her umber cheeks.

"I... I'm very, very sorry... you must understand... I didn't know you were a... please forgive me." Zodak spied an outfit on a statue in the corner. He ignored her blabbering and walked that way, in as tall and stately a gait as he could manage. The woman came groveling behind him. "That's a very nice... unembellished outfit," she offered. The mannequin stood just taller than Zodak. It was draped in a blousy cream-colored linen shirt that laced at the neck and wrists and shimmered slightly in the light. A thick leather belt circled the waist over the pale top and heavy, yet smooth chocolate pants covered its legs. The shoes on the statue's feet looked ridiculous. They were fancy little slippers that came to a sharp point and curled up at the toe. Strands of gold and green waves formed a hideous pattern on the side.

"I would like to try this outfit on, please," said Zodak, pointing to the statue.

"Excellent choice. A fine, yet subtle look. Very good. Very good." She hurriedly stripped the mannequin. She reached for the frilly shoes.

"Do you have any other shoes?" asked Zodak. "Maybe something more... sturdy."

"Yes, of course." She handed him the clothes and directed him to a dressing curtain. Zodak stepped behind the curtain and pulled off the rags he called clothes. In nothing other than his medallion and undergarments, Zodak felt like a snake shedding its itchy, foul skin. The cream shirt slid over him. It fit him as if it had been tailored. The heavy pants were a bit stiff, but smooth and comfortable. These were, without question, the finest clothes he had ever worn. He tightened the belt around his waist.

"Young sir, are these a bit better?" asked the shopkeeper, her voice as cordial and friendly as it could be as she delivered over the curtain a pair of rich brown boots that smelled like the oil from Ardon's finest belt, not a hint of the scent of common stable leather. Inside one of the boots was a pair of rolled stockings, and in the other, a stiff wooden comb.

"Yes. Thank you," he answered. The brown leather boots laced up to his lower calf. They made his shoes feel like folded saddle cloth tacked to old wood boards. Zodak fought the tangles out of his hair until the comb moved smoothly. Then he walked out from behind the curtain. His reflection in the polished metal said it all. Zodak hadn't changed clothes, the clothes had changed him. He was a new person.

"Amazing..." mused the woman, lost in thought and apparently unaware of the slight. Zodak paused for a long moment, staring at this new self. He smiled.

When the shopkeeper asked for seventy corqs, he faltered. He had never spent that much money on anything. But there was no way he could put those rags back on. He took a deep breath, paid the woman, and strode out of the store. Zodak walked the streets until midday, head held high like he imagined the apprentice of a successful businessman might, or a member of the magistrate's house. Others in the street now noticed him with nods, a doffed cap, or a greeting. Each step lifted his spirits. In the early afternoon, Zodak returned to the Oak.

"Greetings, sire, and welcome to the—" Olaf's greeting cut off short. He stared hard at Zodak with his brow furrowed and head cocked. "Young Zodak? Is it?" His face lit up. "Well, would you look at that!" The handful of guests all turned to see what had sparked the outburst. Zodak's eyes dropped to the ground, forgetting his princely demeanor as his cheeks reddened with the attention. "I try never to comment on my guests' appearance," said Olaf, clapping a hand on Zodak's shoulder, "but this is... a transformation! Quite impressive, young sire." Olaf patted him on the back.

After a bowl of meat and vegetable stew, an apple, and a hunk of cheese, Zodak climbed the stairs to the tower for a rest. Again, he collapsed into the soft nest, too exhausted to even untie his high-laced boots.

Zodak spent the next few days exploring the city. The streets had become his playground. He came alive. The constant activity energized him. Even the daily anxiety of the unknown receded, replaced by the thrill of new experiences—new foods, new people, and new places. On one such outing, Zodak ventured back to the marketplace where he had first arrived. He had come to know this place on his many wanderings, and he now relished the thriving and bustling pace of market and the oddities of people and goods that it drew.

He now knew that the day he arrived and first crossed

under the Mead Gate happened to be the last day of the mooncrossing—the busiest days in the market. From the looks of the wagons and pack animals being unloaded, tents being hung, and preparations being made, the upcoming mooncrossing looked to be equally busy. And more exciting still were the hints Olaf had dropped about the Elder's impending visit to the city. But each time Zodak made a careful inquiry about the Order, Olaf looked uncomfortable and changed topics.

"But what *is* the Order? A group? Are they in the castle?" Zodak had asked Olaf, raising his voice a bit for emphasis. Olaf's eyes widened, and he looked around wildly before dropping down beside Zodak with a considerable thud, causing the bench to groan.

"You must be careful talking like that!" Olaf whispered urgently.

"Why?"

"I don't know where you heard that name, but it's one that can get you into considerable trouble in these streets. The Order cannot be found, if it even exists. But the Magistrate's guard have made city folk who talk like that disappear. Whatever it is you know, or think you know, you must keep to yourself. Do you understand?" His eyes pleaded.

"Yes," said Zodak. He most certainly did not understand, but the message was clear. He didn't bring up the Order again.

Around the marketplace, the streets began to look familiar, and in his fancy clothes, Zodak assumed a new level of confidence. He even made his way to the towering Castle gate, hoping to impress with his new appearance, but despite his polite request to see the Magistrate (without so much as a hint about the Order), all he earned in return was a gruff grunt and shove from one of the guards. He would wait. If not the Order, perhaps Olaf could tell him more about the Elder.

Zodak now took his time strolling past the vendors, enjoying being respected as he politely declined the many offers and solicitations aimed at the well-dressed boy. He nodded a polite greeting to the flute-maker, admiring how the gold paint sparkled on a deep eggplant-colored flute. As he passed the tanner's tent, he mindlessly fingered a supple zheibak hide hanging nearby.

"You're not from here," came the shaky voice from the vacant peddler stall past the tanner. Zodak turned to see a curious old man with dark skin and flowing white hair, bushy eyebrows, and a long white beard that twisted to his waist. The man sat perched on a three-legged stool, his knobby fist gripping an equally weathered old walking stick. Spread on the colorful woven mat in front of the old man, lay dozens of glass globes of different colors and sizes. He wore a thin white robe and cracked leather sandals. Age creased his auburn face like folded paper. Beneath the white caterpillar brows, bright eyes gleamed. Without knowing why, Zodak felt invited here, the way one feels visiting an old friend. There was no twinge of discomfort that normally accompanied a solicitous call from a hawker or the desire to dribble out some platitude and feign interest in the next booth to hasten his escape—a method he had been perfecting at market. Instead, he found himself stopping and stepping in towards the man.

"Ahoi." Zodak met the man's gemstone eyes. "No. I'm not," he said. "From here, I mean," he added, scanning the booth. "Is it so obvious?" he asked, disappointed that he could still be singled out as a farm boy despite his flowering confidence and dapper new look.

"Pick one up," the old man said, pointing his shaky stick at a nearby globe. Zodak gave a small shrug and bent down to pick up one of the glass orbs. It weighed nearly nothing. In the center of the globe was a disc of glass or polished metal suspended by fine wire that reflected Zodak's face back at him. He winked. The reflection winked back.

"Who have you lost?" asked the man.

"What?" Zodak looked up from the globe.

"I can see they meant much to you," said the man, nodding knowingly. "Your sorrow will not lie half-buried forever, you know," he continued. "You'll have to meet its steely gaze one day."

"How did you know?" Zodak faltered, looking around, wondering if he were the subject of a ruse or trick. "Why do you say that?"

"You are here looking for something. Searching for important answers."

"Yes! But how can you possibly know?" He trailed off.

"Have you ever heard of the Color Giver?"

"No," answered Zodak. "Wait. Do you mean the Figure in the Clouds? Well, yes, from stories as a child, but how did you know that about me?"

"His breath is life, and Yiduiijn is his work, delicately and intricately fashioned by the trained hand of a master craftsman but with the joy of a child building castles of sand by the sea. True purpose lies only in the Color Giver—all else is a mirage. All good things come from Him. Look into the globe."

Zodak rolled his eyes. He didn't feel like being preached at. He wanted to object but found himself looking again. "The glass *is* beautiful. I can see myself clearly. As if in a likeness reflector."

"Look harder." Zodak found it hard to resist the man's gentle voice robed in authority. He stared at the globe. Only his reflection stared back. He stared harder. The metal disc vibrated slightly, the image losing focus for a moment. When it stilled, the face looking back was Ardon. Zodak gasped and dropped the globe. It shattered on the cobblestone.

He looked up at the old man, horrified. "Oh no! I'm so sorry!" he stammered.

The man's face showed no trace of anger or even surprise. "Not to worry." He smiled.

"But your magic ball," protested Zodak.

"It's just glass, my boy. No magic in it. Your belief changed the image."

"Here we go again!" A loud voice cut through the din from the street, startling Zodak. A young, handsome man with jet-black hair and a square jaw strode up.

"I'm glad to see you again," the old man said.

"Glad like a pit viper discovering a skupp wandering into its burrow." He shot an amused smile at Zodak. "So what rubbish are you filling this young man's mind with today, Badu?" He quickly looked Zodak up and down. "Let me guess, I bet he's told you about something that happened to you that only you would know, right?"

Zodak was confused. "Well, actually, yes. He knew about the death of—"

"This land is none too tame, son," the dark-haired man cut him off. "We've all had someone we love pass."

"But he also knew why I am here," added Zodak.

"Wait." The young man held up his palm. "Stop and think. Was it something that would be true of almost anyone walking through the market?" he asked, gesturing to the busy street.

"Folgin here believes nothing he cannot see."

"Not true, Badu," said Folgin. "I *believe* in the Calendi Maze in the Brikkor Front and the battle of Gyrus Goule. And I believe in heat and in breath, but I have seen none of these. It's just that I don't go racing after spirits and powers for answers when there is a simple explanation."

"You make an assumption," said Badu.

"Is that so?" said Folgin, a bemused frown crossing his face. "What assumption?"

"If I say truth flows from the Color Giver and His creation and dominion of Yiduiijn, then declarations on such grounds are 'logical' and consistent with my premise. What's your premise?"

"My premise is actuality. It is far less arbitrary and whimsical than your fantasy of Colors and the Figure in the Clouds."

"So some call Him," replied Badu as Folgin bent to pick up a globe. "And when there is no explanation based in actuality?" asked Badu. "Then what?"

"There always is. If I see no logical explanation, it means I just haven't discovered it yet."

"What faith you have," said Badu, smiling. Zodak was enthralled. He had never heard such a debate.

"Faith in logic is far superior to faith in ghosts."

"He has never seen anything but his own reflection in the globe," said Badu, nodding at the glass.

"No, I don't force my mind to see something that's not there. You're a crazy old fool," said Folgin with a smile, setting the globe down. He turned to walk away.

"See you tomorrow," called Badu after him. Folgin swiped at the air playfully behind him as he walked. Badu chuckled, then sighed. "One day let him look with his heart and not just his eyes," he said, as if to himself.

"We've not had a proper introduction," said Badu, returning his gaze to Zodak. "I am Baduh'oan Chrintzu, but my friends call me Badu. In fact"—he looked up out of the corner of his eye, touching his lips with a bony finger—"I suppose everyone other than my mother, may the Color keep her, calls me Badu. And with whom do I have the pleasure of speaking?"

Zodak hesitated for a moment. "Zodak," he offered reluctantly. He had been honing his intuition and practicing alertness in the city streets, aided significantly by Olaf, whose servings of food were only outdone by the prolific helpings of advice he dispensed, always sprinkled with a myriad of cautionary tales. Already Zodak had spotted and avoided several tricks and scams: he now walked with his palm resting on his coin purse after catching a street girl's wandering hand fiddling with the drawstring at the fruit stand; he never shared where he would stay for the night; and, no matter how alluring the offer, he never followed a stranger down one of the many dingy winding side streets, lest he end up drugged, stripped, and beaten like Feln, the fabric dealer from one of Olaf's stories. *Yet how quickly I was taken in by Badu,* he thought with scorn. *Of course, Folgin's right. Badu spoke only of generalities: lost someone, searching for something. The same could be said about most any of the market-goers, couldn't it?*

"Zodak," Badu's voice interrupted. "The battle is not easily won. Within all of us, forces are at war, demanding we choose a side. And choose we do. Hundreds of times a day. How about you? What will you feed? Who will you serve? It can be only one."

"You mean choosing right from wrong?" probed Zodak. His confidence swelled, deciding he would test his hand at philosophical banter like Folgin. "But how can you know that what you say is 'wrong' may not be right for me?" Zodak had overheard this argument from the men at the flipibip table at the Oak a few days prior. Badu only smiled, but the corners of his mouth fell ever so slightly. *Was it pity?* wondered Zodak. *Or frustration? Maybe I've stumped him?* he thought.

"This is not what you left the tuks for," said Badu calmly, the kind twinkle never leaving his eyes. The statement punched Zodak like a fist.

"What did you say?" Zodak took a half step back. "How... That's impossible."

"The head of the Order is here in Uth Becca, Zodak. Beneath our very feet."

"What? I never said a word about the Order—"

Badu's head snapped up. "Zodak, you should go," he interrupted.

"What?" asked Zodak. "Wait—How did you know about the tuks? Or that I'm looking for the Order? Have you been spying on me?" he asked incredulously. "I want to know how you knew that," demanded Zodak.

Crunch. A heavy boot shattered a globe.

"Oh, excuse me. I didn't see your trash—I mean your goods there, Badu." The scraping voice, dripping with loathing, sent a chill down Zodak's spine. Before Badu's mat stood a group of six well-built guards, all dressed in gray uniforms with dark chain mail vests, swords strapped to their sides. The towering man at the front of the group with impeccable posture who had spoken to Badu wore black ribbons on each of his shoulders. He smelled of sweat and sandalwood and exuded power and danger.

Badu wore a pained look. "I am not bothering anyone, Stohl. I am just selling my goods like anyone else," Badu offered.

"How much for one of these?" asked Stohl, picking up another globe.

"One dither."

"That's not selling. That's giving away." He dropped the globe, and it shattered. "You're not here to sell. You're only here to infect the minds of simple city folk." Stohl turned his stormy gray eyes on Zodak for a moment before dismissing him. "It's time for you to go," Stohl said to the old man.

"The market doesn't close for over two hours," protested Badu.

"I said it's time to go," repeated Stohl. "Are you disobeying an order of the Magistrate's Guard?" Zodak could see the threat swelling in Stohl.

"I never pledged allegiance to that man," answered Badu calmly but sternly. One of Stohl's guards shook his head.

"That's all I needed to hear!" Stohl boomed, barely containing his rage. "An insurrectionist slandering Magistrate Kuquo! Let's take him in." A nearby guard began stomping on the glass globes, amused at the sport. Zodak drew back. They were destroying all of Badu's beautiful globes. *They can't do that!* One guard didn't move, however, as the others set to work demolishing Badu's booth.

"But... sir," the reluctant guard protested tentatively, offering a tone of respect and discretion. "What's he done?"

Stohl stopped short and whirled on him. "What has he *done*?!" He spat the question, veins bulging in his neck. He grabbed the man by his tunic, yanking him within inches of his face. "He disgraced the Magistrate's name in public. Did he not?" The young guard froze in fear. "Did he not!" screamed Stohl, spraying a mist of spittle on the young man's face.

The young guard nodded rapidly. "He... he did," the guard sputtered. Stohl tossed him aside like a soiled rag. The man barely caught himself on the corner of the tanner's bench or he would have tumbled into the street.

"Get this scat out of here!" bellowed Stohl, returning his attention to Badu. Like the young guard, Zodak couldn't understand what offense had been committed. He clenched his fists, feeling a surge within him. He wanted to shout, to stop this injustice. *But what can I do?* The punishment seemed harsh, but the city was new to Zodak and its customs strange. There he stood as the guards crumpled Badu's mat and threw it to the side of the street, sprinkling bits of broken glass on the ground. Leaning heavily on his staff, Badu rose to his feet, one of which turned awkwardly inward.

"Krollis," called Badu. The young guard, who now stood wiping off a sleeve and straightening his tunic, looked up quizzically at the sound of his name. "Truth and kindness are powerful weapons," said Badu. Stohl lunged towards Badu and drew back his hand to strike. Badu met Stohl's fiery eyes, never losing the façade of serenity. But the blow never came. Apparently thinking better of bludgeoning the old man, Stohl instead snatched Badu's gnarled walking staff, and snapped it like kindling over his knee. Badu grimaced. Two guards grabbed

Badu by the arms and began dragging him through the stall. As he passed Zodak, Badu turned and said, "You will find what you seek, Zodak. Just be patient. Your belief in truth changed the image. Truth is what changes you—"

"Enough, old man!" Stohl shouted. The soldiers hauled Badu into the street and the flow of bodies closed behind them. Zodak stood suddenly alone in the empty booth. The glinting shards of shattered globes flecked the ground like the peaks of an ice scape. He bent down and gently lifted a sliver of glass that still held the delicate wire and polished metal plate. Staring deep into the reflection of his own eyes, Zodak recounted Badu's final words to him: *Truth is what changes you.* He turned the glass over in his fingers. There was no way to know how long he stood frozen in thought when the quiet sting of the first raindrop struck his ear. He brushed it off, still lost in thought. The sudden breeze and the clattering sound of a thousand crabs on stone heralded the coming showers.

Should I have done more? Done something? the voice inside nagged. *I had no choice!* he objected. The image of the hilt of a sword lying in the dirt flashed in his mind. He knew that sword. He had seen it many times. It was the one he spied in the clearing where Ardon fell. The one he could have picked up. Could have fought with. *You would have died!* he reminded himself. *Maybe, but you still had a choice,* came the retort. The smell of rain and its cold pelting stabs finally shook him from his trance.

"Crazy old man," he muttered, tossing the glass to the ground. The clouds boomed and the sky split open with the deluge. Zodak covered his head and dashed from the booth.

20

The next morning at breakfast, sitting at the corner table, Zodak removed his leather pouch. He looked around self-consciously and began counting his coins. He had fifty-five corqs left. As he counted the last corq, Olaf approached. Zodak hurriedly swept the coins back into the pouch, but not quickly enough.

"How long do you plan to stay, Zodak?" Olaf asked after a moment.

"I... I don't know." Zodak's mind raced. *Should I tell him that I'm waiting for the Elder?*

"Mm-hmm," said Olaf knowingly. "I'll tell you what. I have some special guests arriving now in"—he counted on his meaty fingers—"eight days. I need someone to help paint a few things and fix up the rooms upstairs before they arrive. If you're willing to help me in the afternoons, I'll pay you with room and board. But only until the guests arrive."

"Yes. I'll do it," answered Zodak without a pause. Eight days at the Oak would have cost ...eighty corqs. He'd never been paid more than a couple of corqs for an odd job. "Who is coming?" Zodak asked. Olaf didn't answer, but just squinted his eyes at Zodak, deep in thought. He opened his mouth as if to speak and then closed it again, brow furrowed and lips pursed. He glanced to his right and left, kneading his hands.

"I suppose if you'll be working for me, we'll need trust," he finally said. "But you mustn't tell a soul! Do you hear me? Not a soul!"

"Yes, of course," said Zodak quickly, eager to hear the secret.

"Remember you asked if the High Elder ever comes to the city? Well, she's coming in a week's time to meet with the Magistrate—"

"The High Elder is staying *here*?" said Zodak excitedly.

"*Shh!*" scolded Olaf, glancing around again at the handful of seated guests. No one looked up. "The High Elder isn't staying here. She only stays in the castle, but her daughter, the fair Eldress Volithrya, is. She traveled through Uth Becca a few seasons back and stayed in my special tower room upstairs. Ever since, she insists on staying nowhere else," Olaf said proudly. "Her assistants and guards will stay as well. We close the whole place down, you know. Even the nearby shops are closed." Olaf leaned close. "Between you and me, she finds castle life to be stiff and boring," he whispered and winked. "Doesn't much like the Magistrate either from what I've heard. But the High Elder has been visiting quite a bit recently, so we've seen a lot of Voli this season." Olaf leaned back to see if Zodak was impressed. His gaping mouth showed he was.

"My *soup!*" Olaf suddenly shouted, clambering to his feet and rushing off to the kitchen.

Zodak could barely contain himself. *The High Elder!* It was just like Quar had told him. *"There are no accidents."* He couldn't have planned it any better. Like a lamp lit in a pitch-dark room, everything suddenly became clear. He finally realized why he was in Uth Becca. *I knew this waiting had a purpose!*

Every night, now spent in a comfortable, if not a bit humbler room on the second floor, he closed his eyes, visualizing the arrival. *He convinces Olaf to introduce him to Voli, knowing she will be more approachable than the Elder herself. He confides in her, telling her everything Ms. Folba had said. She rushes him off to the High Elder, and everything finally makes sense. There is some sort of testing or staring in his eyes or chanting over him before the Elder invites him to feast at a long banquet table as she answers all of his questions. He can report the crimes of the child stealers and finally there would be justice for Hallah.* He couldn't wait.

The next few days were torture. Roaming the city in the morning and painting the rooms in the afternoon offered Zodak's mind ample time to wander into the imagined meeting with the High Elder. The daydreaming didn't help his painting and once or twice Olaf scolded him to keep his lines straight. He found himself lying in bed many a night, exhausted from the full days, but too excited to sleep. There were too many questions to ask: *what will it be like to meet her? What will she say? Where will I wake up in a week's time? In a castle?* The next few days would change everything.

He had polished his boots a dozen times and recited his lines a hundred times, enduring the unbearable agony of the minutes and hours creeping by. At long last, the day arrived. Zodak had packed up his things the afternoon before, but after pleading with Olaf, was permitted to stay another night on a cot in the feed room. Zodak scrubbed his new clothes again the night before and bathed himself before dawn. He had taken to carrying the little tuk map with him, losing himself in the world beyond these walls as he imagined his future.

At breakfast, he buzzed like a needlefly, peppering Olaf with questions. Olaf again repeated that he had no idea what time Voli would arrive, but assured Zodak it would be today. A Pol Dak rider had visited late the night before to make sure everything was ready. After breakfast, Zodak paced nervously back and forth in front of the stone fireplace in the main hall, muttering to himself. An hour passed before Olaf approached him.

"Zodak? Are you all right, son?" he probed, wearing a worried look.

"Oh, yes. Fine. Thank you, Olaf."

"You look a bit... anxious," replied Olaf.

"No, I... Why would I be anxious?" answered Zodak, forcing a laugh that came out like a frog's croak. He knew his act of feigned indifference didn't work, but how could he begin to explain his complicated story to Olaf? He wouldn't even know where to start.

Olaf smiled knowingly at Zodak. "Not to worry, young Zodak. I understand it all too well," he said with a wink, touching his nose.

"You do? How did you find out? I mean, I don't think I was —well, I'm not, no, I'm definitely not—"

Olaf held up a thick hand. "No explaining needed, Zodak. You're not the first to appreciate Lady Voli's beauty." He winked again. Zodak paused for a moment, confused, and then sighed in relief. "But I'll tell you what. Instead of wearing down my stone floor and your fancy new shoes besides, why don't you go into market and pick up a dozen loaves of stone bread for supper." Olaf counted out a few corqs from a small wooden box. "It'll give you something to do." He dropped the money in Zodak's open palm.

"Yes, of course," said Zodak, glad for the distraction.

"Make sure you go to Knotted Loaf next to the herb tent, not that red-haired curmudgeon Mickle," Olaf shouted as he disappeared into the kitchen.

Zodak turned, leaning his shoulder into the heavy door, but just as he did, the door whipped open, and Zodak tumbled out, crashing into a large figure before falling back on his seat. No, not a large figure, an enormous figure. Zodak couldn't breathe. Before him stood one of the largest men he had ever seen.

Zodak had crashed squarely into the man's thigh. The giant's head stood three measures over the doorframe. He wore black from his head to the toe of his shiny black boots that came to Zodak's waist. A crimson sash slashed across his chest. *A giant!* Before Zodak could scramble away, enormous hands had encircled his chest and began lifting him off his feet. Zodak nearly swallowed his tongue. Bile rose in his throat as his mind flickered back to the dark clearing, watching in helpless horror as Ardon waged war with those two giants.

"Sorry," boomed a voice as deep as a well. The figure set him down on wobbly legs beside the entrance and stooped low to enter the Oak. Zodak lunged forward just in time to catch the heavy door before it swung closed. He stood frozen, watching as the huge man strode across the dining room to Olaf in three gliding steps. Zodak shook like an autumn leaf in a breeze. The giant bent and grabbed Olaf by the midsection, heaving the hefty man up off the ground.

"Jor!" cried Olaf, throwing what, in comparison, looked like a chubby child's arm over the man's shoulder in an embrace. Olaf's face quickly turned a dark shade of red under the powerful grip suspending his substantial frame off the ground. His pats of greeting on Jor's back came faster and harder until the giant finally deposited him back on the floor. Olaf sucked air like a fish. The two boomed greetings to one another. Olaf caught Zodak's rapt stare.

"This is Jor!" bellowed Olaf. "A good friend. He travels with" —Olaf gave a knowing nod, touching his nose—"the caravan. It means they won't be long. We need that bread!" he barked.

Zodak nodded and bowed, shuffling backwards, still in awe of the massive Jor. He stumbled out of the Oak and into the street.

There was no time to waste. He took off at a jog toward the city square. As he approached the market street, he noticed a small crowd had gathered at the intersection. A trumpet blast jolted him. Zodak pushed and squirmed through bodies until he could see the street. Then he spotted it. Gliding up the central street to the castle rode a magnificent golden and scarlet chariot drawn by four immense storm-gray animals, each built like an ox, but with six legs and massive horns that curled around the heads of the beasts. A small army of statuesque knights mounted on towering steeds surrounded the chariot, each draped in piercing yellow and deep scarlet. The brilliant colors of the chariot glowed among the field of ashy townsfolk like the last hot ember in the hearth. Zodak stood transfixed by the regal party. With a blur of sound and color, the procession passed just measures from him. There were excited cheers and hollers from the crowd around him, but Zodak stood frozen, mesmerized by the scene. The music slowly faded as the procession moved on.

Zodak shook off the trance. "Voli!" he exclaimed and sprang back to life. He knifed through the crowd, sprinting the half block to the Knotted Loaf. He burst in and immediately started jabbering about the Oak and the dinner as he fumbled for the coins.

"Slow down, son," said the shopkeeper with the long silver mustache that trickled down either side of his mouth like a pair of tiny waterfalls.

"Olaf. He needs twelve loaves of stone bread," Zodak finally blurted.

"How is old Olaf?" asked the shopkeeper, lazily making his way over to the bread shelves. "I bet he's busy with all the activity in the city." Zodak was nearly jumping up and down as the baker carefully inspected each loaf. It felt like days had passed when the baker finally selected a dozen loaves. He carefully set the bag in a bin of prepared orders. "Anything else, young fellow?" the man drawled.

"No, thank you!" blurted Zodak, snatching the bag and slapping the coins down on the counter. He spun and dashed out of the shop.

"Eiy! Wait! Come back!" came the voice of the baker, but Zodak couldn't wait for the shopkeeper to make change. He was through the door and out into the street without looking back. He dashed across the square and down the side street to the Oak.

When he finally arrived, he was panting and out of breath. The chariot was nowhere to be seen, but there were more people than usual milling about outside the inn, and there at the entrance to the Oak stood one of the statuesque chariot guards. Zodak took a deep breath to steady himself and cautiously approached the door.

The man stood as straight as a battle-axe. A cold black chest plate bore the Pol Dak insignia—seven spires in a circle, painted in a deep crimson red. A leather-gloved hand rested on the hilt of a heavy sword nearly as tall as Zodak. Beneath the chest plate flowed glinting red chain mail that covered the guard's shoulders and upper arms, and each forearm was clad in studded burnished yellow metal vambraces. This soldier wore power like a cape. A metal shield on his back jutted up over his shoulders with a short spear protruding upwards from its center. The guard's dangerous stormy eyes roved beneath his maroon metal helmet that covered the top of his head and wrapped around his jaw, watching everything. In a split second, the guard inspected Zodak from head to toe, and shot a hand out, barring his path to the door.

"The Oak is closed," came a grating voice like steel on a sharpening stone. "Find another inn."

"But I am staying here," answered Zodak. "I work for Olaf. He sent me to market for bread." Zodak offered the grocer bag as evidence. The guard eyed him in cold silence as the hair stood on the back of Zodak's neck.

"Pass," the guard finally barked and then returned his

sweeping gaze to the street. Zodak shuddered and scurried into the Oak, out of reach of the icy stare.

It always took him a moment for his eyes to adapt to the dim interior of the Oak, but today, the dining room was filled with golden light, like the fields of Laan on a late summer afternoon, the sun setting fire to the wheat stalks. Zodak distractedly glanced around for the source of the light but found none. The room buzzed. Strangers crowded in at tables, whispering and staring towards the fireplace. He followed their gaze to burly Olaf who stood with his back to the room, speaking to someone near the hearth. Olaf blocked the guest from view, but Zodak could see he held a slender hand between his two paws. Olaf was thanking the guest for her company, and then tromped backwards a few paces, tilting his head to the side in deference. Hands clasped together, the innkeeper bowed and spun around, crashing off into the kitchen.

Time stopped, and the room disappeared. There, soaked in amber light, stood the most beautiful woman Zodak had ever seen. She wore a shimmering scarlet dress trimmed in sparkling gold that framed her graceful neck. It wrapped down across her chest and gathered at her slender waist before flowing to the floor. A rich, butter-yellow fabric that clung to her like skin, covered her arms and back, opening into flower petal sleeves at her wrists. On her forehead rested a brilliant white oval stone set in gold, yet she wore no crown or headband. How the jewel stayed, Zodak couldn't guess. Fine chestnut hair encircled by two sets of tightly braided strands twirled past her sharp but delicate cheeks. Lips of crimson smiled and danced in conversation. Her skin seemed aglow, like saffra oil. She appeared young, but her age was impossible to tell. Her face carried traces of youth, but her eyes held ages of wisdom.

She spoke now with a man dressed in the colors of the Venerable Council. He pointed to the second floor. Her view followed his arm and then swept down across the crowded room. Like flowers under searing heat of midday sun, the guests each dropped their heads or looked away as her gaze passed over them. Then her eyes reached Zodak, where they stopped. Zodak's heart pounded. Sound faded. He knew custom was to avert his eyes from a regal face, but he couldn't break the millions of invisible strands that locked him under that gaze. It melted him into a puddle on the floor.

"Zodak!" Olaf's voice boomed in his ear and a thick hand shook Zodak from his crystalline tunnel. "The bread. Where's the bread?"

Zodak stared at Olaf for a moment, trying to recall who this man was and what his words meant. "Oh! Yes..." He hefted the cloth bag onto the counter and pulled it open.

"What is this!" cried Olaf, rifling through the bag. Zodak glanced down at the three bundles of baker's yeast and pair of oversized tuba pastries in the bag. His stomach dropped. "I see yeast!" bellowed Olaf. "I don't see bread! Zodak, Voli is here," he added in a lower voice. "We need bread! Go!" He thrust the bag back into Zodak's arms and nearly pushed him out the door before dashing back towards the kitchen. Zodak stole one more glance at Voli and then stumbled out.

VOLI GLIDED over and caught Olaf by the arm before he reached the kitchen, trapping him under the gaze of her shocking green eyes.

"Madame Voli," he said, bowing clumsily. "How may I serve you?"

"Who is that?"

Olaf looked around the room, wondering which distinguished guest she was referring to.

"No. The boy," she said, drawing his attention back to her.

Olaf hesitated again. "You mean Zodak?" he asked, baffled.

"The boy you were just talking to. I must speak with him." Her voice was insistent.

"Yes, but of course. That was just Zodak, my... helper," he stammered. "He's off to the market for bread—"

"Please go find him and bring him back," she cut him off. "Quickly."

Olaf looked at her for a trace of humor but found none. He hurriedly lumbered out the door into the street. He looked both directions, but Zodak was gone.

21

Zodak mindlessly dodged puddles, his legs ferrying him to market while his mind raced through the clouds, fixated on an imaginary encounter with the lovely Voli. He could picture it perfectly: *He bursts into the Oak with the bread from market just as the beautiful woman sweeps down the stairs, her entrance quieting the room. Guests bow and murmur greetings as she floats regally through the Oak, making her way to the private dining room in the back. With a slight bow, Olaf interrupts her, whispering and gesturing toward Zodak. Voli turns and waves at Zodak*—no, no. She's royalty. She wouldn't wave. *Gracefully, she whirls to follow Olaf's stout arm, nodding slightly to Zodak. She strides straight toward him. Zodak bows low at Olaf's clumsy introduction. She invites Zodak to a seat beside the fire to chat before dinner. He takes her arm and escorts her to the fireplace.* No, too forward. *He graciously accepts and follows her to the overstuffed chairs beside the fire where he sits, staring nervously into the flames.*

Zodak glimpsed the packed marketplace and quickly decided to duck down a side street to avoid the crowds.

"So, tell me, young Master Zodak, how long have you been in

Uth Becca and from where do you hail?" Her voice is ethereal and soothing. He quickly recounts his many days in Uth Becca, graciously praising Olaf and the Oak. He tells her of the small village of Laan, but quickly launches into his script: the water sprite, Ms. Folba, the book in the attic, the mission to see the Elder in Pol Dak. At the mention of the Council, she sits up. "What? You visited the Elder in Pol Dak for an assessment?" With heavy, measured words, he tells the tragic turn of his tale. His kidnapping and the fight in the woods and escape. She hangs on every word. When he finishes, she hugs him tightly, a tear falling down her porcelain face. She strokes his face with her delicate palm and stares into his eyes, promising to take him to her mother to discover his destiny. He rewound the scene and played it again and again in his mind, changing details here and there.

"Hai!" The cart driver's warning snapped Zodak from his imaginings. He leapt aside, now well accustomed to dodging the barreling carts. Returning to reality, he was suddenly aware of the passage of time. *How long was I lost in my mind?* he wondered. Looking around to get his bearings, he realized he had no idea where he was. In an effort to skirt around the market crowds, he must have taken a wrong turn. He now found himself in a part of Uth Becca he had never seen. Here the squeezed rows of ramshackle buildings on each side of the street crowded the cramped lane and revealed only a narrow strip of sky above. Zodak had discovered much of the area around the inn but had heeded Olaf's warning to stay away from the old Piper's Quarter to the west, which housed some of the city's most impoverished and disaffected residents.

Around the market square and the Golden Oak, the streets were bright and wide. Here, in place of the well-worn cobblestone, his feet sank into the thick mud lane, and a foul smell filled the air. Zodak hurried ahead, turning towards what he hoped would be the center of the city, but each turn brought him deeper into the slums, and the narrow lanes, lined with rows of shabby buildings, hid the castle, his landmark, from view. Zodak turned down another street, hoping it was right, urgency now spiked with panic. A withered woman with beady red eyes stumbled towards him, reaching aimlessly for him. He jumped aside. The woman staggered past. Shouts arose up ahead, and Zodak saw two scraggly groups of men yelling at each other in the street. Glancing aside, he slipped down a side alley. He had heard much of the dangers of the city, but so far pickpockets and swindlers seemed the extent of the peril. Here though, the danger felt palpable. It hung in the air. The hair on his neck suddenly stood on end.

"Wouldja look at thees one." A tight singsong voice came from down the narrow alley. A small, ragged boy with the face of a baby emerged from the shadows. Zodak gave a nod and turned to walk away. "Where ju going?" called the boy. "I didn't say ju could go!" The boy's sloppy footsteps behind him quickened as Zodak walked faster. Zodak turned to dart down an alley to the right. As he did, he almost collided with four larger, but equally dingy boys. The small boy chirped a piercing laugh as the four moved towards Zodak. He backed out of the alley, and the small boy approached. Zodak now saw that his head was a bit too large for his body and he walked with a limp. On closer inspection, his round face carried no joy of youth. A hardness in his eyes and the sneer plastered to his lips gave him the appearance of a gargoyle rather than a young child.

"I'm sorry," offered Zodak, not sure what he was apologizing for.

"He's sorry!" chirped the boy to the other four. "End sorry ya should be."

"What do you want?" Zodak asked. He had been slowly backing into the lane and now bumped into the building on the far side. The boy pressed in close, the larger thugs hanging back a few paces.

"Fir one thing, high towna," sang the boy, "yer in the wrong place. And ye're never to set foot here agin." He spat. The boys grunted approval. "Ye don't belong here. These a' my streets," answered the small boy. *This imp claims the streets as his own?* Zodak thought, but the larger boys, who appeared to be at least Zodak's age if not a bit older, clearly deferred to the small one.

"Fine," said Zodak. "I'll leave," he added, making a move to pass.

"But it's a little late fah that," said the boy. "Because ye're already here. And for that ye must pay. Ye can start bay giving us yer money and yer clothes. Them shiny boots'll fit one if us." The group laughed.

"I'm not giving you my clothes," Zodak said indignantly, his heart pounding. The answer sounded much more confident than he felt. His hand instinctively reached for the medallion under his shirt. The laughing stopped dead.

"What? What did ye jest say?" asked the small boy. He turned to the tattered crew. "What did he jest say tah me?" The boy let the words hang in the air, savoring the fraught moment like a fine port. "Ye shouldn't have done that, high towna," he hissed. "Boys! His clothes!" The four large boys moved in towards Zodak, each wearing the same dumb, sadistic grin. Zodak caught the first glimmer of joy in the small boy's eyes. Any one of these beefy street boys could probably thrash Zodak, much less all four.

But as the boys approached, panic, mixed with desperation, injustice, and rage surged through Zodak's chest. Absent of thought, he quickly sized up the largest of the approaching boys, the one with a patched cap pulled low, heavy cheekbones, and a smudge of dirt or scraggly mustache, or both, on his upper lip. Surprising even himself, Zodak took a step forward towards the boys and shot out a right jab, connecting solidly with the cheek and nose of the large boy. The blow caught the hulking boy by surprise and knocked him back flat on his back.

For a moment, everything stopped. The group paused, confused by the unexpected offensive. The large boy was out cold, blood flowing from his nose. Then a fist like a hammer slammed Zodak in the stomach. His breath was gone, and he doubled over in agony. Another punch grazed his head and landed on his shoulder, knocking him to his knees. Then another to his ribs. He shut his eyes and curled into a ball against the wall as the punches fell, hoping only to survive.

Suddenly, a bright flash like lightning seared the alley. With eyelids sealed shut, Zodak could still see the brilliance of the burst. Screams filled the air. He tentatively opened his eyes, his arms still shielding his head. Even through closed eyelids, the flash had imprinted, leaving the street scene green and washed out. The boys were doubled over, pawing at their eyes.

"Hie!" A horse and wagon slid to a stop, and a dark slender figure leapt from the driver's seat, a long black jacket fluttering behind him like inky plumage. He began thrashing the blinded boys with a staff, savagely raining blows on the group. After making rounds to each of the thugs, the man turned his leathery creased face, grotesque in the failing green afternoon light, toward Zodak. Zodak drew back in fear

"Quickly, in the wagon!" screeched the man. Zodak faltered, unsure what to do. He considered the filthy alley and the gang of boys, squirming like larvae in the mud, then dashed to the wagon and jumped in. The man brought the staff down with a crack on the largest boy, who crumpled under the blow. Whirling, he then swept the legs out from the small boy leader, sending him to the mud with a splat. He kicked the boy in the side. Like a cat, the man twirled and sprang into the cart, slapping the reins. The horse and wagon lurched out of the alley.

Zodak pressed himself back in the seat, taking a deep breath. He shot a furtive look at his rescuer. *Or is he my captor?* he wondered, images of the ruthless attack on the street boys flashing through his mind. The driver hunched forward in rapt attention as he navigated the cart down a twisting maze of narrow streets. He wore a dirty red bandana on his forehead over shaggy strands of dark greasy hair framing his gaunt face with eyes slightly sunken in his head. He dressed in a long, faded black coat with a thick brown belt around his waist and wore black, fingerless gloves on each hand and chains around his neck. When the wagon had cleared the dark alleys, he slowed the horse, settling back in his seat. Zodak leaned against the far side of the wagon, poised to jump if needed.

The driver let out an exaggerated sigh. "The name's Gormley," he squawked, turning to Zodak and holding out a gloved hand. His hollow cheeks wore a trace of a sneer that only twisted slightly when the man smiled. One eye seemed frozen in a squint, and the skin on the man's face reminded Zodak of dried fruit. Zodak took Gormley's hand tentatively and shook. The man laughed out loud.

"The need for fear's passed, boy," said Gormley, his eyes flicking up and down over Zodak's hunched frame. "You was right to fear them young ones back in the Fel. An' brave to hit the big un, but that was gonna end bad, it was. Lucky if they let you live, and keep yer eyes beside. Hmm-hmm," grunted Gormley, shaking his head. "Was a good fing Gormley came along, it was a good fing."

"Thank you," said Zodak. "What—who were they?"

"Them? Them's just slopfloss. Jus' a gang from da Fel. Nothin' old Gormley can't handle. Nope, a-nothin' he can't, can he? Nope, nope…" His voice trailed off into incoherent mumbling.

"How did you know I was down there?" asked Zodak.

"Didn't, did I? Nope. Just a-driving through and knew them boys was up to no good as soon as I sees 'em," answered Gormley with an awkward smile. He was a better fighter than a conversationalist. "Yous got to be more careful in dis city, boy, that's da truth, it is," Gormley said. "Don't you trust a no one. And keep outta the Fel. No place it is for a high towner, is it?"

"Someone else once told me that," said Zodak thinking back now on Quar's advice. "How'd you make that flash?" Zodak asked.

"Hah, that's the firebulb," answered Gormley. "Some calls it a lightning flash or flash bulb, they do, some do, them crazies they do, up the mountain, that's right, mm-hmm..." He reached into his coat pocket and removed a thumb-sized bright yellow pod. "You just hold de root and throw it. When it hits da ground, lightning bursts out, yep, it does. Blinds about anyone, it will, anyone there, uh-huh." Gormley handed it to Zodak. "You can keep this one, boy, you can. A gift tah remember old Gormley." Zodak inspected the deep red vein-like roots growing around the amber firebulb.

"Well, thanks, Gormley. I'm..." He hesitated. "I'm Zodak." His name was the least he could offer this strange character after being saved.

"Itsa pleasure, Zodark, it is." The two rode in silence.

"The castle!" exclaimed Zodak as they pulled out onto a wide street.

"Yup, always there, she is. Staring downs on us. She is, all right. Yup. Hateful too, uh-huh. Peering right into the heart, it does."

Zodak suddenly remembered the Oak. He had dropped the yeast in the alley, but he had to get that bread and return to the Oak. He had to see Voli. This scraggly, odd fellow had saved his life, and he couldn't leave without some token of thanks.

"Gormley, how can I repay you for your help?"

Gormley didn't miss a beat. "Could use a taste of ogg swallow, I could, um-hmm." He looked out of the corner of his eye toward Zodak.

Zodak snorted. "I'm not sure a drink is a fair trade for my life, but I do have a couple corqs here."

"Oh, lad. It's no' just any drink, a no, it's the sweetest and most loverlilly 'coction in Yiduiijn, it is." He closed his eyes.

"Ha," Zodak snorted. "Okay, it's on me then." He began to open the coin purse to fish out a couple of corqs, but without hesitation, Gormley slapped the reins, and the cart barreled down the street, scattering city folk ahead. Zodak gripped the side of the cart tightly, wanting to object. They wound through the city, passing the street to the Mead Gate heading farther north, a part of Uth Becca Zodak had never seen.

"I could just give you a couple corqs," he offered, eyeing the castle anxiously.

"Nots to worry," replied Gormley. "Be there in just a couple a ticks." The cobblestones gave way to wood plank streets and the houses and inns to small mills and stores. Zodak watched nervously as they zipped past a livestock auction, moving ever farther from the castle; farther from the Oak. A loud man standing on a box bellowed, gesturing to a pen of creatures that looked like enormous sausages on tiny legs.

The cart passed a small outdoor market where squatting women roasted wheelbarrow-sized birds and young men practiced staff skills. Gormley steered them north for another ten minutes without slowing the pace. They were near the edge of the city, far from the Oak. Zodak was beginning to wish he had just tossed the corqs at Gormley and jumped out. But then he remembered the mud and the thugs. This day could have ended much worse for him. The detour was the very least he could do for this strange man. Just as Zodak turned to ask when they would arrive, Gormley pulled hard on the reins and skidded to a stop in front of a building with a shallow thatched roof. A collection of triangular canvas sheets stretched taut above outdoor tables. The air smelled of roast meat and stew. Just ahead past the tents, the road wound out of the city through the gaping Fahyz Gate. Zodak could see soft blue hills in the distance and mountain peaks beyond.

"Here we is. The old watering hole, it is, ayup. Best place for the ogg swallow, mm-hmm," Gormley muttered as he leapt from the cart and tied the horse to a post. A large crowd stood at the bar in the center of the cantina, others spread about at tables, sitting and standing. Most spoke loudly. Zodak marveled at a chubby blue man no bigger than a harvest piglet who sat on a pillow surrounded by a small group of patrons, eating and drinking. His hands rested on a glowing ball. Both eyes were closed, and he sang to the crowd. Despite his tiny size, his voice resonated and bellowed like a howling wind rushing through a canyon. The song was sad and beautiful. Gormley was seated near the edge of the cantina and had already ordered.

"Zodarks, you want food? A drink?"

"No, thank you," said Zodak, eager for this detour to come to an end. He reluctantly climbed onto a stool across from Gormley, his gaze wandering out through the gate to the hillside as his mind spun urgently with plans for escape. Gormley looked distractedly out among the seedy crowd in the bar, mumbling now and then. The unkempt waitress returned with a stout goblet of blue-green froth, and plopped it down in front of Gormley, sloshing some of the drink. Then she slapped her hand down on the table, and when she lifted it, Zodak saw she had deposited a cloudy, translucent marble on the table. It rolled towards Gormley, and his eyes lit up. He snatched the little orb from the table.

"Here's the ogg, it is." With a dirty fingernail, Gormley cut into the ball. Clear fluid spilled out. He peeled back the covering and out of the ball fell a green-brown blob. Gormley watched it intently. For a moment, nothing happened. Then two large eyes opened from the tiny toad-like lump. The eyes looked back and forth, and the blob suddenly shot into the air. But Gormley was ready. His gloved hand snatched the ogg out of midair. In one motion, he plopped it in the mug and took a long swallow. Zodak's stomach turned. Gormley slammed the empty mug back on the table. He shook, sputtered, and then broke into a large grin.

"De ogg swallow, mm-hmm." He wiped his mouth on his sleeve. "Tastiest and best drink in Yiduiijn, it is. The most best, mm-hmm."

"I'm glad you like it," said Zodak. "Gormley, I do appreciate what you've done for me today, but I really have to get back to town."

"Nones the worries, Zorak. Four corqs is the ogg swallow. We's can head back."

Zodak reached down to retrieve his money. As he removed the pouch, his thumb caught on the lacing of the shirt, and he dropped the pouch under the table. "Oogh!" he grunted, leaning down, one hand on top of the table to steady himself. Gormley also leaned down to reach for the pouch. Stretching down, Zodak's shirt fell open. Gormley's eyes darted to the medallion and lit up. Zodak quickly snatched the bag, then closed his shirt and sat up self-consciously. Gormley stared at him. Zodak felt suddenly lightheaded, and his vision flashed. The moment drew out in a fuzzy pause in time as can happen from sitting up too quickly. Slowly his vision re-sharpened.

"I's a gotta go," Gormley abruptly announced. He stood up jerkily, with a glance over his shoulder, turned, and nearly ran from the cantina to the carriage.

"Wait! But... aren't you taking me back?" called Zodak after him, ignoring the stares.

"Nope, I's a-leaving the city. Plenty of merchants comes through here, they does," Gormley called over his shoulder, untying his horse. "Must go, Gormley must." With a slap of the reins, Gormley thundered away, heading for the Fahyz Gate, out of Uth Becca. For the first time, Zodak noticed that all around movement had stopped, and dozens of pairs of eyes looked at him.

"Goodbye, Gormley," Zodak muttered to himself, his hand still slowly waving off to the distance as it hung in the air. Feeling the eyes on him, Zodak looked around at the other patrons who slowly turned back to their own affairs under his gaze. Zodak felt an odd hollowness sweep over him, as if a great friend were departing. *Absurd,* he thought with a smile. Parting ways with Gormley brought relief if anything. He fished four corqs from his pouch, but the waitress was nowhere to be seen. Sitting back, he absorbed the sounds of chattering and laughing around him, suffused with the deep enchanting song of the blue musician. The melody drew him in, and he closed his eyes in the sunshine, recounting the bizarre events of the day: this odd excursion with Gormley, the horrid gang in the slums—he shook off the memory—his interrupted errand from the Oak. *The Oak! Voli!* He snapped out of his daze with renewed desperation to leave. With still no sign of the server, he finally dropped the corqs on the table and rose to leave.

"Why's a young man like you running with a skupp like that?" A deep voice pierced the din of the bar before Zodak had taken a step. He looked around. The bar remained busy, but there was no one near him. "You should choose your friends more wisely," came the voice again. Zodak looked over both shoulders for its owner but could see nobody within earshot. Then across the bar he spied a tall figure in the shadows of the thatch roof, leaning against a support beam and standing almost as tall. The man seemed too far away to have spoken so clearly, but he stared straight at Zodak. The stranger took a long swallow from his wooden goblet and strode from the shadows. In four huge strides he stood at the table in front of Zodak.

The man wore an indigo headband over dusty brown hair that nearly reached his shoulders. Dark whiskers painted his tanned face and his sharp features looked to be cut with a grinding blade, and a broad, trim frame carried his height. A long bow, nearly as tall as the man, its grip thicker than Zodak's wrist, was strapped to his back. Zodak prickled as the man sat uninvited in Gormley's chair and banged the wooden mug on the table.

"That man's no skupp!" Zodak challenged. "He saved my life today." Resentment flashed over Zodak's face at the intrusion.

"Oh, did he?"

"Yes, as a matter of fact," quipped Zodak. "He saved me from a gang of street thugs just an hour ago." Zodak found himself hot with anger. "I could be lying in the street or blinded or worse if it weren't for Gormley." *Who is this prying stranger?* "In any case, I must go." With growing angst, Zodak felt the minutes slipping away. He stood to leave.

"Do you trust him?" asked the stranger. "This Gormley?"

The question took Zodak aback. "I—He's odd, but kind," stammered Zodak, not sure why he was even engaging in the conversation.

"Mm." The man nodded, squinting knowingly. "Well, I won't question your judgment—"

"Thank you," blurted Zodak curtly. "And what business is it of yours?" he snapped, surprised by his own sharp, combative tone.

The man shrugged, lifting massive hands in deference. "None, I suppose," he said, raising his goblet. Zodak stood to leave. "But let me ask you this," the man added, casually drawing again from his cup as Zodak began walking from the table. "Where is the medallion you wear around your neck?"

Zodak froze, opening his mouth in retort, but nothing came out. His hand shot to his chest, groping for the comforting weight of the disc, but even before touching his shirt, he knew what he would find. His breathing was pained and shallow, and he suddenly understood: the unnamed hollowness he felt, the dull ache in his chest. Zodak's stomach lurched and twisted, and he let out a guttural moan, suddenly short of breath. The room heaved and tilted. His precious medallion. The medallion those wicked men had fought and died for; the one his dying father had charged him to protect. His only tie to Ardon. It was gone.

22

Zodak sputtered, gasping for breath. He made a wild lunge toward the wagon, but his foot caught the edge of the table leg, and he lurched forward. The stranger's huge hand shot out and caught the back of his shirt just before he hit the sawdust floor, lifting him like a child and setting him back in the chair. Zodak dropped his head into his hands, cursing himself.

The man looked at Zodak intently for a moment as if wrestling with a decision, and then spoke. "Don't worry, son. I will help you."

Zodak looked up. The tall stranger still stared, then nodded his head in confirmation. He emptied the goblet and tossed it on the table. The imposing figure turned from Zodak, gesturing for him to follow. Striding across the patio out into the street, the man ducked his head to avoid the roof line. Zodak scrambled after him. The man glanced down the street toward the city and back in the other direction out the Fahyz Gate. Zodak followed his gaze. A hundred mounts ahead, the road passed through the Fahyz Gate carved out of the hulking city wall, turned slightly right, and then ribboned out of sight. The man calmly reached down and picked up a pinch of dirt. He rubbed it loose in front of him. With the other hand, he reached back and unstrapped the massive bow. The dark polished wood bow towered over Zodak.

"What are you doing?" asked Zodak.

The man said nothing. In one fluid motion, he slipped his leg behind the bottom of the bow and pulled down from the top, adding his own weight to bend the stubborn wood. The bow sighed and creaked as if awaking from a long slumber as he flicked the bowstring on top. It snapped back forcefully, pulling the string tight. Even curved, the massive weapon stood well above Zodak's head. The man pulled a long arrow from among five that stood like sentries in a quiver over his shoulder, each fletched with azure feathers. The arrow shaft seemed as if it had no end. From the ground it would easily have reached Zodak's chin. Facing the Fahyz Gate, the man took a deep breath, nocked the arrow, and slowly drew it back. The wiry muscles in his arms flexed beneath the skin. With the bow drawn fully, he closed his eyes and froze.

Zodak watched anxiously. He picked nervously at his thumbnail, the fear rising in him. It had all gone wrong. *Wasn't I just steps away from meeting the Elder hours ago? Who is this man? And what is he doing? Sending a message?*

Zodak could tell few had the strength to draw this bow, yet the man before him stood completely still with eyes closed, the electric tension of the straining wood submitted to his will. He wore a leather vest, stamped with intricate patterns, and a rich blue shirt beneath. A leather cuff running the length of his forearm caught Zodak's eye. It bore an intricate design: in the center of the cuff was an emblem like a woven flower surrounded and framed by dozens of delicate patterns. The man raised the tip of the arrow slightly as he stood planted to the earth. A cluster of revelers heading into the cantina stopped to watch the strange sight. Still nothing. Zodak glanced around impatiently at the others. One man in the group shrugged his shoulders to a companion and ushered them into the cantina. With a *swoosh* and *snap* that startled the onlookers and made Zodak jump, the arrow rocketed into the heavens and vanished. A few murmurs from the little crowd, sporadic claps, and a drunken holler followed. The man's eyes flashed open suddenly, and he quickly unstrung the bow.

"Come, boy. We must go," he said. Zodak, still shaken and awed by the performance, faltered. The man strapped the bow to his back and strode over to a tall, stately chestnut horse tied nearby.

"Go where?" asked Zodak, still not moving. He glanced nervously back towards the castle and the city.

"We're going to get your medallion back," replied the man without looking up from the saddlebags.

Zodak grunted bitterly. "That's impossible. You saw him leave. He's cliqs away by now," Zodak said, defeated. But even as he clenched his jaw and shut his eyes to fight tears, he felt the prick of impossible hope. The man spoke with unwavering confidence. *What choice do I have? If there's any chance of finding the medal, I have to try. Perhaps this man signaled friends to come help.*

"We shall see," the man replied in a steady voice, untying the horse. He offered the stirrup to Zodak.

Again, Zodak glanced back towards the heart of Uth Becca, his hands fidgeting. *What about Voli?* He felt torn. The castle towers gleamed brightly in the afternoon light, yet the ache in his chest, a physical clenching that hunched his shoulders, mixed with the agony of losing his last piece of Ardon, brought his gaze back to the Fahyz Gate. *Voli will have to wait.* With a resolute nod, Zodak climbed up on the horse, and with a last glance over his shoulder, the two left the city, the man on foot and the horse at a brisk trot. After they had put some distance between themselves and the city, the man spoke again.

"I'm glad you chose to come," said the man. "I owe you my name. I'm Daen, son of Dane." He bowed his head slightly.

"Ahoi, Daen. I'm Zodak. Tell me: why are you helping me? And where are we going?" Zodak asked in a shaky voice. The sharp edge to his tone had softened, but his mind reeled. His eyes darted warily down the road ahead and he kept weight on the stirrups in case he needed to spring from the horse in flight. "Also, how did you know Gormley stole my medallion? And how can we possibly get it back—"

"Whoa, whoa. One question at a time." Daen chuckled. Zodak did not. "From the moment that man—Gormley, is it?" Zodak nodded. "From the moment Gormley set foot in the cantina, I had my eyes on him. The man reeked of the taint. Far gone was he. I saw him spot the medallion when you dropped your coin pouch. He sat up before you, and with the grace of a gifted magician, or likely a practiced thief, he pulled something from his sleeve as you gathered your things. When you sat up, I imagine the world froze for a few seconds or became blurry—"

"Yes!" said Zodak, recalling the dizzy spell. "But just for an instant."

"He burst a focal spore in the air above your seat. That instant was actually a few moments and was all the time he needed to cut the cord around your neck and snatch the medallion. Thus, his hasty departure."

Zodak wanted to object. He wanted to defend Gormley—or was it his own pride he guarded? But he knew he could not. He had been deceived, cheated.

"But it wasn't that sore of a goblin friend that brought me over to you, or even his underhanded thieving. It was the flash."

"The flash?" Zodak asked, understanding what had happened.

"What is that medallion?"

Zodak said nothing.

"It flashed lightning when Gormley pulled it from your neck," Daen continued.

It's why everyone was staring at me when the dizziness passed, thought Zodak.

"I've heard of ancient relics with that effect."

Zodak only looked away.

"Very well," said Daen finally.

The dusty road wound over grassy hills. The thick scrub brush flicked by as the horse quickened into a canter, Daen effortlessly gliding beside in smooth strides somewhere between a walk and a jog. Zodak gazed fahyznost to the jagged Nost mountain range. They rose sharply at the horizon line, challenging the sky for dominion over Yiduiijn. Lost in the mountains, Zodak suddenly felt the horse slow as they crested a knoll. Below them, the road snaked down a long slope, around a sparse stand of trees, before plunging into a thick wall of dark forest. Not thirty measures from the entrance to the woods rested the wagon, with Gormley still in it.

"There he is!" exclaimed Zodak, an electric thrill shooting through him. *We've found it!* The remote prick of hope exploded into a torrent of sudden joy, like spotting a lost precious jewel on the floor of a streambed. Zodak kicked the horse into a gallop, racing down the road towards the cart. As he sped toward the wagon, his joy melted into anger. *How dare you?* His rage blazed. *How* dare *you, Gormley!* Zodak wouldn't hold back. As he reached the wagon, he yanked hard on the reins. Something was wrong. Gormley's gaunt black horse pulled awkwardly to the side against his reins, straining to reach lush grass. The wagon, tumbling and bouncing out of the city when Zodak last saw it, now sat eerily still, as did Gormley. Zodak couldn't picture the frenetic man at rest, but there he sat, his figure slumped in the driver's seat in an afternoon nap.

"Gormley!" he shouted, as soon as he was in earshot, hoping his cry would startle the thief awake. "I know what you did!" he yelled as he approached. "You stole it!" Gormley didn't move. Then Zodak saw it: Daen's massive arrow buried in Gormley's back, the blue fletching proudly saluting the forest like a royal flag bearer. *Impossible!* The haunting scene froze Zodak in his tracks. He didn't know whether to cheer or cry. *Gormley wasn't sleeping.* The world suddenly flipped upside down. His mind spun uselessly, trying to make sense of what he saw. *Daen killed him?* The lifeless body of the man he had known just hours ago sent chills down his spine. He felt like a child somersaulting down a hill, repeatedly losing his bearings on sky and earth. *One moment Gormley was my protector and the next a thief. And this man Daen... a murderer?*

"Zodak!" Daen called, jogging from behind.

Zodak shot a wild-eyed glare at Daen as he cautiously drew near.

"I know you believed this man to have helped you today. But not everything is as it seems."

Zodak scanned Daen warily.

"This Gormley may have had a noble heart at one point in his life, but that time is many seasons gone," said Daen. "He has been infected by taint, evil, his bedfellow. He cannot be called a man. He has become margoul. A goblin friend." The name put Zodak's hair on end. Images of the child stealers singed his mind. "Come. I will show you." Zodak's muscles tightened as Daen reached for the reins, but he didn't resist. Daen drew the chestnut horse beside the wagon. Zodak grimaced and shielded his eyes. He wasn't used to the sight of blood and feared he would be sick.

"Don't look away, Zodak. You must see this." Daen grabbed the arrow and pulled hard. Zodak flinched but kept his eyes on Gormley. Strangely, there was no blood. Daen's arrow emerged as clean as when he had pulled it from the quiver. Gormley's lifeless body slumped to the side. Where the arrow had entered his back was a hole bigger than

Zodak's fist. The edges of the wound, crusted in black dust, crumbled inward.

"It's sand," said Daen, pointing to the growing hole. "A man gone fully margoul doesn't bleed. It's one way we know they're fully tainted. If he were a goblin, his body would be ash immediately upon death. Cut off a halfie's hand and only ashy sand falls to the ground. A troll, to stone, and other margoul filth to sticky black bile. Nothing remains to nourish life. But infected humans, goblin friends, turn more slowly."

Zodak strained to process everything. He replayed parts of the day with Gormley, now seeing it through new eyes. He spied the medallion hanging from Gormley's neck, glinting in the sun. A rush of grief and joy and profound longing, like an insatiable hunger, crashed in Zodak, followed by another flash of anger. *Gormley stole Ardon's medallion from me!* Something snapped. Zodak leapt from the horse onto Gormley's corpse, screaming and flailing his arms. He pounded on the faded black jacket.

"You thief! You stole it... you stole him from me!" Zodak grabbed the medallion and ripped it from the corpse's neck with a scream. The cord sliced through Gormley's dissolving neck and his head dropped to the wagon floor, exploding in a cloud of dark gray sand. Zodak stumbled backwards and fell to the ground beside the wagon. He cradled the medal, pulling it close to his chest, and sobbed, releasing the first tears he had shed for Ardon.

Floodgates inside him opened, and deep, heavy sorrow rushed out. Zodak had spent weeks in flight, fighting to escape the lake of grief that grew daily within him. Now he succumbed, letting himself fall into those lonely waters. In his hand, he held the physical reminder of the only person who meant anything to him. Now, in the dusty wilderness, beside a stranger, he finally let himself mourn. After weeks of patching the wall to his heart, it came crashing down. Alone he sat in the road, his body shaking, and wept. Tears pooled in the clay dust and trickled into tiny red streams that sank into frozen lines of mud. Daen let the boy cry without interrupting or speaking.

There was no shame or self-consciousness. After nearly half an hour, head between his knees, Zodak's tears had stopped, but his catatonic body still shook slightly. Zodak didn't struggle as Daen carefully picked him up and laid his spent body down in the grass under the shade of an elm. Completely drained from the shock of the violence, the exultation of recovering the medallion, followed by the riptide of grief, Zodak finally surrendered to sleep.

After what felt like hours, he pried open puffy eyelids. The sun hadn't moved far in the sky, and he took a frantic breath before finding the curved edge of the medallion still gripped tightly in his hand. Daen had moved the wagon and freed the black horse, though it still grazed in a nearby patch of grass. He strode over and sat in the grass beside Zodak.

"Who did you lose, son?"

Zodak regarded Daen for a moment. "He was my... Ardon was his name." Zodak faltered. "He loved me. And saved me," he said, naming what he never had. His dry eyes stung, but no more tears came. Daen listened to the words with sympathy in his eyes. Zodak slowly lifted the golden medal and inspected its thousand subtle woven waves and patterns as if hoping to see Ardon in it somehow. Daen followed Zodak's gaze to the medallion.

Suddenly, Daen jumped to his feet and snatched the medallion. "Zodak, where did you get this?!" he demanded.

"What are you doing!" screamed Zodak, leaping to his feet and ripping the prize back. "It's mine!" Fire blazed in his eyes as he edged backward. He slipped the cord over his head and let the medallion suck onto his chest, sending a cool wave of relief across his body. The moment it touched his skin, it burst with a bright flash.

"Whoa! Easy. Easy, Zodak." Daen held up his hands. "I am sorry. I'm not trying to take it from you. I'm no Gormley." He knelt beside the boy. "But I need to know where you got this medallion. Was it Ardon's?"

Zodak silently eyed Daen, betrayal now too familiar a foe.

"Zodak, this is *very* important. Where did you get it? Did you find it? Was it stolen?"

"Ardon never stole anything! *Ever!*" shouted Zodak.

"Okay. I'm sorry. Did he give it to you?" A long moment passed. Urgency shouted in Daen's eyes, craving an answer.

"Yes. He gave it to me just before he..." His voice trailed off.

"Was Ardon your father, Zodak?" The simple question stung. Every fiber of Zodak's being wanted to scream yes.

"He was like a father to me. But no, he was my uncle. My father is dead."

"What can you tell me of him?" asked Daen urgently.

"Of my father?" Zodak's mind reeled.

"No, of Ardon. Where is he?" pressed Daen.

"He's dead," replied Zodak flatly, finally naming what he had struggled to admit.

"Please, Zodak, tell me how you came to have this medallion."

Zodak stared searchingly at Daen. There was no hint of deceit or malice in his voice or eyes, only an earnest desperation.

He took a deep breath. "Some evil men took me from my village. I thought we were bound for Pol Dak, but it was a lie, a trap. They had made some sort of bargain to sell me off to a wicked crew of mercenaries. Ardon came after me. He fought those horrid moths. He killed many to save me. But he fell." The picture of Ardon crumpling into Zodak's arms flashed in his mind. "He died so I could escape. The last thing he did was give me this medal. He told me to keep it safe." Daen listened intently, ever honoring the marq buffer between them.

"Zodak, listen to me carefully," said Daen. "My heart breaks for what you've been through. It truly does. And I'm glad we recovered your medallion. I can see how important it is to you." He paused. "But I need you to come with me to show it to someone. That's no ornament you wear around your neck. It's very old and very important. I promise I will keep you and the medallion safe."

Zodak looked down at the gold disc, reexamining the familiar curves and woven design with a skeptical gaze. He remembered Griss calling for the relic.

"I'm sorry, Daen, but I can't. I need to get back to the Golden Oak. I've been gone too long." He braced for Daen's disappointment.

"Zodak, I don't say this to scare you, but if Gormley knew what it was he had stolen, we would both be dead already."

23

Zodak's mind spun. *What is Daen talking about?* Zodak treasured and cherished the medallion, unconsciously reaching for it many times a day, but how could it be so important? Could it be something more than his most precious keepsake? Zodak had returned to Ardon's final words many times but could make little of the charge. *"Keep it safe at all costs. It is a key to hold the darkness..."* was all he could remember. *Hold the darkness of our sad memories?* he had wondered. *The darkness of the seasons of drought on the farm?*

But now, this new, fantastic claim, a claim both outrageous and intriguing, jabbed him with a needle of fear, fear that what Daen said could be true. What if his strongest tie to Ardon might be something more? Would it be wrenched from him? He wished he could rewind this jumbled mess of a day and end up back at the Oak. *The Oak!* The thought pierced like a trumpet blast over a foggy field, and a wave of anxiety swelled, carrying the feeling that even while he tarried, his destiny had begun slowly pulling away. *No, I must get back to the Oak to see Voli!* He was decided. He recalled Olaf saying that Voli only ever stayed for a few days and always departed quickly, without notice.

"Daen, I fear I cannot go with you," Zodak finally said with conviction.

"Oh?" Daen looked up, taken aback.

Where to start? Zodak wondered. This imposing warrior before him wasn't safe—he had just slain a stranger without a word from two cliqs away—yet Zodak somehow felt that perhaps Daen could be trusted. The trust hadn't been earned as Quar had urged, but there it was again, the unseen. He sensed something over Daen, around him. Something hard to describe, but it left him with a solid feeling. The feeling of warm bark under his cheek as he dozed lazily on the third bough of the massive oak back in Laan.

"Today was the day I...I'm supposed to meet with the High Elder of the Venerable Council today," he blurted. "I think," he added. Daen's eyebrows raised. "To understand why I'm here. What I'm to do." The words sounded as ridiculous as he had feared.

Yet Daen didn't laugh. He only frowned and nodded slightly at the boy before him. "Do you have a meeting set with her?" Daen probed.

"Well, no," admitted Zodak. "But her daughter Voli—"

"You know the Lady Voli?" asked Daen with genuine surprise on his face.

"Yes. Well, I've met her, but I haven't spoken with her," answered Zodak. Daen listened. "Yet," he added. "But I have been staying at the Golden Oak and she just arrived this morning."

"Yes, I understand she prefers staying at the Oak when in the city," said Daen.

"I was on my way back to meet her when I was attacked by those street thugs and then I met Gormley."

"But you had a meeting arranged with Voli?" asked Daen.

"Well, actually, no. But the innkeeper was to arrange an introduction," conceded Zodak. "Or, I hoped he would," he added. Now that he had spoken it, Zodak saw his plan was little more than a wish tethered by threads of hope.

"I see," said Daen. "Yet, I must urge you," he added. "I believe what you wear on your neck to be ancient and powerful. A treasure we thought to be lost. Ozir, the one I told you about, is very wise and deep are his ties to Yiduiijn. Little happens in Uth Becca that escapes his notice, whether seen or unseen."

"Yes, but the Elder," protested Zodak weakly, already feeling the unspoken pull of this figure, Ozir.

"The Elder rarely visits the city without visiting Ozir," added Daen. "If you truly seek an audience with her, he could be the bridge."

Zodak closed his eyes, his fist rhythmically rapping his forehead as his mind raced. He tried peering beyond the forked path before him, but ahead lay unknowns upon unknowns. He had fantasized about his meeting with Voli so many times, to let that go seemed folly. *Did I miss the opportunity? No, she would still be there.*

"I must return to the Oak," Zodak affirmed. Daen again only nodded his head slowly in thought. "Perhaps we could meet with Ozir after," offered Zodak. "Surely we could meet him tomorrow?" he asked hopefully.

A subtle wince danced across Daen's face, but he shook it away and, with a deep breath of resolve, gave one last curt nod. "Very well," he finally said. "I will not force you to go."

Thank you. Zodak's shoulders relaxed a bit.

"I will accompany you to the Golden Oak. But I will not let you or the medallion out of my sight. All I ask is that after this *meeting* with Voli, you promise to accompany me to see Ozir. Assuming he will see you, that is."

Why does he care so much? wondered Zodak. "You have my word," he answered.

"Very good," said Daen approvingly. "The path has been laid then. May the Color guide. Now, we linger too long," he said, helping Zodak up into the saddle of the towering mare. He strapped in the few provisions he had recovered from Gormley's wagon and dumped a small pile of withered fruits and vegetables on the ground for Gormley's newly emancipated horse.

The thought of Gormley pricked Zodak's conscience. *He did save me today,* thought Zodak. *And now he's gone. If I had never met him, he would still be alive.* His stomach sank. *He was tainted, though,* Zodak reminded himself. *And he stole Ardon's medallion.* Reciting the facts didn't quiet the turmoil. Zodak lurched as Daen clicked his tongue and led the mare back up the dusty road to Uth Becca. As they crested the first small slope, Zodak glanced back at the scene one last time. But the black horse was gone. Not five minutes ago, it was munching happily. *Did it run off?* Zodak scanned for a clue but could find none.

"The horse!" he called to Daen, still searching for something he had missed. "It's gone!"

Daen looked back without slowing. "Poor guy," he said, returning his gaze to the road ahead. "The forest took him."

"The...the *what*?" gasped Zodak, horrified.

"That's no picnic glade," answered Daen over his shoulder. "Danger lurks in that wood. It's a good thing we didn't tarry any longer."

Zodak's stomach turned. *What danger?* His mind flipped through scenes of whatever terror could have "taken" a horse. He decided not to press Daen. Not an hour ago, he was asleep beneath the shade tree, just a few marqs from the mouth of those dark trees. He shook off the chill and looked back to the road ahead.

Daen pressed on, with no hint of concern, though Zodak

felt their pace quicken. He considered Daen anew, marveling at the statue of a man before him. Daen moved with effortless grace, his long fluid gait giving him the appearance of floating.

"Zodak." Daen spoke. "Tell me about the evil men who tried to steal the medallion from you."

Zodak breathed deeply, steadying himself. Then he recounted what happened in that terrible forest glade. He held back no detail, pausing only a few times to gather himself. Daen listened to every word. A fortnight earlier, Zodak might have braced himself for utter disbelief of his story about the giants, but he had seen enough of this strange land to know better.

"Remarkable," was all Daen said when he had finished.

"What is so special about the medallion?" asked Zodak.

"If it's what I believe it to be, that medal is an ancient and powerful relic, hundreds of seasons old."

"What does it do?" asked Zodak, though he was skeptical it really did anything. There had been a mistake of some sort.

"I'd prefer Ozir look at it first. He can tell you all there is to know about it."

Or tell me it does nothing, thought Zodak. *That it only resembles whatever important thing Daen is talking about. I'll ask Voli or the Elder. They will know,* he decided. His mind drifted off to the meeting with Voli again.

"How did you do that?" asked Zodak after riding a while in silence.

"Do what?" asked Daen over his shoulder.

"How did you make that shot? With your bow? That's impossible," he added.

"I am a Scor Delfahysian. Most who know my people call us Skypiercers. We have long defended the skies of these regions."

"Yes, but how can you shoot like that? He was cliqs away from the city wall when you fired," persisted Zodak, recalling his own orko hunting misadventures with a homemade bow. "We couldn't even see him."

"Mindsight. It is the ancient tradition of my people. Since I was a boy of half your age I have studied and trained mind, body, and spirit in the way of the mindsight. It's a secret technique we have kept over the ages, impossible to explain in words. We read the wind, heat bands, and land contours, and tune to the earth, to the grass, trees, and spirit."

Zodak squinted as he struggled to make sense of what he had seen.

"The city is beautiful from here," said Daen.

Zodak looked up and beheld the city walls glowing white in the distance. The castle seemed to float regally above the outer ring.

"But it's rotting inside."

Zodak shot him a questioning glance.

"Uth Becca once embodied greatness: power, beauty, and purity from the time of Governors. Now filth pumps from her heart, filling the veins of her streets," said Daen. "The city magistrate, Kuquo, I believe to be tainted himself."

"You mean a goblin friend? A margoul?" asked Zodak.

"Yes, at least partly. He has surrounded himself with a gang of thugs dressed up like soldiers who now carry city guard patches and enforce his bent will. Step out of line, and you end up in his dungeon, or worse."

Zodak recalled his encounter with Badu in the market and Stohl, the Magistrate's guard.

"The people are not yet so far gone as to follow him blindly, but he is subtle and cunning. Many believe him noble. His bold personality wins friends and feeds on power. But there is another ruler in the making. One who could redeem the city. Ozir, the dwarf—"

"Ozir's a *dwarf*?" interrupted Zodak.

"Yes. And a great warrior. He leads an underground resistance. But to his credit, and to his peril, he fears nothing, and with every passing day, the power of the resistance grows. I worry that Kuquo may have already learned of this movement and will soon uncover its source."

"That's who you want me to see?" asked Zodak.

"Yes, Zodak. There are things about you I don't understand. Ozir knows much of this world. He can help. And I sense there are questions you would like answered as well, are there not—" His voice suddenly cut off, and he stopped in his tracks. He lifted a hand and the chestnut horse halted.

"What is it?" asked Zodak.

Daen stared intently at the blurry horizon line far off in the distance where the road met the city gate. "Oh no," he groaned. "They await my return," he finally said.

"Who's waiting? I don't see anything."

"Eight—no, nine armored guards and two shooters on the wall. Someone must have reported me from the cantina. The Magistrate has a bounty on my head."

"*What?!* What happened?" asked Zodak, shifting uneasily in the saddle. He strained his eyes to see what Daen saw, but he could barely even make out the Fahyz Gate in the city wall.

"It was another tainted, like Gormley, only worse. This man, dare I even call him a man, was scum. The taint had nearly completely consumed him. I called him out, naming him for what he was. In the duel that ensued, I slew him." Zodak's eyes opened wide. "You must understand, Zodak, I do not take a life lightly, but evil is growing. We are charged with seeking it out and destroying it. If we do not, the evil will destroy us."

"Is that because you're a skypiercer?" asked Zodak admiringly.

Daen hesitated. "Something like that. But duels are illegal in the city. When the Magistrate found out about the duel, he sent two guards to arrest me. I had planned to simply leave Uth Becca to avoid the bloodshed and whatever twisted pretense of justice awaited me. But when the guards arrived, and I was preparing to leave, that's when I heard it. One of the guards, a royal castle guard, mind you, spoke to the other in goblin tongue—"

"A hissing sound?" asked Zodak, remembering the child stealers.

"You've heard it." Daen raised an eyebrow. "Your trials betray your youth. Yes, they hiss. I killed both guards. And there was not a drop of blood between them, not one. I knew I had been justified. Yet the bounty on my head tripled. As I said, I believe the Magistrate himself to be tainted, and I imagine he knows that if I can ever prove it, he will lose his seat, if not his life."

"You'd kill the Magistrate?"

"If he is a margoul, I cannot allow him to stay in power. My creed forbids it." Daen looked off again to the horizon. "Zodak, you must listen to me." He put a hand on Zodak's shoulder and stared him in the eyes. "No matter what happens, you cannot let them find your medallion."

"Why?"

"It's more than I can explain now," said Daen. "But I need your trust. Do I have it?" Zodak faltered. "Do I have it, Zodak?"

"Yes," he finally answered. "Yes, you have it."

"Follow my lead. It may get...ugly at the gate, but I will get you through it."

"What do you mean ugly?" Suddenly Zodak's heart was racing. "What will they do if they catch you? What will they do to me?"

"I don't believe you're in danger, but these pills don't mean to arrest me. If I'm caught, they'll kill me. But I don't plan to let that happen." He winked. "Now, Zodak." He locked eyes with Zodak. "Listen closely: if we get separated, you must go straight into town until you see the dry goods store. A dry goods store, you hear? It's two hundred mounts straight through the Fahyz

Gate on the left. Take the saddlebags with you but let the horse go. Wait behind the store. I'll find you there."

"Okay…" answered Zodak, tentatively recounting each step of the instructions in his mind. *Dry goods store. Left two hundred mounts.*

The two continued on the path to the city. As they drew near, Zodak could see dull sparkles of the late sun reflecting off black armor at the base of the wall. He swallowed hard. Nearly a dozen soldiers waited for them. *Should I run?* The road dipped out of sight of the city one last time before the final stretch to the gate. Daen pulled the horse to a stop in the shallow depression, removing and quickly stringing his bow. From a pouch hanging on his belt, he pulled two pear-shaped iron objects each the size of a crabapple. He then removed two of the long arrows and replaced their razor tips with the iron bulbs.

"Zodak, in the left saddlebag, you will find a ball," said Daen as he worked on the second arrow. "I will need it." Zodak opened the bag, noticing his trembling hands as he located the round object. He strained to lift the apple-sized sphere of leather in both hands. Its surface stretched tightly over sand or pebbles, though it felt as heavy as lead. A loop protruded from one side of the ball. Daen handed Zodak the two arrows and pulled a long knife from his belt.

"Do what must be done," he said to the horse, patting it on its muscled neck. With the knife, he slit the horse's bridle and reins almost all the way through. Daen nocked both arrows at the same time and drew the bow as before. Zodak thought he might shoot toward the city wall, but he aimed nearly straight up into the sky. Again, Daen froze in this position, eyes closed. Zodak counted to fifteen, sixteen, seventeen before the *snap* and *swoosh* of the arrows rocketing skyward startled him.

"We have no time to waste." Daen spoke quickly, unstringing the bow. He threaded his bowstring through the eyelet of the heavy leather ball and wrapped the other end around his middle finger. Taking up the bow as a walking staff, he marched forward. A sharp whistle brought the chestnut mare to his side.

"They'll begin to wonder if we don't hurry. And we wouldn't want to let them down." He had a twinkle in his eye. *What's he so happy about?* Zodak shook slightly and felt a wave of nausea, but Daen appeared almost giddy.

"And Zodak," added Daen, "hold on tight."

They crested the hill, and there, two hundred mounts before them yawned the massive Fahyz Gate. A wall of nine black-clad guards stood, waiting. Two more guards perched above like birds of prey with crossbows trained on the approaching pair. Zodak's faith in Daen suddenly vanished and he struggled for breath. These men, these hardened warriors, were trained to kill. Their armor and mail and swords looked impenetrable. Panic crashed like a tidal wave over Zodak. His heart hammered in his chest, and he glanced around for escape. A guard edged forward cautiously. Daen moved a few steps away from the horse and held his staff up as an offering for all to see. *Where is he going!*

"What is this? We come in peace," said Daen. The approaching guard only grunted and grabbed hold of the reins of the chestnut horse. He locked Zodak with a frozen stare, and he cocked his head, squinting as he groped for the cord of recognition. Zodak felt it too. *I know this man!* he thought. *The guard from the market. Stohl!* Stohl began leading the horse away from Daen, shaking his head slightly. As he pulled the mare away, Zodak caught his glance and subtle nod up at the archers on the wall. Zodak's stomach turned. He turned to shout a warning at Daen, but nothing came out, only a strained gasp. Even as he struggled for his voice, a new sound, a deep low moaning, joined Zodak's croaking. It grew louder and higher in pitch until it screeched into a sharp whistle from above. The guards searched the sky for the sound.

Daen's arrows screamed down from the heavens and slammed into the helmets of each of the two guards perched on the wall. In a flash, the leather ball shot from Daen's closed fist and caught one of the guards square in the chest, sending him flying back against the wall with a thud. Daen snapped the ball back to his hand with a yank of the string. For a moment nobody moved, the line of guards frozen in disbelief. Then they erupted.

Stohl lunged for Zodak, tearing him from the saddle. Zodak kicked and screamed, but another guard joined Stohl, grabbing Zodak's arms and pinning them painfully behind his back. Stohl gripped Zodak's shirt collar with two powerful fists. Zodak couldn't see Daen behind Stohl's massive frame, but he could hear the clash of battle.

"You!" Stohl's storm-gray eyes flashed, and his musty breath hit Zodak. "You're the grimy cutter from Badu's stall. Keep finding yourself in the wrong place at the wrong—" Stohl stopped short. His eyes had dropped from Zodak's face to his chest.

"What in the sherking downs!" He pulled Zodak's shirt open further. "Slag me!" Zodak felt the rough beard of the guard holding him from behind as he craned his neck to peer over Zodak's head.

"'At's the one Mag's looking for!"

Zodak shrank under the hot sour breath of his captor.

"Bind up that moth," Stohl cried over his shoulder in Daen's direction, reaching for the medallion. "We got a real prize here —" Even as his outstretched fingers brushed the metal, a *whizz* cut the air followed by a thud. Stohl's eyes flipped back, and he crumpled as Daen whipped his leather ball back. As Stohl's body fell away, Zodak finally saw Daen, faced off with four guards. Three lay on the ground, writhing or crawling.

"Huh?" came the grunt of the guard behind him. Zodak leaned his head forward and then slammed it back as hard as he could. There was a crunching sound, and the world flashed white. But the guard behind him released his grip as he staggered to the side, his face in his hands. Zodak jumped up on the horse and kicked hard.

"I'm gonna kill you, moth!" the bearded guard roared, eyes full of hate. He grabbed the reins with one hand, the other clapped over his shattered nose flowing with blood. Zodak slapped the chestnut horse on the flank as hard as he could. The horse reared, snapping the reins in the guard's hand. Zodak nearly toppled backward but grabbed a fistful of mane just in time to steady himself. The mare sprang forward, crashing through the bearded guard and plunging through the Fahyz Gate at a full gallop.

Zodak held on for dear life. He managed one glance over his shoulder and glimpsed two more guards closing in on Daen. The city passed in a blur as the mare raced down the street. Zodak tried remembering Daen's instructions, searching the buildings to the left as they whizzed by. He barely caught sight of a faded sign bearing a wheat stalk and a shovel as it flashed past.

"Whoa, whoa!" Zodak cried, pulling hard on the mare's mane, and squeezing his legs. After pulling frantically again and again, the horse finally slowed to a walk and stopped.

Zodak slid from the saddle, remembering to grab the saddlebags just as the mare began trotting off. He clicked his tongue and gave the horse a hard slap, sending it bolting off down the cobblestone street. Zodak jogged back up the road. Sixty mounts ahead, he spied the faded sign for the dry goods store. As he approached, he heard horse hooves pounding down the lane towards him. He darted from the street to the adjacent alley just as a trio of city guards raced by. Pressing his body hard against the wall of the dry goods store, his heart thundered in his chest, and he prayed to remain a shadow. To his great relief, the clapping hoofbeats faded off down the street. Creeping from the wing of the building's shadow, he scurried to the back of the store. As he rounded the corner, he nearly collided with a dark towering figure in the shadows. An iron grip clasped his arm. The world lurched, and he thought he might faint.

"Zodak!" came Daen's steady voice.

"How did you—? I just saw you—" Zodak stammered.

"No time, Zodak. Change of plans. You must follow me now." Daen lifted the leather saddlebags from Zodak's shoulder as he stammered. Speeding away from the circle of guards at the gate, Zodak was sure he would never see Daen again, yet here the man stood, without a scratch. Daen leapt back against the wall and pushed Zodak back as well. More hoofbeats.

"... down this way..." Zodak heard a gruff voice as two more horses passed. In the distance came a short horn blast and a guard's call. As the fear rushed back in, Zodak glanced around nervously, hoping Daen had another plan to get them out of here. With muscles tensed, Zodak readied himself to dash down a side street, but to his surprise Daen lifted the rusty latch on the creaky door at the back of the dry goods store and ducked inside.

24

It looked as if the dry goods store hadn't seen a customer for months if not seasons. It smelled musty and a fine layer of dust coated everything, yet it appeared well stocked. Tools spotted with rust hung on the walls, and stacks of candles and full sacks stood on shelves. A skupp skittered across the floor, leaving a line of footprints from the chewed corner of a feed bag to a gap in the baseboard. Daen stood staring, his mind elsewhere.

"This will not be easy," he muttered.

"What won't be?" asked Zodak, following the stare to a row of unremarkable wooden pails. Daen didn't answer. He turned and walked briskly down one of the aisles, leaving tracks in the dust. Zodak scampered after him. Reaching a corner of the store containing various gardening and animal care items, Daen slowed. He eyed Zodak up and down.

"This should do," he said, pulling a burlap hooded costume from the wall. As he did, the burlap caught the corner of a small pyramid of carved wooden boxes, sending them tumbling from the shelf. Without words or thought, Zodak's hand shot out reflexively, and in an instant, he had snatched all four falling boxes from the air before they touched the ground. Daen just stared.

"I... I don't know how I did that," stammered Zodak, staring down at the armful of tins.

"Very impressive," said Daen finally, nodding. He turned back to the hooded cloak. "Here," he said, holding it up to Zodak.

"What is it?"

"It's a needlefly tending suit. But don't worry, you won't be handling needleflies." He tossed the cloak to Zodak then continued down the aisle. Zodak caught the heavy burlap bundle and followed, confused. As he rounded the corner, Daen was removing a leather apron from the wall. He laid the apron on the wood plank floor and removed a long knife from his belt. With deft motions, he cut out a lopsided rectangle and tossed the apron aside.

"Give me your arm," he said to Zodak, still holding the long knife. Hesitantly, Zodak extended his arm. Daen wrapped the leather around Zodak's forearm. It nearly encircled his arm twice. Daen cut it again and remeasured. This time it fit better. He punched holes in the edges of the leather and cut a length of cord from the apron.

"Good. Let's go," he said to Zodak, stuffing the materials in one of the saddlebags. Zodak couldn't imagine why they needed a needlefly suit and makeshift leather cuff, but he obediently followed Daen across the store. Daen stopped behind the counter, facing the large shelf of dusty boxes and jars. A muffled voice from outside the store broke the silence, then another. Dark figures broke the blades of late afternoon sun that cut through cracks in the wall. Shuffling armored boots sounded close.

"Guards!" Zodak hissed in an urgent whisper.

Daen looked up distractedly from the shelf he was studying then cocked his head, listening. He reached into his pocket.

"Splash a few drops of this in front of the door. Quickly." He handed Zodak a tiny vial of opal-colored liquid. "And don't spill or touch any," he added, turning back to the shelves. The voices grew louder, even as Zodak crept towards the door, his heart in his throat.

"—spotted his horse," came a muffled voice from outside.

"Check inside," ordered another. Zodak fumbled with the cap of the vial. He opened it and tipped it carefully, splashing a few drops on the dusty planks in front of the door. Small blue clouds puffed up from the spots where the liquid hit the floor. Banging shook the door against the tired lock. Zodak leapt backward, and he watched as if in slow motion as the deadly liquid splashed from the bottle onto his hand. He frantically wiped it on his pants and capped the liquid. *What have I done?!* The door rattled again. He scrambled back to the counter. Daen was gone.

Boom! The guard's kick smashed and splintered the door. A hand grabbed Zodak and pulled him to the ground behind the counter. His head felt dizzy, and his breathing quickened.

"Search it!" boomed a deep voice. "Every inch!" Many pairs of heavy feet stomped in and began to spread across the store. *They'll catch us,* thought Zodak. He was so sure of this, he wanted to stand up and turn himself in. *If I don't surrender, they'll kill me!*

"Footprints, sir!" called a guard across the store. *They'll follow the prints right to us!* Zodak thought. *They will see my small feet next to Daen's and know that I am with him. Why* am *I here? I don't know this man! He put me in this danger!* Zodak's mind spun faster and faster. *He set me up! He is one of them!* Panic seized him, and he lunged to try to stand. Daen's grip held him like iron. *He's trapped me here!* thought Zodak. Footsteps approached the counter.

"These are not their footprints," declared the voice of the leader.

"No, I don't think they've been here," called another.

A voice directly beside them called out, "Maybe that wasn't his horse. We're in the wrong place."

"What'll Captain say when he hears we've lost him?" another asked.

"Men, we have to go!" the deep voice answered. "Now!" As the men shuffled out, Zodak wanted to yell after them. The door banged closed, and Zodak suddenly felt locked in a lion's cage, trapped with the beast. He squirmed frantically, but Daen's grip held fast. *I'm locked in the grasp of a stranger, a killer!*

As soon as the guards had gone, Daen released Zodak. Spying his opportunity, Zodak jumped to his feet and sprinted for the door after the guards. But Daen was too quick. He leapt forward and caught Zodak, clapping his huge hand over his mouth just as he screamed for the guards. Daen carried the struggling Zodak back behind the counter and lifted a dull copper cylinder from the shelf. With a groan and creak, the shelf sank down into a cavity in the floor, revealing a large closet-like space. Daen forced Zodak inside and reached up and pulled a lever on the wall. The shelf groaned again and rose back up, sealing them in darkness. Then, the floor dropped.

They plummeted down the black shaft. Zodak shook his head free and screamed, "*Help!* I'm here! Get me out!" Yet down and down they plunged. Daen's grip on Zodak's arms never loosened. The falling platform beneath them slowed and came to an abrupt, yet gentle stop. Daen fished something from his leather pouch and suddenly there was light. The two of them stood at the bottom of what looked like an old stone well. Daen's outstretched arms would have reached the walls on both sides. *Those solid, impenetrable walls.* There was no opening, no fissure, no escape. Zodak looked up. The blackness continued forever. He wriggled free from Daen's hold.

"Why have you brought me here!" he demanded of Daen. "We're trapped! Have you brought me here to kill me?"

"Zodak. Take three deep breaths."

"I'm not going to listen to you! I don't know you!" Zodak snapped. "All I know is that you're a killer!" He paced back and forth, keeping his eyes fixed on Daen.

"Breathe, Zodak," said Daen calmly.

"*No!* I won't listen—"

"Zodak, breathe!" boomed Daen.

Zodak stopped pacing. He stared at Daen. With a hint of defiance, he took a deep breath, and then another. To his surprise, as he breathed deeply, he felt his hatred and fear of Daen slowly begin to evaporate into the dark. After a few minutes, the frantic terror was gone, like waking from a fleeting nightmare. He suddenly felt confused and embarrassed. *What was I so terrified about?*

"Daen... I'm sorry. I—" he sputtered.

"It's all right," answered Daen. "You spilled the vial on yourself, didn't you?"

Zodak remembered his slip. "Yes... Yes, I did." He trailed off, removing the half-empty vial from his pocket. He handed it back to Daen.

"*Aforia trius*," said Daen. "It's a bottle of doubt. If you breathe it or touch it, everything you trust and know dissolves into fear and uncertainty and panic. It's what happened to the guards, and what happened to you." Daen spoke a foreign word and the soft yellow orb he held in his hand turned brilliant green. An opening suddenly appeared right in front of Zodak in what he could have sworn was a solid stone wall moments before.

"Don't give up hope just yet, Zodak. There will be plenty of time for that later."

25

Daen pushed against the door, stepping through into a rocky passage, ducking his head beneath the jagged ceiling. The tunnel snaked right, then back to the left, winding ever downwards. Zodak trailed closely behind, kicking the dusty floor as he walked.

"We'll stop here," said Daen after a few minutes, dropping down to one knee and opening his saddlebag. He removed the hooded burlap cloak and the leather band.

"Put this on." He handed Zodak the needlefly suit and began threading the string through holes on the leather cuff. When Zodak had squirmed into the scratchy cloak, Daen looked him up and down.

"Good. Now your right arm." Zodak held it out. Daen slipped the leather cuff over Zodak's forearm and tightened the string, cinching the leather. It looked like a pitiful copy of the aged leather cuff Daen wore, with the intricate pattern.

"It's no work of art, but it'll have to do," said Daen. "Now listen, Zodak. You must do exactly as I say. This is no game. An outsider like you is strictly forbidden where we're going, so you must act as if you belong. I know you're scared but try to act confident. And no matter what happens, don't speak. I'll do the talking. If I say run, you run. If I say hide, you hide. Understand?" He fixed Zodak with urgent eyes.

"Yes. I understand." The words unsettled him, yet the overwhelming mountain of doubt he'd felt just minutes before was gone. Beneath his fear, his trust for Daen had returned.

"Good. Let's go." Daen returned the glowing orb to his bag. All went dark. After a moment standing in the darkness, Zodak's eyes adjusted, and he could make out a soft glow ahead in the passage. Daen moved towards the glow, and Zodak scurried behind him, catching his foot on the burlap cloak. Beyond a curve ahead, the passage opened into a square room. The walls, floor, and ceiling of this cube room were smooth, polished gray stone, contrasting sharply with the jagged tunnel walls. Two other similar passages also emptied into this room. At the far end of the cube stood a massive stone door twice as tall as Zodak, covered in intricate patterns and characters, clearly the work of a master cratsman.

Beside the door stood a huge grotesque statue. The stone figure was as tall as Daen, but twice as thick. Carved rock muscles rippled across the statue's chest and arms. Broad shoulders sloped to a thick, square head. A gruesome face peered lifelessly through beady stone eyes. The slate-gray sculpture matched the color of the wall almost perfectly. It must have been carved from the same stone. In the statue's hands it held a huge battle-axe that nearly brushed the ceiling. It gleamed in the light and almost looked real. Zodak leaned closer to inspect the handiwork.

Shwoop! The axe flashed down in front of the door, barely a jot from Zodak's face. He jumped backwards, too frightened to scream, tripping over his cloak and falling backwards. The statue stepped in front of the door, whipping the axe up like it weighed nothing, and thrust the sharp point to within an inch of Zodak's throat. The lifeless black eyes glared down at Zodak.

From the statue's mouth came a voice like clattering boulders. Zodak couldn't understand the words, but the sound shook his ribcage. Daen hurried in front of Zodak, speaking the same strange tongue. The statue answered, with a nod to Daen, who lifted his sleeve and showed his leather cuff. The statue put a clenched fist to his chest and bowed to Daen, never moving the axe. Daen spoke again in the unfamiliar tongue and gestured at Zodak. The stone guard snapped back argumentatively. Daen replied, bowing slightly, hands clasped then pointing to his leather cuff and gesturing at Zodak again.

"Show him your forearm cuff, Zodak," Daen said between breaths. Zodak slowly lifted his right sleeve, to reveal the cuff. The stone creature looked intently down at Zodak, then argued back at Daen. Daen negotiated further with the creature, speaking intently to it and gesturing with his hands. Finally, the statue flipped the axe back upright, and turned to stare at the wall. It furrowed its heavy brow and began counting on its fingers. Zodak let out a sigh and cautiously rose to his feet, yet the giant ignored him, consumed by counting. Daen pointed towards the door and spoke again. The stone creature looked up, as if suddenly aware of Daen's presence and mindlessly pushed a rock in the wall behind it before resuming the counting on its fingers. A low grinding sound echoed in the chamber as the heavy door opened. Daen spoke another word to the guard, took Zodak's arm, and jerked him through the doorway. Behind the door a passage extended for a hundred measures, soft torchlight dancing off the smooth polished rock walls. The end of the corridor glowed softly like the evening sky. The door closed behind them with a dull thud.

"What was that?!" asked Zodak, pointing back to the door, his heart still pounding.

"That, Zodak, was an obsidian rock giant – a half-giant, obviously. But pound for pound, they are the fiercest fighters you'll find. Ozir hand-picked them to guard this place. I would shudder to find myself on the other end of one of their axes... like you just were." He tried to hide a smile.

"Great. Why didn't you tell me he wasn't a statue?"

"Hmm. Yes, I suppose I should have. I can see how you would mistake him for a statue. Their thick hide looks just like stone. In any case, your costume didn't fool him."

"It didn't?"

"No, he was about to terminate you for not knowing the password," said Daen, continuing down the passage.

"Terminate? What password? You didn't tell me about a password!" called Zodak, running to catch up.

"To pass the outer guard, you must be wearing an authentic band of the Order, which you don't have, and you need the password, in the old tongue of course—"

"What? Did you say the Order?" asked Zodak, stopping.

Daen's brow furrowed in a pained look. "I suppose it's too late now," he said. "What I tell you must never leave your lips. Do you understand?" Zodak nodded eagerly. "There is a pact that some have taken. That I have taken, to join a hidden society of warriors, traders, statesmen, and governors. We are called the Order."

"You're in the Order?!"

"The seat I hold was passed from one to another, across hundreds of seasons," Daen replied.

A thrill spiked through Zodak. "You never said Ozir was part of the Order!" he said excitedly.

Daen frowned in confusion. "How can you know the Order?"

"Well, I don't. I mean I've been trying to find the Order." Zodak spoke fast. "You see, Ardon told me to find the Order in Uth Becca. But I didn't know what that was."

Daen cocked his head. "He told you to find the Order? Are you sure?" Daen probed.

"Yes!"

"Color blind me!" said Daen. "Then we have no time to lose." Daen turned and walked briskly down the corridor.

Zodak nearly skipped behind him. He felt like he was floating. *The Order! I've found it!* The sinking feeling of missing his meeting with the Elder vanished. *I'll get answers!*

"So how'd I get by without the password if the band didn't work?" asked Zodak as they trotted down the passage.

"Half-giants are deadly on the battlefield, but they do have a weakness," said Daen. "I answered his demand with a riddle in the old tongue. That particular riddle traps the victim in a mental circle. It won't let them concentrate on anything else. It's like having an insatiable itch in your mind that you can't reach. Once they start solving it, nothing else matters. He let us through so he could get back to solving the riddle."

"Oh. How long will he be trying to solve it?"

"The power of the riddle fades after a few hours. But I don't envy the headache he'll have tomorrow."

The end of the corridor opened like the jaws of a yawning serpent into an enormous cavern. Zodak could barely see the other side. It must have been a full cliq away. Rather than the cramped cave he expected, the expanse felt like being outside, like he had crested a hill and looked down into a rocky valley. Brilliant clusters of glowing fragments that outshone the brightest stars littered the vast rock ceiling that arced across the space, lighting the entire cave with a foggy glow like dawn just before the sun peeks over the horizon. In the middle of the cavern a stone fortress jutted up from an island of rock, surrounded on three sides by the fractured black stain of a chasm that plunged into darkness. Long, thin rope bridges stretched like a spider's legs from the island over the abyss that encircled the fortress.

Far to the left, against the wall of the cavern, through a yawning cave mouth, flowed a river. It emptied into a lake where a dozen small boats bobbed. Workers scurried across a dock, unloading cargo from a moored boat. A road ran from the lake dock to the fortress, and another, over a rock plateau, following the chasm past the fortress island to a knot of buildings the size of a small town on the far-right edge of the cavern where the arching ceiling met the ground. Zodak counted three wagons and two horses creeping along the road. Scattered around the plateau and along the road, slender rock towers like elongated stalagmites rose a hundred measures into the air. *The Order is here in Uth Becca. "Beneath our very feet..."* Zodak remembered Badu's words.

Zodak and Daen stood on a ledge at the mouth of the passageway. A stone path wound down from there and ran across the cavern for two hundred mounts until eventually meeting the road. Across the road, a rope bridge spanned the crevice to the fortress island. Small figures stood on the far side of the chasm at each of the bridges. Their distinct, systematic meandering betrayed their role: guards.

"We have to try," Zodak heard Daen mutter, scanning the cavern.

"Are we going to that fortress?" asked Zodak. "Is that where Ozir is?"

Daen glanced back, as if surprised to find Zodak behind him. He turned and knelt. He paused for a moment, searching for words. "Zodak, that is Blackiron, Ozir's stronghold. We need to get you inside so you can speak to Ozir." Daen looked away, out to the expansive cavern.

"The thing is..." His gaze returned. "Outsiders are strictly prohibited from this secret place. That I even brought you here —I could get in grave trouble for breaking this fundamental rule. But Ozir needs to hear what you have to say."

"So why don't you go tell him? I'll stay here until you come back."

"It's not that easy. We were fortunate to get past the half-giant. The entire cavern is constantly swept for spies and intruders. They may be watching us right now." He signaled with his eyes quickly towards the cavern.

"Who's watching?" asked Zodak, glancing around.

"In this place, they remove intruders first and ask questions second. If I left you here—" He shook his head, agreeing with himself. "And what you have to say is for Ozir's ears only. No, you must come with me. Just do as I say." He stood up and motioned for Zodak to follow him. Together, the two picked their way down the path, moving quickly across the open expanse. When they finally arrived at the road, they slowed. Zodak craned his neck to look up at the stone spike that towered above them. A cart bumped down the road, full of boxes from the dock. Daen casually dipped his head in greeting. The driver gave a subtle wave, showing no signs of surprise or alarm at Zodak's presence. When the cart had passed, Daen hurried across the road with Zodak close behind. On the other side of the road, a delicate rope bridge spanned a chasm no less than fifty mounts across. The rope looked dangerously thin and the structure unsteady.

Daen took a step out on the bridge. "Keep hold of the rope rails, and you'll be fine—" *Whiiid.* A sharp whine pierced the air, followed by a thud as an arrow slammed into one of the wooden posts anchoring the bridge. Zodak dove behind Daen. Daen's head whipped up toward the scout, a guttural rumble rising into a deep laugh.

"Elsin! You old fool!" Daen shouted at the sky. "I'm surprised your eyes still work that well!" He waved up at the pinnacle of the stone spike. On a perch carved from the stone a hundred measures above the cavern floor Zodak could just make out a bowman scout. *Such a precise shot was unimaginable.* The bowman waved.

"So far, so good," whispered Daen. He started across the bridge, effortlessly balancing on the narrow planks. Zodak followed timidly, edging out onto the bridge. It swayed, and he lunged for the supports. Below, the endless black chasm jeered up at him. A wave of dizziness passed over him. He closed his eyes, took a deep breath, and focused ahead on Daen. The second step felt wobbly, but the third felt a bit steadier. By pushing out on each of the two guide ropes, he found he could somewhat steady the planks. He continued until he reached the center of the bridge where Daen waited for him.

"Zodak, there is another guard on the other side of the bridge." Zodak looked past Daen at the tall, cloaked guard who stood expectantly. "If we cannot fool him into letting you pass, I may have to engage him."

"What do you mean, *engage him*?" asked Zodak.

"Hopefully, I can subdue him without bloodshed, but no fight is predictable. If you're not prepared to kill, the challenge is that much greater. I was fortunate to escape from the castle gate today without killing any guards. No matter how skilled a warrior, battle cannot be scripted." Zodak stared wide-eyed. "Any man can win any battle on any day. I have seen timid squires slay hardened warriors. If it appears that I cannot subdue him, you must run for the castle gate. Stop at nothing. You must see Ozir, do you hear me?"

"Yes." Zodak shuddered at the thought of trying to enter the towering black fortress alone. Again, Daen removed his bow, and used it as a walking stick. He somehow balanced on the planks without the rope guides. Zodak wobbled along slowly behind, his stomach in knots. Daen quickly crossed the remaining span, stepping off the bridge, and began speaking to the hooded guard. Suddenly the guard lunged at him. The two fell to the ground. Zodak's heart pounded as he scrabbled along the last stretch of bridge, swaying and stumbling. He leapt for solid ground. The hooded man held a sword to Daen's neck. Zodak made a run for the fort, slipping behind the guard's back.

"Zodak," Daen called. "Stop!" Zodak, already in flight, froze.

The guard, easily as tall as Daen, rose, removing his hood and smiling from ear to ear as he sheathed his sword. Daen stood up, dusting himself off. He too wore a smile. Zodak felt nauseous, and trembled uncontrollably, poised for flight or battle. *Why all the smiling?*

"The Colors have shone upon us again, young Zodak," said Daen. He put an arm around the guard. "Zodak, meet my brother, Sodane, whom I let best me."

Sodane laughed and held out a large hand. The uncanny resemblance now struck Zodak. Both men had the same angular features and broad frames, yet Sodane's coloring was darker, and he stood just a few jots shorter than Daen. As Zodak reached to meet the handshake, Sodane's gaze dropped to Zodak's imitation cuff, and he withdrew his hand.

"He's not of the Order," he said, turning to Daen, sudden alarm on his face.

"It's all right, Sodane," said Daen.

"Brother, it's not all right!" He reached for his sword hilt. Daen moved towards Sodane, pushing his brother's blade back in the scabbard. Daen looked around and then leaned close to Sodane, whispering to him. Zodak searched Sodane's eyes, watching for reaction. The whispering lasted many moments.

Sodane finally pulled away. "No! Are you sure?"

"Yes, brother. You know I would never bring an outsider here, otherwise."

Sodane nodded slowly and then looked at the ground. "I'm sorry to doubt you, Daen. But you risk much. Ozir could have you expelled for bringing him here. Or worse."

"Yes, Soh, I know. It's a risk that I must take. You guard Ozir well, even if you have gotten a bit slower." He winked. "But why did I not know of your new detail?"

"Bah!" Sodane smiled, batting the air. "I arrived just yesterday. After my rotation, I had plans to find you. You've heard about—" He cut himself short, glancing at Zodak.

"Yes. I have heard about the planned... removal." Daen chose the word carefully.

"It must happen soon."

"I assumed as much. We must see Ozir immediately. I will find you after."

"Ozir's installed two skullers at the entrance," said Sodane.

Daen sighed. "That complicates things. What type?"

"Woodland," said Sodane.

"Hmm. Not as slow as the rock giants..." His voice trailed off.

"You could try the pig-in-the-pantry trick." Sodane's eyes twinkled.

Daen smirked. "It's good to see you, Soh. I hope to—I will see you after we meet Ozir." A heavy silence, brimming with unspoken peril, fell on the trio as the brothers embraced.

"Good luck, young master," said Sodane in an earnest voice that matched Daen's exactly. He patted Zodak on the back. Zodak only dipped his head.

Daen and Zodak turned up the slow incline and walked ahead to the fortress gate.

26

Before the open gate to Blackiron stood two half-giants, just as Sodane had said. Their hulking bodies matched that of the rock giant in size, but these two didn't look like stone. They resembled the monsters that Ardon had fought. Zodak swallowed hard.

Both had long, matted tangles of hair. Their heavy brows, sunken eyes, and hard features conjured images of the carved oak warding statue Hallah kept in the corner of the study. One wore a vest of animal fur, though his bare shoulders and arms had almost as much hair. He wore a silver cuff above his bicep and a fur wrap around his waist. On a chain around his neck hung the skull of some small animal. Like the rock giant, he held an enormous battle-axe, its black blade glinting cruelly. The other wore no top, only thick leather straps crossing his furry chest. Hanging around his neck, he wore what looked like a tooth as long as Zodak's forearm. He held a thick black staff with a curved blade at the tip. A small round shield was fastened to his left arm at the elbow. Both guards wore the leather forearm guard on the right.

"Wait here," said Daen to Zodak when they neared the gate.

Daen approached the guards. Zodak was now familiar with the secret greeting and display of the arm guard. As before, Daen began negotiating with the two. *Will he use the ancient riddle again?* wondered Zodak. They appeared to be solid muscle and, like the rock giant, had no necks, just corded muscle sloping from jaw to shoulder. One of those hands could probably break every bone in Zodak's body.

Daen gestured back at Zodak, and the two guards flashed hard stares. After a moment, the half-giant with the spear disappeared, and Daen gestured for Zodak to join him.

"These two would not likely fall for the riddle," whispered Daen. "But I have convinced them that you are here on privileged business. They only require a malscan and we can pass."

"A what scan?" asked Zodak.

"A malscan. It's nothing to worry about. The olerfond plant can sense the taint. Many use it to detect the presence of margoul. If you were a goblin friend or a troll, the plant would turn bright red. We're very fortunate this is all you have to do."

The guard returned, draped in foliage, hauling a shallow stone pot. He dropped the basin with a thud in front of the door. A curled stalk from the base of the plant, ending in a green shovel-shaped pod, rested on the soil. Large flat green leaves flanked the pod on either side. One of the guards grunted a command and the snake-like plant suddenly moved.

The head, if it could be called that, lifted from the pot, rising up like a charmed serpent in front of Daen. The pod-head moved forward to inspect Daen, poking in his saddlebags, and twisting around his side and back. After it had scanned Daen from head to toe, he stepped aside. The plant then nudged Zodak's foot, pressing against his left side. It rose to his head, then continued down his right side. When it reached his right shirt pocket, the plant froze. The entire plant suddenly flashed brilliant scarlet from top to bottom.

"Hungh?" grunted a guard. The plant reared back, the pod

opening like a clam shell to reveal rows of razor-sharp teeth, and let out a horrible screeching sound. Zodak's hand instinctively shot to his pocket. His fingers felt something smooth. He removed it and opened his hand. There in his palm was the yellow firebulb Gormley had given him. The plant lunged at Zodak's face, its mouth agape. Before Zodak could even lift his arm in defense, Daen's dagger lashed out, severing the ferocious pod from the plant body. It fell limply to the ground. One of the guards roared. Daen snatched the pod from Zodak and clapped a hand over Zodak's eyes just as a flash like lightning stung the air. The next thing he knew, Zodak was being shoved and carried between the two blinded guards into the fortress.

Daen pulled Zodak into a stone hallway. They raced up a winding staircase, whizzing by halls and passages leading in all directions. Higher they climbed. Shuffling footsteps sounded from above them. Daen yanked Zodak into a side passage just as five well-armed guards pounded down the stairs towards the gate where the woodland giants now rumbled for help. When the soldiers had passed, Daen pulled Zodak out of the shadows, and they continued their ascent. Below, they heard more guards running to assist. Like a disturbed wasp's nest, the fortress had come alive, scurrying and shouting in every direction.

"We must go the back way," said Daen, turning off the staircase into a cramped corridor. As they left the grand stairway, a dozen more guards thundered past in a blur of armor and weapons. Zodak couldn't make them out clearly, but not all of them were human, of that he was sure. The pounding of rushing feet echoed through the fortress. Muffled shouts and orders pierced the rumbling. Ahead, the dim passage curved to the left, where the sound of more footsteps grew louder. *We're lost!* thought Zodak, staying close to Daen. *They remove intruders first and ask questions later.* Daen's words echoed in Zodak's head.

The footsteps in the narrow passage ahead bore down on them. In the torchlight, Zodak could see approaching shadows on the cobbled floor. Daen snatched Zodak's hand, spoke a strange word, and suddenly leapt straight at the stone wall to the right, yanking Zodak with him. Zodak braced for impact, but the two passed right through the wall and plunged into a pitch-black passage on the other side. Zodak looked back. A hazy film separated them from the hallway. In an instant, men in battle gear flooded the corridor. Zodak shrank back into the darkness, but the guards passed by without pause.

"They can't see us," whispered Daen. "They see only a stone wall." When they had gone, Zodak reached out to the film barrier separating them from the passage. His hand passed right through. He could see his fingers wiggle on the other side. Zodak heard the sound of more guards and quickly pulled his hand back, but it didn't budge.

"Come, Zodak." Daen was already hurrying down the secret passage.

"Wait!" cried Zodak, pulling with all his might. It was as though his arm were frozen in a block of ice. *The guards will surely notice a hand sticking out of the wall!* The thundering footsteps and yells grew louder.

"Daen!" Zodak called again in a panic, seeing only blackness behind him. Through the film, he could see the approaching shadows just measures ahead of the warriors.

"*Foltharza*," came Daen's voice. Zodak toppled backwards. The patrolling unit passed.

"You can't just pass through the wall." Daen's eyes hinted at a smile. "You must ask the permission of the stones, of course."

"But I..." Zodak stammered.

"We have no time." Daen took Zodak's hand in his and pulled him into blackness. Daen's orb flashed to life, casting a dull blue light. The cramped corridor split dozens of times, yet Daen never faltered in choosing the route. At one point, the passage went nearly straight up, forcing Zodak to climb on his hands and knees. After curving and twisting and climbing and turning, the path ended abruptly at a flat wall. But when Daen returned the orb to his pocket, Zodak noticed a thin sliver of light slicing in from a crack running from floor to ceiling. Daen ran his searching hands across the wall.

"Ah," he said. He pulled something and a loud grinding sound bellowed through the passage. *This will give us away for sure!* thought Zodak. He had no idea how right he was.

The wall ahead of them began to move to the left. The vertical sliver of light grew as the wall slid open, revealing a magnificent, ornate room with a cavernous ceiling. Zodak squinted at the brightness and color reflected by thousands of facets of skillfully carved and polished stone. Huge iron lamps hung from the domed ceiling. Intricate carved stone figures gazed down from rock pedestals. A brilliant blue rug ran the length of the room from right to left. It ended in a massive, dark wooden table elevated on a platform.

A group sat around the table in silence, their eyes fixed on Zodak and Daen. At the center of the table sat a stocky man with dark skin that shimmered like a puddle of ink and a long silver beard. He sat on a throne-like seat, maps and metal figurines scattered before him. But alarmingly closer, surrounding the opening in the wall, stood a crowd of the most fearsome warriors Zodak had ever seen, each with a deadly blade, arrow, or spear trained on Zodak and Daen. Zodak recognized a few half-giants among them. A number were men. One of the guards, clad in dark green chain mail, had scaly green skin and a sloping head that reminded Zodak of a frog's but was so thick he made the half-giant look like a slender dancer. Three short, stocky bearded figures like the man at the table but with much fairer complexions wielded large axes, and one to the side held a crossbow. Behind the circle stood wispy men with long bows, each with razor-sharp arrows pointed at the intruders. With a loud *clunk*, the door stopped, and all was deathly quiet.

A small bald and beardless man wearing glasses and a maroon robe pushed through the right side of the semicircle. He fixed a malicious glare on Daen. "Kill them!" he screeched.

27

As soon as the word had left the little man's mouth, Zodak was knocked to the ground, pinned by Daen. A pair of arrows whizzed overhead, slamming into the stone where they had stood, splintering. The mob surged toward them.

"*Halt!*" A booming voice ripped through the room, freezing the swell of guards in their tracks. It was the dark-skinned bearded man from the table. The command echoed in the chamber followed by silence. Daen slowly stood, lifting Zodak.

"But sir!" protested the little robed man. "These are the intruders! The penalty is death."

The bearded man rose from his stately seat at the grand table. "I've no elven eyes, but this is Daen Soldiron, son of Dane, is it not?"

"He's a traitor, that's what he is. And he's brought an outsider to this place." A murmur rippled through the guards, whose weapons remained trained on Daen and Zodak. "He's blinded the guards and broken a cardinal rule!" A sneer hung on the bald man's face. "He deserves no forum."

Now the dark, stocky bearded man stepped from the raised

platform and approached the semicircle of soldiers, which parted before him, though he did not pass through. He wore a thick fur robe with no sleeves, its collar rising to frame his square head. His long beard split into three braids that hung almost to his stomach. Behind the beard, Zodak glimpsed thick chains of precious metal. He wore the band around his forearm like all in the room, but instead of leather, his was a metal that shimmered like liquid silver. The woven flower emblem in the center was onyx black. In his hand he carried a thick wood staff, laced with silver. The top of the staff knotted like the fist of an ancient tree.

"What explanation have you, Daen? Have you come to kill me? You've blinded two of my guards with a tainted firebulb and stormed the fortress with this outsider. Delmuth here speaks the truth. You have broken our laws." Leather creaked as a dozen soldiers tightened their grip on weapons.

"And so, he must die!" interjected Delmuth.

"Ozir." Daen spoke, dropping to a knee. "My loyalty to the Order is stronger now than it has ever been. I know the Code. Of course I know it. Were it not for the desperate need of your counsel, I would never have brought an outsider here. I bring news of the Color Manifest. The Protectorate." *Ozir!* Zodak's heart leapt.

"Not your witchery and prophecies again, Daen!" Delmuth spat the phrase.

Daen never took his eyes from Ozir. Zodak stared in wonderment. Ozir, a *dwarf!* he recalled from Daen's description. There were other dwarves in the crowd of soldiers as well, their stocky figures and long beards distinguishing them. *This is the man who may redeem Uth Becca,* thought Zodak, again remembering Daen's words. Though he was only a bit taller than Zodak, Ozir's air of leadership was unquestionable. He looked powerful. *Should I wave the medallion in front of him now?* Zodak wondered.

"*Al folda moors vanhols caruthil faan,*" Daen said to Ozir. Zodak recognized the sound of the strange speech now. Some of the soldiers in the crowd looked up.

"No! Stop," shouted Delmuth. "Don't listen to his bewitching words."

"Silence!" boomed Ozir.

"Sir," replied Delmuth, slightly bowing his head to Ozir.

"Search these two. Remove all weapons." Immediately, the circle of guards sprang to action. "Are we sure there are no others?" asked Ozir.

"They appear to be alone," replied Delmuth, his words dripping with disdain.

"Shackle them and take them to my quarters. I will speak with them after I am done here."

"But sir—" objected Delmuth.

Ozir raised a hand to silence the advisor. "Spoken."

"Thank you, sir," said Daen, touching his open palm to his forehead and lowering it to Ozir with a bow.

"Do not thank me yet," retorted Ozir. "This day is far from over for you. You have much to answer for."

"I advise against this course of action," blurted Delmuth.

"Your advice is noted, Delmuth. Thank you." Ozir motioned with his hand as he turned back to the long table. Three guards from the circle stepped forward, roughly searching Daen. They took Daen's bow and saddlebags, his knife and orb. Delmuth watched the search intently.

The man who searched Zodak unsheathed a long knife and slit the strings binding the fake leather band from Zodak's forearm, tossing it to the ground. He patted Zodak's pockets and chest. He took Zodak's coin purse and even the tuk map. When he felt the medallion, he pulled back Zodak's shirt, glanced at it, and moved on to inspect Zodak's collar and boots. Zodak quickly closed his shirt again. The guard seemed wholly uninterested in it. *Why is Daen so fixated on this medallion?* wondered Zodak. *How could Stohl know about it?*

The guards clamped heavy iron shackles onto their wrists and pushed them roughly out of the room. The secret passage groaned closed behind them. Ozir didn't look up from the table as they left. Delmuth escorted the prisoners down the hall, flanked by the man who had searched Zodak, a half-giant, and one of the wispy bowmen. The mammoth guard in the green mail, with legs like copner logs and scaly green skin, waddled behind, lugging a block of stone the size of a glugg barrel with an iron eyelet sticking out of the top.

"If I had my way, you'd have been expelled from the Order long ago!" hissed Delmuth to Daen. "You're not but a scheming thickbrow," he added.

"If you missed me, just say so," replied Daen with a wink. Delmuth scowled and continued down the hall. As they approached an oversized metal door covered in detailed carvings and patterns, Delmuth fished a ring of large metal keys from the pocket of his robe and quickly flipped through them. Upon finding the key, he unlocked the door and let the huge green guard enter, carrying the stone anchor.

"Careful!" snapped Delmuth. "Don't drop it this time." The guard gently lowered the immense cube of stone to the floor. Delmuth nodded at the great green soldier who waddled out of the room. The slender man took up a post outside, while the half-giant and the other guard escorted the prisoners into the softly lit room. It had a small carved wooden table tucked to the side, a half circle of chairs around it. An arched doorway led off to another room.

"Hold them here!" ordered Delmuth. The guards chained Daen and Zodak together and locked them to the massive block of stone that came to Zodak's shoulder. He doubted old Sal his mare could have even budged the boulder.

"I will do all I can to stop this meeting," said Delmuth, flashing a sickly smile at Daen.

"I believe your voice has been heard," replied Daen coolly. Delmuth let out an exasperated sigh and spun, scurrying through the door. It closed with a clang and was locked.

"Are you comfortable, sir?" the guard asked Daen.

"Yes, thank you, Kahn."

"You know I would remove these chains if I could," Kahn offered, glancing at the half-giant.

"Thank you. I know you would, and I appreciate your loyalty."

"When Ozir figures all of this out, perhaps he'll finally throw Delmuth topside," offered Kahn.

"Delmuth serves in the way he knows how," replied Daen. "He does what he believes will help the Order."

"But he's always hated you. He would have killed you in there."

"And he would have been right to do so. What would you do with an intruder in the battle room?"

"But it's *you*. You've trained half the men in that room. And if you were really coming to kill Ozir, is this the army you would bring?" He gestured at Zodak.

Daen chuckled. "Well, you, of all people, should know not to underestimate those smaller than we," he winked.

"True, true." Kahn's voice trailed off.

"Kahn, I do have a favor to ask of you."

"Of course. Anything for you." He put his hand to his chest. "Anything I can," he added.

"I need to have a conversation with this boy before Ozir arrives. There are things I will say that would be better for you not to hear."

"Say no more. We cannot leave the room, but we can move." He barked an order, and he and the half-giant crossed the room to the door and took up positions facing the prisoners.

"Thank you, Kahn."

"I'm sorry I cannot do more."

"Zodak." Daen spoke in a hushed voice. "It is time I tell you about your medallion."

28

"I thought Ozir was to tell me about the medallion," said Zodak.

The chains that bound Daen clinked as he crouched. He spoke quickly, but softly, the soft torchlight casting shadows on his angular face. "He will. But there is a bit of history I can share," he said.

"I'm quite good at history," said Zodak, remembering the long hours in the school closet.

"Good. Try to follow along." Zodak nodded. "Have you heard of the Descendants?"

"Yes. The eleven fabled kings and queens said to have some of the original Power. It was said they transformed from earthly bodies into brilliant colors, so rich they blinded the eyes." Zodak beamed. He had heard the recitation from Ms. Folba many times. "The Keepers of Color."

"Exactly," said Daen. "The Sovereign Age, just before the Age of Governance, or so the legend goes. *The Song of the Keepers* says never was a goblin or gorgol seen while the Color controlled the Midlands. But when they retreated to the Heights, the evil forces sought to regain a foothold in the land.

Centuries later, as the tide of evil slowly grew, they say the first Shielders appeared—"

"Wait," interrupted Zodak. "I've heard that name." His mind spun. "It's what those moths called Ardon that night."

"Yes, well, they say there were twenty-two Shielders once, defenders of Yiduiijn, who were charged with keeping evil powers in check—flesh and blood, born of Yiduiijn soil, taken from among the core races. It's said that they each carried a strand of the Power from the Descendants, passed down from generation to generation."

Zodak struggled to grasp the meaning behind Daen's words, trying to connect them to his reality.

"*The Song of Keepers* says that to each of the Shielders, the Descendants bestowed a medallion, symbolizing their unity and purpose."

"A medallion? Do you mean—"

Daen put a hand on the boy's shoulder. "I will answer what I can, but you must hear all of this," he replied.

Zodak now lifted his medallion, examining it anew.

Daen continued. "They say the Shielders didn't—couldn't stop the return of the margoul to the Midlands, but when the balance began to tip toward darkness, they were there. Valiant soldiers still died, and villages still fell, mind you, but over the spans, the Shielders continually upset the plans of the dark forces: intercepting assassination plots, vanquishing fell beasts, and foiling invasions or coups. It was the fate of Yiduiijn they protected.

"If they accomplished their tasks, there was no news—no attack, no assassination, no overthrow. Many thought the Shielders were invincible. But this wasn't so. At the advent of the Second Span, the Monks record the death of the first Shielder to enemy hands and his medallion was stolen. Solgon was the twentieth heir to his line of the Shielder medallion. His death shook the foundations of Yiduiijn. The dark forces had gained an enormous victory, proving that Yiduiijn's defenders were mortal after all. Apparently, during the ghastly margoul celebration, the chief orc (so report the Buruth Monks, keepers of knowledge) ceremoniously placed the medallion over his own neck, hoping to feel the power coursing through his veins."

"What happened to him?"

"He transformed, so the legend goes, into a bizarre mongrel Shielder. He turned on the evil revelers about him, destroying hundreds of the dark host at the gathering that night before they managed to kill him. From then on, the margoul sought to destroy the medallions whenever they could. But the Monks warned that a more powerful margoul could use a medallion to great and terrible effect.

"During the Age of Establishment, the Shielders' numbers were whittled down to ten, then five, then three, and finally two. In the early part of the reign of the Judges, a few hundred seasons ago, a dwarven Shielder, Kozan, was killed. The last standing Shielder, a young elemental human named Hàmer Prax, vanished from the eye of the Order.

"No longer did the Shielder lead great battles or travel across the plains to slay huge monsters. He remained hidden as a shadow until a threat so critical arose that failure to intercede could topple the balance of Yiduiijn itself."

"So, what happened to Hàmer?" exclaimed Zodak.

Daen held a finger to his lips, glancing at the guards. He continued in a low voice. "According to the *Song of Heroes*, it was the Fall of the Burning Grass over two hundred seasons past. The spread of darkness birthed a mighty foe: Helgruz the Fell, a champion of the dark, part gorgol, part orc, part half-giant: a spawn of the Wyther Downs who gathered a massive army of margoul, beasts, and tainted Midlanders like none before it. Villages and cities fell to him like paper dolls to a forest blaze. A mutant, Helgruz towered above men and slew hardened warriors like skupp." Zodak leaned forward, enraptured. "Helgruz searched tirelessly for the medallion and for Hàmer. The Order feared that if he found it, he might be strong enough to finally wield the powerful weapon against the Color.

"The tapestry vault holds the record, a woven picture of the sea of margoul that Helgruz led to the valley around the Castle K'andoria, seeking to destroy the last great stronghold of the Midlands. The *Tome of the Fathers* recalls how Helgruz stood outside the gate and bellowed his challenge to King Kaenor, as he'd done so many times before. This time, though, his challenge was answered. Not from within the walls of the kingdom, but from high on a bluff overlooking the valley, a hunched robed figure answered with a cry of defiance."

"Hàmer?" guessed Zodak.

"Yes. An old man of no less than eighty seasons. As the tale goes, Helgruz roared in laughter but bounded up to the bluff to blot out the thorn of a man and capture the legendary prize that hung around his neck. Those expecting a swift and merciless execution were woefully mistaken. In the view of his legions and in the shadow of the great Castle K'andoria, the two clashed. The old man met Helgruz blow for blow. Fire flashed from Hàmer's blade and shield at each parry until the bluff was engulfed in flames and smoke. When the flurry ceased, a rush of wind cleared the smoke to reveal Helgruz standing stock still, alone on the bluff. His dark army cheered until his head toppled from his body and bounced down the rocky cliff. His body crumbled to dust and blew to the wind."

"What happened to Hàmer?" Zodak asked.

"Nobody knew. With his disappearance, so began the Shielder silence. And to this day, a hundred seasons hence, there is no further record of Hàmer or the Shielders. Most feared the final Shielder had fallen with Helgruz, his body and medallion ransacked by fleeing margoul and destroyed."

"But it wasn't…" mused Zodak, holding the medallion up again. His stomach fluttered. *Was it possible?*

"It was thought the line of Shielders was severed that day—that the last of those mighty warriors, inspired by the medallion and tied to the Color, would protect us no longer. Great scholars have debated what would happen without the balance brought by the Shielders. Perhaps nothing. Perhaps someone else could have destroyed Helgruz that day, but perhaps not. If the schemes of evil were allowed to flourish unchecked, it could plunge Yiduiijn into an era of darkness unlike any we have ever known." Daen took a deep breath, signaling an end to the lesson.

"So, what are you saying?" asked Zodak. "Ardon was related to Hàmer Prax?"

"Zodak, I believe Ardon may have been the last Shielder, and what you hold in your hand is the last known Shielder medallion."

"*What?!*"

"Yes. He carried the relic. Perhaps he was the last descendant of Hàmer. You see, Hàmer's line vanished from view, but hope remained that the line continued intact."

"But Ardon was just a… a…" Zodak stammered.

"A simple man?" asked Daen.

"Yes. He worked in the krius mines, and before that was a farmer. He was no protector of Yiduiijn."

"I know that's how you saw him, but here you stand, before me now, with the medallion. The last medallion. And you said he fought like a lion and destroyed an entire gang of mercenaries with nothing but an axe handle? And two half-giants? After being stabbed?" Daen put his hand on Zodak's shoulder. Zodak felt tingly and lightheaded. "Now Zodak, I know what happened to Ardon is very painful for you, but I must ask you a few questions about it. Is that all right?"

"Okay," replied Zodak dumbly, still reeling from the story.

"Did you see Ardon die, Zodak? You said he was stabbed, but did you actually see him die?"

The cruel question hung in the air. After a long pause, Zodak answered. "I... I think so." The memory pained him. But now there was something else, a tiny prick of hope. *If Ardon was the Shielder, maybe he didn't die. Maybe he arose and destroyed those evil men when I left,* hoped Zodak. *But no, the child stealers were alive and searching for me the next day. And if Ardon didn't survive...*

"If Ardon is dead"—the phrase still stung—"what does that mean about the Shielder?"

"That's why we're here. It's why I risked bringing you into this place. I'm no scholar," answered Daen, "but I believe the line of the Shielder has always passed with the medallion. Surely you have felt the power of the medallion."

The power of the medallion? Zodak's mind swirled and spun through memories. The way he fought the goblins with the sickle when the tuk caravan was attacked; how he snapped and flipped up to his feet when Quar had awoken him that morning; the knockout punch he delivered to the thug in the streets; how he caught those boxes in the dry goods store. His body, his reflexes, his strength, his instincts. He had known without knowing. He had been changed. The medallion had changed him.

"Zodak." Daen put a hand on each of Zodak's shoulders. "I believe you are the last Shielder."

29

The statement tore through Zodak like the shock from leaping in a cold mountain pool. And while the words were foreign and ridiculous, something resonated deep inside. The empty hollow he had been searching to fill suddenly felt complete. He searched for objections, for doubt, if only to ground the incredible statement in truth. *Could it be?* The sprite. Ms. Folba. The Elder. The pieces suddenly snapped together in his mind. It was so outrageous, yet it explained so much. *I know why I am here! Why I'm alive!* He let himself cradle those words, and as he did, he swelled until he thought he might burst. He felt as if he grew a full measure in height in that moment.

The bolt of the door clunked and the guards from the hallway entered, followed by Ozir and Delmuth.

As Ozir stepped into the room, Daen and the two guards instantly stood at attention, pounded their left breasts with their right fists and dragged the fists across their chests while nodding to Ozir. In his daze, Zodak didn't think to stand.

"Even now, held fast by chains, you salute me, Daen, son of Dane?" said Ozir. The stocky dwarf moved with grace. Bright hazel eyes shone under a heavy brow, set against ebony skin. His long, braided mustache flowed into his beard with jewelry woven throughout that glittered like stars against a desert night.

"To the death," responded Daen automatically.

"It may be an act, sir," chirped Delmuth.

"Daen, this is a grave matter." Ozir's voice was stern. "You've broken many sacred rules today. You put your life and this boy's life in grave danger. What if the guards' arrows had found their mark? Also, most of the men in there knew nothing of that secret passage. It was reckless and foolish. I hope you are able to explain—"

"I come with news of the last Shielder," Daen cut in.

One of the guards gasped in surprise.

"Impossible!" snapped Delmuth. "The Shielder line is cut! How can he say that?" demanded Delmuth with scorn. "Sir," Delmuth quickly added.

Ozir stood silently, absorbing all focus in the room, his eyes locked on Daen as though he probed the skypiercer's very heart for truth. Delmuth's desperate glance from Ozir to Daen and back again, hungrily awaiting a response. Ozir's gaze swept down to Zodak.

"Who is the boy?" Ozir finally asked.

"An outsider," shot Delmuth.

"Selvior holshas madruidon," Daen said.

"He's doing it again!" exclaimed Delmuth. "He'll trick you with those slippery words."

"Just because you do not understand the old tongue, do not diminish its value," scolded Ozir.

Delmuth sank low in his robe, his cheeks and forehead turning red.

"Unchain these two," ordered Ozir. The two closest guards sprang to respond.

"Sir! You mustn't!" protested Delmuth.

"Spoken." Ozir shot Delmuth a stern look. "I will speak to you in my chambers," said Ozir to Daen. "Alone." Ozir swept through the room and into the next, trailed by a volley of objections from Delmuth. Kahn eagerly complied, fighting back a smile. Daen followed Ozir into the inner room.

The minutes passed like hours for Zodak in the main chamber under the searing glare of Delmuth. Finally, Ozir reappeared and ordered Zodak brought in. Delmuth squealed, but the guards complied, leading Zodak into the small, comfortable sleeping chamber. A carved wood bed rested in one corner, and a small desk in another. Two large chairs sat on opposite sides of a wooden chest. Ozir pulled the chest from the center of the circle. "You will have to sit here, lad."

"This is Zodak," said Daen. "Zodak, the Kommandor of the Order, Ozir of the Sokel Citadel."

"Zodak..." Ozir nodded his head. "I'm sorry about the circumstances, but as a strict rule, outsiders are never allowed in this place. In fact"—Ozir looked at Daen—"I believe you are the *first* outsider ever to break in here by force. And your friend Daen here has a fantastic theory about why you're here. Unless, of course, my judgment of character has failed me, and you are indeed here for my life."

Daen flashed a hint of his winsome smile. Earning no response from Ozir, his expression hardened again. "Ozir, this boy was raised by the last Shielder," Daen stated flatly. "He saw him die and now the boy carries the medallion. I believe him to be the Heir." Zodak winced, waiting for Ozir's outburst.

"So you say," Ozir replied coolly, taking a measured step toward Zodak and studying the boy. An hour earlier, this situation would have been utterly preposterous. But something had changed. He could feel it. Deep inside there flowed a new spring. He stood tall before this powerful man whose searching face betrayed not a hint of incredulity.

"Show him, Zodak," said Daen.

Zodak obediently removed the medallion from around his neck, causing it to flash brightly, and handed it over. Ozir cradled the disc as if he held a spider's web. He ran a stubby finger over every line and curve etched in the metal and mumbled a few words, reading the worn script etched into the medallion. Over and over, he turned it, and then he closed his eyes, holding the medallion in both hands. He remained like this for many minutes. Finally, Ozir opened his eyes. He looked around as if he had suddenly awoken in a new place.

"Delmuth!" he called. The door flung open and Delmuth leapt in, followed by two guards.

"Yes, sir!" he said, searching the room for danger.

"Please bring us glugg—and one falswine," he said, glancing at Zodak, "and some food. We will be here for a while."

"I... but..." Delmuth stammered. "The Council—"

"Thank you," said Ozir.

Delmuth backed out of the room.

"Now, Zodak." Ozir turned again to face him when Delmuth had gone. He carefully placed the medallion back in Zodak's eager hands. A ripple of relief passed through him as he cradled the familiar form of the disc. "I need to know all there is to know about you. Tell me everything, including when and how you came upon this relic."

"Yes, sir," he replied. *Where do I start?* wondered Zodak. "I received this medallion from my uncle Ardon in the clearing just outside—"

"Earlier," broke in Ozir, waving a hand.

"Pardon me?" Zodak glanced at Daen.

"Start earlier. Where are you from? Where did you grow up? Where are your parents? Please, no detail is too much."

Zodak took a breath and began again with his earliest memories on the farm in Laan with Ardon and Hallah and Ergis and Alana. He recounted the stories he was told as a child. How his father, also a farmer, had suffered from a bad heart and when he died how his uncle Ardon pledged to raise him. Zodak poured out every detail of his simple and sad story that he thought might be helpful. He tried skipping past his childhood with Alana and Ergis, but Ozir pressed him about his cousins.

Delmuth returned with a servant carting a platter of roasted game birds, cheeses, breads, fruit, and drink. Zodak's mouth watered, and his stomach rumbled at the smell. How long had it been since he had eaten? Delmuth lingered, fussing over the food. His roving eyes landed on the medallion, and he let out a shriek.

"Not a word," cautioned Ozir, with a nod of dismissal. Delmuth staggered from the room.

"Please, continue," said Ozir.

Zodak continued talking, breaking only for a bite of food or to answer an interjection by Ozir. He spoke of the water sprite and of Ms. Folba.

"You never mentioned this water sprite," Daen cut in when Zodak had described the visit by the creature.

"I've told almost no one," replied Zodak, snatching another handful of pepper fruit. When he looked up, he caught the glance between Daen and Ozir.

"Please, go on," urged Ozir.

After nearly an hour, when he told of his journey from Laan and the death of Ardon, he faltered, stopping to wipe tears that now came unbidden. Daen rested a large hand on Zodak's back until the boy had composed himself. Ozir listened keenly to how Zodak received the medallion. At least three times, he asked Zodak to repeat what happened in his final moments with Ardon. Each telling stabbed like a knife, but Zodak complied.

"How could they have known about the medallion?" asked Daen.

"Müziel," said Ozir simply. "He somehow found it before we did."

"We're fortunate his plan didn't succeed," said Daen.

"Fortunate?" Ozir snorted. "We'd not be sitting here if Müziel had recovered that medallion."

"Who is Müziel?" asked Zodak.

"He's an ambassador of evil, said to be a direct pawn of the Ice King," answered Ozir. "But I'm sorry, we diverge. Please continue. What happened after Ardon fought Griss and his men?"

Zodak told of how he fled in the night. He shared about the tuk family, and when Zodak ate the last bite of bread, and swallowed the final sip of falswine, his story had carried him to the gates of Uth Becca. Daen listened closely too, hearing much of the tale for the first time.

"Old Olaf!" snorted Ozir when Zodak recounted finding the Golden Oak. Ozir and Daen both leaned in attentively when Zodak described his encounter with Voli. He told how he had gotten lost in the slums and about the gang of boys. He explained how Gormley had rescued him and taken him to the Fahyz Gate.

"Ah, the firebulb," said Ozir.

"That's where it came from..." muttered Daen. Zodak described his first encounter with Daen.

"So, this Gormley snatched the medallion, hoping only to make a quick profit?" asked Ozir. "Amazing. And very fortunate that you were there." He looked at Daen.

"He would have soon learned what he had stolen..." Daen's voice trailed off as he chased the thought through his mind. "Our search had grown stale by generations. Who could have expected this? Here and now, in the hands of this boy?"

"Quite so, quite so," said Ozir. "But the timing is no mistake," he added.

"After centuries of searching, the filth had the prize in hand

and let it slip through their grasp," Daen said with mischievous delight.

"We can only hope it remains hidden." Ozir spoke to no one in particular. The room grew quiet.

"They saw it," blurted Zodak. Daen snapped his head around. "One of the guards at the gate," Zodak said meekly, his hands fidgeting. "I think he spotted it."

"And recognized it?" asked Daen.

Zodak nodded.

Ozir closed his eyes and tapped a clenched forefinger against his forehead. "So, we must assume Kuquo knows it's in the city and with us," he said, opening his eyes again and returning his studying gaze to the medallion. After a moment, he stood and walked to Zodak, still perched on the wooden chest. Ozir took Zodak's chin in his stout palm and inspected his face. He stared deeply into Zodak's eyes.

"It's amazing!" Daen's excited voice came from behind Ozir. "The Heir here at Blackiron. After how many dozens of seasons? How long ago had the Order given up finding him?"

Zodak felt the swelling within him again. Partly pride, but something greater: purpose. Worth. He had begun putting the pieces together even as he spoke. *It's all true. The medallion marks the Shielder.* The sprite's words pounded like a whitewater chorus in his mind: *"Your call has come. You are needed."* There was *purpose. I am the Shielder.* He finally let himself form the words in his mind. He marveled at the thought, looking down at his hands and forearms and, for the first time, letting his mind run with the fantasy spoken to life.

Ozir spoke again. "I would have thought it impossible, but this boy's father was the last true Shielder."

30

Zodak repeated Ozir's words in his mind: *This boy's father was the last true Shielder.* Suddenly he felt he was no longer in his body but watching the scene in Ozir's sleeping chambers as a detached observer.

"He has the look of his father," said Ozir to Daen. He took a draw from his goblet.

"The farmer?" asked Daen, confused.

"*Ha!*" snorted Ozir, spewing a fine mist of glugg into the air. Zodak and Daen both jumped. Ozir's smile vanished as quickly as it had come. "He was no farmer!" he roared. "And that a farmer is all he knows of his father burns me!" Ozir slammed a thick fist onto the table, shaking dishes. Silence flooded the room. *Did this dwarf know my father?* Zodak wondered, confused.

"So Zodak's father was the Shielder... not a farmer," Daen said, trying to follow the thread.

"Yes," Ozir answered calmly. "Zaid, Zodak's father, was the most ferocious defender of the Midlands any of us had ever known. He alone thwarted scores of enemy plots, any one of which could have swallowed us all. His noble deeds should be sung about, yet they lay untold and locked away in the Color Ambit, where the deeds of all Shielders must." Ozir gazed off, following unspoken layers of memory. Zodak couldn't stand it. He had desperately longed to know his place, and only moments after the dim picture had begun to take shape, it dissolved again into a swirl of questions.

"But..." Daen frowned. "Hàmer was the last."

"I was but a squire, but I recall overhearing how the Council urged Zaid to use caution," Ozir continued, his voice now softer, "to follow the clandestine ways of the lone Shielder, of his father, and his grandfather, all the way back to Hàmer."

Hàmer Prax was my great-great-great grandfather?! mused Zodak.

"Secrecy was his best weapon. The Council asked him to do the one thing that could ensure his survival: to become invisible. It's how the Shielder had survived undiscovered for so many seasons. But Zaid diverged. He rejected tact and subtlety, refusing to choose among the 'errands,' as his missions were called. In so choosing, he insisted, he was passing judgment on the victims of the errands refused. I am yet marked by his words: *'That may be the cautious path,'* he told me when I first took the Kommandor seat, *'but it's a path I'll leave buried in the graves of my ancestors.'* Zaid answered every call, great or small, regardless of the risk. The Order believed him dead on many occasions, yet he returned, again and again." Zodak listened, spellbound.

"Why have I never heard these stories?" asked Daen with a hint of offense.

"I'm sure you have. But not from me. I swore a blood secret as a squire and again as Kommandor. A very select few knew anything about Zaid. It was all we could do to hope to protect him. Does the name 'Fire Walker' sound familiar?"

"No!" Daen drew back, his eyes wide. "Fire Walker *existed*? I thought him a margoul myth."

"Who is Fire Walker?" asked Zodak. Ozir nodded an invitation to Daen. Zodak shifted on the wooden chest.

"When I first heard the name," answered Daen. "We had captured a clap of halfies on the Thurrk Fault, hoping to extract information, but they broke down into fits of terror, babbling about some horrific being called Fire Walker. They said he drank fire and destroyed with a touch. His name set the halfies into hysteria. It happened again a harvest moon after with a pair of crickets, and on dozens more occasions besides. We began using threats of the Fire Walker to scare information from margoul. But you're saying it was no myth?" Daen trailed off.

"No," said Ozir. "It was Zaid." Ozir snatched up a leg of the roasted game bird and sucked the meat off.

"Where is Zaid now?" asked Daen. "I've heard the name Fire Walker as recently as last season," he added. Zodak's heart leapt. *Last season? Could it be?*

"The power of legend," mused Ozir. "Zaid's weakness, if you could call it that, came in the form of a provincial girl in the tiny town of Tusco: Niah. When she had their first baby, a boy, Zaid left for thirteen seasons, as all Shielders do, to protect the Heir. But the baby did something the Order never could: it tamed the wild bear within Zaid. To the relief of the Order, he began to be more cautious in his errands. He continued to serve Yiduiijn, but no longer would he march brazenly into the gaping mouth of death. After thirteen long seasons, he returned to Tusco to raise the Heir. He trained his son Zaiden in the ways of the Shielder for three seasons."

"I have no brother," interrupted Zodak.

Ozir just shook his head. "No, you don't. But you *had* a brother, Zodak. An older brother. A courageous boy, too." Zodak opened his mouth, but nothing came out. "Yes," Ozir continued, "Zaid remained in Tusco, training Zaiden for two seasons more, hidden from the rest of the world. Or so he thought. But somehow, the news of his location reached the Wyther Downs. The margoul must have spent many seasons assembling that army.

"We felt tremors in the Shadow Ambit, but when we received reports of a thick swarm of evil warriors flooding the Tambord Valley, closing in on Tusco, it was too late. A small contingent of Order Guard flew with all haste, but upon reaching Tusco, we found only the ghost of a battle."

"Yes," said Daen. "I recall the excursion. Many of us stayed behind."

Ozir nodded. "Acres of fields lay scorched and trampled. At the epicenter of immense mounds of sand and scattered stone carcasses of margoul, we found Zaid's home utterly decimated. Among the charred remains lay the broken bodies of the Shielder, the Heir, and Niah…and an empty cradle." Ozir paused reverently. Zodak's mouth hung open. "We didn't dare imagine what those hideous margoul could have done with the baby, and we never found the medallion. We concluded that the evil host had taken it and destroyed the thing, once and for all. I still recall administering chiproot tea to calm the rattled villagers' nerves (and to ensure they woke the next day with no memory of the event)."

"So, how…" began Daen, echoing Zodak's question.

"My answer would only be speculation," replied Ozir. "Though there was one odd account. An old blind woman of all people, sworn off as crazy by the other villagers, said she saw – saw mind you – a figure as tall as a mountain stride into the village through the sea of margoul and scoop something up. This I do know: your new home was well chosen. You and the medallion have been kept hidden from the evil all your life."

"Until they discovered it again," said Daen.

"Yes. From the shreds of reports from the scouts as recently as this mooncycle, we know Müziel has been pursing some prize to the Mead, but we didn't know what."

"The medallion..." mused Daen. "So Zodak must be the Heir!" he insisted. "He's the son of the last true Shielder. He carries the medallion!"

"Yes, I can see how it would appear so," replied Ozir thoughtfully.

Daen jumped up. "Sir, we must alert the Council. We should arrange the swearing ceremony to anoint the Heir. Shall I fetch Morjn and the Council?" He took a step toward the door.

"Patience." Ozir's voice cut like a hot knife.

"Oh. Of course, sire," said Daen. "You should tell them. I'm sorry. I forget myself. I will alert Kahn that—"

"It was Zaiden who was the designated Heir and would have been Shielder if he had continued in his training and reached the age of acceptance for the Transition," Ozir continued. Daen slowly sat. "If he had chosen the Shielder Path, the medallion would have been passed to him according to the ancient laws. But this was not the case." Ozir stared at the ground, shaking his head, deep in thought.

"Delmuth!" he suddenly bellowed, causing Zodak to start.

The little suspicious man rushed into the room on cue. "Yes, sire!"

"Delmuth, please bring the Scroll of the Descendants and the Lineage."

"Bring it here?" asked Delmuth, eyeing Zodak and Daen.

"Spoken."

"Very well, sir," answered Delmuth reluctantly. The nascent hope and pride within Zodak now churned into a swirl of confusion. Delmuth returned, carrying a hefty leather tube. He carefully removed the formed leather cap and withdrew a yellowed scroll.

"To the lineage of the Shielders, if you would," instructed Ozir. Delmuth deftly spun through the ancient document, coiling the top of the scroll with one practiced hand as he unfurled the bottom. After a few moments of frenetic spinning, he exclaimed, "Aha!" as his hands stopped.

"Please, Delmuth, read about the generational passing of the Shielder mantle," asked Ozir.

"Read the ancient text? In this company?" objected Delmuth, looking over the top of his spectacles.

"Please," answered Ozir. "It's all right, Delmuth," he added.

Reluctantly, the advisor began. "Lines and Lineage of Shielders," he announced. "The power, title, and responsibility of Shielder shall become that of the Shielder's heir. As flows lineage, so follows the mantle of Shielder. The firstborn male (or if the Shielder has no male heir, firstborn female) shall carry the mark of the Shielder. It shall be the duty of the Shielder to train the Heir in the Path. When thirteen seasons have passed in the life of the Heir, the age of eligibility, the Heir shall undergo the Testing—there is a reference here to the testing protocol in a footnote," added Delmuth. "Once the Heir has passed the Testing, he or she must willingly take the Oath to choose the Shielder Path. An unwilling Heir may, by ceremony, refuse the Path, but only if there is another offspring of the Shielder. An Heir who has taken the Oath will, at the age of twenty-two seasons, undergo the Transition and be entrusted with the medallion and named the Shielder. There is another footnote here about alternate succession," Delmuth mentioned dismissively.

"Please, read that one," requested Ozir.

"Very well," Delmuth replied. "Notation on Succession: In the event of the death of a Shielder devoid of offspring, or the death of the Shielder whose Heir has not reached the age of eligibility, instead of succession of the Shielder mantle to such untested Heir or other untested alternate heir, the Shielder mantle and medallion shall, if available, pass laterally to a blood sibling of the deceased Shielder. Such recipient shall not be a declared Shielder, but rather a Steward of the mantle and medallion until the offspring of such Steward reaches the age of eligibility, passes the Testing, and takes the Oath, restoring the lineage. If the Shielder and/or the Shielder's sole Heir(s) should die with no further heir or offspring and no sibling for lateral transition, the line of the Shielder is cut, and its protection ceases. End notation," declared Delmuth.

"Thank you, Delmuth. Very instructive," said Ozir.

"It was?" asked Zodak.

Delmuth bowed, stealing a look at Daen.

"If you could give us a moment," requested Ozir. Delmuth returned the scroll to the leather case and left the inner chamber.

"So, with the death of Fire Walker—of Zaid and Zaiden," said Daen, "the Shielder mantle would have transitioned."

"Correct. The mantle would have passed to Zaid's only brother," added Ozir.

"Ardon?" asked Zodak. "So he *was* the Shielder." Scraps of the battle with Griss and the giants flashed back into Zodak's mind. Ardon *had* decimated those thugs and slain the half-giants.

"The Shielder Steward," corrected Ozir. "He received power from the medallion as all do—power he seldom used, from what I can tell. But he was not the true Shielder. I expect you have felt the power of the medallion as well once your body accepted it." Zodak only nodded.

"The Shielder mantle is in flux until the rites can be properly performed for the true Heir. The offspring of the Steward." Even as Ozir spoke it, Zodak felt the dread creeping over him.

"The *true* Heir? The offspring of the Steward..." he managed. "You mean..." He couldn't bring himself to speak the words.

"Yes, Zodak," Ozir replied. "The true Heir. Ardon's blood son, Ergis." The words stabbed like hot metal. Zodak felt like he had been strapped to a boulder and plunged into a deep lake, helplessly watching Ozir and Daen recede up on the surface as the weight dragged him into the depths.

"Color abounds!" Daen exclaimed. "We *have* found him!" He was exuberant again, even as Zodak sank. "We must secure the Heir right away." Ozir nodded in agreement. "Zodak, you can help us locate the Heir?" Daen was rising to his feet again. "If Müziel realizes what has happened, he could return to destroy the Heir. We must mount a troop and ride to Laan."

Zodak had once considered the return to a life in Laan without Ardon to be the worst fate imaginable, but now he knew one worse: riding back to Laan to anoint Ergis the defender of Yiduiijn.

"Yes, agreed," said Ozir. "Fortune has shone on us." Even Ozir's stately demeanor had brightened, and his eyes sparked. "We have secured the medallion and located the Heir. There is hope for the resistance yet. We must inform the Council immediately."

Ozir and Daen rose, still talking excitedly. Their voices seemed quiet and far away from the lake bottom where Zodak now lay, hoping the depths would just swallow him once and for all. Mere moments before, he had dreamt the impossible. He had torn down the curtain of fear to imagine the unimaginable. *You, the Shielder?* he scoffed. *As savior of Yiduiijn? Fool!* he scolded himself. *How dare you? Such fanciful nonsense! You're a stableboy. Nothing more.* The accusations assailed him. Daen's muted voice broke through the swirl of thoughts.

"Zodak?" Daen bent low before him and put a large hand on his shoulder. "I know this is a lot for you, but you must believe it is very good news. The Order had thought the medallion lost and the Shielder line cut."

"We must go to the Council." Ozir's voice was urgent, and in it, an unspoken request.

Daen nodded to Ozir and turned back to Zodak. "We will need the medallion," Daen said apologetically.

The pit in Zodak's stomach opened even wider, and the heaviness engulfed him. Sadness, anger, and regret slowly gave way to deadness, defeat and utter resignation. *Of course they need it.* Zodak nodded mindlessly and removed the cord. He almost savored the familiar tug of metal on flesh and the bright flash of removing the medallion one last time. With trembling hands, he handed over the treasure. Delmuth snatched the only remaining piece of Ardon, quickly wrapped the medallion in an oiled cloth, and hurried from the room.

"Kahn will show you to your quarters," called Daen over his shoulder as he and Ozir hurried to the exit. And then they were gone.

31

Delmuth cried in protest when Ozir invited Daen to return to the Great Hall to meet the Order Council for the strategy summit just before midnight.

"I urgently recommend the summit remain closed, sire," Delmuth insisted breathlessly as he scurried down the hallway, trying to keep up with Ozir and Daen. "We must continue to exercise the utmost care in security with Council affairs."

"Daen once sat at this table." Ozir replied curtly. "How many times has his keen foresight and battle intuition benefited us in the past?" "It would be to our folly to exclude him while he's within our walls."

"But my lord—"

"Besides, his information about finding the medallion and the Heir must be heard."

Delmuth finally gave up the chase. He stooped slightly, steadying himself on the hallway wall and shaking his head as he panted. Then, in the sight of no one but his pride, he drew himself up, dramatically whirled about, and tromped away.

"Glad to see he hasn't changed," said Daen.

"Delmuth means well," said Ozir. Daen nodded. *So many of the difficult ones do,* he thought.

As he walked down the corridor, Daen fought the urge to run an outstretched hand over the rough rock walls. How many seasons had it been since he'd been truly welcome here? Much had changed, but much had not. He had felt free during the long months since he had last set foot in Blackiron, yes, but restless, aimless, if he were honest. The Order had called on him periodically, requesting the occasional dignitary's escort or mediation of a livestock dispute, and he was happy to take these scraps tossed from the Order's table, but it paled in comparison to the camaraderie and thrill of addressing the Order Council, to leading men into battle.

Tonight, Blackiron felt truly electric. The Heir, the medallion; this was a monumental development. Excitement surged through him at the thought of delivering such news to the Order Council. Once again, he would have the floor. Once again, he would report a triumph at that weathered old broam wood table that had heard so much history. If he led the party to Laan to recover the Heir, perhaps Ozir could find a place for him in the Order Guard. Perhaps he could once again be swept into the current of destiny that ran through these halls.

"I am sorry about the boy," said Ozir without looking up, giving words to the small nagging voice in Daen's head. Even in his wandering into the grand possibilities of his own future, that quiet pinprick in his conscience remained. *You left a crushed and broken boy back there,* the voice reminded him. Just hours ago, Daen had felt overcome with the divine orchestration of events that entwined Zodak and him. He had marveled at how the Color had brought them together in the cantina.

Against logic, Daen had shaped a fantasized reality in his mind, so different from the one he walked just the week before, a reality where he trained the boy, tutored him, sculpted him into the Shielder. There was still hope for that future with the true Heir, this Ergis. *There had been an unmistakable bond though, hadn't there? Yet here you stand on all too familiar ground. Turning your back on the people you love and plunging ahead into the bright, cold headwind of duty and destiny.* How quickly he had loosed the dream of shepherding Zodak, the dream of raising the son he couldn't have. *The son you chose not to have,* the voice reminded him. *You left that world behind. You left her.*

"His future was dashed tonight," said Daen finally. "I think he had started to believe he was the Heir. I know I had." Daen shook his head. Ozir slowed and turned to Daen, meeting his gaze with a stern and concerned face.

"What is it?" Now it was Daen who searched Ozir's face. It was pained. Daen recognized that look. His stomach turned. "No..." he stammered, refusing to face the twisted thought. "You couldn't be... you can't."

"The Council will demand it," said Ozir, his voice taking a hardened tone. "He's an outsider. He knows far too many of our secrets."

"He's but a boy. I brought him here! For the sake of the Order." An icy cold stabbed through Daen, turning hot and frantic. "He brought us the medallion! And you'll crush him like a storehouse skupp? For bram's sake!"

"Mind your tone, Skypiercer!" Ozir snapped back. "Yes, *you* brought him here," Ozir hissed. "It was *you* who broke your sacred vows. *You* who put the boy in harm's way!"

Daen dropped his head, pinching his eyes shut. "Forgive me, my lord. The moment took me." He placed a hand on Ozir's forearm. "Please, my liege. He had the medallion. I thought him the Heir. You know I act only for the Order."

Ozir breathed deeply. "You act in haste. And you were wrong. He is no heir. He is nothing."

"He has Hàmer's blood running through his veins!" protested Daen.

"The line has been broken," quipped Ozir. "He might as well be heir to a farmer."

"You must not kill that boy," Daen said simply, his voice soft but firm.

Ozir shook his head, looking away. "And what would you have the Council do with an intruding Topsider?"

"Join him to the Order as a squire. Have him take the pledge."

"You know the Code, how admission works." Ozir's tone was exasperated.

"The Council can surely make an exception," pleaded Daen.

"The Council is a rock that has stood for hundreds of seasons by *not* making exceptions." Ozir shook his head. Daen could feel the familiar pulse of electric energy building within him. *They will not kill that boy,* the defiant voice inside vowed. *Or they will have to take me too, and I some of them with me.* How many times had this familiar surge flung him into action, into battle? He closed his eyes and drew a deep breath, practicing the inner calm Shalen had taught him. *"Search for the doorway,"* the soothing voice came and steadied him.

"There is another way," Daen said finally, his body's defenses easing. "Distilled chiproot."

"Distilled? The prisoner's drug? You know we can't control it," said Ozir. "And what if he retains knowledge of this place?"

"Give him a double dose if you must," said Daen quickly. "But do not cast ultimate judgment on that boy."

"You know what you're asking," said Ozir with a sigh. "You're asking me to violate our Code. And with a double dose…" Ozir's words faded.

"Yes, I know," said Daen. "He could lose all his memory."

"That much could kill him," said Ozir.

"The Council would be pleased," retorted Daen. "But I think it will not. The boy is strong." Daen's mind hummed now, the plan unfolding even as he spoke. "He will wake the apprentice to a vintner up in Setland Woods, knowing only that he had an accident... kicked by a horse. I can arrange it." Ozir straightened as a guard approached. The guard saluted, stealing a glance at Daen as he passed.

"Sir, he has shown great bravery bringing us the relic," added Daen in a whisper. "He may have changed the tide here for us. The Figure has spared him already. Not so that he be cut down at the hands of allies." Ozir was quiet. *Please, Color, please!* Daen begged silently, knowing Ozir's next words carried ultimate judgment.

"I will ask the Council for leniency," Ozir finally said. Daen let out the breath he had been holding. "But listen to me carefully, Skypiercer." Ozir stepped close, jabbing Daen with a stout finger. "If this boy survives the chiproot and has even a ghost of a memory of this place, it will be you we send to finish what's undone."

"Yes, my lord." Daen bent low on a knee. "Thank you, sir."

"And I cannot promise the Council will agree. Trouble follows you like a cape, son of Dane!" growled Ozir, turning and marching down the hall. "Rise!" he called over his shoulder.

Daen sprang to his feet and quickly caught up, the crushing weight melting from his heart like a warming glacier.

Ozir paused at a split in the passage. "We have space for you in the visitors' quarters if you'd like to rest a bit before the summit."

"Not in the barracks?"

"No. I think not." Ozir cleared his throat. "Many of the soldiers would welcome that, I'm sure," he said. "But just as surely, there are some who would not."

"How is Horgor doing?" asked Daen. "Does he lead well?"

"The Guard's Chief has the heart of a lion," Ozir replied without hesitation. "The men follow without question."

"Yes. Of course they do," Daen agreed. "He's a born leader."

"And a fighter..." Ozir baited Daen with the unspoken reminder.

"Yes, well. Hopefully, time has cooled some of his fire for me."

"I'm not so sure, Skypiercer," said Ozir. "But worry not. He's topside at the moment."

"Very well." Daen was relieved. "Until the summit then, my lord." Daen bowed slightly and saluted Ozir.

32

Zodak jerked awake in darkness, gasping for breath. The air felt too thin. As had become his ritual, he let his waking mind try to hold the splintered hope that he was waking from some protracted nightmare. The charade never lasted long. His head pounded, and he searched his consciousness for recall. This wasn't Laan. It wasn't the tuk wagon or the Golden Oak. He clutched at his chest, his hand slapping tender clammy skin. The missing medallion echoed the void he felt inside.

Blackiron. The Shielder. Ergis. It all came rushing back. Now he recalled the anchor that pulled him into darkness. The haunting image that returned to his mind again and again was a look. The look he imagined on Ergis's face as a company of exotic and dangerous looking soldiers marched into the tiny village. Yes, there would be a moment of satisfaction when Zodak and Hallah's eyes would meet for the first time. A split second of victory when her shock and secret guilt and shame would erupt into paranoia and cold fear for her long-deserved judgment. But that brief hot moment would so quickly melt into confusion and then solidify into Ergis's triumph. Ozir couldn't possibly know the mistake it would be to bestow power like that on Ergis.

Muffled voices came from the dark. Zodak tried to orient himself in this room. The forms of the spartan sleeping chamber slowly came into view as his eyes adjusted. Now a flickering line of torchlight appeared as the door creaked open, the sliver growing to a box framing Daen's unmistakable silhouette.

"Zodak?" Daen entered, carrying a small steaming mug, and sat in the chair beside the bed. Another tall, wispy silhouette hung back in the doorway. With a grunt, Zodak pulled himself up, so he sat on the edge of the bed, taking the clay mug with a slight nod. He felt exhausted despite the nap, an empty cavity in his chest. Each arm seemed to weigh a hundred doka.

"I'm glad you slept," offered Daen.

Zodak only nodded and took a sip of the sweet, toasted drink, feeling the warmth fill him.

Daen rested a hand on his shoulder. "Zodak, I know the last days have presented you with many surprises, as they have me. You have been strong to hold it all."

Another absent nod from Zodak, his eyes unfocused, staring off in thought.

"And I need your help now."

Hope flickered inside Zodak. "I thought you were done with me," he replied, searching.

"I need you to tell me all you can about Laan and where your home is."

Zodak's rising spirit collapsed like a punctured loaf of cloud bread. "It's not a large village," he scoffed. "I can just show you." Again, he flinched at the image of Ergis's smug, satisfied face. Daen opened his mouth to speak, but hesitated, as if reconsidering. "What is it?" asked Zodak.

"You're not coming to Laan," Daen finally said. Zodak's

flame of hope fizzled. So, they would strip even this final purpose from him like the medallion, like the future he once dared to imagine.

"He's not who you think," said Zodak, sipping the drink.

"Who?" asked Daen.

"Ergis. He's evil."

Daen snorted. "Well, boys *can* be devious. I know that," he offered.

"No. Not devious," Zodak said flatly. "He hated me. Always. Raw hate."

"I'm sure he was jealous. Especially if you and Ardon were close."

"You're making a mistake," Zodak objected weakly. "He won't be the hero you want. He's incompetent and dangerous."

"These are troubled times. The need is great and finding the medallion and the Heir is no accident. I believe the Color Giver brought this all about for a reason." It was useless. Daen's mind was made up.

"And what of Hallah?"

"Ozir and I have yet to discuss her," said Daen. "But what she's done to you is unforgivable. She will be held to account." *And what of Alana?* Zodak wondered. *If she had indeed shed her wicked shell, would she be abandoned in Laan as Ergis is whisked off to Uth Becca and Hallah hauled away to a Pol Dak dungeon?*

When Daen removed a small leather roll and ink pen and asked for the description of Hallah's home, Zodak didn't object. The deadness had returned. He described what he could: the path into town that ended at the large well, the curving road through the dilapidated harvest festival gate, the hedges along the farm road out past the tanner. Daen asked for details of the houses and a description of Ergis. Zodak gave an annoyed snort. Any farmer or villager could show the way. He finally complied.

"Excellent work," said Daen.

"What happens now?" asked Zodak.

"Leithra," called Daen. The shadowy figure in the doorway glided into the room. "This is Leithra," said Daen. "She will be your escort." Leithra stood nearly as tall as Daen, but Zodak doubted two, maybe three of her would equal his weight. Her sinewy frame looked to be spun from baling wire, and every movement seemed choreographed. But despite her slender build, she looked anything but fragile. She wore a flowing midnight-blue cape and beneath, a billowy suit of pale fabric, crossed with leather straps holding knives, pouches, and a deadly razor sickle. Zodak had never seen anyone like her. Taut purple-brown skin stretched like a drum hide over her long gaunt face, and tall black oval pupils set in yellow eyes gave her face the look of a cat. Her translucent blue hair was pulled back and tied, but a few wisps around her face had escaped the binding and undulated in the still air like jellyfish in the current.

"Very nice to meet you." Leithra's deep voice sang more than spoke, smooth and cool. Her forked tongue flicked from her mouth as she talked.

"Nice to meet you," Zodak replied.

"Leithra is a skeyth. Brought up from the Slag desert. One of our best in battle," Daen said proudly. Leithra fixed Daen with a menacing glare before she dipped her head to Zodak in greeting. "She will lead you back to the city."

"And how will I find you again? How will I get back here?" Zodak asked.

Daen drew a deep breath. "Zodak, I must speak plainly with you," he said quietly. "You are an outsider here. I have asked that we find a way to keep you here, but some in the Council believe you should be... removed. That you've seen far too much."

"So, I'm just being kicked out?"

"No, Zodak. I mean, permanently removed."

Zodak chuckled, but then cut short, noticing Daen's face. "Wait, what? Removed permanently?" A chill passed through him. "Like *killed*?"

Daen patted the air to hush Zodak, glancing nervously at Leithra. "Don't worry, that isn't going to happen," Daen said quickly, with a pat on Zodak's leg. "I put you in danger by bringing you here. For that, I am truly sorry. I... This is not how I expected it to go." Zodak almost laughed. If it weren't for the deepening pit in his stomach, he might have. "But I have argued on your behalf, and Ozir and the Council have agreed to expel you from Blackiron and administer chiproot to protect the Order." Daen smiled, though his face betrayed pain.

"You mean the tea? That's supposed to make you forget?"

"The herbalists here have distilled it to a concentrated tincture, but yes. I know it's not what you wanted, Zodak. Believe me, it's not what I wanted either."

"What will I forget?"

"Please. I know what you're thinking—"

"Will I forget you? The Oak? The tuks?" More loss. More friendship ripped away.

"We expect... I hope you will retain your memories from before we entered Blackiron, but it's not a perfect science. The elixir works differently on different people."

Zodak dropped his head, rubbing his temples. He spun through the mountain of memories spilling over from just the last two dozen hours that he would lose.

"But—" Daen's voice brightened. "I believe I have a spot for you."

"A spot?"

"Yes, as an understudy with a vintner about a day's ride upriver from here. Silbah, the proprietor, owes me a favor."

"I'll be a *winemaker*?" Zodak blurted with more offense than he intended. "With no memory of anything I came here for?"

"You'll be safe. You can start a new life."

"But I don't want a new life on a vineyard," Zodak protested.

"I know you don't," answered Daen. "But you cannot return here—you won't even remember it exists. You can't go back to Laan. Where else would you go?" Daen's tone hardened. The words stung, but the truth stung more. Zodak had nothing.

"I will check in on you," said Daen.

"Check in on me?" Zodak's anger spilled over. "Will I even remember who you are?!"

Daen said nothing. He closed his eyes. "I do not know," he answered finally. "It pains me too, Zodak, but it is all I could do."

"Well, it's not enough." Zodak's boldness startled even himself. "You dragged me here, nearly got me killed, you've taken the medallion, the only thing I care about, and you're going to march it off to the woman who tried to kill me and place it around the neck of her sadistic moth of a son." Even as he said it, the shame and hurt boiled into rage. "And me, you'll drug and leave with some stranger, stomping grapes for the rest of my life wondering how I got there and who I am, all because you screwed up! Because I'm not who you thought! I can't believe I ever trusted you."

"Zodak..."

"I wish I had never met you!" Zodak was on his feet, fuming. The words felt unfair, but he couldn't take them back. Daen hung his head. "You've ruined me!"

"Sir." A squire's voice at the door made Zodak jump. "The Council reconvenes. Ozir beckons."

"Very well. Thank you, Zinhar," said Daen. The boy slipped off. Daen stood slowly. "Zodak, listen, son—"

"I'm not your son."

"I know you're angry. I know this feels like a lot. Too much. But your story hasn't been written yet. You have strength in you. Keep hope."

Zodak snorted bitterly. Daen offered his hand, but Zodak

didn't move, Daen's words deflecting off his disillusion like darts off a stone wall. He felt nothing but the scorching fire of betrayal. Not just by Daen, or even by the Order. He felt betrayed by every one of the hundreds of choices and circumstances that had merged over the seasons into the wretched path that was his life. Betrayed by the Color Giver himself.

How did I come to this? Everything that made him who he was, that made him matter, was being cut away. With a few drops of that potion, the life-altering events of the day, and maybe much more, would be wiped from his memory like soot from glass. *But what does it matter?* he thought bitterly. *If you had your memory, you would only replay your rejection again and again like a tired, stinging loop in your mind's eye.*

"Quickly now, Leithra. We need you back here," said Daen with a knowing look as he passed something into her hand. He looked back again to Zodak, a thousand meanings behind his eyes, and then slipped out the door.

Leithra seemed to float more than walk, her liquid movements like those of a forest predator. Zodak trailed her silently through the maze of halls. They passed servants' quarters, and arches opening into a large room with ivory-colored padded floors and lofted ceilings where groups of soldiers sparred. They exited the fortress and set off across one of the spindly bridges.

"What did they tell you about me?" Zodak asked Leithra's back. She didn't slow. He wondered if she heard the question.

"A messenger." Her smooth, flowing voice reached him just as he was about to clear his throat and ask again. "A messenger boy with a powerful relic and news of the Shielder," she added.

"And yet there were some who wanted me dead?" pressed Zodak.

Now her head cocked. "I cannot speak of what is spoken in the Great Hall of Blackiron," she said firmly, leaping over the last few bridge slats to solid ground.

"Why not?" His indifference had turned to boldness. *What can she take from me now?* Zodak also leapt, landing less gracefully on the sandy charcoal rock. "In an hour, I'll have no memory of this conversation anyway," he said casually. "I probably won't know you ever existed." Leithra stopped and stared at him, searching his face. He met her withering gaze but didn't flinch. He betrayed nothing.

"Very well, clever boy," she finally cooed, turning toward the edge of the cavern on the far side of the castle from where Zodak and Daen had entered. "I will speak plainly and freely, as one does to a dying man." The sudden honesty startled Zodak. "No outsider has ever tried to enter Blackiron by force and lived to speak of it. The voices were many in the Council who clamored for your execution. If the decision were mine, you would not have lived through the night." She delivered this last verdict without emotion or even breaking stride. The words prickled down Zodak's spine. "Skypiercer saved your life."

"What?"

"Skypiercer argued for you, said you knew the Heir, said you brought the relic to us freely and should be spared. These arguments failed to sway the Council. They prepared their votes, the judgment decided." Leithra had reached the edge of the cavern. A shallow cave as tall as a man and as deep again was scooped out of the cavern wall. A torch burned within, illuminating the pocket and revealing rungs of a wooden ladder fastened to the rock leading up into the belly of the wall.

"After you." Leithra gestured to the cave. Zodak edged tentatively into the space no larger than a closet and glanced up at the ladder. It disappeared into the darkness above. "Climb, young one." Leithra's voice was firm. He tentatively ascended the ladder.

"So why am I still here?" Zodak asked over his shoulder as he ascended. Even as he did, a cold chill flashed through him. *What if Leithra is here to carry out the will of the Council? Maybe*

Daen's story was a lie and she was ordered to kill me after all, he thought. *"I will speak plainly.... as one does to a dying man..."* He recalled her words. He expected the spike of panic and rush of adrenaline, but none came. The thought of his death now felt like everything else, a hollow and listless eventuality.

"Skypiercer"—she snorted what sounded like it could have been a laugh—"threatened the Council. Threatened!" she exclaimed. "Said he was the reason you came to Blackiron. Said he would invoke an honor duel against the soldier carrying out the sentence and if he survived, each Council member who voted in favor. Wouldn't have made it past my sickle," she added. Zodak's heart sank as he listened. He replayed his final words spoken to Daen. A soft glow above revealed the end of the chute. "Such a quickdraw," continued Leithra. "It's why he was removed as Guard's Chief, you know. Too reckless, some said. Too fast for battle. Still slower than my people," she added.

"Daen was Guard's Chief?" asked Zodak, the only safe question that came to mind. *Daen would fight for me? He would have... died for me?* His arms burned with fatigue, and he gasped for breath as he climbed. A dull pain radiated from his chest. Just a day before, a climb twice as high would have barely caused him to breathe out of rhythm, but now his arms felt like noodles and his legs wobbled. Just as he feared he would lose his grip, he reached the last ladder rung and the sandy ground above. He heaved himself up into the passage and panted on hands and knees.

"Need more exercise," Leithra scoffed. "This way." She stepped into darkness around a large boulder that revealed another branch of the tunnel winding slightly upward, its walls, floor, and ceiling clad in wooden planks. "Yes, he was exiled."

Zodak found himself slowing. *What have I done? You fool! You've made a huge mistake.* Every fiber in him longed to sprint back to Blackiron and find Daen. To throw himself at his feet and beg for forgiveness. He knew it was an impossibility. The hollow in his stomach grew as he recalled the chiproot. *I will forget all of this. What will happen when I see Daen again? Will it be as if I've never met him? Will I even remember him as the friendly stranger who helped me retrieve the medallion?*

"What did the Council finally decide?" he had to know.

"Sharing Council deliberations with a Topsider... this is a first," Leithra mused. "Must have been moved by his speech," she said with disdain. "That and Ozir argued for leniency. Against the Code. Strange day..." Her voice trailed off. "Some still voted for removal, but most for mercy. They cited extraordinary circumstances. Weakness, if you ask me." She stopped abruptly. "I speak too freely, even to you. It is all I can say."

The passage ended in a flat wall, the planks stained in a patchwork of brown and gray. Leithra removed a wooden tool that resembled a long-handled finishing hammer from a hook on the wall. In a rapid flurry of movement, she struck a dozen different colored planks in rapid succession with the head of the hammer, each producing a different tone, like clinking bottles filled to different levels. As soon as she stopped, there was a rumble and groaning sound as heavy gears within the walls turned. She replaced the hammer as the massive door slid back into the wall, revealing a musty, low-lit room, and in its center, pushed back from a simple wooden table with an oil lamp burning and colorful wooden chips strewn about its top, stood a trio of dangerous looking men, each with crossbow bolts trained on the pair.

33

Leithra quickly performed the Order salute and spoke a cryptic phrase in what Zodak took to be the old tongue. Two guards lowered weapons, but the third, with the barrel chest and thick red beard, did not. He stepped forward and nodded to Zodak.

"His passage is sanctioned," she said coolly. "By Ozir himself." Her hand flicked from her pocket, revealing a piece of leather stamped with an intricate design. The red-bearded guard lowered the crossbow and reluctantly returned the salute. Zodak noticed Leithra smoothly remove her hand from her sickle.

"Ye be careful them gray pills topside don't see you with that," he said. "They're crawling like ants tonight," he added. Leithra only nodded, grabbing Zodak's wrist as she glided past the trio of guards to a rickety stairway on the far side of the room. If he didn't know better, Zodak could have mistaken the room for a jam cellar in a modest farmhouse. A heavy door blocked the top of the stairs, secured by a pair of thick wooden beams. Leithra pulled a rope, raising the beams clear of the door, and pushed it open. As soon as Zodak had passed through, the door shut tightly behind him with a thud.

They stood again in utter darkness.

"Where are we—"

"Shh!" snapped Leithra. From the way the sound carried, Zodak guessed the room was not much bigger than a closet. It smelled like a barn. After a long moment, Leithra cracked open another door in front of them barely a jot, and then froze again.

"Okay," she finally said, opening the door and slipping through. Zodak followed as she quickly closed the passage behind them. A few sheep and a donkey milled around in the hay in the dim light. A pair of stalls held horses to the left. Zodak glanced back and marveled at how the door had disappeared into the wall of stacked hay bales against the end of the barn.

"This way," said Leithra, leading Zodak through the barn into a small courtyard. They were suddenly outside. Zodak breathed deeply of the crisp night. Uth Becca. The city's fragrance rushed at him like a familiar friend. *Will I remember that smell when the chiproot takes me?* he wondered. Dark night draped the sky, but a few figures and the occasional wagon passed in the streets. *Preparation for mooncrossing,* he guessed. They stepped into the street and turned left toward the castle.

"I know this place!" said Zodak excitedly. He now recalled this courtyard from one of his exploration walks. *I walked right past a secret entrance to Blackiron each time I passed here!* he mused.

"Yes, we are not far from the Golden Oak," said Leithra.

"Is that where we're going?" Zodak's heart leapt. He would return to something he knew.

"Yes, you will stay until the Vintner arrives."

For the first time that day Zodak felt a flicker of hope, buoyed by the thought of seeing Olaf again and maybe even Lady Voli. Surely he would remember them after the chiproot.

Even as it comforted him, the thought brought a stab of loss as he grasped for the medallion that no longer hung on his neck. Just days ago, hours ago, he was on top of the world. The hope of a meeting with Voli burst with unspoken promise. *Will Ergis meet Voli now?* He shook the thought from his head. No, he would welcome the familiarity of the Oak even if it now felt hollow of purpose.

"We cut through the market," said Leithra, scanning the streets. "Look to be guards about, so I will keep my distance." Her eyes darkened. "But, boy! Know that if you try to run, I have strict orders." She pulled her cape back, and the moonlight glinted off the curved sickle that hung at her waist beside a collection of throwing knives and some sort of tube. Zodak shuddered. *I wouldn't get three steps before she opened me like a fish. It's what she wanted, wasn't it? It's what she voted for...* He only nodded his understanding with a sour smile.

"Good. Meet me on the other side of the smithy stall beside the auction tower." She motioned to the solemn structure that hunched like a hangman's gallows at the end of the line of tents and stalls two hundred mounts away. "I'll be watching you," she added, her cat eyes flashing. Zodak sighed and shook his head as he began picking his way through the market. When he looked back, there was no sign of Leithra, but he could feel her gaze on him from the dark. He had no idea of the time, but from how the streetlamps burned low and the handful of stray peddlers fiddling with their booths he guessed it to be an hour or two before dawn.

A pair of guards sauntered down the street in his direction. *Should I just walk by? Act normal?* His mind raced. He recalled his encounter with Stohl outside the Fahyz Gate. *No, too risky.* As the guards stopped and called out to a man working on a stall nearby, Zodak slipped from the street to behind a booth. He hunched down low and waited, peering out from the hiding place. After a moment, the guards finally ambled past. The nearer one he recognized as the young guard from Badu's stall. The one Stohl had tossed like a rag doll. *Krollis? Is that what Badu called him? Was he at the Fahyz Gate?* Zodak couldn't remember.

Movement caught Zodak's eye over his left shoulder. Perched high atop a stack of empty crates, boxes, and dismantled market booth parts, squatted Leithra, her yellow eyes watching his every move like a sentry. *I'm going,* Zodak mouthed, pointing to the guards that were passing his hiding spot. As soon as they had, Zodak crept forward, slipping through two stalls back to the road. He couldn't linger. Krollis might recognize him, and a chance encounter could turn dangerous quickly.

Trying to act natural, he forced himself not to run as he hurried down the market street past a busy group of tentmakers. He glanced casually over his shoulder to ensure the guards weren't following him. Movement to his right. The fishmonger stopped chipping ice and stared. Zodak gave a practiced nod and kept walking. His heart pounded as he crossed the last stretch of open market before reaching the auction tower and the Knotted Loaf. The side street to the Oak was in sight.

A shout and sudden rushing of feet rose from ahead as another pair of city guards flew around the corner beside the auction tower, running at full tilt towards him. Their shouts filled the sleepy market square. Without thinking, Zodak sprang from the road, diving into a pile of woven baskets. He froze, praying the low light would obscure him. The guards streaked past, joining shouts from Krollis and the other guard at the far end of Market. For a moment, all was quiet other than his breathing. Then he heard it. A swooshing and rhythmic stomping of feet and hooves and the rumble of iron on stone. The sound of an enormous dance troop or herd of bushcow on the move. Zodak knew that sound. He had heard it before right here in this very spot. It was unmistakable. The Elder!

Sure enough, even as he craned his neck to peer out of the mountain of baskets, a pair of towering steeds emerged from the darkness, rounding the curving road past the auction tower. In the daylight, the Elder's caravan was beautiful and awe-inspiring. In the night, it was ominous and terrifying. The scarlet and yellow of the Pol Dak guards fluttered like muted flames in the darkness. The soldiers' sharp eyes flashed from atop the massive steeds. Once again, Zodak was frozen, mesmerized by the sight. He'd struggle to rise from his throne of crushed baskets even if he tried. If they noticed him, the two columns of riders didn't show it as they entered the high side of the desolate market square. This time, no trumpets blasted, and no minstrels played. The procession passed in mighty silence except for the drumming hoofbeats and the grinding of the wagon wheels. He watched the cavalcade, gliding like some regal insect through the heart of the market square. *I could have met her, could have been part of that.* The wistful thought bit as it rose.

A billowing wisp of silver fabric slid from the shadows three booths down as Leithra's nimble silhouette slipped from the tool mender's tent into the main square, interrupting his thoughts and finally breaking the spell. Somehow from thirty measures away she had spotted him among the baskets.

"The mere sight of her knocked you on your tin, did she?" called Leithra with a sly smile. "You wouldn't believe what she—"

Crack! A blinding white-blue light ripped the night in half. Like a lightning strike in the middle of the market, the flash seared Zodak's vision and an earsplitting *boom* tore through the darkness. An invisible force slammed Zodak in the chest, flipping him backwards like a paper doll in a windstorm. He crashed head over heels into the woven straw booth wall and crumpled upside down against the sagging wall before toppling sideways painfully onto the ground. It felt like he had been kicked by a horse. He sucked for air and his vision swam in blackness. All he could hear was a high-pitched whining. The smell of charred cloth and flesh filled the air, and somewhere in the distance, voices shouted. He blinked again and again, each time bringing a few more shapes back into focus. A sharp pain shot through his ears. He touched his neck and felt something wet. Blood trickled from his throbbing ear.

As his burned vision slowly returned, he could make out the blue bonfire burning hungrily in the center of the marketplace sixty mounts away. Dark shapes littered the street around the fire. His stomach turned as bitter bile rose: those shapes were burnt bodies, charred horses, and soldiers. The burning mass was the Elder's chariot.

A nearby moaning and gurgling sound startled Zodak. A shape on the ground slithered towards him, heavy arms dragging the dead weight of a broken body.

"Leithra!" Zodak forced himself to his feet, sending a lancing pain through his left leg all the way to his head. He stumbled towards her. His feet caught a shredded basket, and he tumbled to the ground. He pulled himself up on his elbows and inched forward towards her. She had only one leg and a splintered shard of wood protruded from her back. Her pale linen robes were soaked in red, and her yellow-and-black eyes were fixed on him with wild intensity as she dragged herself closer still. Waves of spastic aqua light rippled through her undulating blue hair.

"It'll be okay," he lied, placing a hand awkwardly on her shoulder. Her shaking hand plunged into her pocket and jerked out, gripping a small glass vial.

"You... take..." The hand tremors were so violent that she fumbled and dropped the chiproot tincture. "I swore..." Her head dipped to the ground, still shaking.

"It's okay," he repeated, now touching her leathery temple, the jellyfish hair wrapping around his thumb. "You needn't struggle. The Garden awaits you. The Figure will welcome you." He recalled Ardon's stories of the great beyond. "When life's adventure surrenders to the tranquility of the Garden, you shall shed this heavy body and dance in the golden light of your weaver." Where the words had come from, he couldn't say. They sprang up unbidden from deep in a childhood he couldn't unlock. Her eyes flitted up to his face and fixed on his once more. Then, with a gasping sigh, Leithra was gone. Her body slumped and the living tendrils of her hair went limp, fading to a thin gray that fanned on the ground like a halo around her severe face. He didn't know Leithra, but he felt the loss. Daen had spoken almost reverentially of this warrior. One of the Order's best. *How many battles had she fought? How many margoul had she slain?*

He dropped his head to hers and just sat, feeling. Feeling the night, the faint heat from that cursed fire, the bite of thick smoke carried by the wind. He felt the throbbing of blood in his ears and the growing ache ripple across his torso and stab into the muscles of his neck. *Maybe you can slip away with her,* the voice inside begged. He picked up the vial and stared at the thick dark orange liquid within. With trembling hands, he removed the cork top. *It would erase your pain. It alone can give you something you will find nowhere else: escape.* He slowly lifted it to his mouth.

"*Stop!*" cried a piercing voice. Zodak whipped his head around. He was alone. Whether the voice was his own or came from somewhere else, he would never know. Lifting the vial, Zodak inspected the sloshing liquid. "Aaargh!" he shouted, and hurled it, shattering the glass on the cobblestones. He slumped backward, his head throbbing and the smoke from the marketplace scraping and scouring his dry throat. Lights danced in his vision as the world began slipping away.

The sound of rhythmic marching pulled him back from the edge of consciousness, back to the basket weaver's tent, back to the market. He pried open his puffy eyes. Around the very same corner where the Elder's caravan had emerged moments before came a line of figures. *Castle guard.* Yet the castle was half a cliq away. *How had they come so quickly at this hour?* Methodically, they fanned out into the market.

"Bring them!" boomed a familiar voice. "Any who might have been responsible!" Stohl barked the orders. "Over there!" Stohl called. Zodak didn't need to look up to know he had been spotted, but he didn't have the strength to try to get away.

"You there!" Stohl stormed into the tent, a half dozen guards behind him. "What brings you out so late—" Zodak looked up and caught his glare. "Well, sherk me! You!" Stohl's eyes widened as he took in the sight of Zodak and Leithra. He lunged forward, grabbing Zodak by the collar, and lifted him straight off his feet. Even as he heaved, Stohl was ripping open Zodak's shirt.

"We've been looking for you. Where is it, pill?!" Stohl screamed. "What have you done with it?"

"It... it's gone," Zodak stammered.

Stohl glanced down at Leithra and back at Zodak, understanding crossing his face. "There's someone who's gonna want to talk to you, moth! You have a lot to answer for!" He tossed Zodak to the waiting guards. "Straight to lock with this sore. Kuquo's gonna want to see *him*." Before Zodak could object, fists hammered him in the stomach. He keeled forward, nausea surging through him. Strong hands wrenched his arms behind him and bound his wrists as a damp, musty hood was yanked over his head, plunging him into darkness.

34

Daen snapped awake, whether just before the knock landed on his door or just after he couldn't say. He sprang to his feet, accustomed to the quick naps of a soldier. The Council recess would be over. The young guard in the hallway stammered a hello, a look of awe plastered on his youthful face.

"Yes, thank you—Hushtel, is it?" The guard lowered his eyes to the floor, cheeks flushing crimson. "Last I saw you, you were just a banner carrier."

"Yes, sir," said Hushtel, glancing up. "I've come to fetch you for the meeting." Hushtel's eyes dropped again.

"You carry the stripes well, Hushtel," said Daen, placing a hand on the young man's shoulder.

"Yes, sir... uh, thank you, sir," fumbled Hushtel. "Please, to the Great Hall."

"Very well," said Daen with a salute. "Lead on."

Soldiers flowed into the Great Hall from its many entrances, collecting in pools and eddies of others wearing the same colors on ribbons and sashes. At the far end of the hall on the raised platform, obscured behind a thin sheet of water falling from the ceiling like a bolt of silkeen, sat the great oak table, perpendicular to the length of the room and dwarfed by the great hall. *The Order Council.* It appeared a lively debate ensued at the table, but all sound was engulfed by the curtain of water. At the table, Daen knew, would sit Ozir and the eighteen Council members.

He lowered his eyes and hunched his shoulders as he snaked quickly through the soldiers. Some familiar faces sought his gaze, but this was not the time for reunion. At the front of the room, the soldiers left a five-mount buffer of empty floor between themselves and the water wall. The apron they called it. The apron was never to be occupied by a soldier—a lesson some new recruit always learned the hard way. Hushtel halted obediently at the edge of the apron. Daen ignored the stares and whispers at his back, catching a surprised, even indignant glance from a nearby commander as he strode through the apron and stepped up onto the platform. As he did, the curtain of water parted wide enough for him to pass before falling behind him.

Sure enough, as Daen passed through the parted water, the blast of noise from the heated discussion engulfed him. He walked around the table and took his place on an empty stool behind Ozir's left shoulder, his back only a few measures from the weathered tapestry of the Goblin Invasion that spanned the width of the back wall. Aside from a few servants and Delmuth, who perched on a stool over Ozir's right shoulder, Daen was the only one on the platform not seated at the table. Delmuth glared when their eyes met. Daen just nodded.

"...or it could be worse." Daen focused on Awalmir, the bronze-skinned man from Epis Kopol with black wavy hair and a heavy jawline who now spoke. "We have no way of knowing who, or even why—" Awalmir caught sight of Daen and stopped short. "What's he doing here?" he barked, half standing. There was a mumble from the table.

"Awalmir, please." Ozir motioned for calm. "I asked Daen to join us this evening. He brings information quite pertinent given the... developments."

"He also brought an intruder into this very room, did he not?" sneered another man beside Awalmir, a newcomer to the Council whose name Daen couldn't recall. The man vaguely resembled Awalmir and also wore the leopard skin cord around his neck with the firstkill tooth dangling from it. Another rumble of agreement.

"We settled that matter before the recess," said Ozir with authority. "We will not reopen it now."

"Has he heard the news?" asked an older woman with streaks of white veining her dark hair, draped in a heavy midnight-blue cloak. Deep plum paint shadowed her shining eyes buried below a wrinkled brow. Though her voice wavered slightly, she spoke with confidence and authority.

"What developments?" Daen stood. "What news, Pegarah?" He ignored the underhanded jabs.

"It's the High Elder," answered a tall elf, slender of build with a youthful yet dignified appearance, at the far end of the table. His silky hair, pressed flat under a silver headband, fell just below his sharp chin. He glanced to Ozir who nodded. "We fear something has gone terribly awry. There are reports of an... accident. We have only a rumor, secondhand information that just came in."

"What kind of accident, Silden?" asked Daen.

"It's the Elder," said Silden. "We have reports of an attack."

"We know very little now," Ozir cut in. "The entire thing could be a misunderstanding."

"Yes. There has been a mistake. Must be some kind of mistake," said Awalmir. A dozen voices joined, agreeing or disputing.

"Order!" Ozir suddenly boomed, rapping his staff on the drumstone in the floor. "If the report is true, this is grave news," said Ozir. "Each of us knows the place the Elder holds in Rislaan, but even more, the critical role she plays in Yiduiijn's delicate balance. Harm to her would cut deeply," he continued. "I recommend we send a pod to confirm the rumor."

"If this news is correct, and I have no reason to doubt your network, Ozir," said Silden, "then the city and Yiduiijn have certainly suffered a grave blow."

"We will soon learn for certain if the time for action has come. But we must be prepared," said a weathered man across the table with a faded scar that snaked from chin to cheek.

"But we don't know—" objected Awalmir.

"Yes, we must prepare," Ozir interrupted. "Draw the veil," he said to a nearby servant as he rose from the table. The servant pulled a long cord, and the wall of water stopped falling, first from the center, then toward the edges, giving the appearance of a great curtain being drawn. As it did, it revealed the vast chamber filled with soldiers, suddenly hushed.

"Milblocks!" bellowed Ozir. The sea of figures sprang to action and within seconds transformed before their eyes into an intricate pattern of ten perfect blocks of warriors. The formations stood six soldiers wide by four deep, each with three soldiers one step in front of the rest of the block. The soldiers in the milblocks wore the leather Order cuffs on their forearms, but each block of warriors wore a different colored leather strap across their chests.

Near the apron, ten soldiers stepped from the others in a staggered row facing Ozir: men, dwarves, two sinewy skeyth, elves, and a half-giant. Each wore a black leather mantle that covered their neck, shoulders, and the top of their chests with a different color sash: oily blue, brilliant red, orange, dark emerald, flame yellow, maroon, and ivory. The leaders wore a black leather cuff with a colored woven Order emblem at its center, matching the color of the cloth sashes. Daen admired the soldiers, standing erect, full of confidence and poised for action.

"Ready yourselves for battle, soldiers." Ozir's voice echoed off the vaulted ceiling, returning through the hushed hall in agreement. "It may not rear its ugly head today, but then again, it may crouch at our doorstep as we speak. Ready your men. Return to the barracks, and await my command. Milblock commanders will receive orders within the hour." Every one of the hundreds of soldiers, in perfect unison, saluted Ozir with their fists on their chests. The troop turned and marched out of the room, never breaking formation, even as they passed through the door. Scrawny young squires scrambled to close the oversized doors behind the army. The sound of marching faded, and the doors closed with a loud *thunk*. Within moments, the hall was cleared and quiet.

"We have never seen a brazen attack on the High Elder, and certainly never within city walls," Silden continued. "But now is a time for measured steps and utmost vigilance. We know not whence this attack came, and we cannot ignore the possibility that the Magistrate himself was involved." He let the leaden words hang in the air. "The elves have long warned you of this man."

"Harrumph! You elves mistrust all humans!" snorted a bearded dwarf across the table from Ozir, earning a grunt from Awalmir. "It's quite an accusation you make, Silden, given the lineage of our Magistrate." He pointed a stubby, ring-adorned finger at the elf.

"*We elves* predicted the taint and rebellion at the Mandavian Outpost seventy-five seasons ago, Hilbane. It took the death of nine hundred sleeping villagers and the destruction of three outposts for the Order to heed that warning," retorted Silden.

"The dwarf guilds have an age-old pact with the magistrates, dating back to the reign of the Governess," said another dwarf to Hilbane's left. "And the Order, for that matter, has fostered a steady alliance with this city." Hilbane nodded his agreement.

"We honor the pacts of our fathers," said Daen, "but let's not allow them to cloud our vision or obscure our resolve lest we're lulled into complacency." Delmuth stood, lifting a finger to reply.

"The Scor Delfahysian speaks wisely," Ozir cut in, sending Delmuth quietly back to his seat. "But I will add knowledge to his words. The purpose of the Elder's visit to Uth Becca today was to evaluate the Magistrate's leadership. She has heard our complaints and the growing case against Magistrate Kuquo and came in person to judge his fitness."

"Why was this not shared with the summit members?" pressed Hilbane.

"I always pass the information I receive to the Council, Hilbane, you know this," replied Ozir. "But the Elder specifically requested that I share the purpose of her visit with no one. She warned of an unknown danger. Whether she had information of the attack or just a premonition, she did not say, and we may never know."

"Are you suggesting the Magistrate has the power to destroy her?" asked a man with inky dark green skin and even darker eyes, a white animal skin clinging to his back. Blue war paint spotted his bare chest and climbed his neck and face. He wore the head of a white wolf on his hood.

"His powers are inferior to those of the Elder, Talbor," answered Ozir. "But there have been sightings of Müziel in the city." An audible gasp escaped the group.

"The Elder gave her blessing to Kuquo's appointment as magistrate," added Pegarah. "An accusation of the Magistrate could undermine the Elder's judgment, or worse. Are we prepared to suggest that the High Elder of the Venerable Council erred in appointing her cousin to the Magistrate's seat? Or must we explore an even more insidious possibility—if he was tainted, might she be as well?" A grumbling wave of objection rose from some of the members at the table.

"The Elder was purer than any at this table," said Silden simply, quieting the grumbles.

"Was?" challenged Talbor.

"Is," Silden corrected himself. "For many seasons, her rule has been an unfaltering symbol of truth and Color, and she has done much to protect Rislaan from evil."

"Arrgh. Color," groaned Awalmir, waving at Silden.

"Elsir, the elven king of the Mead, regularly confided in the Elder," continued Silden. "Let us not be quick to forget her role in the Battle of the Beasts or the Meridian Conflict. Besides, were both the Elder and her cousin the Magistrate tainted, what cause would there be for attack? He may have begun with good intentions, but I believe the magistrate's seat has steadily poisoned him like an untended sicklethorn barb. Perhaps he even learned of her intent to replace him and—" He stopped suddenly, looking up from the table.

"Continue, Silden," urged Ozir.

"Someone approaches," replied Silden, his gaze turned out across the yawning hall. Another elf, a few seats down from Silden, focused on the same spot. Daen looked but couldn't see or hear anything. Questioning looks volleyed around the table. The group sat quietly but for a scuffle of boots on a rug or a low whisper.

Finally, Hilbane the dwarf spoke. "Silden, your ears are tall and pointy, no doubt." He slipped a playful grin to another dwarf. "But I fear your age has gotten—"

"A runner approaches!" bellowed a breathless watchman bursting through the sprawling opening at the far end of the hall. Hilbane's grin evaporated. He slouched low in his seat. Someone at the table gasped. A shape sped through the archway and past the breathless guard in a gray blur. Swords and bows were drawn, but within a split second, the shape had traversed the expansive hall with unnatural speed, blown through the apron, and stopped short before the great table. When it halted, Daen saw the blur for what it was: a diminutive figure dropped to one knee. The party at the table was on their feet, weapons brandished, but Ozir held up a hand. No one moved.

"Sire." The kneeling figure spoke. "Your servant, Heldin, runner for the High Elder of the Venerable Council, bearing news in an hour of darkness." From where Daen stood, the figure appeared to be but a boy. He was clothed in a charcoal-gray jumper with an orange belt. Shimmering silver shackles circling his ankles pulsed and glowed eerily. Yet this boy didn't address Ozir in a child's manner. Ozir slid his long knife back into its scabbard and motioned for the rest to do the same. With a creak and sigh, bows were loosened, and swords slithered back into sheaths. Ozir approached the runner.

"By what margoul magic do you fly like an eagle, runner?" demanded Delmuth, stepping up beside Ozir. "And how did you come to this secret place?"

The runner appeared calm. "Not margoul, my lord. I run with the enchanted Utheriel Bands, passed down hundreds of seasons through the House of Lightfoot, messengers of the Council," replied the boy. "As for this place, I have visited here once thirty-two seasons past, my lord, when I was new to the Elder's service." Murmurs from the group. "I have not accompanied her since, yet my memory serves me well." *Thirty seasons? He must have misspoken,* thought Daen. From his size this boy could not have seen more than twelve.

"I see..." said Ozir, eyes squinted in contemplation.

"The password. Do you know it?" Delmuth screeched.

"I do, my lord," replied the runner, speaking the phrase in the old tongue. More whispers. "The Elder insisted I memorize it not an hour ago. She spoke of some emergency. As for my last visit, she had come to discuss the reports of encampments on the Northern Brikkor Fronts. You, sire, were yet in the service, nursing a wounded hand if I remember correctly," he said to Ozir. "My lord, I would not dare venture here alone now, but I knew not what else to do."

"Yes, I remember this meeting," said Ozir, absently rubbing the palm of his left hand. "An unusual reunion in Fortress Blackiron, Heldin, Council Runner. We eagerly receive your news. We have an early report of an incident with the High Elder. If you have news, grave or promising, crier, deliver now without delay."

"I am afraid I have the gravest of news, sire." He rose slowly, now turning for the first time to the others at the table. His eyes swept across the group, yet his stare skipped over each like a polished stone on the surface of a glassy pond. His face wore the vacant, confused look of a child awoken to be carried to bed. As Daen caught a view of the runner, he started. He was indeed no boy. Lines on his face belied the youthful stature. Most of the dwarves, while short, had chests like flour barrels and powerful frames, but this man was small and slender, yet he spoke with confidence and seasons of knowledge crouched behind his dazed eyes.

"Continue, small master," urged Daen. The little man craned his neck to seek the source of this voice. Without reaction or effect, he turned back to Ozir.

"She is dead..." he said flatly. All went quiet. The silence ripped across the Great Hall, filling it to the ceiling. No one at the table breathed. "I saw it myself," he continued in the same monotone voice. "Blue flames leaping from her carriage, engulfing it... splintering its very frame..." He trailed off. Again, silence.

"You're sure the flames were blue?" Pegarah's voice broke the spell.

The runner turned to her. "Yes, as blue as the Lake of Glasir."

"And what of her Special Guard?" Ozir demanded. "Where was her guard? Where are they now?" The small group at the table drew a collective breath.

"Decimated." His small head dropped.

"Impossible!" roared Talbor, the white wolf head echoing the roar. "The Special Guard hasn't lost a man in combat for a dozen seasons!"

"From two city blocks away, I felt the heat of the blast," said Heldin.

"And what of Eldress Volithrya?" asked Ozir.

"She has fled the city or soon will. I ran to her directly after the blast. I knew she was in peril. You see, she was to be in that carriage, but she slipped away from the dinner meeting early. I delivered the news and urged her to leave immediately."

"To return to Pol Dak?" Daen asked.

"I do not pretend to know the Eldress's mind, my lord," he replied. "She has her pod of Special Guard with her. She should be safe."

"With the Elder dead, safety is no longer a guarantee anywhere," said Ozir. He turned to the messenger, laying a hand on his shoulder. "Thank you, Heldin. You serve Pol Dak faithfully, and the Order as well." The runner met his gaze with an inscrutable expression. "May I ask you one more favor before you rest?"

"Of course, my lord," Heldin said.

"I am in dire need of counsel with Horgor, my Guard's Chief," said Ozir. Daen's head snapped up at the name. "He is at post in the city at the twin mills near the river mouth. Will you send him here?"

"As you wish," Heldin said with another bow.

Daen knelt before the runner. "Thank you, sir, for bringing us this news. You risk much, and the Color has aided us by sparing you from that blast. Your courage is heartening."

"Live to serve," responded Heldin, thumping his small fist to his chest, an inscrutable look on his face.

"When you return, I will have quarters awaiting you," said Ozir to Heldin with a wave.

"Thank you, sire." Heldin turned, the shackles on his ankles gleaming. He shot off through the room with blistering speed. Daen had never seen any animal or person move so fast. In a heartbeat, Heldin had crossed the expansive hall and was out the door.

Two dozen pairs of eyes followed the blur of the runner as he sped through the archway at the end of the hall, and for a moment no one spoke.

35

"The medallion! Where is it?" The scream erupted from the gray circle of guards as the punches, kicks, and slaps landed again and again.

"I told you!" cried Zodak under the barrage of blows. "It was... stolen. Stolen at the cantina..."

"Stolen by who, moth!" Another kick landed in his gut, sending the air rushing from his lungs. He struggled for breath, his stomach feeling like it was being pulled inside out.

"Gormley!" he finally gasped. *Did they find his body already? Will they see through the twisted truth?*

"Stop!" Stohl finally called. "Gormley, you say? I know that pill. Sticky fingers for sure, and that *is* his watering hole."

"I swear it," stammered Zodak. "He stole it from my neck." Zodak dry heaved and panted. "Confused me by using some sort of spore." He peeked through a swollen eye up at Stohl who nodded to another guard.

"Throw him in the cell," added Stohl. "He may know something more about the Order. Caught him with that sore Daen at the gate and with the desert pirate at da markey. We'll make sure he talks, no matter how many fingers it takes." Someone laughed.

"I've told you what I know," sputtered Zodak.

"Well then, you'll lose yer fingers for nothing, won't ya?" sneered a portly guard, flashing a toothless grin from his grimy face.

"Get him out of here," boomed Stohl. "I'm off to Kuquo. He'll spit bile if I keep him." The guards heaved Zodak to his feet and dragged him down a narrow stone corridor.

"Oh, trust me, you sherking pill," whispered a skinny toothless guard with the foul breath closest to him, "you'll tell Stohl *everything*. Whatever ye can think of to make the slagging pain stop, I promise ya." The guard winked at Zodak as he tossed him into the cell and slammed the door with a loud *clang*.

Zodak crumpled to the hay-strewn floor, exhausted and thrashed. The room was black, lit only by the small window of cloudy predawn sky and the glow of torchlight from the hall. It reeked of stale urine. His jaw throbbed, and he felt that he might vomit at any second. *If you had taken the chiproot, at least you'd have forgotten tonight,* he scolded himself.

"But you'd have lost a piece of yourself too," came a quavering voice from the darkness. *Too many blows to the head,* thought Zodak, rubbing his temple. "Yet here you remain," came the voice again. "Not who you thought you were, perhaps, but here all the same."

Zodak looked up, peering into the darkness. "Who's there?" He crawled painfully towards the edge of the cell, where bars separated him from another darkened cell. "Who are you?"

"That's the question you need to ask yourself right now, my son," replied a quavering voice as a shape shuffled in the darkness on the other side of the bars. A familiar face drew close, barely lit by the dim moonlight.

"Badu!" Zodak exclaimed, wincing at the stab of pain in his

gut. He pulled himself through the filth until his face pressed against the bars.

Badu laid a hand on Zodak's head. "It is good to see you, my boy. You've been through the fire since we last met, lad."

Zodak only nodded. Dropping his head, he closed his eyes against the geyser of emotion that he felt welling up inside. He fought its rising, but he couldn't stem the tide. He sobbed, letting his anger, grief, and exhaustion rip through him and rush out. Had his cell mate been another, he might have locked the feelings down and maintained a hard facade, but something about Badu gave him permission to break.

"There, there, my son." Badu stroked Zodak's shaking head with an unsteady hand, knuckles bruised and scraped.

"I've failed." Zodak spilled the admission between gasps. "It was all a lie. I have nothing. I'm nothing."

"Ah. Many a great man has uttered such words."

"I'm not great. Not the Shielder. I'm not the Heir. Ozir... the Order... they were going to *kill* me. To toss me aside..."

"Well, maybe you're not who you thought, but as long as you draw breath, your story is not written," said Badu. "What about the water sprite?"

"Did I tell you about that?"

Badu's patient face only smiled.

"I... I don't know. Maybe I imagined it all. Look at me, I'm not a hero." The sobs had faded to sniffles.

"You're exactly what the Color Giver created you to be. And whether you have a medallion around your neck or not, there is greatness within."

Zodak silently shook his head. "They're going to kill me." Zodak stated the fact with sudden clarity and alarm. "I don't want to die."

"You're not dead yet, my boy."

"Why are you down here? Have you been here since the market?" Zodak asked, looking up for the first time. "Your face!" He hadn't noticed it before in the darkness, but Badu's left eye was swollen nearly shut, his top lip was puffy, and scrapes and bruises littered his face. "What have they done to you?"

"I have one last role to play," said Badu. "Then it's off to the Garden with me."

"What do you mean? What role?"

"I'm to be tried and sentenced for the murder of the High Elder," he said, smiling as if sharing his favorite flavor of tea.

"What?! That wasn't you! It wasn't. Was it?"

Badu laughed, but then grimaced. "No, my boy. There is an evil wave mounting, and I am just a pawn. But soon it will be over for me."

"No! You can't die," insisted Zodak.

Badu chuckled. "Son, these bones are tired. I've lived a dozen lives —some I'd re-live tomorrow, and some I would erase..." His gaze wandered for a moment. "But no, there's no place I'd rather be than the Garden." He smiled down at Zodak.

"How can you be so calm?"

"Let these fractured men take what they can from this old body. My spirit has one final adventure ahead of it yet," he said, the twinkle in his eye as bright as ever. "But as for you, my boy," continued Badu, his voice intensifying, "you must not give up. Your time has not come."

Zodak shook his head. "You don't understand—"

"You were built for a purpose," Badu cut in, "and you must not give in."

"Badu, I'm not who you believe I am."

"All right, pillboy!" came the cry from the heavyset guard in the hallway. "I told you it wouldn't be long. You ready to sing?"

"Take courage, son," said Badu. "There is strength in you!"

"You git away from him!" hollered the guard, fumbling with the keys. "He's not to be talked to by no one!"

"Zodak," said Badu urgently. "You *are* an Heir." Zodak

looked back quizzically even as the guard wrenched his arm, pulling him to his feet. "Heir to the Color Giver! Don't forget it."

"Shut up, you old buzzard! We'll silence you soon enough." The guard grabbed Zodak by the arm and the back of the collar and half marched, half dragged him down a long hallway, and up a flight of winding stairs. At the top, the panting and wheezing guard threw Zodak at Stohl's feet who stood like a statue before a pair of large ornate doors, a towering spear in hand.

"Hello, skupp." Stohl sneered down at Zodak.

"Jabbering with the old man in the toss," said the portly guard.

"Yes, you and Badu are acquainted, aren't you?" Stohl's eyes roved over Zodak. "Always find yourself in the thick of it, don't you? First Badu, then the skypiercer. And guess what? We've identified your skeyth companion killed in the market. A sherking Order Guard soldier. Quite a bounty on her head too. Kuquo will be very... interested to learn more about these acquaintances." A chilling scream came from within the throne room. "You're next." Stohl smiled at Zodak.

Zodak's heart thundered in his ears and his breath quickened. As dead as he felt inside, the prospect of imminent torture triggered ancient fear within him. He wanted to run. *Why are you here? You belong in a stable!* The minutes ticked by, punctuated by muffled screams from beyond the wall. After what felt like an eternity, the huge carved doors creaked open. Two guards dragged out the motionless, mangled body of a prisoner, leaving a smear of red in its wake.

"In you go." The portly guard pulled Zodak to his feet and Stohl reached for him. As he stood, Zodak swung his left elbow back fast, catching the hefty guard in the temple, and spun away from Stohl. He spied daylight down the long hallway and sprinted for the door.

With a *thud*, Stohl slammed the butt of his spear into

Zodak's thigh, sending him twirling and crashing to the marble floor on his shoulder and back. Stohl stood over him, pinning him to the ground with the spear.

In a cursing flurry, the jail guard rushed up behind Stohl, gripping his bleeding head and split brow, knife drawn. "Give 'im to me! I'll kill 'im!"

But Stohl blocked the guard with his solid forearm. "Not to worry, Ulyush, soon he'll be begging for that. And you may still get your wish when we're done with him."

Ulyush seethed, glaring down at Zodak, his face red as a pig turnip, one eye nearly swollen shut.

Stohl pulled Zodak to his feet and marched him into the throne room.

Magistrate Kuquo sat like an overstuffed frog on the golden chair at the end of the long room, attendants buzzing about him like flies on carrion. To the side of the throne was a table with leather straps for hands and feet. A servant pushed a mop messily over the bloodstained floor. Nearby, a hunched figure with a wide reptilian head and long arms, wearing an apron and spectacles, arranged tools on a stand beside the table. Zodak's stomach turned at the sight. The smell of rusted water filled the room despite the servants feverishly fanning the incense bars over candles near the Magistrate.

"Yes, fine. Have them take the farms and assemble there," Kuquo said to a servant, shooing him away.

"Your Highness," said Stohl as he approached the throne, bowing and forcing Zodak into a bow as well.

"Yes, Stohl? You bring me children? A thief?"

"No, sire. It's the boy I spoke to you about. The one with the skypiercer at the Fahyz Gate."

Kuquo's face still wore an annoyed, confused expression.

"The one with the medallion," Stohl said with a knowing nod.

Kuquo's head snapped up and his eyes flashed, jowls

spreading into a wide smile. "Oh, thank the Fire." He clapped his hands and closed his eyes. "Excellent! Very excellent. You found him. Well done, Stohl! Remind me to send you two extra slave girls tonight—"

"Sir," Stohl cut in. "He no longer carries the medallion." Kuquo's hands dropped, as did his smile. "He says it was stolen."

Hot anger flushed red on Kuquo's cheeks. "Stolen!" he roared, rising from his seat. "Boy—bring him closer," he snapped at Stohl, who shoved Zodak forward under the shadow of Kuquo's ample figure, towering over him from the dais. "Boy, do you know what I have done to find that medallion? What I have been through?" Zodak began shaking uncontrollably. "Wait." Understanding passed over Kuquo's face. "You were there that night, weren't you? Yes, it *was* you. You watched my giants fall. You watched Griss, my best bounty hunter breathe his last. You took the medallion and you fled." He collapsed back to his throne, his face darkening. "I need that medallion, boy, and you're going to help me find it."

"Says it was that moth Gormley who stole it," reported Stohl.

"When?" snapped Kuquo.

"Uh…" Stohl turned to Zodak. "Must have been yesterday, after our run-in at the gate."

"Y-yes," stammered Zodak. "Last night."

Kuquo's beady eyes bored into Zodak, something insidious in the gaze. "Is that so?"

Zodak nodded.

"Very interesting." He popped a pepperfruit into his mouth. "Because hunters found Gormley's body and wagon out by the entrance to the Dark Forest at dusk yesterday, a gaping wound in his back," said Kuquo simply. Freezing needles stabbed across Zodak's skin. "And there were reports from Scarab's Cantina of a skypiercer firing his bow out over the Fahyz Gate yesterday. Gormley may very well have stolen the medallion, but this boy, with the help of the skypiercer, stole it back. That's what took them outside the city." Silence sat heavy in the room. Zodak's stomach was in his throat.

"You lying moth," Stohl hissed at Zodak, the anger building behind his eyes.

"How did you catch him?" asked Kuquo, disinterested.

Stohl ripped his boring gaze away from Zodak. "He was in the middle of the market right after the blast. And there's more: he was with the very same skeyth Order Guard that killed six of our men last mooncycle."

"Was he? You have much to tell us, boy," snarled the Magistrate. "But first, the medallion. I have other plans for the Order."

"Are we ready?" growled the creature manning the torture table. Zodak decided its head looked most like that of a massive frog.

"Excellent, Quog," sang Kuquo, collapsing back in his throne and tossing a chip of krius in his mouth. *Quog the frog.* The thought almost made Zodak smile. Almost. The guards dragged Zodak to the table and pinned him down against his kicking and struggling as the reptile secured the leather straps. As he thrashed, Quog simply poked one scaly finger into his shoulder and another into his hip, sending excruciating pain lancing through his body and making his muscles go limp. Once Zodak was secure, Quog tilted the table upward so Kuquo could see him.

Zodak watched in terror as Quog carefully selected a scalpel.

"No, no," said Kuquo, "slowly. He has much to tell us." Quog replaced the knife and picked up a thin polished metal rod no longer than the handle of a mixing spoon, with a small ball at the end. Zodak sighed in momentary relief.

"Where is the medallion now?" asked Stohl. Zodak swallowed hard.

What are you protecting? The Order? The group that wanted to kill you only hours ago? The voice was back. *You owe them nothing. Why not just tell? Tell everything. About Blackiron. About the Order. Why walk this path of pain?*

"Your call has come. You are needed." Another voice rang out. It was the water sprite, speaking as clearly as a bell ringing in an empty room. "Much will be asked. But in you there is much courage." Zodak nodded slightly to himself. *You owe Daen.*

"It was stolen from me. I have no idea where it is," he finally blurted.

Kuquo shook his head, and Quog snapped the metal wand, striking Zodak on the temple. A flash of red shot across Zodak's vision and pain crackled through his head. The world tilted and a wave of nausea surged.

"That will feel like a tickle soon," croaked Quog as he snapped the wand again, this time landing a blow between Zodak's eyes. Searing pain shot like fire behind his eyes. For a moment he thought he would faint, his vision crossed, and a small trickle of blood rolled down the side of his nose.

"Shall we try again?" asked Kuquo, eating pepperfruit indifferently. He made a spinning motion with his finger to speed Quog along. Quog selected long handled snips, the brass top fashioned to resemble the head of a bird of prey, its beak, the blades. The heavy shears could easily sever a sapling.

"The fingers!" Stohl sounded excited as he pried back Zodak's fourth finger on his right hand.

"No!" Zodak screamed.

"Where, boy, is the medallion now?" Kuquo asked.

"Okay! Okay!" Zodak yelled. Fear roared like a lion inside him. Kuquo held up a finger to stay Quog who rolled his bulbous eyes.

"Yes?" urged Kuquo.

"*You were built for a purpose.*" It was Badu's voice now. "*You must not give in.*" From deep inside came a blast of defiant courage like a howling wind.

"It's at the bottom... of... Phi Bay," Zodak hissed.

"Fool!" Kuquo roared and threw a handful of pepperfruit out into the room. "Do it!" he commanded Quog.

Quog lifted the shears into place, sliding them over Zodak's finger. Zodak grimaced and looked away.

"Sire! Messenger!" A sharp cry from the guard at the doorway froze the room. Zodak opened squinted eyes to see a gray blur streak into the room with incredible speed and stop at Kuquo's feet. There crouched a tiny figure, a child to Zodak's eyes. Magistrate Kuquo's face beamed at the sight of him. He rose from his chair.

"Sire?" Quog croaked eagerly, shears at the ready.

"No, no!" Kuquo waved him off distractedly. "Go! Leave us!"

"But sire," Quog objected.

Stohl shot out a hand to Quog's arm. "We'll resume presently," he said. Disappointment flashed across the creature's flat face as he let the shears fall. He returned the implement to its stand and ambled down the length of the throne room, pausing only once to steal a hungry glance at Zodak.

"Heldin! My dear Heldin. You returned sooner than I expected. Did you meet with difficulty?" Kuquo's face fell with apprehension.

"No, sire. On the contrary, I gained entrance just as you said I would." The little man's face was aged, and he spoke like no child. *Who is this?* Zodak wondered. His eyes fell to the curious sparkling silver bands on his ankles.

"And what have you learned?"

"I have been inside. Blackiron is vulnerable, sire," he replied.

The words stabbed Zodak like a knife. *Blackiron? This wretched spy has infiltrated Blackiron?*

"The news of the Elder's death caused quite a stir. They spoke of marching against the castle, but some argued for patience. When I return with the report of the captured sorcerer, I believe it will quell their ire." The little man proceeded to describe the fortress, the various entrances, the password, and the defenses. He described the hideout in tremendous detail. He even told of the Great Hall and the council convened at the grand table. *Did he meet Daen? Ozir?* Rage flashed through Zodak. He pulled against his wrist strap, hoping beyond hope that it might rip free so he could launch himself at this despicable pill and tear him apart. The leather bonds held tight.

"Excellent work, Heldin," said Kuquo. "If you keep this up, you will have a place among our spies."

"I would ask only that our agreement be honored, my lord," replied Heldin as he bowed. Kuquo's eyes flashed with anger at being rebuffed. He shot a quivering hand over the bowed runner's head. But he steadied himself, drawing his hand back in.

"Return quickly with news of the sorcerer Badu," Kuquo said. "He is to be beheaded at midday. The Magistrate will deliver justice to the High Elder's murderer before all his subjects. It is just as Müziel predicted," Kuquo added quietly to himself. "Very good. Be off!"

"Yes, sire," said Heldin, turning to leave. "Oh, sire." He paused and turned back to the Magistrate. "I nearly forgot. The medallion. The one you asked about. The dark dwarf Ozir wears it around his neck."

"What?!" Kuquo was on his feet again. "Are you sure?"

"Yes, sire. It's exactly as you described it."

Zodak's heart sank.

"Heldin, you shall have a farm and a dozen cliqs of land before the day is out!" declared Kuquo. "I shall see to it."

"Yes, sire," said Heldin, turning to go. His gaze lingered on

Zodak for a moment and then he sped out, as if launched from a crossbow.

"Well, I suppose that's good news for you, boy," Kuquo said to Zodak. "And certainly good for me. I really haven't the stomach for another torturing today. Anyway, I need a wink." He collapsed back thunderously into his throne. "Let's not prolong the inevitable, Stohl. Just take him to the chambers and dispose of him." Kuquo sounded almost bored.

"What of his connections to the Order?" Stohl objected. "Quog can still draw information from him—"

"We have the medallion, Stohl. We have Blackiron. What else do we need?" Kuquo fished out another flake of krius and deposited it on his tongue. "By the time the day is out, we'll have Ozir's head on a pole. He'll die knowing the legendary Order is no more."

"We could do it publicly." A sly grin crept across Stohl's face as he nodded towards Zodak. Kuquo looked at him quizzically. "I caught the boy in the market with Badu just a few days past. Perhaps he's the sorcerer's apprentice." Stohl winked.

"You do enjoy your theatrics, don't you, Stohl? Very well. Just remember there is much to do, much to plan for. Müziel's hordes are already arriving. He will be here any hour."

"Yes, my lord." Stohl's tongue flicked over his teeth as he smiled down at Zodak. *What is wrong with this man?*

"You appear to have all your fingers," said Badu as Zodak pushed himself up off the cell's dirty floor to wavering hands and knees, still recovering from Ulyush's parting gut punch. The guard had promised to come back for more. The guard's poor whistling could still be heard as he ambled down the hall.

"They're going to kill us both," said Zodak, pausing to spit on the floor. "At midday. They'll drag us to the square and declare you the sorcerer who killed the High Elder, and I your apprentice."

"Ah. So, they plan to pull you in too."

"And the Magistrate said there are hordes marching here and they would take over Blackiron and ruin the Order." Zodak stood painfully. "And some woman named Muriel or something would be bringing them."

"Müziel?" Badu's head snapped up.

"Yeah, that's it."

"Oh dear," said Badu, his face suddenly hardening. "It's even more serious than I thought. Then there isn't any time to waste, is there?" He cocked his head, his eyes roving in thought.

"Huh?" Zodak was lost.

Badu spread a flea-bitten shawl on the floor and lowered himself awkwardly to a cross-legged seat. In each hand, he gathered a handful of the foul sawdust and dirt covering the floor and closed his eyes. Zodak shook his head and threw up his hands. One minute grew to three and dragged to five as Badu sat perfectly still.

Finally, Zodak cleared his throat. "No time to waste for what?" he whispered loudly, trying to interrupt politely. Badu didn't move. "What does it matter?" said Zodak with a sigh, turning away. "We're trapped like skupp in here."

Down the hall, the sound of whistling grew louder as Ulyush paced his practiced route, staring into each cell, daring any prisoner to meet his gaze. Zodak slunk back to the edge of the cell and tried to make himself look small to avoid the guard's attention. As he waited, he caught sight of the frail old man beside him. Meditating, or whatever it was, in view of the guard seemed risky, yet from the serene look on Badu's face he might have been dreaming. *How old is he?* wondered Zodak. *Is he a grandfather?* Zodak felt a stab of guilt, realizing he hadn't ever asked anything about Badu or where he came from. Even as he studied the old bird, Badu's eyes shot open. He sprang to his feet with the grace of a man half his age, then steadied himself on the bars.

"Get ready, my boy." His eyes gleamed mischievously, and he winked. Turning to the hallway, he called out loudly, "Esmerelda!"

"What?" Zodak asked. A confused grunt rose from the hallway.

"It's Esmerelda!" called Badu.

"What?!" boomed Ulyush from the hallway, anger flashing in his beady eyes. "What the downs did you just say?"

"She has a message for you!" said Badu.

"You shut your sherking mouth!" roared Ulyush, fumbling for the keys to Badu's cell.

"Esmerelda," repeated Badu loud and clear.

"I said shut your slagging mouth!" the guard was screaming now as he flung the door open and rushed at Badu. The beating was swift and severe. Badu tried to cling to the guard, but was shoved to the floor, kicked, punched, and even thrown against the wall as the tornado of Ulyush's fury whipped inside the cell.

"No! Stop! Stop it!" Zodak yelled. He might as well have been a mute. Zodak had to avert his gaze until the sound of the blows subsided. When he finally looked up, Ulyush stood, chest heaving over Badu's crumpled old body.

"If you weren't to be paraded into town today to be cut in two, I'd a' done worse tah you, you old scat sack!" Ulyush spat on the old man. "But speak that name again, and I'll take your tongue!" The guard slammed the cell door and stomped off.

"Badu!" Zodak rushed to the edge of the cell where Badu lay in a heap. To his relief, the old man moved his head and opened his eyes a slit.

"What was that?" Zodak stammered. "Who's Esmerelda?"

"I have no idea," Badu's thin voice replied with the hint of a smile. "The Figure gave me that name. It was a gift."

"A gift?" Zodak was sure Ulyush had broken some bones.

"Yes." Badu smiled. "And I have one for you." The old man lifted a shaky arm from his robe. As Zodak gripped the cool skin of the bony hand between his own, he felt Badu pass him something smooth and thin. He looked down and there in his hand rested the cell door key. "And when Ulyush calls for a song, it's your time to go."

"What? How do you have this?" Zodak's mind spun. "You stole this from him? *Just now?*"

Badu closed his eyes and nodded, still smiling. "You haven't long, boy," said Badu sleepily, eyes still shut. "I hope to see you in the Garden," he coughed softly, "but not today. Remember, wait until he calls for music." His eyes closed.

"What will I do? They'll catch me! They'll kill me," Zodak protested. "Badu!"

Badu jerked slightly as if waking from a dream. "To the right, at the end of the hall there is a rubbish chute. It will get you out."

"But... how?"

Badu only tapped his ear.

"You pathetic pill!" came Ulyush's shout from down the hall. "I didn't smuggle that in here for nothing. Stop your whining and play me a song!"

"Go, son. Go! Covered in Color."

"But... I..." Zodak objected, even as he rose.

"Music!" came Ulyush's shout again. Zodak squeezed Badu's hand one last time. He rose on unsteady legs and stumbled to the door.

With trembling hands, he reached through the bars and tried the key in the rusty lock. *Could this work? Is it the right one?* It glided into the keyhole and with a *clunk*, the door unlocked and creaked open a few inches.

"Thank you!" he hissed in a whisper at Badu. The old man didn't answer or move. It was as if he'd fallen asleep.

Zodak slipped into the hallway. To the left of the cell where the passage curved out of sight, he could just make out the guard's shadow, cast on the wall by the torchlight, and he could hear Ulyush's shouting and the faint strumming of a lyre. The shadow grew larger as Ulyush began his plodding return down the corridor. Zodak tried closing the cell door quietly and set off quickly in the other direction, his heart thumping like a tribe of mountain trolls in his ribs.

He moved as fast as he dared over the cracked stone floor in the dim light, terrified that he would trip or crash into some discarded pile of refuse, sounding the alarm. The growing volume of Ulyush's heckling insults told him the guard was on the move. Zodak barely even glanced at the pathetic, broken souls chained in the dungeon around him. He couldn't bear to see the faces of these poor wretches. A roaring cry erupted from the passage behind. There was a shuffling sound, and a bell began to ring. *They've discovered me!* Zodak abandoned caution and sprinted ahead. "Boy!" came the scream from down the hall.

Dirty torchlight splashed the grimy walls at the end of the hallway. There ahead, fastened to the center of the wall, hung a square wooden door with a handle affixed to the top. He dashed forward as the sound of boots filled the chamber. Reaching the dead end, he yanked the handle down, opening a black hole in the wall. The stench assailed him, striking like a rotting serpent, knocking him backward.

"Down this way! Look, there he is!" came a voice from behind.

Without looking back, Zodak dove into the chute, into the mouth of that putrid beast. He fell down the shaft, tumbling and bouncing off the walls. The bottom rushed up suddenly and he braced for impact, but his body dumped out into a large room into a forgiving mountain of filth. For a moment he froze, listening. The garbage chute ended in a dimly lit cavern beneath the castle. A massive fire burned in a huge round hearth off to one side, and a diverted finger of the Zhar river ran through here to carry refuse from the bowels of the castle.

He heard no sound other than the roar of burning trash and the gurgle of swift flowing water. Hastily arranged fire-tending tools leaned against an empty stool beside the hearth that still smoldered. If there was an attendant here, he looked to have recently abandoned the post. Zodak rose painful to his feet, the reek causing him to momentarily lose his footing. Shouts echoed through the chute followed by a loud clattering noise. The chute shook and roared like a choking dragon. They were coming! Without hesitation, he sprang from the pile of trash and leapt into the cold black rushing water. As he plunged into the frigid depths and felt himself swept into darkness, he had but one thought: *Escape!*

36

"There is much to mourn," said Ozir, addressing the council. "But now is not the time. Rislaan is in grave danger. We sit in the eye of the storm, and if we do not act now, we may not later be afforded a chance to grieve."

"And against whom do we march?" asked Pegarah. "The Magistrate's guard? Some outside evil?"

"It's a mistake to challenge Magistrate Kuquo without evidence of his involvement," argued Hilbane.

"We should await Horgor's report," added another dwarf. "This misdeed could've been carried out by anyone."

"No. No, it could not," replied Pegarah flatly. "Blue fire? The Special Guard gone in a single blast?" She shook her head. "No, this is the work of a powerful foe."

"What foe, Pegarah?" asked Silden. "Are you suggesting..."

"The return is foretold," answered Pegarah, her purple eyes flashing. "Some say he gathers strength even now."

"The Ice King?" blurted Hilbane incredulously. "Pure fantasy!"

Pegarah shook her head.

"I have reported the visions seen by Moarun, my tribe's

Seer," said Talbor. "Müziel, communing with the Ice King in Flat Water."

Awalmir snorted and rolled his eyes.

"Whether the work of the Ice King or some other force, we must assume such a bold step was made with calculated purpose," said Silden. "Uth Becca's fate may be shifting. The attack on the High Elder could be the first strike of many. We mustn't waver."

"It would be better to wait than to attack a potential ally," retorted Hilbane.

"Ally?" erupted Daen. "Magistrate Kuquo is as tainted as they come. He's Müziel's puppet already, or that of the Ice King or both. I say we cut the head from the snake and take back this city!" Sporadic calls of assent rose around the table.

"You remain quick to fight," scolded Ozir. "Though we have reason to suspect the Magistrate, I believe Hilbane is right. I want retribution as much as any of you, but without proof of the Magistrate's involvement, we cannot risk an attack that would topple the balance of power, especially with the Elder gone. We must wait." Some of the group grumbled, some chirped in agreement.

"Sir," Daen addressed Ozir.

"Speak," replied Ozir.

"I understand the call for caution," said Daen. "But whether we choose blindness toward his fell heart or no, we must all admit that the Order's presence in Uth Becca has long been a thorn in Magistrate Kuquo's side. He may have learned of your desire to dethrone him. We know he does not eagerly share power, and we have all heard of his relentless searching for Blackiron—"

"He searches for you!" exclaimed Awalmir's companion. Disdain contorted his face, and he shook a quivering claw of a finger at Daen. Awalmir nodded in agreement.

"Perhaps his search will lead him here," added Delmuth.

"Perhaps it has!" Delmuth glanced around self-consciously at his outburst, returning to his seat.

"The Magistrate wants Daen's head, there is no denying that," said Ozir. "But more even than Daen, he wants this place found and razed. Let's hear what Daen has to say."

"My point, Gyalp," continued Daen, facing the interrupting man, "is that if this attack is from the Magistrate, whether of his own accord or orchestrated by Müziel, the Ice King, or some other power"—he gestured toward Pegarah—"as Silden suggests, it may be part of something larger. If so, he will redouble his efforts to find Blackiron. And if this is not his doing, he will certainly smell power in this tragedy. A man like that doesn't miss such an opportunity."

"A strengthened magistrate could be an ally!" retorted Gyalp.

"In the meantime," continued Daen, unfazed, "I believe it would be wise to at least lock down traffic in and out of the fortress and post a pod at each of the five tunnels."

"And ready the troops for battle?" asked Silden. "Should the need arise," he added.

Ozir nodded. "Do I hear objections to securing Blackiron and preparing the troops?" asked Ozir. The room was quiet.

"Such a course of action seems an exercise in futility, sire," remarked Hilbane. "If the Magistrate isn't involved, against whom do we march?"

"We do not march. We only prepare, as a precaution, Hilbane," answered Ozir. "We would be foolish to ignore the threat posed by this night."

Hilbane finally nodded in reluctant agreement.

"Seal the gates and ready the milblock commanders!" Ozir ordered. Delmuth motioned to a nearby servant, sending the boy rushing from the Great Hall.

At the heavy table, the discussion of strategy and preparations roiled for the better part of an hour. Dried fish, jerky, flatbread, fruit, and honeycomb were served with goblets of ale and falswine. As the group pored over various logistics, readiness plans, and stronghold suitability in tedious detail, a crier's alert shook the room.

"Runner!" shouted the guard at the entrance to the hall. The familiar gray blur streaked through the room and halted before Ozir. Heldin bent low.

"Heldin, arise," said Ozir, shaking off the drowsiness that had begun to creep in through the logistics review. "Did you manage to find Horgor?"

"Yes, but—"

"Excellent. Thank you, Heldin." Ozir began a salute.

"There is more, my lord," Heldin continued.

"Go on," Ozir urged.

"They found him," said Heldin meekly.

"What? Found who, man?"

"The assassin!" blurted Heldin. "The one who destroyed the caravan!"

"What?!" Ozir leapt to his feet. Soon the entire group was up, edging towards the runner.

"Yes, the Magistrate's City Guard has captured a dark magician or sorcerer. That moth who killed..." he stammered, squeezing his eyes closed and clenching his teeth. "The city guard has him in the stockade," he continued. "I passed just as they made an official announcement identifying the traitor. He is to be beheaded at midday."

"And they are sure this is the one?" asked Ozir.

"The Magistrate himself has proof of the assassination. They found the sorcerer's magic staff, still smoldering with blue flame."

"You see?" said Hilbane in triumph. "Marching on the Magistrate would have been pure folly. He has captured the fiend who committed this vile act."

Daen shook his head. "A single sorcerer? Who could wield such power?"

"Perhaps Müziel himself?" offered Talbor.

"If only we were so fortunate," scoffed Awalmir.

"Not to worry, we will discover the identity of this assailant," declared Ozir. "But we have good news after a long night. We should retire and rest, for tonight we have avoided war." Ozir raised a glass. All at the table joined to cheer a toast; all but Daen who fixed the runner with a searching stare.

37

Zodak thought only of survival as the rushing river swept him from the castle, tumbling him end over end in the frigid water. He was a passable swimmer, yet everything ached and throbbed, and the angry water threatened to pull his beaten body under. In his thrashing, his hand found a floating plank that he clung to for dear life, even as he gasped for breath in the biting cold water. His eyes darted from bank to bank, fearing pursuit from the guards, but the water moved him swiftly and soon, the twinkling lights of the castle had grown distant. When the current had slowed, he gathered his strength and pushed off from the plank, swimming for the bank with all his power. But even as he paddled desperately, the pain and fatigue overtook him, and he began to sink beneath the surface. As darkness enveloped him, panic set in. He swallowed mouthfuls of the foul river water. Kicking and choking, he somehow managed to pull his head up out of the water and flailed towards the black smudge of riverbank.

Gasping, Zodak clawed his way through the mud to the dirt bank. He clutched fistfuls of the scrub brush and dragged himself up hand over hand before collapsing under the shadow of the city's great wall. Another fifteen mounts in the water and he'd have been swept straight out of Uth Becca. For what felt like an eternity, he lay panting, cheek pressed to the dirt like a beached dartfish under dawn's cold scowl. He suddenly felt sick and rolled over in time to throw up mostly river water before crumpling back to the bank.

His head pounded, and his body felt as if he had fallen from a great tree, hitting all its branches on the way down. He trembled uncontrollably in the cold.

You'd be better off dead, a voice whispered in his head.

Or sleeping back in the Oak with no memory, he retorted.

Look at you. Why are you here? taunted the voice.

Where can I go? he asked.

There is nowhere for you. What do you have left? You're nothing.

Badu said—

That old fool? the voice mocked. *He'll have his head on a pole by sunset. You don't need to end up like him. Why fight? Why not just give in? Let go. Let it all go. You're weak. Crawl back into the river. The icy water will finish its work.* There was something appealing about that thought, about ending the pain that tormented his body and mind. A quiet escape from it all. Over his own weak objections, his body began to comply. Trembling arms pushed him up off the ground to his knees. He looked at the swirling black water.

Good, coaxed the voice. *One leap in, a deep breath, and your troubles are over.* The Perkins boy had drowned in the feed pond one winter in Laan. Zodak hadn't been there, but he remembered the boy's cousin had described how peaceful the passing was once the thrashing had stopped.

Yes, a peaceful slipping away. That doesn't sound bad, does it? asked the voice.

Zodak rocked back on his knees, shaking his head. *No.* He

covered his face with his hands. *Aarrgh!* He cried alone in the dark, battling the oppressive despair that filled him.

It doesn't need to be a fight. The voice was gentle now. *Come,* it urged.

He dropped his hands to his sides, rocked back and forth, and wept. The overwhelm, the exhaustion, the unfairness of it all. In anger and desperation, he squinted his eyes shut, clawing at the gritty riverbank soil, and he screamed.

Even as he did, in the dark of his mind, behind shut eyelids, he felt himself suddenly falling. Down he plunged into a black abyss rimmed with glowing white. When the blackness had wholly swallowed him, everything stopped. He hung in a silent void. The darkness exploded in a flash, and he was suddenly spewed from the darkness into blinding white light that seared his eyes. *Am I asleep? Dead?*

He came to rest on hands and knees on brilliant white against brilliant white. Slowly color and texture began to return. Beneath his knees and hands, he felt something spongy and green. This wasn't the riverbank. Instead of mud, his fingers gripped cool, velvety moss, and a floral smell of earth and forest engulfed him. The world slowly came into focus. He found himself kneeling on a bulbous mound of moss under a brilliant sun. There were hundreds of these mossy domed outcroppings extending in every direction, each swaying gently in independent motion, giving his perch an oceanic feel. Lifting his gaze, Zodak's breath caught. The undulating carpet was no floor, but a pedestal atop the world. A marq ahead, the emerald carpet dropped away. Before him spread an unimaginably vast landscape thousands of mounts below. The jagged jaw of a mountain a thousand cliqs off reached up to snap the skirt of the piercing blue ceiling of cloudless sky. Golden-green hills tumbled down the foot of the distant peaks and immense carpets of black forest sprawled as far as he could see, etched with the occasional vein of river or rock outcropping. The scene was both magnificent and remote, as if viewed from a cloud. Beyond the end of his mossy pad, the world plunged straight down for an eternity.

"*Some who are within it lose the majesty of the work,*" came a voice from nowhere and everywhere, rumbling thunder within him.

"Am I dead?" Zodak asked aloud, looking around for the source of the voice.

"*Not dead, child. But so grieved, so weary,*" came the voice again, low like a river. "*Rest now.*" No sooner had the words been spoken than the moss patch beneath Zodak began to dissolve, the firm earthen carpet giving way to a feather-soft fiber, like freshly spun clouds. Fear flashed through Zodak as he began to sink into the melting earth.

"*It's all right.*" A jolt of cold energy ripped through him, followed by a warm wave of calm. All fear was gone. He let himself sink into the fleecy nest. Down he slipped, silently, the fatigue suddenly an overpowering wave within. Like a sleepy toddler in the arms of a parent, he let himself go, a complete relinquishing. He plunged into slumber, or if not sleep, some profound, bottomless respite. It lasted but a moment, or had it been a season? If it *was* slumber, it was deep and dreamless.

He awoke chasing wisps of memories of wondrous travels through time and memory and found himself back again on the swaying moss carpet above the world, brimming with a new, indescribable elation. He hoped never to leave. *This is where I want to stay. Forever,* he thought. A picture of the world, of Uth Becca, flitted at the fringes of his mind and repulsed him. Dirty, angry, falsehood saturated the place. Towns, villages, cities, castles. Full of millions of insects trapped in the noise. The constant, incessant, futile striving for naught. Nothing down there mattered.

"*I know.*" The voice like a zephyr rushing through a canyon resonated in his own chest, answering the unasked question.

"They pursue much of no significance, and yet the struggle is of the utmost consequence. You long for escape, yet this now is not your place or time, Zodak. You must return."

Before him there opened a small dark pool in the moss, its surface shimmering like polished black glass. In the inky pool before him, he saw the picture of the crumpled figure on a riverbank at first light, broken and crushed by despair and self-loathing. His heart wept for that hopeless boy. His yearning for death, for escape, broke Zodak's heart.

"What am I to do? Where am I to go?" Zodak looked up to the crystalline heavens.

"Doors will open. They will close. The choices, though, are yours. And choose, you must, and you will."

The pool before him glowed lava red, and a string of images flashed across its glassy surface in rapid succession. First came pictures from the past, flashes from Laan, from his home. He saw the great old farmhouse, the sweeping porch outside the bluestone kitchen floor, the drought, the schoolhouse. It was like watching someone flip through a book of images of his life. Many flicked past almost too quickly for comprehension, but others played like a scene. The queensweight won in Komo. He flinched watching Ardon slay the giant in the clearing. He glimpsed the image of a sword he never picked up; his flight; the tuks; the Oak; Blackiron; in the basket-maker's tent. It was all there.

He saw his capture and flight from the castle. There was Badu in prison but standing tall like a soldier, in conversation with a gleaming warrior. And there were new pictures of things he had never seen: the Order council debating, the traitorous Heldin addressing Ozir, and rows and rows of hideous goblins and krikkis in battle gear marching on a dusty country road.

There appeared a hazy, smoke-filled cave. Zodak was running. Someone lay on the ground. It was Daen, unconscious. Zodak yelped as a krikkis leapt on Daen and stabbed again and again. Zodak tried to jerk away, but he couldn't escape the scenes. A monster emerged from the smoke. The image flashed to Ozir's limp body on the ground, a gnarled margoul hand ripping the medallion from his neck. The Lady Voli, engulfed by margoul in a forest clearing. Then he saw himself outside in the sunshine atop the world, then standing beside a very much alive Daen in the countryside. Ozir sitting regally on the Magistrate's throne. A wedding. Then Zodak, running beside Voli through the woods; towering waves; an enormous tree, as tall as a castle, a sea of warriors in battle, a duel. There was too much.

The pool flashed back to serene, starry blackness. The visions were gone.

"What was that?!" Zodak gasped, his heart racing.

"*You must not despair,*" rumbled the voice.

"Will that all happen? Will they die?"

"*Many great stories are yet unwritten. Many paths are yet to be laid. Off you go now.*"

The surface of the pool began to ripple as a breeze swept over him. The breeze turned to a whipping wind. Zodak shut his eyes against the wind, and as he did, the world spun. Hard mud and grass replaced the spongy moss in his hands. He slowly opened his swollen eyes. It was as he'd feared: he had returned to the riverbank.

"*You are treasured,*" came the voice once more, softer now, like the final rumble of a passing storm. With a jolt of newfound resolve, he rose to his still-unsteady legs, and turned his back on the water. He thought he heard something, the shadow of a sound, really, barely louder than a memory. The sound of frantic swishing, like something fleeing, accompanied by a muted anguished cry fading away into the dark as the sun rose on his face.

THE SLANTING MORNING sun sliced through the drab blue row of buildings, coaxing steam out of the cobblestones. Zodak stepped shivering into a slice of sunrise and closed his eyes, letting the chill creep up his spine as his sodden clothes softly hissed. His body felt heavy all over and a sharp pain seared his left temple and behind his eyes. He could tell bruises were beginning to form where the guards had landed punches. His neck ached from his tumble down the garbage chute, and his left thigh burned from where Stohl struck him with the spear butt. Yet, somehow, he had found it.

"Dry Goods" read the faded sign over the doorway. The city slowly awoke and with it, the steady trickle of traffic from the Fahyz Gate. When the street was clear, he slid around the back of the building and to the same entrance he and Daen had passed through the afternoon before. *Could it be? That felt like seasons ago. A lifetime ago. When I thought I was special. The Shielder.* He snorted mirthlessly. *When I was a fool.* He brushed aside the mocking voice, knowing he'd invite it back in at another, quieter time. But now he had to get to Blackiron. He had to warn them. *Could he even make it inside? If he did, what would they do to him?* The thought sat like a stone on his shoulders. A stone giant. He shuddered, recalling the obsidian black guardian in the throat of the passage, the statuesque behemoth and his terrible axe falling like a guillotine. *Maybe he's not there? You have to try.*

The shelf behind the counter was lined with dusty containers and trinkets. *What had Daen pulled to open the door?* He grabbed cans and bottles, tossing them on the floor. Then he spotted the unremarkable copper cylinder with a faint sunburst pattern painted in faded navy ink that flashed in his memory. He lifted it off the shelf, feeling resistance as he pulled. Instead of coming up in his hand, it tilted forward and something behind the wall groaned as the shelf sank into the floor. *It worked!* He stepped cautiously into the dark lift, recalling the wild terror of his last visit to the closet, but that fear was gone. Groping about blindly, he finally grasped the smooth wooden lever protruding from the wall. He took a breath and pulled. As before, the floor dropped, plunging him down into darkness.

Darkness. He had forgotten to bring any sort of torch or light. He sat for a moment in the bottom of that pit, in stillness, waiting for his eyes to adjust to the inky cavern, but they did not. Cautiously, he rose to his feet and stepped forward, abandoning sight and following the unseen memory of this place in his mind's eye. Groping along the wall, he found the opening to the winding passage. Walking without seeing, hands patting the craggy walls of the tunnel, he made his way. After what felt like an eternity in darkness, the sandy ground gave way to solid, smooth stone and a dim light flickered ahead.

Zodak skipped ahead, but froze when he heard the conversation. *The guards! They're here!* Panic set in. His pulse raced and his stomach twisted. He glanced around, frantically looking for somewhere to run or hide. *Maybe I could just turn myself in? No, they would never bring me into Blackiron. They might kill me on the spot.* The deep rumbling discussion continued.

With trembling steps, Zodak crept forward, the hair on his neck standing on end. Around the curving passage, he spotted the open room and caught sight of the doorway with the etchings. *It's open!* He edged closer until he could see just a sliver of the owner of the powerful voice. His heart dropped. The stone giant was still there. And he spoke to someone. *Go back. You'll die here!* snapped a voice in his head. *No. I can try to explain why I'm here,* he told himself unconvincingly. He inched closer for a better view of the guard's full body, and his heart leapt. The giant was exactly where they had left him the night before, and he continued to count incessantly on his fingers. *The riddle!*

Heart thundering, Zodak emerged from the tunnel, every muscle taut and ready to sprint back down the passage. As he stepped forward, the guard looked up. His black eyes landed on Zodak's for a moment, but then immediately flicked back to his hand to resume counting. Without pause, Zodak scurried through the doorway and sprinted down the long smooth corridor. He stopped to look back only when he had reached the end of the passage that spilled into the soft glow of the vast cavern. The giant hadn't followed.

Zodak sighed in relief and slumped to the ground, panting. Everything burned. His eyes danced over the beautiful cavern, surveying the grand fortress and the impossible path he had to travel to reach its doors. Tiny gnats stood at attention atop the lookout spires, and Zodak counted a dozen more guards surrounding the fortress. The boats were gone, and he could see only one wagon inching like a beetle along the road on the far edge of the chamber towards the barracks.

What will they do to me when they catch me? he let himself wonder. *They'll kill you,* the voice inside answered too quickly. *Maybe not. Maybe they'll listen to my warning and just give me chiproot. Then I'll be no worse off than last night. Or maybe... just maybe, when I've proved myself, they'll welcome me back in.* The thought seemed like an impossibility. *Don't they kill outsiders who break in?* And he had, twice now. It didn't matter, the choice was made. The path was set.

The smooth stone floor called him to rest, to lie down for a moment. *No!* Zodak forced himself to his feet and trudged ahead, picking his way down the rocky bank to the cavern floor, battling through pain at each step. When he reached the bottom, he stopped. *Should I run? No, slow is better.* He raised both hands in surrender and began walking towards the castle. The bridge and spires stood a hundred mounts off. At this pace, it would be an eternity until he reached Blackiron. No sooner had the thought passed through his mind than a whining scream filled the air and an arrow slammed into his chest, knocking him to the ground.

And suddenly he saw it all in such crisp, cruel clarity. *This plan, the hope, had all been a fool's errand, destined to end in disaster. This is no children's fort, no game.* Fear welled up like a spring and regret drowned Zodak as he lay on his back, struggling for breath, the arrow protruding from his sternum. *Should have stayed,* was the only thought that came to mind as he choked for breath and his head spun, a distant trumpet blast piercing the air.

But as he lay, waiting for the end, life did not seep from him. Breath suddenly rushed back into his pounding chest. Wincing, he looked down at the wound. Instead of a clean arrow shaft pooling with blood, there on his chest sat a thick green gelatinous mound stuck to his shirt with an arrow protruding. He laughed to himself, then winced in pain, even as the rushing guards surrounded him with weapons drawn. A tall guard wearing a crimson sash yanked Zodak to his feet, wrenching the arrow and thick glop from Zodak's chest.

"How'd you get in here!" demanded a thick guard with an eye patch.

"Why'd he use the stun?" asked another.

"Just a kid," said a third. "An' he's all wet!" They slipped two rope loops over Zodak's hands and pulled tightly.

"Wait! I have news!" said Zodak. "It's urgent. I must speak with Ozir. Blackiron is in danger! Daen is in danger!" The three guards laughed heartily. The closest one yanked him close, and for the second time in the last day, a heavy black hood covered Zodak's head. Strong hands grabbed either arm, and marched him forward. Zodak kept crying out his warning, but either they couldn't hear him in the hood or didn't care. Every blindfolded step on the rope bridge felt like it might be his last, but he finally felt solid ground on the other side.

"What's this?" Zodak heard a voice.

"Looks like he sneaked in somehow," answered the crimson guard.

"Sneaked in? Why does he yet breathe?" asked the voice. Silence.

"Lookout hit him with a stunner. Thought we'd bring him to you."

"Fools," spat the superior. "Intruders are not tolerated here." Zodak heard the swish of a sword sliding from its hilt. "I'll do it myself. Remove that and let him die like a man." Someone ripped the hood from Zodak's head.

"Wait, I—" shouted Zodak. The figure before him drew up for the final blow.

"*You?*" stammered Kahn, his sword frozen in the air. "How... how did you get here?" He slowly dropped his sword hand.

"I must speak with Daen," urged Zodak. "It's urgent!"

Kahn just stood for a moment, perplexed. "I thought they had... thought you were..." His voice trailed off.

"No, they hadn't—I'm not. But please, you're in danger. All of you."

"No, son. The danger to Blackiron has passed," Kahn reassured, sheathing his sword.

"It hasn't. Please, I must speak with Daen. Or Ozir," Zodak pleaded.

Kahn snorted. "After what I've seen today, I'd take my own eye before I brought *you* back in the fortress."

"I speak the truth! There is a spy! I had a vision of Daen's death!" cried Zodak.

"Yes, there is a spy," said Kahn, stealing a glance at one of the other guards. "But don't worry, we've caught him now." He winked.

"You *have*? Oh, good—" Zodak caught the amused faces of the guards. "Wait. Me?" More laughter. "No, there is—"

"The castle rests. But when my watch ends, I will discuss what is to be done with you," said Kahn. "Not something you should look forward to, though. To the pen!" he ordered.

The guards marched Zodak to the foot of one of the tall

lookout spires, where there stood a sturdy cage, no bigger than a pair of covered wagons.

"Never seen anyone in here," said the crimson soldier to a stocky black-haired guard with a long scraggly beard to match. The bearded guard only shrugged. They tossed Zodak in and locked the door.

"Wait! You have to believe me!" Zodak shouted as they turned to go. "It's the runner! He's spying for the Magistrate." It was no use. The guards couldn't have paid less attention if he were a barking dog.

Before long, they had resumed their patrol. Zodak tried yelling up through the bars to the scout atop the spire, but it was no use. The man was hundreds of measures up. "You sooty, charred, blind, sherking, slagging sims!" Zodak yelled every vulgarity he could think of. "*Aaaggghhh!*" he screamed into the wind, shaking the thick metal bars. When his breath gave out, he collapsed to the floor. He drew his knees up and seethed.

For what felt like hours, he sat in the pen. He slept in fits. He woke and yelled until his voice began to fail. He practiced his speech before Ozir—or perhaps the executioner. From the cage, he could see the doors to Blackiron. *Maybe Daen will appear there,* he hoped. He fixed his eyes on the gate, but the only movement was the perimeter guard patrol and the two half-giants occasionally bantering back and forth. Zodak wondered what half-giants talked about to fill the dead hours.

Lying on his side, his mind many cliqs off, Zodak was carefully shaping tiny domed sand piles into houses, when movement at the fortress gate suddenly ripped him back. A small figure emerged from Blackiron and raced by in a streak of gray.

"Hey! Stop! It's him!" screamed Zodak, jumping to his feet. Nobody heard him. "Wait! Stop! Somebody stop him," he shrieked. "Heldin! You moth! I hope you burn!"

The runner suddenly stopped just before stepping onto the rope bridge and glanced his way. His face screwed up.

"You sherking coward! You pill!" shouted Zodak.

Then, changing course, the runner sped over, and in a flash stood before the cage. "Impossible! You can't be the boy I just saw fit to be disemboweled before the Magistrate," Heldin sputtered.

"You're scat, less than that," shot Zodak. "I'll tell them who you are! What you've done. You'll hang! You'll burn!"

"You haven't much of an audience at present. Besides, I'll be far from here." A pained look of grief suddenly passed over the runner's smug face. "What is done is done."

"Because *you* did it. How can you sentence so many to death? You're nothing but a traitor! A coward! Didn't you serve the High Elder? Did you kill her too?!"

"No!" Heldin barked. "I had nothing to do with that!" He shook his head.

"You lie!" Zodak seethed. "I've seen what you do. I know who you are."

Heldin was quiet for a moment, his head hanging. "You have seen what I do," he said finally. "But you don't know why. And you don't know who I am."

"You are what you do, moth!" said Zodak. "Remember that when you're sitting in your new farm. I hope the screams of the men you've handed to Kuquo ring in your ears."

"My daughter!" Heldin screeched, his voice cracking. "Kuquo has my daughter and my wife. I cannot repeat the terrible things he said he would do to them if I didn't help him." Heldin shook his head. "I had no choice."

"You did. You always do," said Zodak. "I may be nobody, but I am here. And I will do what I can to stop you."

"There is much you don't understand," said Heldin finally.

"No. I see clearly, runner. I see a traitor before me who gave up." Movement caught Zodak's eye at the mouth of the fortress. Kahn emerged at the entrance, speaking with someone and pointing toward the cage.

"Hey! Here he is! The traitor! Hurry!" Zodak yelled.

"I'm sorry," said Heldin with one last glance, and he sped away. Kahn led a small group sauntering toward Zodak across the rocky ground from the castle. After what seemed like an eternity, they reached earshot.

"Hurry! He just left!" cried Zodak. "You can—" Zodak stopped short. Though still fifty mounts off, he recognized the gait of the tall figure beside Kahn. Skypiercer. Daen.

"Daen!" shouted Zodak for all he was worth.

"Fire burn me!" said Daen as he rushed over, his face pale. "Where's Leithra? Zodak, what are you..." His face turned grave. "You shouldn't have come back here—"

"Heldin is a spy!" shouted Zodak.

"What?" Daen asked, snapping his head up to find the runner. But Heldin was gone.

"He's given Kuquo everything," blurted Zodak. "I was there. Captured. Leithra is dead. The Magistrate knows all about Blackiron. He killed the Elder! Müziel leads some kind of horde marching on the city. We are all in danger!" Zodak panted. Daen studied Zodak's face for a moment. Zodak's head dropped. *He doesn't believe me. Of course not. You tried,* he offered to himself.

"Release him!" Daen finally ordered.

"Sir?" Kahn faltered.

"Release him now! We must see Ozir right away!"

38

Blackiron buzzed with movement and preparation. Soldiers, squires, and servants scurried in all directions, like ants in an agitated hill. Zodak had spewed every detail of his last hours to Daen as they hurried back inside Blackiron. Ozir looked like he had seen a ghost when Daen marched Zodak into his quarters, a collage of emotions passing over his face. Every detail of Zodak's fantastic story rang true.

"I should have known! I could feel it," Daen had told Ozir. Zodak was given fresh clothes and sent away to scrub off the stench of garbage that he now barely noticed. He ate ravenously until a squire arrived to fetch him.

Zodak trailed Ozir and Daen as they walked briskly down the hall to Ozir's personal chambers. *What will today hold for me? Will they try to wipe my memory again? Treat me like a prisoner? They won't ask me to fight... would they?* The questions swirled in his mind.

Back in his quarters, servants swarmed Ozir, readying him for battle. Ozir peppered Zodak with occasional questions as he and Daen discussed strategy. Zodak spied the medallion hanging from Ozir's neck. He wondered longingly if it fed the dwarf with energy and vitality the way it had him. It disappeared under a mantle like those Zodak had seen on the leaders in the Great Hall, but not fashioned from black leather. Ozir's mantle was metal that glinted and shimmered, too bright a silver to be iron. Each arm was covered in mail and each hand was fitted with a jagged metal gauntlet. Zodak had heard stories of kings who wore decorative armor, meant only to inspire the soldiers, but Ozir's dress was meant for battle. Despite the high polish, beneath the buffed surface, the mantle bore scars and dents from battles past. Squires worked quickly to fasten heavy metal boots to Ozir's feet.

"And what to do with Zodak?" Daen asked quietly. Zodak looked up.

"I wish I knew," answered Ozir, chuckling, casting a side glance at Zodak. "I was ready to send him to the Garden only hours ago." His smile faded, and he shook his head, lifting his hands in the air so the servants could fasten a thick leather belt around his waist. The heavy metal clasp bore the same woven design as the emblem on every man's arm guard. "Fate has spoken otherwise. He just may have saved us all today." Zodak's heart skipped. The servants fastened a round metal shield to Ozir's back. "I put him into your hands, Daen."

"Out of the way!" came a shout from the hall. Zodak scurried from the doorway as two squires jogged into the room, hauling a long wooden case. The way they strained under the weight of the box, it looked to be packed full of river stones.

"Vigram!" exclaimed Ozir when the servants entered his dressing room. "Let's have a look at her." The squires knelt and slowly lifted the lid on the wooden case. Zodak saw a gleam in Ozir's eyes as he bent and lifted a wooden shaft, followed by the head of an enormous axe. He flipped the axe into the air effortlessly. One side was sickle shaped, razor-sharp no doubt. The other side of the head was a massive hammer-shaped block of metal. The tip of the shaft ended in a spear point, as did the butt. Ozir made a cut through the air.

"She feels good back in my hands." He sliced the air twice more. The squires watched in awe. Wary servants approached cautiously to place a helmet on Ozir's head. The helmet was a solid burnished silver cap, crossed front to back and side to side by two gold straps. The lateral straps fanned into wide cheek guards. A pair of angular polished golden wings pointed backwards as if in a strong wind.

"You need not join us in this battle, Daen," said Ozir, returning from battles past.

"Am I not still of the Order?" replied Daen quickly. *Was he defensive?* wondered Zodak.

"Yes, of course, but not in active guard," answered Ozir. "You have no obligation to march with the ranks—"

"My lord," replied Daen in a steady but firm voice. "Thank you, but my path was set the minute the Magistrate defiled Rislaan, the Order, and Yiduiijn herself!" Now Daen fumed.

"Yes. Defiled," answered Ozir through gritted teeth. "You have made your decision, then. In that case, know I am glad to have you beside us. Will you dress in your old armor? We have kept it in the armory, oiled, and your blade sharp."

"I think I should not," answered Daen.

"Oh?" Ozir gave a questioning look. "Because of Horgor?" he asked.

"Yes. He is the Guard's Chief now. Dressing in my old kit could only cause strife."

"This is battle, Daen. Every warrior knows there is no proxy for his own armor, tested in combat, molded to his body from mud, rain, and the blood of enemies."

"True, my lord. But what of the men? What of Horgor?"

"I don't think the men will confuse you for Horgor," Ozir chuckled. "Equip yourself. We shall meet at the gate when you are ready."

"As you wish, sire." Daen saluted and turned from the room. Zodak followed him out and down the hall.

After a few steps, Daen slowed and then stopped, turning to face Zodak.

"Zodak, I owe you an apology," he said, dropping to a knee. "I took much from you by bringing you here and was prepared to take even your memories."

"I understand," said Zodak. "I am sorry, too. For what I said. Leithra told me what you did at the Council for me. Thank you."

Daen held out a hand. Zodak lunged forward and wrapped his arms around him. Daen squeezed Zodak in an embrace and, for a moment, they didn't move.

"There is something else," said Zodak. "I think I had a…vision."

"Oh?" said Daen.

"Yes, and I… it showed me something. Something about you. I don't think it's happened yet—"

"Stop." Daen held up a hand. "What the Figure shows you is for you alone. We are all on our own paths, we make our own choices."

"Yes! He said that!" said Zodak excitedly.

"Very good. Then treasure it in your heart." Zodak started to object, but Daen held up a hand again. "You have the courage of a lion. The Color is with you, my boy. Quickly now." Daen turned down the hallway, Zodak following closely.

"Who is Horgor?" Zodak asked after a moment.

"Horgor is Ozir's Guard's Chief," Daen answered over his shoulder. "He leads the entire Battleguard."

"What's the Battleguard?" asked Zodak.

"The Battleguard is Ozir's entire army stationed here in the city. It is made up of forty milblocks."

"That's hundreds of soldiers!" Zodak exclaimed.

"One thousand forty," replied Daen. The two arrived back

at Daen's quarters and he began hastily stuffing his few belongings in the leather saddlebags.

"And Horgor leads them all?" asked Zodak.

"Yes. Heavy is the mantle of duty borne by the Guard's Chief."

"So, what's the conflict you were talking about?" asked Zodak.

"Full of questions?" replied Daen sharply. "I'm sorry," he added in a softer tone, turning to face Zodak. "Of course you have questions." He threw his saddlebags over a shoulder. "I was Guard's Chief here for eight seasons. There was an… incident, and I left the city. Horgor replaced me."

"What happened?" asked Zodak, wide-eyed.

"We haven't time for the long version, but I accused Horgor's weasel of a brother, Horgalus, of being a spy and selling secrets from Blackiron. He challenged me to a blood duel—to the death. Horgor tried to put a stop to the madness. If only he had succeeded…" Daen's gaze drifted.

"A *duel*? What happened?" asked Zodak.

Daen continued to stare. "I tried everything I could to get Horgor to stop it. I spoke to him in private and begged him to speak sense to his brother. But Horgor wouldn't hear it. To him, I was the instigator because of my accusation. His devotion to his brother filled him with hatred for me. I believe Horgalus had no choice but to try to silence me in the duel so the charges would be dropped. I couldn't get Horgalus to change his mind. I even pleaded with Ozir to end it, but the duel was sanctioned under the ancient laws. The night before, I was poisoned—"

"*Poisoned?*"

"Yes. I expect by Horgalus—Horgor has too much honor to do such a thing. I became violently ill, tasted death that night. As I lay there, swaying over the precipice, I was visited by the Color Giver—"

"You were visited?" Zodak exclaimed.

"We truly don't have time for that story. We've already tarried too long. Come, Zodak." The two left the room and continued down the hall.

"I miraculously recovered," Daen resumed, "leaving the fort healers at a loss, unable to explain it. I announced my intention to continue with the duel."

"Why not just say you were sick?"

"Under the Code of the Order, making such a grave accusation and then backing out of a sanctioned duel is viewed as a sign of false witness. You are stripped of your position within the Order and banished from the city. No, Horgalus was the one who had to end it. And since he did not, he left me no choice."

"So, you won the duel?"

"Yes. I am sorry to say that I did."

"Sorry! Why? He was bad. You said yourself that he was spying."

"It is true. His heart had been tainted, and I believe he intended to deliver Blackiron itself for the right price. But Zodak—" Again Daen stopped and turned to Zodak, looking him in the eye. "Listen to me carefully: even a tainted man has good in him. When you kill a man, you pass the ultimate judgment on him. This can never be done lightly. You take everything from that man. His past and his future. Death is final. It cannot be reversed. Do you understand?"

"Yes. But you said he was evil. Was he like a goblin friend or something?"

"That I don't know. But what I do know is that I've seen dark hearts, as hard as granite, be turned. There is hope for anyone." Daen stood and continued through the maze of winding corridors.

"So why did you stop being Guard's Chief?" asked Zodak.

"To this day, Horgor believes his brother was innocent. He charged me with the death of his brother by false accusation. This was a serious charge, punishable by expulsion from the

Order and imprisonment, or worse. The Order Council ruled in my favor, but as for the false accusation, it was my word against Horgalus's, and he was dead. I had not broken the Code, so I wasn't imprisoned or expelled from the Order, but the Council decided it would be best for me to step down as Guard's Chief and leave Uth Becca. That was three seasons ago. When we entered Blackiron today, it was the first time I had been back." Daen chuckled softly. "Before I met you yesterday, Zodak, I was planning on slipping though the city unnoticed on my way down to Groark, a quiet fishing village to the south." He shook his head and smiled. "We think we choose our own paths," he said to himself. They walked the rest of the way in silence.

Following a long corridor that sloped downward, the two finally arrived at the armory. The blade of an enormous sword crossed the handle of a huge axe above the oversized double doors, their polished metal dancing with flickering torchlight. Soldiers flowed in and out of the catacomb, equipped for battle. Zodak had never seen so many swords and bows and axes and shields. Behind the rows of spears, he spotted a well-lit archery range and beside it, a sparring floor with wooden dummy soldiers, chipped and battered from training.

The attendants bowed slightly when Daen approached, a look of reverence in their eyes. Zodak caught the surprise on the face of one of the servants when Daen requested his old armor, but they complied quickly. Past rows of chain mail, they came to dozens of leather mantles and sets of armor that Zodak recognized as those worn by the milblock leaders. The servant led them to the back of the armory. On the wall hung an impressive armor set, nicks and cuts covering the oiled leather. An imposing black chest plate was stamped at its center with the silver Order emblem. The servants helped heave it up and Daen pulled it over his head in a fluid and familiar motion. The attendants fitted its straps and buckles as he pulled on black leather gloves with veins of metal running down the back of each finger.

"Chilsar?" asked Daen, glancing around.

"Oh, yes," replied one of the servants, scurrying off deeper into the armory. He came back moments later, lugging a giant sword. The attendant hefted it up into Daen's arms. He buckled the thick sword belt around his waist and reverently drew the blade. Torchlight glinted off its polished razor edge. He whipped it through the air. The leather suit creaked at the movement.

"This is Chilsar, the Guard's Chief Sword. It has been passed through the leadership for generations. Horgor refuses to touch it because I wielded it, so here it has remained." The sword was the better part of a marq tall and, from its heft, Zodak doubted he could hold it steady, yet Daen flicked it about like a catswillow switch. The blade made a slight hum as it sliced through the musty armory air. Zodak stared in awe: before him stood a truly great warrior.

Daen's bow skills were dazzling, but somehow, watching him whirl that sword faster than the eye could follow, Zodak marveled at what this warrior before him must have been like in battle. That razor edge surely had slain scores of enemies. Daen returned the sword to his scabbard. He pulled a dull black helmet over his head. It had a slit for his eyes, and a grate covered his mouth. The rest was cold, solid black.

"Well done. You have kept this equipment in fine condition," Daen said to the attendants. They bowed in appreciation. "Come, Zodak. I march into battle, and we must get you out of the city."

39

Daen and Zodak hurried back down the passage, through the gate, and out into the gaping cavern. Blackiron had awoken. Blocks of soldiers jogged in unison, gliding like an enormous mollusk along the sea floor. Daen turned right out of the fortress gate, crossed the bridge, and followed the road along the chasm. Carts carrying supplies and men on horseback streamed past. Zodak trotted behind him into the current of traffic.

"I don't want to leave you," said Zodak to Daen's back. "Why can't I stay here?" Daen slowed to a walk beside Zodak. A cart rumbled by.

"Zodak, I don't think it's safe here."

"But you have a thousand men—"

"There are some dangers against which numbers offer no safety. I will ensure you are in good hands."

Zodak wanted to shout and beg to stay with Daen, but he held his tongue. Daen had his trust, and Zodak knew the skypiercer would do what he could to keep him from harm. Still, something deep inside him longed to be by Daen's side.

Along the entire length of the cavern wall, at intervals of

one hundred mounts, groups of soldiers stood waiting for orders. Each group gathered at the mouth of a small cave that disappeared into a snaking tunnel. Daen increased his pace, continuing straight ahead past the assembled troops. Zodak panted as he jogged to keep up.

"Oi!" a voice cried out from the ranks of soldiers. "Sir Daen?"

"Not him!" answered another. "He's exiled in Stahlgarr."

Daen kept walking, his eyes to the ground.

"Looks like him."

"It can't be," added another

"Daen Skypiercer!" yelled a soldier. "It is him! See the armor?"

Daen stopped. He turned to the group of soldiers and removed his helmet. Immediately, some men dropped to a knee. Some, however, remained standing, staring coldly.

"You are no Guard's Chief!" yelled one of the men still on his feet. "Why do you dress up like one?"

"No. I am not Guard's Chief. I am here today, led by the Color to the trenches beside you as a brother-in-arms. I don my old armor so that I may enter this battle beside you. Today, we fight against a common enemy. But be warned, before this day is out, your courage and strength will be demanded of you. This is no routine city sweep. The balance of the Order may rest in the hands of Blackiron and this Order Guard today."

"What's going on, Daen?" asked a man kneeling in the front row. "Why do we march?"

"The High Elder of the Venerable Council was slain today!"

Gasps and whispers escaped from the men. One of the men on bended knee sprang to his feet and hurried to Daen's side. He wore the block leader's regalia and a burnt-orange wrap around his bicep.

"Sir, that information hasn't been shared," he whispered urgently to Daen. "Our orders are to hold all details for now."

"Captain Selphir, I know your orders. But your army, and you yourself, underestimate this battle. These soldiers are best equipped if they march from here with rage."

Selphir was quiet for a moment. Then he began nodding slowly. "Yes. I see."

"When you walk through that gate into Uth Becca, you must make them understand Rislaan is in grave danger. Fill them with fire!" Daen urged.

"Live to serve!" Selphir saluted.

"Rise, men," said Daen to the soldiers. They obeyed.

"The Elder is really dead?" asked a soldier.

"YES!" screamed Daen, suddenly full of rage. Zodak shrank back. He had never seen Daen like this. "And her blood, not yet dried, stains the hands of our city's Magistrate."

"Do we know that, sir?" whispered Selphir.

"It is for this we march," continued Daen to the soldiers. "It is for Yiduiijn we fight. Her very foundations have been shaken. And it is only our blades and our blood and our courage that will keep her from falling to the evil that claws at her. It is because of you that, as the sun sets this evening, Uth Becca and Rislaan will stand in victory. For this, you were trained. This, and none other, is your purpose today." He paused.

"The Magistrate has killed the Elder!" Daen bellowed, the cry echoing in the cavern. "He has spilled her blood! He has spilled the blood of Yiduiijn. And this I ask you—" Daen panted, chest heaving, and then roared, "HOW DARE HE?!" The soldiers erupted in raw, angry cries. Even some of those who had refused to kneel now cheered. Zodak found himself shouting along with the men. Daen saluted. The men saluted back. He turned and continued down the path. Zodak followed, blood coursing through his veins. He felt ready to fight.

Ahead, a larger group of no fewer than one hundred soldiers stood at attention. They were arranged in long, orderly rows. As they approached, Zodak could make out Ozir's bulky figure standing in the carriage of a chariot. It was hitched to what looked like a huge shaggy hog, but thicker and more solid. The animal's legs were straight stumps, each as wide as Zodak's chest, and gray armor plating covered its body, a thick bone crest rising from the back of its head up over its crown and down between its eyes. White tusks gleamed in the cavern's glow. This beast looked as though it could crash through the wall of a house with ease.

In front of Ozir, a hulking figure addressed the lines of soldiers, pacing before them. This man stood over a marq and had a barrel chest like one of the dwarves. He wore a black leather mantle that Zodak recognized as that of the Guard's Chief. On his back, two long swords crossed in scabbards beneath a round black shield. The Order emblem shone in deep crimson on the shield. The man held his helmet in his hand. Long black hair was pulled back in a messy knot.

As they approached, Zodak heard him speak: "For you are the Order Guard! You live to serve and kill for the Order." A small commotion began among the men. "We prepare to—"

"Look!" A soldier pointed at Daen. The brawny man addressing the troops stopped short and turned. For a moment, he was silent, his eyes flashing. "What is he doing here!" he demanded of Ozir, seething.

"Daen will fight beside us today, Horgor," said Ozir calmly.

"My lord, I mean no disrespect, but he has no place—"

"Spoken." Ozir cut him off.

"Yes, sire." Horgor whipped back to face the men and continued his speech. Ozir drew his carriage beside Daen. He waved a hand, and Sodane and Kahn slipped from the ranks and jogged to his side. The chariot creaked to a stop. Zodak shuffled back from the massive head of the gray beast. It snorted.

"Brother!" Daen and Sodane embraced. Kahn and Daen exchanged salutes. Kahn gave a short nod to Zodak.

"We will march through the Millgate any moment," said Ozir. "When we open the gate, we march straight into the heart of the city. Just follow the orders we discussed."

"Yes, sire," they answered in unison.

"Zodak, once the army has marched out, Sodane will escort you to a safe house outside the city until danger has passed. Until then, I want you by my side. Do you understand?" asked Daen.

"Yes," Zodak answered. Sodane stepped away from the group and motioned for Zodak to join him. He squatted to Zodak's height. His eyes had the same sparkle as Daen's, the look that had first earned Zodak's trust.

"I know you may be scared."

"I don't think I'm scared," said Zodak truthfully. "Daen explained everything. I just wish he could come."

"Yes, I know. And he would like nothing more than to join you, I am sure. But we need him here."

"I understand," answered Zodak.

"You have a spring of courage within you, young Zodak." Sodane smiled. "You and Daen are kindred spirits, I think. I can see he hates that he cannot remain with you."

"He does?" Zodak had never thought about the possibility that Daen, the warrior, the Guard's Chief, wanted to be with him.

"Yes. It is plain to me how much he cares for you," said Sodane.

Zodak looked at the ground, blushing, suddenly self-conscious.

"But you must put your trust in me now. I will keep you safe." Sodane smiled again. "Come on." He rose and patted Zodak on the back as they rejoined the group.

"Are your men ready?" Ozir called to Horgor.

"Yes, sire!"

"Fall in behind the chariot!" The woolly beast jolted forward into the mouth of the cave.

"Men, Uth Becca needs you! We march on the city!" Horgor boomed. The men cheered. Zodak fell into step beside Daen, his heart thumping now. Sodane and Kahn followed closely, with Horgor and his army marching behind. Up the passage, they climbed. Zodak breathed heavily. The men around him did not. Ahead, the passage ended abruptly in a wooden wall that stretched the entire width of the passage. The men halted. Ozir nodded to Daen, who walked to the side of the passage to a stairway, hewn in the rock, that Zodak hadn't noticed at first. Beside the stairway hung a cord that disappeared into a hole in the passage ceiling, and a long wooden lever protruded from the wall. Just above the lever hung two bells, one small and gold, the other larger and silver. Daen yanked the cord. The men waited.

"He's not ringing either bell," said Daen finally.

"Throw the lever!" commanded Horgor, approaching Ozir. "The scout is asleep, and yet the sun grows higher in the sky. Sire, we have no time to waste! We must position these troops," said Horgor. "Men, ready yourselves!" he shouted.

"Wait!" said Daen.

"Send me up to the perch," called Sodane. "I can run quickly and ring the bell if all is clear."

"If all is clear?" challenged Horgor. "How many times have we marched through the Millgate into this sleepy corner of the city? It's always clear! We must stop wasting time, my lord," Horgor implored, fixing Daen with a cold stare.

Ozir looked at Horgor, then to the bells. "Sodane, quickly, then!" Ozir ordered. Sodane sprang to the stairway in a flash, bounding up with speed and grace.

Horgor glared at Daen. "You don't belong here." He spat the words. Then he whirled around and stomped off to join his men. The company waited in silence. All eyes were fixed on the two bells hanging motionless beside the lever.

Kahn caught Zodak's confused expression. "The large bell means all is clear outside the Millgate. The small one means danger. There never is," he added, "but the scout should have rung by now." The silence persisted. Then, barely audibly, with the faintest quiver, the tiny bell twitched. The movement was so subtle a gentle breeze could have caused it. But there was no draft in the cave.

"Something's wrong!" said Daen, moving towards the stairs.

"What now?!" came Horgor's voice.

"Do not open that door!" Daen shouted as he dropped his helmet and flew up the stairs. Without thinking, Zodak bounded after him. Breathless from the interminable climb, with lungs about to burst, Zodak stumbled up the last of the stairs.

When he reached the last step, he froze at the scene before him. Something crashed into Zodak, hurling him to the ground. He landed hard as a whizzing sound zipped over his head and a projectile shattered on the stone wall of the stairwell. Zodak lifted his throbbing cheek from the wooden floor and looked around. Not more than two measures from his face lay an elf in a pool of blood. The elf wore the Order cuff on his forearm. A short black arrow protruded from his neck.

Zodak pushed himself off the floor and scrambled away from the dead elf. He shook and fought off the nausea. He looked over to Daen, who sat slumped on the ground, making guttural grunting sounds that chilled Zodak. Daen was covered in blood. In his lap lay the motionless body of Sodane, a black arrow buried in his chest. Sodane's blood flowed over Daen's cradling arms.

Daen did not speak or look up. He only mumbled incoherently as he stared blankly into his lap. In an automatic motion, Daen reached back and pulled hard on the signal cord running into the wall. Zodak watched in shaken silence as the pillar of a man before him crumbled.

The room shared some similarities with the tower room in the Golden Oak: a simple watch post with windows facing every direction. Zodak's back rested against a stone wall beneath a broken window. He lifted his head just over the windowsill and quickly peeked out. He instantly dropped back to the floor, his heart pounding.

"D... Da... Daen, there are hundreds of them!"

Daen didn't look up. "Probably thousands," he answered listlessly.

"Wha... what will we do?" asked Zodak. Now Daen pulled his gaze away from his brother. For a long moment, he said nothing, but just stared at Zodak with hollow eyes.

"Daen!" Zodak screamed. Daen kept staring. *Is he giving up?* wondered Zodak, biting his lip. Daen looked back to his lap. His hand, resting on his brother's chest, brushed the black fletching of that tiny, hateful arrow. Daen pulled away as if stung by a wasp and suddenly snapped his head up. The distance in his eyes was gone, replaced by fire.

"We must warn the others!" He looked back at Sodane once more, and Zodak feared he would slip back into the trance. Instead, Daen closed his fist around the black arrow, hesitated a moment, and then ripped it from his brother's chest. As he pulled, Daen threw back his head and roared so loud that Zodak involuntarily clapped his hands over his ears. The deafening peal rattled the windows in the loft and shook Zodak's chest. Veins bulged in Daen's neck as he screamed with savage anger.

When he had no breath left, his eyes shot up at Zodak. "Go! The stairway!" he said. Zodak obediently scrambled across the floor, descended two steps, and turned to wait for Daen, who dragged Sodane's body with him. Daen froze for a moment. Suddenly he dropped Sodane and sprang at Zodak, knocking him backward down the staircase. As Zodak slammed against the stone steps, he heard breaking glass and a crash, followed by a deep *whoosh*. The perch and stairway above exploded in a ball of fire, flames groping after them as they hurled and crashed down the stairs.

40

Daen braced against the wall, stopping their fall. He snatched Zodak up over a shoulder and ran the rest of the way down the stairs. As they burst into the cavern, both Daen and Zodak collapsed to the ground. Zodak pressed his hand against bruised ribs. Daen was on all fours, breathing heavily.

"What happened up there!" demanded Ozir.

"They stand a thousand strong outside this gate," Daen panted. "They killed the scout and…" His head dropped. "He's dead…" The words were almost a whisper. Daen's back bowed, his long hair brushing the ashen gray powdered floor of the cavern. He spat.

"What?" Ozir continued. "Speak up."

"Sodane is dead," Daen said, suddenly lifting his head and rocking back on his heels. The men stood silenced as Daen stared up at Ozir with an empty gaze. Ozir closed his mouth and clenched his teeth. Even Horgor dropped his eyes and shook his head. Zodak saw no hint of joy in Horgor at the parallel tragedy. The group's silence continued. Daen brushed his hair from his face and slowly stood.

"The arrows. I recognized the arrows," he finally said. "Fangorian shadow hunters. Outside this gate." A murmur rippled through the soldiers.

"How could this happen?" asked Horgor, stepping forward. "How could they have discovered the Millgate?"

"However it happened, the tower is destroyed and the exit is surrounded," answered Daen.

"Messenger!" came a cry from the ranks of soldiers. A rumble of hooves filled the cavern as a horse thundered up the passage.

"Wait! Hold!" cried the harried rider, a slight man with a beaklike nose, wearing the Order uniform. "The enemy is outside the gate!" The man slipped from his saddle and rushed to Ozir, dropping to a knee.

"Yes, Farish. We know," answered Ozir.

"Every primary exit is covered," said Farish, rising. "All the scouts are dead."

"Fire burn me!" Ozir exclaimed. "Have any blocks marched out yet?" he asked.

"No, my lord. The army at the Pasturegate was pulling the gate lever as I arrived, but it has been re-sealed."

"We must redeploy the Battleguard," said Horgor. "We can defeat whatever awaits us behind this gate." He turned towards his men and raised his voice. "We are the Order!"

The men struck their chests in unison and called, "Live!"

"None match us in battle," continued Horgor.

Again, the men answered in unison, "Serve!"

"Bring them! Bring the thousands! We will cut them down! We will triumph!"

"Live to serve!" sounded the men. Horgor turned back to Ozir and Daen.

"They *have* lost the element of surprise," Ozir agreed. He drew to Horgor's side, and the two spoke in quiet but urgent tones.

Zodak noticed Kahn break ranks and whisper to Daen. Daen nodded. After a moment, he saluted, and Kahn glanced and nodded towards Zodak before slipping back to his group.

"Zodak," Daen called. "You have to get out of here. Back to Blackiron."

"You're coming with me?" Hope glimmered in Zodak.

"No, Zodak," answered Daen with a grave face. His jaw clenched and then relaxed. "Without Sodane... I'm afraid you must go alone." Zodak opened his mouth, but nothing came out. That word: *alone*. It assaulted him. He hated it. It made his stomach turn and his head spin.

"Fall back to Blackiron." Daen now sounded like a general giving orders. "Report what you have seen, and wait for a—"

Boom! Something slammed into the Millgate. The entire company started as the crash echoed down the passage. A dust cloud burst from the heavy planks of the wooden gate.

"They're upon us!" Daen shouted. Horgor bellowed an order, and his army sprang to life, quickly taking formation in front of the wall.

Boom! Another crash rocked the wooden gate. It creaked and moaned. Zodak felt lightheaded, but the soldiers wore no hint of fear on their faces as they stood, planted for battle. He kept his eyes fixed on the wooden gate even as he began shuffling backwards down the passage.

"Zodak!" Zodak glimpsed Daen between a row of soldiers. He stood beside Horgor and Ozir at the front of the line, just measures from the gate, bow in hand. "Go! Blackiron!" As the words left Daen's mouth, a deafening crash shook the tunnel. Splintered wood flew from the gate. A blast of dread ripped through Zodak as he peered through the dust at an enormous arm protruding from a jagged hole in the gate, searching and groping about. The swamp-gray fist was as big as Zodak himself and covered in a pebbled, scaly hide. Zodak let out a cry and scrambled backward.

"Fire!" Horgor's voice rang out, and arrows peppered the giant arm. A muffled wail rose from behind the wall and the mighty arm slithered back through the hole. Zodak scurried backwards more quickly now, still unable to tear his eyes from the scene.

Boom!

An enormous crash thundered from the passage. The blow shattered the Millgate. Zodak glimpsed the airborne wooden shard only a split second before it filled his vision. Suddenly a flash of white and red and then black.

41

Daen scanned the passage for Zodak, a ringing in his ears. The air hung thick with dust, but he thought he spied a shape slipping through soldiers at the far end of the tunnel. *He's off,* thought Daen with relief. *Such courage.* A sudden pang of loss and longing jabbed the warrior. He'd known the boy for what, one day? Was that possible? Would he meet Zodak again? Uncertainty and fear crouched behind his resolve. This day, this battle, it swirled like a nightstorm that could only truly be known in its retelling. He might dine in Blackiron tonight, or maybe never again.

Somehow, sending Zodak down the passage felt like sending his own son, a piece of himself. *Where did such thoughts spring from?* The boy was resilient, but Daen knew too well the fragility of life. The picture of Sodane seared his mind. He shook the image away. Every soldier in the Order Guard took the oath, vowing to cut ties with the world and offer his life for the Order, he reminded himself. They had all accepted the simple truth: death slithers into every battle alongside every soldier. *But this boy. He was no soldier. He has taken no oath. Yet off he fled, alone into the jaws of this terrible day.* Daen fought an unfamiliar wave of fear. *This is why we have the Code,* he knew. *To extinguish fear for the ones we love, lest it consume us.* He looked down the passage again but couldn't see past the throng of soldiers. *We will meet again one day, Zodak.* Daen spoke the pledge silently to himself, yet the hardened soldier hadn't the heart to test its veracity. Instead, as if with a swipe of his massive blade, he severed the thoughts that chased after the boy and turned back to the Millgate.

The dust cloud where the Millgate had once been glowed a charred orange, illuminated by the angry light beyond. A stiff morning breeze rushed into the stillness of the cavern, swirling the orange curtain and replacing the stale air with the fragrance of the streets of Uth Becca, tinged with the smell of fish and nets from the docks. Daen removed a blue-fletched arrow from his quiver. The creaking of leather and soft clink of metal from a hundred soldiers poised for battle kindled images in his mind of battles past. The familiar surge of defiant anticipation rose in him. But this battle rush carried a tainted stench. *The enemy ambushed the Order at our own gates. Caught us unaware. How could it be?*

Only in his grandfather's stories of the Goblin Swarm or the legends of the Great Wyther Invasion had Daen ever heard of margoul mounting such a coordinated assault. The night before, he had hoped the Order would march on the castle today to dethrone the Magistrate in a swift and decisive blow. The Magistrate's guard would have crumpled like stalks of leopard grass before the elite Order Guard warriors. What waited outside the gate was something else altogether though. No, if she came at all today, victory would be neither swift nor bloodless. He fought back the tide, not of fear, but of inescapable sorrow that swept through every battle. Many would fall today. *Sodane*—the thought stabbed him. He shook the name from his mind and forced back the rising bile. Mourning his brother would have to wait.

"Ready, men!" Horgor's call shattered the frozen anticipation. Ahead, the dust thinned and dissipated, revealing a massive, dark silhouette. It thumped closer, emerging from the fog like an apparition. The creature stood almost twice as tall as a man. A sunken block of a head emerged from a massive neck of corded muscle. Arms like tree trunks hung nearly to the ground. Its large barrel chest tapered into squat legs. *Gorgol,* Daen thought to himself, the name dripping with disdain. He nocked the arrow to the bowstring. Small, wiry figures danced from behind the massive frame of the gorgol, scurrying between its feet.

"Watch the keepers," called Horgor. Spidery creatures swarmed the beast. Each with the build of a small, slender man but hunched over, their faces looked withered or badly burned. Daen had seen gorgol keepers before. Obsequious minions that cleaned, fed, and armed the behemoths, they constantly tended to the larger gorgols. The keepers were often the first to suffer the monster's wild temper, yet they would defend a gorgol to the death. At the mouth of the gate, three gorgol keepers, wrapped carelessly in bands of dirty battered cloth, pushed a roughly hewn wagon, loaded with boulders the size of hogs. Two others crouched at the gorgol's feet, spears in hand.

"Archers, the keepers!" cried Horgor. As the word left his lips, arrows whistled through the air and struck all five of the gorgol keepers. They collapsed in writhing heaps, melting into dark ooze that seeped into the earth. The gorgol's gaze swept over the fallen keepers with indifferent disdain. It reached for a boulder from the wagon and heaved it up over its head. Beady eyes darted and then landed on Ozir. The monster cocked its arm.

"Fire!" At Horgor's order, archers let fly dozens of arrows. The creature stumbled backward and roared as it launched the boulder spastically. The rock flew wide of its mark. Soldiers dropped and dove out of the stone's path. But the boulder bounced and caught an Order Guard square in the chest, hurling him to the tunnel wall where both stone and body shattered. The line of soldiers replaced the fallen guard without pause. Two soldiers ran from the back of the lines to their fallen comrade. They dragged him back down the tunnel.

Daen drew the great bow and narrowed his eyes. The beast wailed in rage, clumsily ripping tiny arrows from its hide. With swelling fury, it snatched two boulders, knocking the cart over and spilling the rocks.

"Strike!" called Horgor. The first two soldiers in each of the six lines sprang into action. They clustered in groups of three and surrounded the gorgol. Behind them, soldiers filled the ranks. Even still, Daen did not move. His mind was present, but his thoughts were intertwined with the surroundings. In this state of mindsight, he saw with his thoughts more than his eyes. He felt the slight breeze coming from beyond the gate, the damp air, and he kept time with every muscle that moved beneath the beast's hide. Bending his presence in the Color Ambit, with feet planted in the sandy tunnel, Daen was at once aware of every whispered word or cough from the dozens of soldiers around him, the rage of the beast, the thrusts and parries of the soldiers, and the angle of the boulders it swung in its giant fists.

The beast, confused by the synchronized movement of the soldiers, now swept a massive arm at the closest trio of guards. As if one body, they ducked the blow. In reply, three guards at the gorgol's flank struck at its unprotected side. Two spears and a sword slashed at the monster. It wailed and swung wildly back at the men, but again, the Order Guard was too quick and the beast's flailing fist met only air. Now another strike at the gorgol's other flank. It roared in agony and let fly a boulder. The rock spun sharply downward and slammed into the tunnel floor, knocking two of the soldiers to the ground. Possessed by rage and raw instinct, the gorgol lunged at the closest fallen Guard with alarming speed.

"Up!" shouted Horgor to the downed man with sudden urgency, but the dazed soldier struggled to lift himself. The gorgol's hulking frame flew at him, a boulder cocked over its head, bellowing a cry of war as it brought the massive load down on the soldier. The soldier braced for glory. But as he did, Daen's bowstring snapped and the javelin arrow sprang forth, slicing through the air and catching the monster beneath the jaw in the soft flesh at the base of the gorgol's neck. The massive arm with the boulder froze just measures above the fallen soldier, and with a series of cracks and snaps, the enormous body of the gorgol froze to stone, petrified in death. The gorgol statue slowly toppled sideways and crashed to the ground. Suddenly the cavern was quiet except for the sound of the soldier scurrying out from beneath the looming statue.

"Battle!" Horgor boomed, shattering the silence.

"Victory!" shouted the men. Two men helped the fallen soldier to his feet. As the rescued warrior returned to the battle line, his eyes met Daen's. Daen nodded and the soldier hurried back to his unit.

"We will not await their next assault!" Ozir called out to the men. "We march out to meet our foe!" The men cheered.

"Pods!" shouted Horgor. The warriors formed groups of nine soldiers—three deep and three wide. The back row of soldiers carried bows. A pod leader stood at the center. A line of sturdy warriors jogged forward carrying polished silver shields, nearly as tall as a man and twice as wide again. They moved swiftly under the load, but taut, muscled arms betrayed the heft of the shields. Each shield bearer wore a shiny helmet and carried a short wide sword on his back. Horgor began the march, followed by the line of shield bearers and behind them, a line of four pods of soldiers. Next rode Ozir in his battle cart, Daen beside him.

"That was impressive, skypiercer," said Ozir. Daen just nodded. "It has been too long since we have stood side by side in battle."

"My service is yours, my lord," replied Daen, returning the compliment. He had unstrung his bow and unsheathed Chilsar, cutting the air as he advanced. Behind Ozir and Daen marched three more lines of four pods each. Each in perfect step; each in perfect unison. The Battleguard was on the move.

Like a river, they surged forward, trampling the remnants of the keepers and flowing around the gorgol statue sprawled before the Millgate entrance. Beyond the demolished gate, the tunnel curved left and then rose sharply as it opened into the floor of a large storage barn. The barn stood on the outskirts of the city and to the common eye resembled any of the dozens of merchant storage buildings, loaded with boxes and topped with a ship-spotting tower. The concealed exits that the Order had diligently protected for decades were a secret no more.

Horgor halted the company at the foot of the steep incline leading up into the barn, just out of sight of the Millgate. Here, the rough hewn walls changed to straight planks that lined the exit. The roof of the passage gave way to the dark cavernous storage building. The false floor that covered the tunnel's exit had been smashed. At the crest of the path, where the tunnel emerged into the barn, a yellow-white square of sunlight seemed to be cut from the darkness. But all was not still. Atop the incline, a jagged line of figures spanned the barn's entrance, staring down the tunnel. Even as the pods marched, the cry of some foreign tongue rose from outside the gate.

"Cover!" called Horgor. The shields flashed up into a silver wall. The guards knelt behind, arm shields raised above bowed heads. As the last shield went up, a scratchy horn blast rang out, followed by the unmistakable sound of a chorus of creaking bowstrings from above and then a *whoosh*. Hundreds of arrows and darts filled the tunnel, striking its sides and ceiling and slamming and shattering against the glinting wall of shields.

"Forward!" cried Horgor. In a steady, measured pace, the shield bearers marched forward, never breaking the wall. Stray arrows sporadically pinged off the shields.

"*Aiiieee!*" With a rasping cry, a line of short black-clad figures rushed down into the tunnel.

"Wedge!" boomed Horgor. Like a mechanized ballet, the line of shield bearers split at the middle, and each side collapsed into an angled *V* shape, creating a funnel from the tunnel's walls to its center. A stout half-giant shield bearer planted his shield at the narrow exit of the funnel.

Like bushcats, the charging goblins blindly poured down into the trap, pinging harmlessly off the impenetrable wall of polished metal. At the base of the funnel, they slammed into Horgor's shield bearer. The soldier's massive legs didn't budge at the repeated impacts. The dazed goblins streamed around the half-giant, screeching and flailing into the maze of waiting Order Guard. Within seconds, the soldiers had cut the hissing wave of creatures down into dozens of piles of ashen sand. Another horn blast, and a second wave of goblins charged down into the tunnel, only to be struck down. Wave after wave of the fiends assailed the Order Guard's position, each meeting the same fate as their evil brethren. The piles of cloaks and sand grew and mixed with the tunnel's soft floor. Three zealous goblins broke from the herd, seeking a vulnerable fissure in the steely wall of the funnel. In a pause of useless swiping and stabbing at the shield, a short broadsword lashed out from behind the wall, and in one powerful swipe decimated all three of the attackers. The cavern grew still.

"Steady, men!" cried Ozir. "The halfies are just fodder for the fire!"

"Advance!" cried Horgor. The shield wall assembled before the troops again and ascended the final stretch of tunnel. The pods marched behind. Daylight now filled the inside of the barn and shone down into the tunnel, shimmering off the polished shields. The entrance to the barn was empty, but what lay beyond, Daen could not guess.

"Wall the entrance!" The shield bearers halted at the top of the tunnel. The soldiers waited. No sound came, yet they held fast. Daen's grip tightened on Chilsar's familiar worn leather grip. He was eager to swing it in battle again.

"Spotter!" Horgor's voice broke the silence, and an elven archer sprang from the closest pod to the center of the shield wall. Two shields parted before the spotter ever so slightly, revealing a sliver of landscape. The elf peered through.

"A thousand strong in the lower valley!" he called. "Two battle siege—" The elf suddenly spun backwards and collapsed, clutching a short black arrow in his chest. A shield bearer turned towards the spotter and a whizzing arrow struck his leg. He cried out and dropped his shield. Instantly, another arrow struck his back.

"Close the gap!" yelled Ozir. "Close it!"

"Fangorians!" spat Daen. A shield bearer rushed to fill the opening, but not before another arrow whistled through and struck a pod leader square in the chest.

"Burn me!" shouted Horgor, as the crippled pod lifted their leader and retreated to the back of the troop. A full pod replaced the position.

"We need eyes in the tower," Daen said to Ozir.

"Horgor! Elven archers!" yelled Ozir.

Horgor paused a moment and then turned to the ranks. "Cliel! Froren!" cried Horgor. Two soldiers rushed up from the troop. "We need you in the tower. The flash fire should have burned out by now. Take arm shields, and—"

"Stay alert!" interrupted Daen. "A glimpse is all they need." They nodded.

"Live to serve!" The elves bounded back down the tunnel to the staircase and disappeared up it. Daen and Horgor exchanged looks.

Horgor shook his head as he turned away. "Two of my best," he said under his breath. He sheathed his two swords on his back.

"How can they shoot like that?" Horgor asked Ozir. "Even our steadiest elven archers are not so skilled."

"I've seen them in battle once before," answered Ozir. "Daen and I fought against Fangorian shadow hunters in the Talson Exodus up in the Fahyz. They are truly unmatched. More precise than the best elf."

"Then they cannot be stopped," replied Horgor with disgust.

"They have limits," quipped Daen.

"I have seen none!" retorted Horgor. "In two dozen seasons, who has ever surprised our elven scouts?"

"They are well trained, and their shadow darts fly true," answered Daen. "But each shot must be set up and can only adjust slightly without repositioning. They cannot hit a target on horseback on a battlefield, and their tubes are slow to reload. They are poor combatants at close range."

"How many do they bring into battle?" asked Ozir.

"I never saw more than two with a margoul cluster, but there must be twice that trained just on the gate."

A call rang out as the elves sprang up the tunnel to Horgor. Their round wooden arm shields were decorated with small black shadow darts, the fletching still smoldering from a blast.

"An army of foot soldiers, five hundred strong, crouches outside the Millgate barn—crickets mostly," reported Cliel. "One hundred mounts past the road, gather hundreds more:

crickets, sows, halfies, and forest trolls. I spotted horsza among them—"

"Horsza?" interrupted Ozir. "In Uth Becca?" A murmur arose from the nearby warriors.

"Yes, sir," he answered. "Froren and I have slain horsza in the Jade Swath one hundred and seventy seasons past, sir," Cliel added.

"You're among the few, then," Ozir said.

"Orcs?" asked Horgor.

"None we could see, Sir. But a half dozen mountain gorgol and keepers are gathered in the Holling farm just down the east hill," said Froren. "They've a battle tower set up a hundred mounts beyond the barn, and another half a cliq to the south," he added. "Reinforcements—mostly halfies and crickets—stream in through the Mead Gate. Fangorian riders arrive from the north. We spotted seven heavy catapults arranged around the city."

"Catapults!" exclaimed Horgor.

"And how many shadow hunters?" asked Daen.

"At least eight, sir," answered Cliel.

"Eight!" exclaimed Ozir.

"Yes, sir," answered Cliel. "Most appear to be trained on the gate or tower. They are positioned on the battle scaffold, in the second story of the smoke house, on the roof of the Carris and Pickons farmhouses."

"Krikkis soldiers? Shadow hunters? Battle towers? It's an army!" boomed Ozir indignantly. "How could they amass such a force within the walls of the city!"

"This has been carefully planned. They must have entered through the Fahyz Gate after nightfall," offered Horgor. "I came to the keep from the Slag Gate and saw nothing."

"What of the Castle Guard?" asked Ozir. "Is the castle under attack?"

"It appears not, sir," answered Cliel. "The castle is sealed, and guards line the walls, but no invaders within a hundred mounts."

"Aided by the Magistrate..." Daen shook his head.

"Burn me!" roared Ozir. "And what of the people? The ones the Magistrate is commissioned to protect!"

"The margoul have overrun every farm and building in sight," added Froren. "And they have what looks to be a crude command station at the mill near the river."

"A command?" asked Daen. He brushed his hair from his face and stepped closer. "Do they fly any flags?"

"One I do not know," answered Cliel.

"Nor I, sir," echoed Froren. "Black and brown. A white spear planted in the ground, crossed by another, broken on one side."

Ozir's and Daen's eyes met.

"What?" asked Horgor, catching the look. "What does it mean?"

Daen lowered his voice. "That is a flag we have seen before. And one I had hoped I'd not see again. Müziel is—"

The sound of a howling wind suddenly filled the cavern as an enormous ball of fire ripped through the barn and exploded on the left side of the shield bearer wall.

"*Back!*" shouted Horgor. The other shield bearers shuffled backwards to remake the barrier, but they were now too few—the wall had been broken. The terrible hiss of shadow arrows filled the cavern. A warrior dropped, and then another. As the shield wall collapsed, Daen glimpsed the battle scaffold. He dove to the ground, just as arrows whistled overhead.

"Horgor, Ozir, drop back!" he called. "They've identified command!" Ozir's spooked warble boar lurched and bounded down the tunnel, tossing Ozir off the back of the chariot. Daen scrambled across the sand to him.

"Quickly! We must move!" he said. But a belabored groan was Ozir's only reply. Ozir rolled to his back, his hand gripping the black fletching of an arrow lodged in his stomach.

"Sire!" shouted Daen. He snatched up a discarded shield and planted the half-charred metal in the sand just as the sickening sound of whistling arrows rose again, striking soldiers and pinging off the shield. Outside the cavern, a drum boomed, followed by a rasping cry, like the tearing of heavy canvas. The ground trembled slightly as the cry rose and a thousand rushing feet charged down into the tunnel.

42

Muffled shrieks and the sound of clanging metal rose from the painful swirl of darkness. Yelling ripped through the din. *Battle.*

As the fog slowly lifted, Zodak found himself in a sitting position, hard rock pressed into his lower back and the thick smell of dust and death in the air. He pried his eyes open. *The tunnel. The Millgate. Yes.* He remembered the monster's giant arm and the smashed gate. The beast now lay awkwardly to the side, rigid and still. Stone. The gate was gone, and the soldiers had pushed ahead. Someone must have dragged him, unconscious to the side of the cavern and propped him against the jagged wall. No time for anything more. His head throbbed. It felt like the entire battle waged between his ears.

He slowly pushed himself to his feet. He recalled Daen's instructions: *Flee to Blackiron. Yes, I have to escape.* He began stumbling toward the fortress. Behind him, from beyond the shattered gate and out of sight came a swooshing sound and an explosion that shook the ground. He instinctively crouched. Men screamed.

Run! urged the voice inside. *You don't belong in a battle!* It was true, yet something pulled, something slowed his retreat. *Why are you even here?* demanded the voice. He didn't know. *Listen: what do you hear? Those are the screams of hardened soldiers. You have no choice. Go!* Of course, the voice was right. He had no place here. The fear started rising like a surging river, and he began to jog. But as he ran, he spotted it: a sword handle jutting from beneath the body of the soldier crushed by the gorgol. *Forget it. Run!* urged the voice.

Yet he froze. The image of that sword burned in his mind. *Why?* No, he didn't have to ask. It was all too familiar. He had fled a battle once before. He had chosen escape when Ardon was alone in the clearing, even when he had spied that blade. *You couldn't have done anything.* Maybe he couldn't have saved Ardon. But maybe, just maybe, he could have. The vision he had seen in that dark pool flashed in his mind. The sword handle. Daen on the ground. That filthy creature ripping the medallion from Ozir. *No, you have a choice.*

He suddenly found himself, sword in hand, marching back up the passage toward the battle. *Daen is up there somewhere.* A snort and rumble echoed from the bend in the tunnel ahead, and a large shape burst into view. Zodak dove to the side as Ozir's warble boar thundered past, two black arrows in its hindquarters. *Not good,* he told himself, the fear returning. But he pushed ahead, stepping over the remains of the Millgate and moving up the curve in the passage.

Zodak could hear them before he saw them. What had been a dull blanket of sound rose to a frenetic din, and as he rounded the curve in the tunnel, he beheld the harrowing scene. The impenetrable and indomitable Battleguard with its perfect blocks of soldiers was now a thick sea of skirmishes. Blades whirred, staffs twirled. The enemy was everywhere. Margoul filled the cavern. Clumps of krikkis warriors in dirty black and brown uniforms, if they could be called uniforms, with messy war paint caked to their faces fought beside goblins and the short, squat pig-faced creatures Daen had called pullpoz.

Hundreds of margoul battled the Order. Among the throngs were the ape-like trolls, some with crude blades or clubs, but others who had abandoned weapons in favor of claws and fangs. Like men among children, three half-giant margoul swung and whaled on everything in their path. Zodak shuddered, recalling the clearing. He searched the sea for Daen, but couldn't find him in the chaos.

Margoul outnumbered the Order Guard at least three to one, with more dark shapes constantly pouring in through the entrance, yet the skill of the Order Guard shone. Zodak marveled at the ferocity and precision of these bold soldiers. A nearby dwarf fought four painted krikkis at once, blocking jabs with the deft swing of a large axe and landing devastating counters that quickly cut his foes to two, then one. Zodak spotted a skeyth soldier like Leithra and stood mesmerized by his awful offensive. He spun and sliced and twirled in a fluid dance of death, leaving a ring of slain foes at his feet. Yet the enemy were many. As he watched, an Order Guard soldier fell to a blind attack from behind as he squared off with a trio of pullpoz and krikkis. Another, a man, fell from an arrow strike, even as he cut down a painted face.

The throng of soldiers ahead suddenly parted, and a squat, tangled shape crawled toward him from the scrum, as if birthed by the battle itself. Zodak leapt away, but as he stared, the image before him took shape, and he saw it was no creature but a hunched figure, dragging another.

"Daen!" shouted Zodak.

With a last burst of strength, Daen surged backward, dragging Ozir's limp body, and collapsed to the floor. Two guards stood beside him. Daen's fiery eyes shot up to Zodak and then to the sword in his hand. His face fell.

"What...? What are you doing here?!" he demanded. Zodak was taken aback. He had expected to be welcomed. "You're to be in the keep."

"I... I was struck," Zodak stammered.

Daen grasped his chin, inspecting the swollen goose egg on his head, nodding. "Ozir is injured. Find a length of cloth." Daen spoke without emotion. He lifted Ozir's helmet off and began removing the mantle from Ozir's slumped shoulders.

Zodak darted away to a nearby body of a shield bearer who had fallen to a Fangorian arrow. He hacked at the shirt with his sword, cutting away a long strip of fabric.

"Thank you," Zodak said to the fallen soldier, rolling him back over. He rushed back to Daen, who had ripped the black arrow from Ozir's abdomen and was pushing hard on the wound.

"Here!" Zodak thrust the cloth at Daen. The skypiercer snatched it up and pressed it tightly against Ozir's midsection. Daen yanked a bottle from his waist, ripped out the cork with his teeth, and poured yellow liquid on the cloth. Immediately, blue foam bubbled at the wound.

"Hold this!" Daen ordered, nodding at the bloody cloth.

Zodak replaced Daen's hand with his own, pushing the wet bandage down on the spongy wound. His gaze flicked up at Ozir's fluttering eyes, and then he spotted the gold disc shimmering behind the thick beard. *The medallion! My medallion!* An electric pang jolted through him. How he longed to reach for it, to touch it. To take it. To feel that power again.

"Get him back to Blackiron!" Daen ordered two soldiers who stood beside him. "But carefully. He—" Daen stopped, his head cocked. "Listen."

Zodak could hear it, too. Something had changed. The margoul; they were chirping strangely and now running. Some fled up out of the cavern and some ran down the tunnel. Daen drew his sword and jumped to his feet to meet a charging krikkis, but the frantic margoul just streaked past in flight.

Swoosh! Boom! A huge explosion, twice the size of the first, ripped through the mouth of the cavern, filling the cave with brilliant red and orange. Zodak threw himself to the ground and covered his head just as a blast of wind and singeing heat swept over him. Bodies, man and margoul alike, blew past him, thudding down around him like falling rocks. His ears rang with the explosion, and dust and debris rained down. For a long moment, he just lay, face buried in the ashy sand beside Ozir's still body. Slowly he raised his head.

He looked for Daen, but the skypiercer was gone. Zodak groaned and pushed himself up to his knees. Everything burned. Ozir's fallen body lay before him, the lower half of a krikkis draped across his torso. Of the two guards who had been standing beside Daen, Zodak now spotted only one. His broken body had been blown back twenty measures and now lay twisted on the ground, smoking. Then he found Daen. To his horror, Daen lay unmoving, sprawled out four mounts away, knocked back by the blast. The left side of his face and body were singed.

A dazed krikkis wandered into view, dragging a dark sword. With innate savagery, the krikkis suddenly raised the blade and brought it down mercilessly into the writhing body of the soldier beside Daen. The soldier spasmed and then was still. The krikkis wrenched the sword free and its deadened roving eyes landing on Daen. *No!* Zodak knew this scene. He had seen it before.

"Wake up! Daen!" Zodak frantically pushed himself up on unsteady legs. The shell-shocked krikkis paid him no mind. It dutifully marched forward, straddled Daen, and, standing above the skypiercer, lifted its jagged blade.

"No!" Zodak lunged forward and threw himself into the

beast. His shoulder connected with the small of the krikkis's back with a satisfying *crunch*. Blinded by fury, Zodak punched the side and back of the krikkis's head again and again. He snatched up the krikkis's fallen blade from the ground and thrust it into the margoul warrior again and again. Even as he stabbed, the krikkis body beneath him began to shrink and then melted away into a thick black tar. Zodak spat on the corpse and let the margoul blade fall from his hand into the sticky filth. He ran to Daen, dropping to his knees beside the skypiercer.

"Please, wake up!" Zodak shook Daen, but he didn't stir.

"Fall back!" coughed Horgor, his muffled cry carrying through the smoke. Ahead, where the shield wall had once stood so strong, through the clouds of dust and smoke, three dozen haggard soldiers struggled to re-form some semblance of a pod, their silhouettes backlit by the orange sunshine burning through mist. But another sound pierced the shouts and cries.

Boom. A drumbeat thundered at the tunnel entrance ahead and slithered down its length. Then another. Zodak looked up in terror to see a huge foggy silhouette looming on the lip of the tunnel entrance, every bit as tall as the gorgol statue.

"Droggth!" The figure bellowed the angry cry as dozens of shapes poured into the passage behind and around this monster.

"Form up!" roared Horgor in response. The haggard remnant of Order Guard slid together into a knot, braced to meet their foe. Droggth surged forward, plowing into the pod of soldiers with a jarring crash of metal and wood. He whipped an enormous hammer over his head with deadly force. Zodak could just make out Horgor's hulking shape among the soldiers, squaring off against Droggth. Horgor stood a full head shorter than Droggth, but he held his ground, the twin swords whirring. Other Order Guard not skirmishing with margoul also encircled the monster in their practiced battle formation, but Droggth moved like a great cat in battle, swift and dangerous. Zodak looked away when Droggth's massive hammer slammed down onto a dwarf, crushing him where he stood.

Ecstatic squealing erupted a few measures away where a cluster of goblins picked over Ozir's body, yanking on his beard and bejeweled fingers. One of the goblins lifted Ozir's limp hand, yanked on a finger with a sparkling golden ring. Not having success, it opened its mouth of sharp broken teeth and lifted the finger to bite.

"No!" screamed Zodak. "Leave him!" The goblin suddenly tumbled forward, struck from behind. A dark krikkis with glowing yellow eyes pushed the other goblins aside and began inspecting the fallen dwarf. It picked through his beard and then drew back. It lifted the medallion up through Ozir's beard, inspecting the prize for a moment, then drew back in surprise. With an air of reverence, it traced the lines of the medal with a crooked finger, then the krikkis lifted its head and screamed a shrill choking sound, flashing waves of color rippling through the tendrils that sprouted from its head.

"That's not yours!" shouted Zodak, springing from Daen's side and charging at the krikkis. Rage controlled him. His sword was gone, and he had no plan; he just hurled himself at the krikkis. But this was no goblin. The krikkis snapped its head up and as Zodak left his feet, the creature swung a shield arm around, in a cold, dismissive swat. The powerful blow struck Zodak in the head and shoulder, plastering his vision with bright stars and sending him crashing to the ground off to the side.

He had barely struck the ground when a black fluttering shape pounced on him. The attacking goblin's forehead collided hard with his own, sending another jolt of pain through his head. The goblin struggled for a fallen knife just a measure out of reach, but Zodak spotted it too. He kneed the goblin hard in the midsection and arched backwards, reaching for the blade. Zodak held the goblin back with one hand as it clawed at his face and snapped broken teeth at his cheek. His fingers groped for the knife handle as the goblin pressed in on him.

He stretched as far as he could go. Finally his fingers found the handle, the goblin just jots from his face. Like a stone viper, he snapped his hand around, thrusting upward, burying the knife in the goblin's chest. For a moment, both he and the goblin paused in frozen surprise. He met the goblin's eyes as they flickered from shiny, hateful black to a dead, ashen gray. As the beast began to deflate, the foul shape crumbled away.

A scream erupted from a few measures away. *The medallion!* Zodak spotted the krikkis screaming holding its burnt hand as it dropped the medallion. It bent and carefully lifted the relic by its cord, straightening up over Ozir with the treasure in hand. The marauding goblins cautiously edged closer to Ozir's body, still transfixed by the bejeweled fingers and beard. The krikkis threw its head back and shrieked again, flashing its colors and lifting the medallion high. This time, another krikkis up the passage answered in the same scratching shriek and then a third. From fifty mounts down the tunnel, Droggth paused his scrum and roared in victory back at the messengers.

"Stop him! He has it!" yelled Zodak helplessly. The krikkis turned and raced up the tunnel towards Droggth with the prize.

Zodak pushed himself to his feet, summoning strength for one last futile pursuit, even as he watched in defeat as the krikkis scampered up the passage.

A gray missile suddenly streaked past him with unnatural speed, kicking up a swirl of dust as it passed. He knew only one thing that moved like that: *Heldin!*

The runner ran too fast for the eye to follow, but in his dusty wake stood the fleeing krikkis, still mid-stride, its outstretched arm that once boasted the precious prize now severed just below the elbow. The two pilfering goblins at Ozir's side each clutched fresh stab wounds in their torsos as they slowly crumbled into sand.

Zodak scanned the hazy passage until he found Heldin, fifty measures away, prying the medallion out of the severed krikkis arm. Their eyes met. Heldin only gave a short nod as he slipped the medallion over his head.

"Traitor!" cursed Zodak. A pair of goblins and a krikkis approached Heldin, seeking to regain their stolen prize. He drew his sword.

"Zodak!" Daen's wavering voice rose from the cavern floor. Zodak flashed one more hateful glare at Heldin and ran to Daen.

"You're alive!" Zodak threw his arms around Daen and was enveloped by the smell of charred cloth and hair.

"Help me up, son."

Zodak heaved, pulling the skypiercer to unsteady legs.

"What happened here?" asked Daen, swaying on his feet.

"An explosion. The margoul army is coming."

Daen's gaze swept across the passage, littered with bodies and wreckage. "Ozir..." He stumbled forward to the fallen dwarf. "The arrow..." A cry came from the tunnel ahead as Droggth decimated another Order Guard soldier, cutting the remnant of the pod to two dozen soldiers. Daen squinted up the passage and moaned. "Droggth."

"Who's that?" Zodak asked.

"A spawn of darkness. We must get Ozir to Blackiron."

"Is he..."

"Dead?" asked Daen. He bent low and touched Ozir's temple. "The arrow's poison is spreading. There is one in the castle who can help him—" Daen gasped. "The medallion!" he shouted, pawing through Ozir's beard and tunic. "Where is it?"

"Heldin," seethed Zodak. "He came back for it. There—" Zodak pointed to the runner, but Heldin was gone. In the spot where he had been, the goblin cloaks slowly fluttered and the krikkis writhed on the ground.

"I know what you think of me." Heldin's boyish voice sounded from behind. Zodak whirled to see Heldin standing with the medallion. "But I did only what I had to—"

"Look around!" shouted Zodak. "You did this!" He swept an arm across the fallen.

Heldin dropped his gaze. "I have done many things I regret. This more than any."

"You sold the souls of these soldiers for your gain!" snapped Zodak.

"No!" Heldin retorted. "Never for my gain. It was always for Silda and Yindi. For my loves. I hadn't a choice." Zodak stepped forward, but Daen placed a hand on his arm.

"But you did choose, Runner," Daen said.

"Yes, a terrible choice I had," answered Heldin. He winced and staggered, planting his sword into the ground to steady himself.

"Droggth!" boomed the wild voice a hundred measures up the tunnel. Through the smoke, the shapes of Horgor and the dwindling remnant of Order Guard circled the monster. Horgor traded blows with the enormous fiend.

"But Kuquo is a liar, and his promises are scat. Filthy, putrid... bram." Heldin's voice wavered. "My sweet ones... they're dead." Heldin grimaced. "Kuquo killed them. I came back here for this." He lifted the medallion. "To bring it to you." He slowly removed the relic and stepped forward cautiously.

"Don't trust him!" warned Zodak.

"If Kuquo wants it so badly, then I will deny him," said Heldin. "That is my choice."

"Heldin," Daen said calmly, "that wicked man has left a swath of death in his wake. No man is immune to such hate. Your deeds will be weighed someday, but you show great courage returning here now."

Heldin gave a pained smile. "I'm afraid someday has come, my friend. For it has cost me." Heldin held the medallion out in offering. Even as he did, his legs gave out, and the runner fell awkwardly to the ground. Then Zodak saw it: the familiar black fletching of the Fangorian shadow hunter arrow, lodged deep in Heldin's back.

Daen knelt by Heldin, taking the medallion and resting a hand on the runner. "You have fought for Color today, runner," said Daen, lifting the medallion over his own neck, but then stopped suddenly. "No, this cannot stay in Blackiron today."

"Take the bands of running," croaked Heldin. "They will carry you like an eagle far from here."

"I cannot," Daen replied sternly. "I'll not leave Blackiron this day. The margoul press in on us. The Order needs me—"

"Give it to me. I'll take it," Zodak cut in. He started at the sound of his own voice. Daen snapped his head up. For a moment the skypiercer was silent, a thoughtful frown on his face.

"Yes." Daen slowly nodded. Heldin nodded too. "Yes," Daen repeated. "I remember now. After the explosion. A vision in the darkness. *You* wore it."

"Wait... but... I can't..." *What have I done?* Zodak's mind swam with fear, even as he hungered to hold it again.

"I know you doubt yourself," said Daen. "But I have seen strength in you. You are more than the boy you see. Inside you lies a warrior."

"I'm no warrior!" Zodak retorted dismissively.

"Zodak, the army at our gates is larger and more terrible than anything we dreamed we would face. I fear Blackiron may not stand today."

"And what would I do? Where would I go?!" Zodak almost shouted the accusing question.

"The bands will carry you far from here," said Heldin with a cough. "There are none like them in all of Yiduiijn. No man or horse can catch you as you run but run you must. Stop and you are just as vulnerable as you stand now. The bands offer no protection from arrows or blades." He reached down with a grimace and released each shimmering liquid silver band with a *click*.

Zodak's mind spun. This was happening too fast. *Shouldn't we deliberate? Speak to the Council?* But Daen was already fastening the bands to Zodak's ankles.

"Guard them well," Heldin continued in a feeble voice. "Holdinor, my great-great-grandfather, first found them. Ours has been a family of runners ever since." He closed his eyes in pain. "My time draws to an end. I... I trust the purpose that calls them now." Zodak noticed the black tendrils creeping up the back of the runner's neck just beneath the skin. His breathing was labored.

"You have done a valiant deed, Heldin," said Daen. "We will see you again in the Garden." Heldin nodded and shut his eyes. Then he was still. "Travel swiftly," Daen said, laying the small body on the ground. He spoke a phrase in the old tongue and touched the runner's forehead.

"You will need this," said Daen over his shoulder, removing Heldin's sword belt and handing both belt and blade to Zodak. Zodak hesitated before accepting the bundle.

A blinding light crackled through the tunnel from ahead, leaving everything ghosted in greens and reds. As Zodak tried to blink the shadows away, he heard the approaching stomping.

"Stand aside, boy!" a voice boomed over Zodak's shoulder. "We must pull back to the stronghold. Ozir?"

"He's alive," said Daen.

"To Blackiron with him, then!" Horgor's massive frame loomed over Zodak and behind him stood a small cluster of Order Guard soldiers, now reduced to a dozen. "We don't have long," barked Horgor. "Droggth took a flashbulb to the face, but it won't last." Zodak nodded absently, peering down the washed-out passage to see Droggth's massive frame spinning wildly, the enormous hammer devastating nearby margoul.

"Can you fight?" Horgor asked Daen, the gruff voice softening as he offered a hand.

"I believe so," answered Daen, taking the hand and rising beside Horgor. "Dazed by the last blast is all."

"Good!" answered Horgor. "We need your sword."

"Sir." A voice carried up the cavern ahead of ten jogging soldiers. The group was dirty and bloodied from battle.

"Hushtel, where is the rest of the Guard?" asked Horgor, looking up from where he stooped beside Ozir.

"The Guard is decimated, sir. Gorgol at every gate. Fangorian sharpshooters, crickets, skullers, sows, and a sea of halfies. Many of the Order were injured in fire explosions, but a strong remnant have pulled back to defend Blackiron. We must go before they cut the bridges."

"Burn me!" Horgor grunted as he hefted Ozir onto his back. "We move!" Horgor stumbled ahead. "Hushtel, our flank."

Daen drew beside Zodak. "We have no time." He spoke in low tones as he placed the medallion over Zodak's head. Daen engulfed the boy in a sudden hug, smothering the medallion's flash. The disc immediately sucked to Zodak's chest, and energy surged through his body.

"Don't you need to discuss it with them?" asked Zodak, waving at Horgor and the company of soldiers. "The Council?"

"We're out of time. They'd want it to stay here, but there's too much at stake. Listen: on the far side of Blackiron there is a hidden tunnel behind the stables that leads outside the city walls. You must find Dirgash the animal tender in the barn. He can show you the way." Zodak remembered the quaint fence and scattered hay in the mouth of one of the caves and how out of place it had looked. "You must head north – fahyz, past where we left Gormley, through the wood. Find Shalen in Galspur. Dirgash will tell you the way."

"Come, Skypiercer!" called Horgor over his shoulder as the company began moving down the tunnel.

"I... can't," protested Zodak, fumbling to buckle the sword belt around his waist.

"I know you're scared, Zodak, but we have no choice. Your call has come. You are needed." Daen's earnest eyes pierced Zodak.

"They're in pursuit," yelled Hushtel. As if in answer, Droggth roared. Zodak glanced up the passage and his stomach dropped. A roiling dark mass rolled over the lip of the tunnel as hundreds more margoul poured into the passage behind Droggth. Hushtel blew a sharp horn blast, sending a shrill echoing cry ringing through the cavern. The convoy hurried down the passage, Horgor carrying Ozir's slumped body.

"Go now!" commanded Daen, drawing Chilsar. "And remember: you're not alone!"

Zodak wanted to argue, to persuade. He wanted to curl up and hide somewhere. But instead, he saluted, as he had seen Daen do, turned, and ran.

At his first step, Zodak launched forward like a bolt from a crossbow. The bands sent him shooting down the passage, the cries of battle quickly fading behind him. In an instant he reached the entrance to the cavern. The speed felt exhilarating and frightening, yet somehow when he focused, the world slowed. Zodak sprinted for the barn across Blackiron as fast as he could. The chaos of the cavern flashed by him in a streaking blur, and yet his feet never faltered. Within seconds he had arrived at an opening in the cavern's wall with a wooden fence running across the entrance. The fence zoomed towards him. He feared he had not slowed soon enough and covered his face for impact, but his body stopped sharply from a full sprint. Zodak let out a sharp breath. He opened the gate in the fence and hurried along a rocky path leading gradually upwards. Hay covered the floor, and the air was thick with the smell of farm animals.

A cluster of stocky stonepeckers chirped and hopped aside, and a small herd of shaggy pigs scurried past, snorting at the interruption. The passageway opened into an enormous barn with a vaulted wooden ceiling five marqs above the hay floor. Wooden corrals and cages filled the room. A pair of stocky black rams with patterns etched on their massive horns chewed casually in the corral closest to Zodak beside an enormous toad of burden. A six-legged striped bison with only half an ear pulled against a thick chain tethered to the wall.

"Well, excuse me!" exclaimed an odd-looking man with sloping shoulders and a vaguely piglike face. "What's this? Who are *you*?"

"You're Dirgash?"

"Yes," said the man warily. "But who are you? And what are you doing here? What's happening out there?"

Zodak breathlessly recounted the attack at the Millgate.

Dirgash nodded quickly, eyes darting about. "They will be coming here?" Fear gripped the man.

"I don't know. They may," answered Zodak. "But Daen said you could show me to the secret passage out, past the wall. I have a very important... message that I need to carry to Galspur. He said these enchanted bands of running will carry me."

Dirgash stared at Zodak, quiet thoughts whirring.

"A message? Bands of running?" Dirgash mused to himself, inspecting the bands. "It *is* possible," he said to himself.

"What is?" asked Zodak.

"Quickly, follow me!" Dirgash turned and disappeared through a doorway. "To the map room," he called over his shoulder. Zodak scampered after him down a hallway and through another door that opened into an octagonal room with a sprawling map sketched on the floor. The map, which stretched from wall to wall, measuring ten mounts across, depicted cities and mountains and seas in incredible detail.

"Is that Yiduiijn?" asked Zodak.

"It is, my boy!" said Dirgash, as he stepped out onto the surface of the map, which shimmered like water but held like polished marble. He studied the floor at the far side of the room for a moment.

"Here. Galspur," said Dirgash, gesturing to a point at his feet. "The bands, boy. Give them to me." Zodak was lost, but there wasn't time to argue. He clicked the bands off and handed them to Dirgash, who kneeled next to the map of Rislaan. He spoke a foreign word and, with his index finger, encircled an area no bigger than a button in the southeast corner of Rislaan. Immediately, the entire map floor changed, the shapes swirling like a sandstorm before reassembling. Now, instead of the outline of a continent, Zodak could see the shape of a town, depicted from above. Dirgash examined it for a moment and then walked across the room and pointed to a cluster of huts.

"Shalen?" asked Dirgash. Zodak nodded speechlessly. Dirgash spoke the words again and drew another circle, and again the floor shifted shape. Now the entire map was filled by four huts. Zodak could distinguish individual pieces of straw on their thatched roofs.

"If memory serves, that's the one," said Dirgash, pointing to one of the buildings. He placed the shimmering bands on the doorstep of the hut. "Perfect."

Zodak watched, bewildered. *How will this help me escape from battle?* he wondered.

"Now, the rhumb." Dirgash groaned, rising to his feet and

shuffling to a set of shelves at the edge of the room. He hurried back, carrying a small brass cylinder from which he pulled a crystal eyedropper holding some sort of silver-blue liquid. He carefully dripped two drops on each band. A wave of blue flashed over the bands and rings of blue light rippled from Shalen's hut on the map, like a disturbed pond. "They took!" he hollered in triumph.

"Took?"

"We must go," said Dirgash. He returned the bottle, snatched up the bands, and hastily shoved them into Zodak's arms as he bustled toward the exit. Dirgash led Zodak through the barn and at least half a cliq down an earthy tunnel that split and wound, dipped and rose. The tunnel finally dead-ended in a wall overgrown with vines and leaves. Dirgash lifted a blue glowing shard that dangled on a cord around his neck, and the vines on the wall came alive, twisting and wriggling, like snakes fleeing a flame. They parted under the azure glow, revealing an opening in the wall. Dirgash disappeared through and beckoned for Zodak to follow.

Zodak snapped the bands to his shins, ducked, and entered the darkness, following the soft blue light. Ten mounts ahead, the tunnel wall opened for Dirgash and light streamed in. Zodak followed the animal handler out of the cramped passage down onto grass outside the city walls. As soon as he stepped out of the tunnel, Zodak could feel himself being pulled to the right by the bands. His feet turned and his torso twisted awkwardly to align.

"I do believe they are pointing you in the right direction already," exclaimed Dirgash, pointing to the bands. "This may actually work! They should pull you all the way to Galspur! Good luck. I suspect you may need plenty of it," said Dirgash, with no hint of humor.

"Thank you, Dirgash." Dirgash nodded briskly. "Where should I—"

"I'm away," cut in Dirgash. He turned abruptly and scurried through the tunnel again.

"Wait!" called Zodak.

Dirgash's head popped out of the tunnel. "Follow the pull of the bands. They will lead you. I must get back!" He disappeared again. Vines and roots twisted and closed in on the tunnel opening until it was invisible.

And just like that, all was quiet and Zodak was alone. He took a deep breath. The world seemed peaceful here. Birds' songs filled the bright blue sky, and leaves whispered in the breeze. No sound escaped the city, no hint of clash or struggle. But a battle raged, he knew. *What will become of this place today?*

Zodak remembered Sodane; the smile and kind words he had given Zodak just before he died; the brothers' boyish tussle just outside the fortress gate. Then he remembered how Sodane's blood covered the floor and how Daen's scream ripped through the tower. He smelled the singed skin and hair and dust and blood. He saw that great slithering arm punch through the Millgate as if it were paper, heard the splintering crash. Zodak shuddered, remembering the wet crushing sound of Droggth's horrible hammer. He shook his head to escape the memories and wiped the blurring tears from his eyes.

Turning his back on the city, he gazed out across the golden field, rippling like water under the breeze, and beyond, to the dark forest that crouched at the field's edge. *How did I end up here?* he wondered, looking down at himself. The bands on his ankles shimmered and danced like liquid silver. Heldin's small sword hung from his waist. Before today he had never swung a sword. *Will I again today?* He tried to recall the map, the picture of Galspur. *How far will I run with these bands? Hours? Until sunset? Days?*

He longed to rip the vines away and crawl back through the tunnel to find Daen. *What if I had stayed?* Serving as a vintner's hand on a quiet winery suddenly sounded lovely. There would be such simplicity in waking up with no memory of this day.

"*It is time.*" The voice inside spoke as clear as a bell as the sudden urge to move jolted him.

He turned to the right, feeling the draw of the bands. And then he ran. The world smeared into a blur, and the ground streaked beneath his feet, taking his breath. Off he flew.

AUTHOR'S NOTE

THANK YOU so much for coming on this journey! I hope you loved reading the story as much as I loved writing it.

★★★ PLEASE LEAVE A REVIEW ★★★

Reviews are the lifeblood of the indie author. If you've liked this book, it would mean a lot if you could take 60 seconds to leave a review.

Author's Note

Also, if you haven't already, check out ***Throne Born*** (MaxMoyerWrties.com/throne-born), a novella that predates this story by 200 years.

Keep any eye out for novellas released between novels (yes, one is in the works right now) and lots of other stories, histories and writings from the world of Yiduiijn.

ACKNOWLEDGMENTS

I never dreamed, when I first penned the opening scene of this book 18 years ago that this is what would follow. For one thing, it was never supposed to be a book. But here we are.

First and foremost, I need to thank my truest partner in all things, my wife, Sara. Thank you for putting up with, and always seeming impressed by, my writing, whether polished finals or terrible first drafts. You always saw through to the heart of the story. You've generously given me time and space, often at your own cost, to pour the hundreds (thousands?) of hours into this project.

Every member of my family has played a huge part in writing this book. Each has experienced the story in one (or multiple) of its various iterations. For the Treehouse Gang: thanks to Ella for early listening - actually the earliest captive audience at 2 months old - Finn for inspiring much of the heart of adventure in a teen boy (and the cover modeling), Harper, you've been one of my most faithful readers (I don't know how you notice all of those details!), and Millie, who listened to many chapters (at least the first parts of many chapters) of the draft story at bedtime. You guys are the best.

Bronwen, thanks for the early editing and constant feedback. You've been a great writing companion along this journey - and much more to come. I have appreciated your insight and your paving the way with your own publishing journey – as a big sis should. Mom and Dad, you guys are the persistent examples of unending encouragement and support as well as inspiration for what's possible and how to chase dreams.

Elrod (House of), you remain my original partner in crime. Thanks for starting this journey with me and adventuring along the way. The world wasn't ready for the video game or board game decades years ago, but just wait! I'm excited to see what's coming. Into the world of Mind's Eye we forge!

Special thanks to my beta reader team, especially Mike and Greg for their reading multiple versions and acting like it's no big deal, but which must become more of a grind each time. You guys have been a huge encouragement to me. Also, to the many others who read an early edition.

Zodak simply wouldn't be what it is without Fiona McLaren's great editing. You helped shape the direction of the story and saved the world from that early draft of Zodak. Deborah, your keen eye and insight helped polish the story. To Frankie Emrick, the eagle-eyed reader and fan-turned editor. Thanks for your extremely valuable additions!

Great working with Jeff Brown on the cover design. I love where we ended up. Amanda Gavigan has been a great engine to help push this out there. And thanks to Janeen Ippolito for her sage consulting on all things publishing and marketing.

As always, my biggest thanks goes to you, the readers. Without you, a story is just a voice lost in the wind. Keep reading, join our newsletter for more updates and stay in touch!

www.MaxMoyerWrites.com

ABOUT THE AUTHOR

Max grew up roaming the streets and exploring the deep dark forests of Washington D.C. terrorizing neighborhood wild game and putting his brother Eli through various club initiations. He now resides just outside D.C. with his wife and four kids (lovingly referred to as the "Treehouse Gang"). The Treehouse Gang and the rest of the family are, without a doubt, the biggest fans of his writing and creativity.

As a day (and sometimes night) job, Max runs Triumph Law, a boutique corporate law firm, where he works with amazing founders building, growing and selling inspiring companies. In the off hours (read: early in the morning before anyone else is awake), he loves getting lost in his writing.

In his limited free time (see above about running a law firm and raising four kids), he loves playing/skateboarding/trampolining/fishing/skiing with the Treehouse Gang, Crossfit, riding his classic motorcycle, woodworking, drawing, painting, watching great movies and playing board games.

Zodak is Max's first full length novel.

He previously wrote Throne Born, a novella and prequel to Zodak, which can be found at www.maxmoyerwrites.com/throne-born

Want more? Sign up for the newsletter and come join the adventure: https://www.maxmoyerwrites.com/join